The Conditions of Love

The Conditions of Love

DALE M. KUSHNER

GRAND CENTRAL
PUBLISHING

NEW YORK   BOSTON

Grand Central Publishing
Hachette Book Group
237 Park Avenue
New York, NY 10017

www.HachetteBookGroup.com

Printed in the United States of America

RRD-C

First Edition: May 2013
10 9 8 7 6 5 4 3 2 1

Grand Central Publishing is a division of Hachette Book Group, Inc.
The Grand Central Publishing name and logo is a trademark of
Hachette Book Group, Inc.

The Hachette Speakers Bureau provides a wide range of authors for speaking events.
To find out more, go to www.hachettespeakersbureau.com or call (866) 376-6591.

The publisher is not responsible for websites (or their content) that are not
owned by the publisher.

Library of Congress Cataloging-in-Publication Data

Kushner, Dale.
  The conditions of love / Dale M. Kushner.—First edition.
    pages cm
  Summary: "A first novel about a young girl who is looking for love and guidance from her Auntie Mame mother and her absent father"—Provided by the publisher
  ISBN 978-1-4555-1975-0 (hardcover)—ISBN 978-1-4555-1976-7 (ebook)—
ISBN 978-1-61969-026-4 (audiobook)
  I. Title.
  PS3611.U7375C66 2013
  813'.6—dc23
                                                                    2012040786

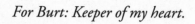

For Burt: Keeper of my heart.

Henrietta knew of the heart as an organ; she privately saw it covered in red plush and believed it could not break, though it might tear.

Elizabeth Bowen, *The House in Paris*

We insist, it seems, on living.

Virginia Woolf, *The Waves*

The Conditions of Love

Part One

❧

Mern:
Via Separatio

1953–1958

Chapter 1

Mern

My mother was dead set against me calling her Ma. When the offending sound passed from my lips, she pinched my chin and enunciated very slowly, the way she later talked to her parakeet, Mr. Puccini—"Baby say *Mern* not *Mama*. Baby say *Mern*." She was hoping, no doubt, that with time and a little encouragement, I might grow into an adaptable companion whose demands were minimal, someone with whom she could discuss Cary Grant's perfect profile, Shelley Winters's yen for men.

Mern was different and I was different too. I was the only kid I knew who didn't have a father. Do you miss him? neighborhood kids would ask. "He's gone," I'd say, shrugging. Will you see him again? Why did he leave? "Don't know," I'd answer. And I didn't.

I soon learned about playground cruelty, the broad scope of taunting, school—a place where tedium and terror hunkered side by side. I learned the response of no-response, the Stare-'Em-Down factor, how to hold back tears by pressing my tongue into my palate until my tormentors got bored and skipped off. I kept my distance from games of jump rope and hopscotch, girls in gangs of three or four. Mern signed my report cards each semester without looking at the growing number of checks in the Needs Improvement column, the loopy *M* in "Mern" sprouting butterfly wings. My mother didn't care if I memorized the states and their capitals, the names of the presidents, the five biggest rivers in the world, so why should I?

There were no nursery rhymes or bedtime stories at our house, no "Jack Be Nimble" or "Hickory Dickory Dock," no *Sleeping Beauty* or Donald Duck, but my mother taught me how to cream anyone at rummy, and I was a whiz at solitaire. As for domesticity, she was allergic to cooking and cleaning, and the naked skin of any fowl made her shudder; she never cooked a turkey in her life. We never had a Christmas tree until Sam moved in, rarely a birthday cake, and only New Year's Eve was consistently celebrated—with Coke and pretzels for me, rum and Coke and pretzels for Mern, our horoscopes dissected after the sun went down. My mother did not believe in church or religion. Her words: "I'll believe in God—the Man Upstairs—the day God believes in me." As for Jesus Christ: "What good is a god that gets himself killed?"

Mern liked to say she was a makeup *arteeste*, but actually she was a *manicureeste*. She worked at Annie Stiltz's beauty shop, wore cat eye glasses with rhinestones at the temples, and studied the lives of movie stars. Her Bibles were *Photoplay* and *Modern Screen*. Each month she'd select an actress and alter herself accordingly—Rita H in January, a raven-haired Elizabeth T in March. Lana, Ava, Grace: pageboy, spit curls, French twist. Once, from too much peroxide, her hair turned pea green and fell out. For weeks she wore a kerchief, said she was playing Garbo in *Camille*. Without adornments she was enough of a blue-eyed beauty to make men spin around and whistle, but this flattery could not be trusted, since men, she said, were about as choosy as goats.

Her oddness clung—to her, to me. It spread over everything like road tar on a summer's day. She'd have me laughing, then in the next breath demand I quit bugging her. Her mood changes left me puzzled and on guard. Some nights she wept muffled, private sobs. I would have crawled on my knees to comfort her if I hadn't been afraid she'd freeze me out with a dead-eyed stare.

My mother believed a person's name was her destiny. "I'm named after a British actress," she told me, and when I asked if it was Myrna Loy, she threw back her head and laughed with disdain. "I'm no Myrna Loy! Myrna Loy has no pizzazz." Around the time I was two, I mispronounced my own name, substituting *Cissy* for *Eunice*, which I later shortened to CC, initials being more mysterious. Later, when I asked my mother how she'd chosen the name Eunice for me, she recited the moment her finger had landed on it in a book. Mr. Tabachnik, our downstairs landlord, maintained *Eunice* had noble origins—meaning "victory" in Greek—but usually he called me "Cisskala" or "CC Dumpling," nicknames that were kisses to my ears.

Mern's big dream was to go to Hollywood and be discovered by Jack Warner or Louis B. Mayer. The closest she came to Movie Land, however, was the theater a few blocks from us, the Hollywood Cinema. The first time I went with her I was about six; we were going to a matinee of an old movie, a real tearjerker called *Portrait of Jennie*. "Get ready for Hol-lee-wood," she said, spiriting me from my bedroom in her cherry toreadors and cardigan with the fake rabbit collar. So vast was my happiness, so intoxicated my senses with the perfumed, blazing sight of her, I forgot to tie my shoes. "Girls out on the town," my mother sang, grabbing my hand. She hated to be late for the feature: in an instant, storefronts and houses were passing in a blur. The ticket lady let me in for free. Then Mern was dragging me past the astonished usher, up the stairs to the mezzanine, to the box seats, the best seats in the house where a crystal chandelier threw rainbows over our heads. We plunked ourselves down as the houselights dimmed, and Mern leaned over to spill Milk Duds into my hand.

A hush descended, the blue velvet curtain rose, the sheer curtains parted, and the screen came alive. For the next hour and a half, Mern squeezed my pinky until the fat face of Winston Churchill replaced Jennifer Jones. Woken from our trance, we scrambled to the Ladies, a room done up in red brocade with two reclining lounges and marble sinks. Before the hordes barged in, my mother opted for a tufted chair and pulled out her compact, pretending to be a high-society lady powdering her nose.

When I was a bit older, I asked Mern why our little town of Wild Pea, Illinois, had a fancy theater, and she answered it was because of the railroad—vaudeville troupes had once passed through. In those days, the Hollywood had been the Orpheum Theater. Eddie Cantor and Sarah Bernhardt had sung on its stage. The magic's all gone now, she mourned. Vaudeville was kaput. A few trains still rattled down the tracks, but the passengers were cows.

We stayed for the second showing, our sighs braiding into one. Which was why I dreaded the sound of those final arpeggios. Coats bunched between our knees, we lingered until the credits scrolled down in cursive flourishes. When the lights popped on, Mern's eyes were ringed with streaky mascara, her lipstick sucked off. Our old familiar selves were waiting in the dusk outside, and we weren't in a rush to claim them. Mern and Eunice. Eunice and Mern.

When I pestered Mern for details about my absent father, she would alternatively bray and rant unstoppably or get tight-lipped and evasive. "His sweet talk might as well have been poison," she said. She pulled her shirt into two pointy bosoms, stuck out her tongue, and waggled her behind. "He went for big bazoongies." But he was a great dancer. Sometimes she'd forget herself and roll those huge blue eyes of hers and gush about the jitterbug contests and smoke-filled roadside bars strung with colored lights. "Frankie used to drive me wild. He had this way of holding me," she said, closing her eyes, swaying her hips to a radio crooner, her arms circling the waist of my invisible father. I could see them together, Mern and my father, spooning and dipping to Nat King Cole's "There Will Never Be Another You."

Wildness must have brought them together, a wildness they counted on to keep them fabulously in love. "He was real bad in a good way," she'd tell me with a throaty laugh, both of us under the spell of those long-ago nights when the stars pitched a teasing love song. But soon enough, her self-righteous anger would kick in, and the bashing would commence. He couldn't hold a job. Money slipped through his fingers. She accumulated a litany of complaints, a list of accusations. The bum took money from the mouths of his wife and child, she'd say, and I'd picture Mern and me, doggy-like on our hands and knees, dollar bills clenched in our teeth, my father plucking money from our jaws. *This isn't the life you promised!* she must have yelled at him. No cash. No more fun. *A kid with a wail like a banshee.*

I used to wonder if anyone or anything could have prevented my father from leaving us. I was trying to get an outline of the man, to know his size and shape, the fragrance of his soul. Until I met him in the flesh when I was ten, the picture I had of my father came from a photograph I'd found beneath a tangle of nylons in Mern's underwear drawer—a lanky, dark-haired guy striking a pose in someone's yard, his long legs slightly bowed, his thumbs hooked onto his low-slung dungarees. I could see what Mern meant when she said he was movie-star handsome. He had a lady-killer smile that teased the camera up close. I had his dark looks, the heavy chestnut hair, lashes Mern said she'd kill for. My features were exotic, or so she told me, though my chin was too pointy and my hair wouldn't hold a perm. "You're like your father in more ways than one," she remarked, tapping my cheekbones as if she were searching a wall for studs. Evidently Frankie hadn't loved her the way she'd loved him, and I wondered if every time she saw my face, the calamity of that insult returned. Through the walls of our shared bathroom, I sometimes heard the squeak of the medicine cabinet and Mern rummaging for pills. When she thought I was asleep, she'd sit on the toilet and wail his name.

The Big Bum, she called my daddy. "Let me set the record straight on that Big Bum," she'd say. "He stranded us when you were a mere squirt in diapers. Up and vamoosed in his goddamn got-no-words-for-it-babe way. No note. Nothing!" He'd left a hundred bucks tied with a white ribbon, five twenties, in a fry pan. My father, it should be noted, had a showman's touch. The story of his departure grew more elaborate, more pathetic and heartrending with each passing year. Occasionally my mother conceded he had a big heart. Then she'd add he had a Big Something Else, too, and the Big Something Else got him into trouble. "A big something else?" I'd ask, concerned. "Yeah," Mern would say, her nostrils pinched from despair. "What would you know?" A wave of self-sorrow would sweep over her, and she'd grab at the nearest soft thing, me, and smother my face against her scrawny chest. Beneath her sternum rumbled an impressive pattering: Big Bum or not, she still loved my father and imagined his CinemaScope return.

What does a child know? What does she know for certain? Her name? The names of her parents and family? Her address and telephone number? She knows the way to school and back, the streets of her neighborhood. She knows her birthday, the date and year, the name of the president of the United States, the Pledge of Allegiance, the "Star-Spangled Banner," the order and names of the months. She knows simple arithmetic, spelling, how to form a perfect cursive *e*. These are the basics, the facts. She also has learned hunger and sleepiness and boredom, when she is safe and when she's in danger, the itchy feeling in her body in the presence of a liar, the stiff-tongued ache when she's the one telling a lie.

For the first ten years of my life, I harbored fantasies about my father. My mind was a movie factory, and all my "What If" stories were full of anguish. What if my father had disappeared because he'd had an accident and couldn't remember who he was and was wandering from city to city, his family in Wild Pea wiped from his brain? What if, right after I was born, he discovered he had a fatal disease and, not wanting us to see him suffer, left without explaining? It wasn't until he came back that day in June that I recognized the misguided bent of my imagination. My father wasn't sick, and he obviously wasn't dead, but he was also not the bogeyman Mern claimed him to be. Inside the bad father, the object of Mern's snide remarks, I discovered another person whose existence she was ignorant of. *My Frankie* didn't have a vicious bone in his body. He only pretended to prefer sexy blondes because that's who real American men were supposed to like. Deep down, *My Frankie* yearned for someone worthy to share his love. Once upon a time, before she'd become her full-fledged Mernself, when she was Grandma Sophie Sunny Polestar's daughter, a teenager in bobby socks, brushing her hair a hundred strokes before she went to bed, my mother had been that person. Once upon a time, she'd been my father's chosen, and for a single day in my childhood, I'd been his chosen too.

On that Saturday, the thirteenth of June 1953, I had a date with Mr. Tabachnik to listen to his favorite opera singer, Caruso. Opera was a great artistic tradition, a true expression of human dignity, Mr. Tabachnik believed, and if I wanted to grow up to be a mensch, I should know opera. Mr. Tabachnik exalted in my education. In the sunlit kingdom of his kitchen, he'd put a hand on my shoulder. "Take it from your old friend Tabachnik, Cisskala. You got an A-plus-plus mind." I was a "schmarty," he said, which was different from being a smarty-pants, and I owed it to myself to not goof off in school. Education was worth more than gold. I understood that Mr. Tabachnik wanted something for me, though I couldn't say what; that he believed in my potential made me eager to try. With his encouragement, I read all his encyclopedias, starting with *aardvark*. Africa was a great continent "shrouded by a veil of ignorance and mystery." Atomic energy was "the promise of tomorrow." I'd just turned ten, and during my hours with Mr. Tabachnik I read, I dreamed—we discussed.

My mother wondered what the hell I did down there with the old man, but I just shrugged. Once, when I thought she might even be jealous of my friendship with him, she accused Mr. Tabachnik of being a Russian spy. Of course she was dead wrong. His eyes watered behind thick lenses, and he was deaf in one ear. How could an Old World gentleman who wore bedroom slippers and soft gray sweaters all year round be a spy? In his youth, he'd confessed, he'd ridden freights from the East Coast to Chicago to get away from *a situation*. Chicago had a big opera house where he could live his dream and join an actors' guild and maybe write a play or two, but by a twist of fate he'd ended up in Wild Pea.

At ten o'clock, our prearranged time, I knocked on Mr. Tabachnik's door. He'd been working in the garden and the smell of sun and earth mingled with his sweat. His roses had magical names, which he trilled off in a list—Jeanne D'Arcy, Belle Amour—roses he was rescuing from extinction.

"Cisskala Dumpling," he said, wringing his hands, "have I got something for you! Come. Make yourself at home." He pulled me forward into the stifling apartment, opening the drapes he kept closed until I arrived.

"Sit, sit," he said, indicating one of the deep maroon chairs that matched the faded Persian carpet and the ruby cut-glass decanter on the sideboard that never held a drop of wine. To accommodate my size, Mr. Tabachnik always bolstered my chair with a bed pillow and set out the usual glasses of weak tea, two sugar cubes apiece, and a single spear of pickle on a plate, pickles he knew I loved.

The Victrola sat on a nearby table. Its long arm rested in a metal clasp. Mr. Tabachnik lifted the arm, rubbed his thumb over the needle to clear away fuzz, then carefully shook the record from its paper sleeve and lowered the platter onto the platform. The needle made a dull scratchy sound. "Listen, Cisskala, you'll hear for yourself, the greatest tenor who ever lived."

We sat facing each other, our necks arched against tattered doilies. Mr. T closed his eyes and insisted I shut mine: the street noises receded, and I tried to concentrate. I listened hard. Inside the music I heard weeping, anger, shame; then the dark, foreign power of Caruso's voice invaded me. I recognized the truth when I heard it—not the words but its sound. Something heavy was being chased away off my chest and something else was unlocking. My foot stopped jiggling, the itch behind my knee where the scratchy nap of the upholstery pressed against my skin stopped itching, and I sank farther into the chair. Behind my eyes I saw a mountain range, pure and lonely, and I knew it was part of the truth too. A noise came out of my throat, a warm sound trying to blend with Caruso's. Mr. T's head jerked off the doily, and he thrust an accusatory finger to his lips. My tongue froze; my mouth snapped shut. "You think this is Mr. Ted Mack's Amateur Hour, young lady!" I slunk down into my chair. *Rigoletto*! Mr. Tabachnik closed his eyes again and Caruso finished the aria. The needle went around and around in the last groove. Mr. Tabachnik stuck his feet into his bedroom slippers and shuffled to the record player, tousling my hair as he passed. Next was Caruso singing from *Pagliacci*. Such is the lesson that life teaches us, he said. A clown's face can't mask the sadness beneath.

When our listening hour ended, Mr. Tabachnik returned the records to their covers with the same care he'd used removing them. "Such beauty from such an instrument!" I should pay attention. In Caruso's mouth each word was fondled and caressed. I might not understand Italian, but it didn't matter because Enrico Caruso sang from the source of all languages, which was no less than the human heart. This was how Mr. Tabachnik spoke when he wanted to convey the grandness of things: *no less than the human heart.* "Terrible things happen to people," he said, the lines in his face deepening, "but from the terrible, beautiful can come." That was opera, and Caruso was a genius of grief. Mr. Tabachnik placed a trembling hand on the crown of my head and bent to kiss me. Out of the ugly and terrible comes beauty. I shouldn't forget it, he said.

The doorbell rang once. Silence, then three loud raps. "Your mother's expecting someone?" Mr. Tabachnik inquired from the kitchen. He liked to know who was coming and going in our lives. Again, three knocks by an impatient fist. Upstairs, our door scraped open, and Mern's wedgies clumped down the steps. Mr. Tabachnik and I blinked at each other. A man began to laugh. It was the laugh I'd heard a thousand times in my dreams. We heard Mern exclaim, "Holy moly! *Frankie?*"

"She knows him?" Mr. Tabachnik said, ear cocked.

My heart jumped like a frog in my chest. I pushed my knuckles into my mouth. The man laughed again. I told Mr. Tabachnik I had to go. He stooped to kiss me, his brows knitted with concern. If there was trouble, I should come right back.

"There won't be any trouble." I was mad with glee. "My daddy's home."

Chapter 2

Dupere

The door to our flat was wide open. A man was in the kitchen with Mern leaning against the refrigerator.

"Daddy!" I cried, the ridiculous word I'd never before uttered spilling from my mouth.

Mern said, "Well, it ain't Amos and it ain't Andy . . ."

"Bunny!" my father said.

In person, my father was even better-looking than the purloined photo from Mern's underwear drawer. Big dark eyes. *My* dark eyes. A smile I couldn't help smiling back at.

"Her name is Eunice," my mother corrected. "Or maybe you've forgotten?" She was backed up against the sink in her pink quilted robe, her hair still in curlers, smoking.

"I haven't forgotten," my father said, "but she's not Eunice to me."

I had halted several feet from him, my eyes glued to his face, my heart socking me in the chest. Mern glared at me. *I'm warning you.*

"It's okay, sweetheart," the most handsome man in the world said. "I won't bite. Don't be afraid." Hiking up his chinos, he crouched and welcomed me into his arms. Though his nearness made me dizzy, I let myself be hugged. And then I was hugging back with all my might, clasping him around the neck, taking in the unfamiliar smells. Hair tonic and aftershave. I felt the pressure of his hand on my back—*my father's hand*—and nuzzled closer. He laughed deep in his throat. I knew I was supposed to hate him, but how could I hate the way his arm coiled around my waist, the way he planted his lips on my forehead as if he'd never been gone and had every right in the world to kiss his daughter?

Mern roared from across the room, "Jesus Christ! Go ahead and break her heart, Frank. It's what you do so well."

My father's embrace loosened. In a voice that could rule the universe, he asked me to be the judge. "You don't believe her, do you? You know I wouldn't hurt you."

I nodded slowly, thinking she'd been lying about him. He did love me!

He lifted a strand of hair off my face and smoothed it behind my ear. "You're the spitting image of my mother when she was a girl." I was so close I could see the teeth marks of his comb along his part. I could see a tiny white scar in the middle of one of his eyebrows where the hairs had stopped growing. He asked me how old I was, and when I told him, he whistled. "Time sure flies." I allowed him to stroke my cheek, breathing in his fumes like I couldn't get enough of them. "Pretty baby," he said.

"That's enough, Mr. Charming," Mern snarled, advancing on us as if I were in immediate and grave danger. "Who do you think you are coming here like this? We don't hear one lousy word from you in ten years, and then one morning you wake up and decide you want to see your kid, and you come busting into our lives like nothing ever happened?"

Next to me my father unfolded his long spine, vertebra by vertebra, and stood up, his every movement a revelation.

"It's not fair," my mother said.

My father looked insulted. "Hey, Noodle, I thought you'd be pleased to see me. Both of you."

His honeyed tone filled my head. Why did my mother have to spoil things?

"All right, maybe I should have called to warn you I was coming, but I figured you'd hang up." He brushed his pompadour back from his forehead, his eyes soliciting Mern's forgiveness. "I was right, too, wasn't I? You'd have hung up?" His grin was luxurious. He strode over to my mother, his body giving off fierce heat like the sun on a winter's morning as he passed.

Mern put up her hands. There was pain in her eyes, but also

pleading edged with a flirty dare. "Don't come near me. I'm not your Noodle anymore." Some of her rollers had come loose, and she pulled out the rest and fluffed her curls. Glossy, toffee-colored waves rippled down her neck. My father's smile broadened. "Still playing hard to get, Noodle?" He asked if she remembered the first time he'd ever called her that. She tossed her head in a moment of pretend anger. "Only a rotten traitor would bring that up at a time like this." He laughed, catching the meaning of her pout. "You always were gorgeous when you got angry." My mother looked at her hands, then back at him. She padded to the kitchen table and sat down. My father followed and sat next to her. He picked up a pack of Camels and shook out two cigarettes. She took the cigarette and gave him a crooked smile. My father hovered closer, flipping open his lighter and cupping the flame. My mother dipped her head, inhaling in a long draught. Silently I cheered: *Kiss, kiss!*

"That's an expensive lighter," Mern said, drawing back. "Things must be good, huh?"

"Can't complain," my father said.

She looked down at his cowboy boots embossed with tiny hearts. "Those real leather?" Her voice had grown tight again. Wary. The enchantment had vanished. Mern blew smoke at the ceiling. "I can't believe it's been ten years. Christ!"

Leaning forward, my father pushed a ringlet behind my mother's ear, his lips inches from the lobe. "Tell me there isn't some place inside you that isn't happy I'm here." His finger drew small circles on the back of her hand. My mother did not move but watched his mouth, waiting for his next words. His fingers moved to the cavity between her collarbones, a private spot she dabbed with perfume. "You always did say no when you meant yes," he said, and even I knew it was a cunning thing to say. Mern's face colored. "Stay for lunch, Frankie?" She glanced over at me. "Eunice, don't you have something to do in your bedroom?"

I shook my head.

"Hey, Bunny!" my father said, turning to me in his chair. "You're so quiet over there I almost forgot you were around." His scrutiny electrified me. Mern got up to fill the kettle and grab some beers. My father pointed to his lap. "Come over here and tell me about yourself."

I went over, cautiously.

"In case you're wondering," he said, continuing to look at me but addressing Mern who carried in two foaming mugs, "I'm here on account of Bunny. Thought she might want to meet her old man. I had a little time on my hands so . . . I didn't want her to grow up thinking I was a loser."

Mern's head shot up. "For Eunice?" she said. "You came back because of Eunice?"

My father tugged his ear and didn't say anything.

"You can't come back after all this time, like nothing happened, like you're some kind of hero or something. What about me? How about an apology?"

My father ignored this last part. Twisting around to look at me, his lips parted in a dazzling smile. "You're happy to see me, aren't you, Bunny?" To my mother he said, "Let the kid speak for herself."

Mern wiped her hands on her robe and came over to me. "She can't speak for herself. She's just a kid. *My kid*, as a matter of fact." Her fingers dug into my shoulder. Everything was all ruined now.

"Your kid?" my father said. "You had some help, you know. You're not exactly the Virgin Mary."

"And you're not exactly Santa Claus," my mother said. She let go of me and began to move away, looking around the kitchen, uncertain of what to do next. She went back to the sink and ran herself a glass of water. She didn't want him to leave. I saw this clearly. Neither one of us hated him, and neither one of us wanted him to leave.

My father seemed more amused than upset. "Don't be mad, Noodle. Listen, why don't you and I go out, have something to eat, drink, you know, have a little reunion? That's not against the law, is it? Eunice can stay here till we get back." He got up and began to massage her shoulders. Mern closed her eyes, letting herself melt into his touch. "You wouldn't mind that, would you, Bunny? Your mother and me going out for old times' sake?" My mother lowered her head to expose her nape.

They'll both leave me now, I thought. *They want to be together without me.* I opened my mouth to say something, but nothing came out.

"Okay, then," Mern said, a little tipsy from his touch. Blowing me a kiss, she headed for the bedroom to change her clothes. My father came over and held my hand. "I knew I could count on you, Bunny." He started to sing. *"Beautiful, beautiful brown eyes."* Someone had sung that to me long, long ago.

After the two of them left, I got into bed and hugged my pillow. It was midday, but it might as well have been midnight. I was alone and nothing made sense. *Why did he leave us? Why isn't Mern mad anymore? Did he love me when I was a baby? Now that he's back, will he stay?* Eventually the questions trailed off. I heard the love duet from *Rigoletto* floating up from Mr. Tabachnik's. I could go downstairs, but I wasn't ready to tell Mr. Tabachnik about my father. I wanted to keep him secret, separate. For a short time, I played cat's cradle with a piece of string, listening to invisible birds laughing in the big tree outside. Hours later, my parents returned, jabbering as if they'd never been apart. Mern came into my room, and I waited for her to say, *What the heck are you doing in bed in the middle of the afternoon?* But instead, she just stood there grinning and twisting her shoulders back and forth, music playing in her head. She had gone out in her Joan Crawford dress with the big padded shoulders and jacket that was now buttoned wrong, and there was lipstick smeared on her front tooth. My father bounded through the doorway holding a box from Lane's Bakery.

"Bunny," he said. "Don't look so worried. You'll get wrinkles before your time." I took the box and pulled off the string. One cupcake was frosted pink, the other chocolate. "Thank you," I said. I felt sick to my stomach. Mern had gone into the living room. From the edge of my bed, I could see her flopped on the couch. *"It's only a paper moon,"* she sang with her eyes closed. My father laughed. "When she's not a nag, your mother's a barrel of fun." He offered his hand and helped me up. "The rest of the day is for you." He kissed my cheek.

"You're not leaving?"

He reeled back, affecting a hurt look. "What a question!"

"What are you two up to?" Mern called from the couch.

I got out of bed and followed my father into the living room. Mern looked me over and yawned. It was long past lunchtime, and I wondered if she'd ask if I'd eaten anything, though I was not surprised when she did not. My father went off to the bathroom. Mern crooked a conspiratorial finger at me. "He cares about us, kiddo. He really does. He told me he's turned over a new leaf."

What leaf, exactly, had been turned? I wondered. My father came back into the room, and she put her finger to her lips.

"You and I are going on an adventure," he said, and in one smooth motion, he gripped my waist and swung me above his head. He had it all planned. We were going to an amusement park, just the two of us, and we wouldn't come home till stars lit the sky. The train that would take us to Oceanside was one of the few passenger trains that still came through Wild Pea. He knew where the station was and knew the schedule; he'd been to this amusement park when he was a boy, and now he was going to take his best gal.

We hustled past Wagner's pharmacy, past the Laundromat, past George's Florist. Without knowing it, I'd been longing my entire life for the simple pleasure of strolling down the street with my father. The extraordinariness of the event was lost on passersby who smiled vaguely at what must have seemed our ordinary happiness. Only the motherless and fatherless would have noticed my rapture. It was early June, the trees lining the sidewalk standing like tall girls with identical bouffant hairdos. My mother's grousings echoed in my head, but I now dismissed them, the past sucked back into a vapor of forgetfulness, the clap of the sun on our faces undeniably real.

Inside the station, my father bought tickets, and we went back into the brightness to wait on the platform. A couple kissed openly, and several teenage boys pretended not to watch. My father asked if I had a boyfriend, and I almost said, *You!* "Well, let me tell you something, Bunny. Guys are going to be crazy for you. Trust me. Don't give your heart away to the wrong son of a b." He squinted down and examined my features for the nth time that day. "You sure are a chip off the old block, aren't you?" I shrugged. He looked at the sky. "What a knock-out of a day! You won't forget today, will you?" A cloud covered the sun. The light dulled and a shadow crossed our faces. I imagined his life of beautiful women, palm trees, yachts, the life of a movie star, the life Mern craved for herself instead of being stuck with me. A girl resembling Patti Page asked my father for a light, their eyes exchanging a momentary spark, and his fingers loosened from mine. A portion of my joy split off and blew away. *Suave*—that was the word my mother called him.

My father looked at his watch. The train was late. "Do you have any hobbies?" he asked casually.

I was ashamed to say I read encyclopedias in bed at night. "Baseball," I said.

My father grinned. "No kidding? Me too! That's my girl!"

Pride raced through me. We were alike. We liked baseball. We talked about Mickey the Great and Stan the Man. I told him I collected baseball cards. Which cards did I own? All the big names, except Whitey Ford. I wasn't a stupid girly girl. He bobbed his head, impressed. Then we got onto animals, which ones we liked best. I told him I wished I had a horse. I hadn't known I wanted a horse until it came out of my mouth, and then I felt I couldn't live without one. He leaned down from his great height to fix the shoulder strap of my red purse, which Mern had packed with Lorna Doones. "A girl like you deserves a horse," he said, my own self reflected in his dark eyes. He said he wished he had all the money in the world to buy me a horse and anything else I wanted. Removing a dollar bill from his pocket, he folded it in half and put it in my hand. "For your horse, Bunny," he said. "The first of many dollar bills from your father."

A few seconds later, the train rolled in. The black engine had a toot-toot whistle and a smokestack that spouted gray smoke. A storybook train. With the aid of the conductor, I climbed the steep metal steps, recalling the newspaper article Mern had recently read to me about a train accident that had killed a pack of Cub Scouts from Des Moines. She kept a scrapbook of disaster articles.

Our coach number was 4725. The seats were brown leather, two across. They held the depressions of departed bodies. I sat by the window behind a girl who cracked her gum. "We're going to have a fantastic time," my father said after we'd settled ourselves. "The best you've ever had." He took my hand and tossed it between his two, like an India rubber ball. The floor shimmied under us as the train lurched forward. The couplings clanked, the cars jiggled, and then the train assumed a steady rhythm, the station disappearing from sight.

Whole worlds raced by—shingled houses with screened porches, factories, empty schoolyards. Through a window, a man in an undershirt crouched in front of an open refrigerator. A woman watered pots of geraniums on her sill. I put my head against my father's shoulder. There was no need to talk. I watched my face watching me as we entered a tunnel, a ghostly moon in the dark glass. When we popped out into daylight, my father asked if I had any nicknames. I told him what Mr. Tabachnik called me; I told him what I called myself. "Your mother named you," he said. "Nothing personal but I never liked the name. I said to her, '*Eunice*, for crissake! That's an old lady's name. You can't name a baby *Eunice*. She'll hate us.' But you know how stubborn your mother is." He studied my face for confirmation. I eased my hand out of his and put it into my own lap. The way he was talking about my mother made me uncomfortable. "Another thing about her," he said. "She's heavy on demands, like she's entitled to get whatever she wants. Ever notice that?"

My father rested his hand on my knee. "You can tell me, Bunny. It'll be confidential. You're old enough to understand certain things. See, I want to set the record straight." He winked and squeezed my knee. "Let's admit it. Mern's bossy. Selfish too. A leopard can't change its spots, sweetheart."

I listened without saying much. I was modeling myself on Lauren Bacall in *Dark Passage*, practicing being the kind of woman a man could tell his secrets to without feeling betrayed.

The train slackened as we approached a meadow dusted with amber light. The sun was in the west, going down behind some trees. I put on a pair of Mickey Mouse sunglasses and turned away. My father searched his pocket for our tickets as the conductor proceeded down the aisle. After they were punched, he placed the yellow stubs in my hand. "There! A souvenir. From your old man. So you won't forget." I put them in my purse with the folded dollar. We were passing field after field of nothing but green nubs of corn. My father said, "What does she say about me?"

I had to think quickly. "She says you're a good dancer."

He scratched his chin. "True, true," he said. "What else does she say?"

My mind went blank. I couldn't think of a thing except *Big Bum*. The Big Bum. My father pulled out a package of Life Savers and offered me one. I picked a cherry Life Saver and sucked furiously.

"She blames me for all her unhappiness, doesn't she? Probably told you I have a bad temper, and I drink too much."

I stared into my lap and wished he would quit questioning me.

"Silence speaks louder than words," he said wistfully. "A woman like your mother can't be made happy. I did what I could. Remember that."

The train was pulling into a station. A small crowd of smiling, scrubbed faces waited under the portico of a redbrick building.

"I wish you never left," I said. But my father didn't seem to hear. He was staring out the window with a fixed expression. "She wants to make us enemies, Bunny, but we won't let her, will we?"

Resentment gathered in my throat, constricting my breath. He wanted me to like him more than I liked my mother. My mother wasn't perfect, but at least she hadn't run away. Some passengers boarded, entering our coach and making a bit of a ruckus. I saw only happy mothers and happy fathers with happy children. I watched them move down the aisle, deciding on seats. I touched my father's arm and smiled with every ounce of love I could muster.

When we arrived, the sun was no longer visible, and the air was dusty blue cut by streamers of pink-edged clouds. My father and I joined a pocket of people pushing toward the amusement park, which was all lit up a short distance away. The smallest children clutched their mothers' skirts, their faces throbbing with glee. My father bent down and asked if I wanted something to eat. I shook my head. My body felt warm and content, as though I'd filled myself with food and laughter and could rest easily in the after-sensation of their pleasure. I raised my nose to the wind and smelled big water nearby. Above, keen-eyed gulls with a pharaoh's profile wheeled in the sky. Every few minutes, one would make a spectacular dive, then ascend with something in its beak. My father hoisted me onto his shoulders, and I spread my arms wide and flapped away like a regular old seabird, the sounds and lights from the amusement park carrying us along.

As we approached the cyclone fence, Frankie let me down from his shoulders. Moms and pops and kids crowded near the entrance. The neon, the show tunes, the colors and smells wove an exquisite pattern, a quilt with a red star of sound, a navy rosette of twilight, and yellow piping all around. Frankie held my hand tightly as we paid the entrance fee and passed through the gate. "*See the pyramids along the Nile,*" he sang.

But something was wrong. Above the gate, the entrance sign did not say Oceanside. It said LAKEVIEW AMUSEMENT PARK.

"I thought we were going to Oceanside," I said.

My father shook his head and laughed, a curtain of dark hair flying away from his eyes. His teeth were as white as the gulls. "I did say Oceanside, didn't I?" His smile wasn't quite sincere. "Yeah, well, I wanted you to be excited." He cuffed my shoulder and fended off my protest. "What's the difference anyway—Oceanside, Lakeview? Lake Michigan is big enough to be an ocean, so that's all that counts."

I looked at him hard in case I'd missed something, but my father just beamed his smile. Of course I knew we lived in the Middle West, far from any ocean. *Oceanside.* The word had held a promise, and I felt cheated.

We proceeded into the glittering, spinning world, and my mood changed. An avenue of hot dog and popcorn stands faced us, a truck with a taffy-making machine, a booth that sold beer and soda pop. Next to these were open tents housing the games of chance. To the right, at some distance, the skeleton of the huge Ferris wheel stood against the sky, its hundreds of tiny pink lights tinting the air. The roller coaster rumbled, accompanied by shrieks of terror and delight. I gripped my father's hand.

In front of the games of chance, a boardwalk of gray-planked wood ran the length of the beach. My father bought us hot dogs, which we ate standing up, and then he bought a bag of peanuts to feed the pigeons perched on the boardwalk railing. In front of a bingo tent, my daddy said, "Watch this," and held out his nut-filled hands. Pigeons began dropping from the air. There stood my father haloed by the last golden threads of light, a chorus line of pigeons sidestepping down his arms. He shook his shoulders, and the birds jumped into the air like kites caught by a sudden wind. I could feel him watch me watching the pigeons disperse. "You got quite a mug on you," he said, his jaw stuck out with pride. He told me a story about when Mern was pregnant with me and how one night she woke him up crying and said the baby hadn't moved all day. She was afraid it was dead. "So I pulled back the covers and placed my hands on her stomach. 'Come on, kid,' I coached. 'Give your old man a somersault.' That was you I was talking to. I put my mouth to her belly button and whispered, 'Hey, baby, don't be afraid. It's going to be okay out here.'" My father clutched my shoulders. "Damn if you didn't start your gymnastics again, kicking your mother for all get-out. Damn," he said, running his hand over my cheek. "Damn if I don't remember everything about that night."

We had time for only a few games, a few rides, my father said. A wind came up off the lake, bringing with it the faintest odor of fish. I thought I heard the train's double whistle, but it might have been music from one of the rides or the midget who sold beaded Indian belts and played his flute. My father smoked a cigarette. The smoke rose into the violet twilight. I tried to follow the thread of smoke to see where it became soft bluish air, but it simply disappeared. He crushed his cigarette and held out his hand. "Come on. Let's go."

We climbed into a pair of bumper cars. Night was falling all around us, and I had the distinct feeling I'd been lifted onto a bright stage in a darkened theater. Nothing seemed to exist beyond our lit-up platform, the honky-tonk music, and the slashes of colored lights that now whirled across our faces. My father had to double up, knees to chest, to fit inside his kid-sized seat. Suddenly there was a jerk and our bumper cars came alive. My father waved his free arm and yelled, "I'm going to getcha." His car zigzagged across the vinyl floor, coming at me head-on. My hands went slick on the plastic wheel. I floored the pedal, and then we were chasing into each other, my father shouting, "Here I come," or "Bombs away," every jolting bump of our rubber fenders as thrilling as a kiss from my handsome father.

We hit the Ferris wheel next, all lit up like a giant clock ticking in the evening sky. My father marveled at its construction, at the brilliance of a man named Ferris who'd adapted the design from a bicycle wheel. My father knew about such things, strange and useful things pertaining to mechanics. Just because I was a girl, he said, was no reason I shouldn't have an erector set. He'd get me one. Someday he'd teach me to use a hammer, a plumb line, a miter box, a saw. *Someday.* When it was our turn to board, the man lifted the bar and held the seat steady. The metal was cold against the back of my thighs. My father looked down at my bare legs and frowned. "Doesn't your mother know how to dress you?" he said, rubbing my legs to warm them.

The Ferris wheel lifted us from the earth into the sky, where the air was even cooler and darker, and the stars were distant jewels whose nearness fell away once we swung over the top. The lake stretched out midnight blue, a silvery thread of moonlight across its surface. Beyond that was pure blackness. I uttered a cry as my stomach dropped, and the breath flew out of me. My father's right arm tightened around my shoulder. He squeezed my hand. I squeezed back. *I'll never let him go,* I thought.

The sign MR. DUPERE ESQ.: FAMOUS FROZEN CUSTARD blazed bright yellow neon at the end of the midway. Under it was a billboard with a picture of a cone topped with a huge swirl of vanilla custard. Behind the counter, a man was fussing with his malt machine. He had a flat face with a very black, very thin handlebar mustache, the edges of which were waxed and curled at the tip. He spoke with an accent that afterward my father said was French Canuck. The owner's name was

Denis Dupere, and he gave us cones with extra toppings. When we'd walked a few paces from his booth, my father and I laughed and held our fingers under our noses to imitate Denis Dupere's mustache.

"Chocolate or vanilly?" my father said in a froufrou French accent.

"Chocolate or vanilly?" I imitated.

My father pinched his nose and responded nasally, "Monsieur Dew-Pear to you." And that's when I stopped calling my father Frankie and started calling him Dupere.

When we finished our cones, I knew we'd have to be heading back. I could feel the abysmal pressure of loss coming over me, like the uneasiness before a storm, before the clouds bunched together and rolled down so close to the ground you could swear they weighed a ton. Before the thunder and the lightning you counted off for, then held your breath. When everything on earth sank into its own density, and the sky deepened several hues.

I tried to think of what I could do to forestall leaving Lakeview, like wrapping my arms around my daddy's knees and not letting him move. I pretended to get a speck of sand in my eye. My father knew I was acting. Snapping his green varsity jacket around me for warmth, he scooped me up onto his shoulders and carried me silently back to the train station. The air had a chilling bite and my legs prickled with cold. Lake and sky formed a single curtain of darkness. I looked back at the lights of the Ferris wheel. They seemed to touch the top of the sky, where a few more stars blinked their presence. I wondered if I was in a dream and if I would wake up in my own bed, smelling Mern's overstuffed ashtrays and bacon frying.

"Sleepy?" my father asked. We sat down on a bench outside the train station. "I have a secret," he said, snuggling close, and when I asked, "What?" he whispered, "I've got a crush on you." Under the harsh electric lights, my father's face looked as if something essential had drained out of it, something I couldn't name then, but I saw the remorse.

"Am I what you expected?" he asked quietly.

"Better," I said.

*   *   *

Mern was waiting up for us. She seemed jittery, pushing at her eyeglasses, full of quickly disappearing smiles. When we came in, she hugged me with all her strength and kissed the top of my head, something she never did. "You're back! You two were gone a long time. Jeez!" When she let me go, I didn't know whether to stand next to her or go over to my father. We moved in a pack into the living room, Dupere boasting about what a good time we'd had. Mern listened expectantly, as if any moment he was going to compliment her for doing a good job of raising me. While we were gone, she'd tidied the place. A bowl of pretzel sticks sat on Grandma's pine chest. I knew that they were fresh and that she'd gone to the market, because all the pieces weren't broken.

Dupere glanced at his watch. Mern blew a raspberry at him. "Bet you all had fun. Don't expect me to be the old maid next time!" She lit a cigarette from the tip of another. Dupere pushed his hands into his pockets. A second later, he shook them out and cracked his knuckles. He wasn't the same person he'd been earlier. My mother watched him with a sardonic little twist of a smile. Finally she told me to go to bed. I looked at Dupere for help, but his eyes skittered from mine. He wasn't thinking about me anymore. I got up and went over and stood in front of him. "We had a good time, didn't we?"

He put his hand on my head. "Sure thing, Bunny," he said. No more dazzling smile.

"G'night," I said, just barely controlling myself from locking my arms around his legs. At the last minute I stammered, "Y-you won't forget about the horse?"

Mern glared at my father. "What did you promise her, Frankie?"

My father ignored her. "Hey! I won't forget about the horse." He hesitated a moment before giving me a hug.

In my room, I put the yellow ticket stub and my horse money in the Whitman's Sampler tin. My room was chilly. I pulled up my covers and closed my eyes. I saw my parents in a field, tipsy with love, dancing to bluesy horns. Through the haze, a Ferris wheel was spinning toward them. In the top seat, a man resembling my father swung dangerously in the wind. When I opened my eyes, night had become day, a radiant, sunshiny day. I threw off my sheet and rushed into the kitchen. This was the first morning of my new life.

Mern was sitting at the table. Her eyes looked as if she'd put drops of iodine in them. Crumpled tissues sat in a heap next to an ashtray filled with a million butts. She spoke without looking at me, the sound of her voice like that of a person on death row.

"He didn't even stay the night. Didn't even have the courage to say good-bye to you. The shit. The bastard." She started to cry. Every cell in my body knew it was true. Even as he'd said, "You're my Bunny!" and promised me a horse, I knew he was going to leave again. If he walked back into our flat in the next minute, I'd probably run to him, at the mercy of his white teeth and dark eyes, but we weren't enough to keep him. I'd heard that lightning doesn't strike the same place twice, but that was a lie. My father was like one of those comets that whizzed by every hundred years. His light had vanished from our earth. I looked up at the calendar next to the sink and memorized the date. Sunday, June 14, 1953—the Second Time My Father Leaves Us.

Chapter 3

Overnighters

My mother had driven my father away. Of this I was sure. The shithead, she said. F'ing creep. If I defended him, I got blasted: *Eunice, you are a traitor to the cause.* If I covered my ears, she slapped my hands away. "Pay attention, kiddo, or you'll fall for a louse like him." Forget about the horse he promised. "Your father's as close as you'll get to a horse—a horse's ass!" Nevertheless, I waited for a sign that would let me know my daddy hadn't forsaken me. I refused to acknowledge it to her, but as the weeks passed, I suspected my mother was right: Frankie was a rat fink, a womanizer, and a deceiver; he played the horses and ran with the mob. Or the taunt that burrowed into the heart of my heart: he had another family he stashed somewhere that he loved more. Mr. Tabachnik offered his own pearls. "A man such as your papa is not worthy of calling himself a man." Over such a person, my heart would shrivel to a wasteland of sorrow.

Mern's unhappiness was my unhappiness, and there was no escaping it. The Man Upstairs didn't give a shit, she said, hoping to spark a revelation in me. "Where did you come from?" she'd say when she failed to incite me against my father, when her tirades fizzled into an uneasy standoff that might, in the world of her topsy-turvy emotions, send her into my bed that night. What she simply didn't understand was that we *both* loved Frankie and we *both* wanted him back and that every poisoned arrow she shot at him hit me in the gut.

I thought her ranting would go on forever, but about a year after my daddy left us, she said she'd be damned if she was going to let the bum ruin her life. To celebrate the Fourth of July, Mern bought sparklers and mint ice cream, and when the sky grew lustrously black, she went downstairs and invited Mr. Tabachnik to join us. "So. Misery takes a holiday, just like that!" Mr. Tabachnik said. Mern bowed her head and stared at her sandaled feet. She least of all could predict her moods.

In the garden we set the lawn chairs in a circle and dished ice cream into Dixie Cups. Mern lit a cigarette. A sweetness lifted from the roses, and in the deep twilight, wearing her new red kimono with the dragon on the back, she could have passed for one of our movie heroines. Annie had dyed Mern's hair platinum, and in her Marilyn Monroe do, without makeup and glasses, she looked untroubled and innocent, the way Marilyn might have looked when she was still Norma Jeane. My mother began to sing, "*Home, home on the range.*" Her voice was strong and pure and lovely. Mr. Tabachnik took off his spectacles and wiped them with the corner of his sweater. The booms began before we saw the sky blow open with light and dazzle. Mern's hand searched for mine in the dark, and a tear leaked from my eye. That night she let me climb into her bed, and I slept against the curve of her belly, her breath making wet patches behind my ear.

Annie continued to drop over and console Mern about Frankie. Annie was my mother's best and only friend, and Mern and I adored her. Whenever I visited the shop, Annie set down her scissors and made a fuss. "Why, you can't be Eunice," she'd say. "Why, I thought you were Elizabeth Taylor!" She'd turn to my mother. "Mern, this doll-baby is growing up much too fast!" Mern called Annie *buxom*, which meant she was reassuringly sturdy, if slightly masculine, but not flabby or fat. What cemented their friendship was a wicked sense of humor and an attitude of being different from the rest of the "cows." Annie's father had been a policeman who'd cracked a couple of skulls, including Annie's, and Mern hinted that now Annie didn't like men. Occasionally Annie accompanied us to the Hollywood Cinema, sleeping over afterward on the scratchy couch. In the morning, my mother and Annie enjoyed picking apart the cosmetic mistakes of the stars. One Friday night toward the end of summer, we had just gotten back from seeing a rerun of *The Reckless Moment*, a juicy murder story starring Joan Bennett, and Annie brought up my father. Where did Mern think he was? "Rotting in hell," my mother said, shuffling a deck of cards.

"Any man will trample you, if you give him half a chance," Annie said.

My mother sighed. "In a perfect world, women could have flings, just like men, and not be strung up for them."

Annie wrinkled her brows and thought for a moment. "In a perfect world, flings wouldn't be flings, but every single time would be real love."

My mother laughed. "Real love? Too exhausting!"

Annie shook her head. "But what a perfect way to die!"

"In a perfect world," my mother continued, staring at the ceiling where a fly was walking upside down, "I could afford anything I wanted and wouldn't have to slave night and day."

"Amen," Annie said solemnly. "In a perfect world, that would be true." She turned to me. "What do you think about all this, pal? What would be a perfect world for you?" she said, slapping her paw over the nine of clubs I'd just drawn.

I felt my mother's eyes on me. "In a perfect world, there'd be nothing to wish for because everything would be so perfect." My mother breathed a sigh of relief. I hadn't brought up my father.

"In a perfect world, you could eat chocolate cake for every meal and not get fat," Annie said, blowing out her cheeks.

"Bingo!" my mother said. "And in a perfect world, liquor wouldn't make you drunk and cigarettes wouldn't give you bad breath and a cough."

"In a perfect world, there'd be no such thing as constipation."

"No varicose veins either," my mother said, sliding her hand down her calf.

"No hemorrhoids or arthritis, bleeding gums, no losing teeth. Who wants to be Betty Crocker when you can be Betty Bacall!"

Their rummy game was losing steam, and they decided to go out. To Delrico's or the Rusty Nail. Wild Pea wasn't a big town, but it was big enough to have more than one bar. I knew about those places. They gave off a sad, dark feeling when you passed their tinted windows and dirty brick fronts. "You don't mind if your mother and I have a little fun?" Annie said. Mern had already left the room to put on something flashy.

The following winter and spring, my mother came home from these excursions wobbling on her heels, her lipstick and thick layers of Max Factor pancake rubbed off. Her kisses were spongy, her words slurred. "Life's no bowl of cherries, kiddo. You'll find out!" Her education had been at the School of Hard Knocks. It was her turn to have fun. I'd watch her in the bathroom, extending her eyeliner into little black hooks. Who was she today? Hedy Lamarr? Dorothy Lamour? Dorothy Malone? I practiced in the same mirror in my best Rosalind Russell voice. *Mern! You must mend the error of your ways!* "You're a misfit," I'd say, "and if I don't do something about it, I'll be a misfit too."

If my mother wrestled with guilt about her nights on the town, her solution came in the form of crackpot offerings—feathered fishing lures, a rhinestone shoe buckle, or some garage-sale junk she laid at the foot of my bed. Other mothers bought their daughters roller skates or potholder kits. Mern offered trinkets, a kiss, and a rhyme she giggled while tracing a scarlet fingernail over my skin. "Tickle, tickle on your knee. If you laugh, you don't love me." Maybe she thought that in case of fire or thieves, Mr. Tabachnik would charge wheezing up the stairs to rescue me, but Mr. Tabachnik was slightly deaf in one ear, turned out his lights at 9:30, and slept the sleep of the undisturbed. We often heard the whale songs of his dreams rising up through the open windows.

But one morning before dawn, he caught her sneaking in. This was in early May. Mr. Tabachnik and my mother were arguing under the door light, their voices breaking through my sleep. I went to the window. Mr. Tabachnik was in his pajamas, jabbing a finger at Mern's head. "What you got in there for brains? Leaving a kid alone like that? Shame on you."

"I was walking a friend's dog," my mother said, starting to crumble, her voice low but grudging.

Mr. Tabachnik repositioned two milk bottles cradled against his chest. "You think because the sun don't fail to come up every morning your kid is safe?"

My mother swayed on her feet. "Wha?"

Mr. Tabachnik grabbed her arm with his free hand. "You think nothing can happen here in America? You should know how lucky you are." He paused to gather momentum. "Safe? *Gott im Himmel.* What is safe?"

They were both silent for a moment, pondering. He touched her shoulder lightly. "Let me tell you, there's no such thing as safe. You've never been to such places where they snatch the children from the mothers and shoot them right in front of the mamas' eyes." The grief in his voice shocked them both. Mern hung her head without moving.

Mr. T's voice rose again. "Why should I care? What are you to me? Are you family?" He spat on the walk and brushed my mother away. "Go. Go upstairs to your daughter. And stop acting like an alley cat."

But my mother refused to listen.

One night I woke and I knew I was alone. Mern had stayed out late before, very, very late, but this was different. The silence in our flat felt heavy and inert; darkness swirled past my door down the hallway. I was afraid to see Mern's untouched bed. Clutching my sheet, I watched the moon climb over the catalpa, speckling its bare branches with a hundred dashes of light.

That night Mern crossed an invisible line. I was sure she was biding her time; she would leave me just like my daddy had. But I was biding my time too. Sooner, not later, if only I could figure out where I'd go and how I'd get there, I'd disappear, and Mern would decompensate in regret. Meanwhile, I'd develop tactics to reshape the lonely hours. That night may have been when I started to draw—the lamppost throwing its weak cone of light on the walk; my tennis shoe, its streaming laces the only white thing in Mr. Tabachnik's darkened garden. I drew an intricate spiderweb on the inside of my arm and thought up something to make me laugh: Mern's corpse, plastic-white with bright red lips, in a fancy satin coffin, sitting up to ask for a smoke.

I finished fifth grade. At school when I had to read aloud, the words dissolved into squiggles. I remembered Bette Davis in *Dark Victory* and wondered if I was going blind. Mr. Tabachnik said the trouble wasn't my vision. "Confidence, Cisskala, and practice!" We made an agreement: I would read to him every afternoon, and for every book I finished, he'd give me a dime for my horse. One day I heard my own voice as if for the first time; it sounded pleased and sure. Something was going to happen. I couldn't see what, exactly, because the change was outside words. Mern tore off the calendar pages month by month. For a while, a man named Reggie phoned. Not much changed even as change bore down on us.

Then my mother did something to win me back. One morning in June, three years after my daddy left, she marched into my room honking a nasal rendition of "Reveille" through her fist, the piercing twang of those first notes jarring me from sleep, and coerced me from bed with the promise of a surprise in the bathroom. "Upsy-daisy," she bugled. "Rise and shine." Brimming with smiles, she shushed my pro-tests and pushed me forward, cold hands low on my spine. In the bath-tub was a turtle with my name painted in red nail polish on its shell.

"Eunice?" I said.

My mother laughed. "Eunice!"

I looked again at the turtle straining to climb up the side of the tub and was not prepared for the sudden and unbearable pressure inside my chest, an odd mingling of doom and love. Eunice Turtle was the size of my palm, a dark mossy color, like the bottom of a lake, with yellow pinstripes running down her almost-black legs. Her face was pinched together at the tip, a long green thumb without a chin. She was trying to crawl up the slick side of the porcelain and was making straining motions with her back legs. Mern lit a cigarette and gestured to the turtle. "I forgot to get it food. You think it will eat bologna?" I turned around to see if she was kidding. Already I was picturing a box filled with grass and a bowl for paddling around in and a flat rock for sunbathing. I would catch flies and spiders for her. I caught a whiff of Cashmere Bouquet as my mother moved behind me.

"Promise me you won't smooch that turtle," she said, cigarette smoke wreathing us. "Turtles have streptanosis-something, Eunice. They can give it to humans." She dropped her head over my shoulder and made a face. I laughed. Mern had never been brave about disease. Dogs gave you fleas. Cats had leukemia. Squirrels and bats carried the dreaded rabies, from which, if bitten, you could not be saved. Eunice Turtle was doing a slow-motion turtle two-step back toward the drain. When I looked again, she'd flipped over onto her back and her legs were swimming in the air. I reached down and put her right-side up. Mern rubbed her eyes with her fists and yawned. "Poor thing. Wouldn't you know I picked up a brain-damaged turtle."

"That's not funny," I said.

She pretended to sniff the air. "Smells like turtle pee-pee in here. Maybe I should splash some Evening in Paris on its shell." I could hear the phlegm breaking up in her before-breakfast chuckle. She swept past me and opened the bathroom window. A wave of lilacs floated in. It was a Saturday that my mother didn't have to work until later in the afternoon.

"Okay, that's enough turtle for me. Coffee time, kiddo. Let's get the show on the road." Her mules flip-flopped on the tiles as she left the room, and I wondered where Mern could have gotten a turtle in the middle of the night.

When she was gone, I slid my hand under Eunice Turtle, picked her up, and stroked her horny shell. We stared at each other for a meaningful minute, her pert upturned face and liquidy black eyes gazing into mine. It gave me a miraculous feeling, as though we were speaking without words. The nose holes in her face quivered. Then she pulled into her house.

"You in there, Eunice Turtle?" I said, rapping a knuckle against the crooked red lines of my name. "Are you really in there?" I couldn't feel anything through her armor, not her squishy body, not her delicate heart and lungs. Very gently I kissed the collar of rubbery skin into which her head had disappeared. "That's okay," I said. I laid her back in the bathtub in a pod of sunlight. She looked like a little green space-ship marooned on Planet Whiteness.

Chapter 4

Eunice Turtle

So, do you want to hear where I was last night? Swear to God, I saved a man's life." My mother was in her gypsy queen mode, spinning tales and smoking by the sink in her kimono.

"A guy collapsed in my lap at Delrico's last night, and I went to the hospital with him in an ambulance. I *volunteered* to go in the ambulance."

Did she think I was so gullible? She'd faint at the sight of blood.

"And you know who I was thinking of when I marched through those hospital doors? You."

I snorted.

"I am telling you the truth. When I marched through those hospital doors and saw the nurses running around in their white hats, all I could think about was almost dying because you were too stubborn to come out." By some magical means, we'd now arrived at the story of my birth, the story of how much Mern had suffered to give me life. When I was very little, she told the Birth Story so often I'd memorized it word for word. She repeated it now with her usual gusto: Dr. Jekyll leering from his mask over a tray of knives about to perform an emergency cesarean. The killeroo, not-to-be-believed pain. Her brave, selfless stoicism in the face of it all. "Someday, Eunice," she said, tapping her ash, "when I'm dead and buried, you'll realize your mother wasn't a bad person. Someday when it's too late, you'll understand my life's been no picnic. Now, here's the truth, believe it or not. A man named Sam Podesta might've died if it hadn't been for me. In fact, he might even be dead now."

Mern was on her feet, the front of her kimono flying open. "Someday you'll realize that everything, *everything I've ever done for you, I've done out of love.*"

I stamped my feet and shouted back, "Nothing! You do *nothing* for love!" A hundred broken promises lay between us. I announced I was going downstairs to live with Mr. Tabachnik.

"Go, then. Run away to that sad old fool," Mern said. "You're just like your father, leaving the scene when things get hot. You don't care what happens to me, do you, Eunice! You're not the least bit interested."

"She can't help herself," Mr. Tabachnik said, walking in circles on his Persian carpet.

"Don't protect her," I growled.

"She should get down on her hands and knees and thank God she has a daughter like you." Mr. Tabachnik took out his hanky and blew his nose. He didn't want to be a buttinsky, but a little girl named Cisskala *was* his business. For a while we listened to ball games on the radio and later pored over the *P* encyclopedia, and Mr. T showed me the place he was born. "One day you're from the Ukraine," he said. "The next day the village sign is in German. A year later, Russian soldiers are sleeping in your barn." He removed his glasses and wiped the lenses. "Let me tell you something, the land doesn't know from one conqueror to another. The dray horse remembers the shape of the field in his sleep."

By evening, Mr. Tabachnik convinced me to go back upstairs, but when I walked into our flat, Mern refused to look at me, her version of the silent treatment. "I'm taking a bath. Answer the phone," she said, addressing the wall behind my head.

That night I refreshed the grass in Eunice Turtle's shoebox and changed the water in her bowl. She was the only one I could really talk to.

"I'm glad you're here," I said.

Me too, she answered.

Before I fell asleep, I opened the Whitman's Sampler tin, removed the dollar bill, and sniffed the picture of George Washington to see if I could detect any trace of my father. I'll never get a horse, I thought, but at least I have a turtle.

The next morning, Mern stood in my doorway. For a long moment, we stared at each other. Meeting her steady gaze felt like sliding down the throat of a pure blue morning glory. I blinked and she puckered her lips.

"Let's make up, my little Moucheroo."

I practically wept. Her little Moucheroo! She took me by the hand and we cruised into her bedroom. Opening her nightstand, she withdrew a cross on a silver chain. "Sam Podesta gave this to me last night. For saving his life." She swung the necklace in front of my eyes like a pendulum. "Proof is proof," said Mern, the tiny eye at the center of the cross watching me as it swung. I fell back onto her bed, grabbed a pillow, and crushed it to my chest. "You're weird," I said.

She swooped down for the newspaper next to her bed. "More proof," she said, and pushing up her glasses, she read, "'Aries. Watch for entrances and exits. This is a time for romance. Relax and get a facial.'" She rattled the newspaper in my face. See, Sam Podesta was in her stars.

"You're not normal," I said. "Normal, normal."

"Who wants to be normal?" my mother said. "Normal is boring, Eunice."

I burst into laughter. Who wanted to be normal? Mern removed the pillow from my clutches, uncurled my fist, and poured the silver chain into my hand. She climbed into bed and draped an arm around my shoulder. "Sam Podesta practically dropped dead in my lap. You want to hear or not?" Without waiting for my reply, she began.

She and Annie stayed late to do cash-out; then they decided they deserved some refreshment, so they went over to Delrico's. "I sat at the bar. Vic the bartender told me he's trying to save money to buy a small boat—nothing fancy, a putt-putt he can take fishing—and then, in the middle of our conversation, this guy walks in." Did I remember Gene Kelly in *Anchors Aweigh*? This guy was no Gene Kelly, but he had those natty Irish looks. Maybe Irish on his mother's side. The blue eyes, the teeth. He was brawnier, with a bit of a pot.

"He climbed onto the stool next to me, introduced himself, ordered a Schlitz and one for me. A real gentleman." She said it had been hotter than an oven in Vic's. The fan was broken, and it was muggy, like the air was used up. Sam drank his beer, then right away ordered another. He told her he was new in town, didn't know many people. He was the new produce manager at Dvorjek's. Said it was a big responsibility.

"He unzips this leather pouch and rolls himself a cigarette. 'Turkish stuff,' he says. 'I've been all over this globe. I'm a navy man,' he says, 'in case you couldn't tell.' He was wearing a sailor's cap, so of course I could tell. He says, 'Compared to what I've tasted, American tobacco can't cut the mustard. I've gotten used to good tobacco, good wine, good bread,' he says. 'Real bread. With fennel and pine nuts baked in it. Indian bread with onions and ground lamb. I've seen the world,' he says. 'I've tasted the world. I know quality.'" She scrambled out of bed to get her own cigarettes.

"Then Vic started singing, '*How ya gonna keep 'em down on the farm.*' And God, we all started laughing at that one. But all this time, I'm noticing how Sam's face is getting shinier and shinier. Sweat's dripping down his forehead. I said to Vic he ought to save for an air conditioner instead of a fishing boat, and he got riled, said I must be one delicate lady to be so sensitive.

"Then the next thing I know, Sam has got awfully quiet, and he's pulling at his collar. When he goes for his glass, his hand starts shaking. Crash! Bam! He drops the glass. Next thing, he's sliding off his stool and practically into my lap."

Mern stopped talking to strike a match. "Do you think I could make this up?" she said, exhaling, peering into my eyes for a good long second.

A thought flashed through my mind. Mern was telling the truth, but what was so special about the truth? The truth wasn't Superman or the FBI. It couldn't protect you from anything. Sometimes it even got you into trouble.

"Did he die?"

Mern shook her head and blew out smoke rings. "You never saw Vic move so fast. He yelled for Marty, who shot out of the back room where he'd been doing the books. Marty said Sam was having a fit and we'd better get hold of his tongue." Mern stuck hers out, demonstrating.

"Not for a million bucks was I gonna put my fingers into a stranger's mouth. But Vic said it wasn't a fit, probably a heart attack, and we laid him on the floor, and Vic put a cool cloth on his head, and Marty called the ambulance, and I rubbed Sam's hands so his blood would come back.

"When the ambulance arrived, Vic kept trying to explain to the drivers it wasn't the beer. Maybe he thought he'd get blamed. They wrapped Sam up and put him on a stretcher. He rallied for a minute, opened his eyes, and said, plain as day, 'It's all your fault, sugar. My heart is going crazy 'cause I just met a beautiful doll.' He shot me a smile before he went out. 'Christ!' I thought. 'What if that's the last thing he says?' Meanwhile, Vic shoves Sam's sailor cap into my hands. 'You go. Go with him,' he says, pushing me out the door behind the drivers. So then I'm in the ambulance with Sam, praying he's not going to croak on me. I'm thinking, 'This guy's got a good attitude.' I couldn't forget how he'd called me a beautiful doll, making a joke when he was at death's door. Hey, I could learn to like an upbeat guy like Sam.

"At Sisters of Charity, we backed up to Emergency. Sam was awake but groggy. Now it's around midnight, and you'd think the place'd be empty, but some drunk had just driven into a tree and the police were bringing him in. The nurses were running around with bags of blood. One of them—the type who wears a nylon net over her hair and thinks it's invisible—comes up to me and says, 'Who are you with?'" Mern snorted. "I say, 'I'm Sam Podesta's girlfriend.' What am I supposed to say? That I sat next to him at a bar? Jesus. The emergency room was a dismal place. Forget about sleep. I walked those halls for God knows how long. I couldn't go home without knowing about Sam. Maybe I was there an hour or two. Finally another nurse finds me and says

Sam's okay, but they're going to keep him overnight, for observation. Then she hands me the cross and says Sam instructed her to give it to me—that is, if I was still there. 'Tell her it's a lucky charm from Sam Podesta.'" Mern sighed. "The end."

"What about Sam?"

"I don't know," she said. "I've been afraid to call the hospital." She reached into the pocket of her kimono and brought out a packet of matches. The cover was forest green with "Delrico's" written in white. She placed the matches on the night table. Real evidence.

"Here's the bit that concerns you. To get to the front of the hospital, I had to walk through the children's ward. Room after room of sick, sleeping children. At the end of a hall, I passed an open door, a red light blinking above it. The bed was stripped, the sheets bundled in a corner. I didn't want to think what might have just happened. You couldn't really see in, except something, a streak of light, caught my eye. Believe it or not, on the windowsill, was a fishbowl. I go over. There's a turtle at the bottom."

Mern opened her arms wide to convey the wacky wonder of it all. My throat closed on horror-filled laughter. Eunice Turtle had been stolen from a dead kid!

Mern rested her hand over mine. "So, for your information, kiddo, not only did I do one good deed last night. I did two. I saved Sam Podesta, and I saved a turtle."

Chapter 5

Sam Podesta

A storm blew down on Wild Pea. Branches cartwheeled across lawns. Sparrows flew from hedges; lightning seared the sky. "Holy Toledo! We're in a goddamn blitz!" my mother said, tightening the sash of her kimono. Sam Podesta still hadn't called, though her horoscope promised that her moon was moving into the House of Love. What was the deal? "A person doesn't just walk away from death's door, Eunice." She took a post by the bay window in the living room, and her eyes burned through the glass at the bruised air. "I'm not getting any younger," she muttered. "Beggars can't be choosers."

Before I could say what I was thinking—that it was true she was getting older, but that *everything* was getting older: the catalpa tree in the yard, Mr. Tabachnik's roses, the earth itself eroding—she fled into the kitchen and returned with a mug of rum, which she did not even try to hide. For her nerves, she said. What was the point of arguing? She turned back to the window and I started to walk away. "I'm not getting any younger and *neither are you*," she called after me. "Shirley Temple's star faded long before she turned twelve." My head went hollow and I froze. I was thirteen. I couldn't have spoken if I'd wanted to.

Just then a wand of sunlight broke through the clouds and hundreds of raindrops coursing down the windows glowed pearly rose. Mern looked dazed for a moment, caught in the sudden brilliance; her face softened as she slouched over to tug my sleeve. "So solly, Chahlee! You're only a baby!" She stood back from me, pouting and puckering up. "Hey, don't be so sensitive. Who's my little Moucheroo!"

* * *

"Human beings are such problems. Why do we even like them?" I asked Eunice Turtle that night.

Eunice Turtle halted on the way to my lap, right leg in the air. *Ask me when I've been around a little longer,* she said.

The next morning it was raining again. "We might as well be living in Red China," Mern mumbled. Hundreds of Chinese people had recently been swept away by a flood. "We might as well be starving in India," she continued. Stewed in a pot in Africa. Freezing in Antarctica. Tsetse-flied in Panama. Her chest collapsed under the weight of yet another sigh. She was at the kitchen table licking Green Stamps into a book. A hundred books or more and she'd get a trip to Miami. Downstairs, the buzzer rang. Electricity jolted through my body. *Dupere.* Mern tore off her glasses and stuffed them into her pedal pushers, then tugged down her bra. I ran into my bedroom to brush my hair. Mern opened the door. It took me a long, slow minute to realize my prayers hadn't brought my daddy back. Sam Podesta had arrived.

This was Sam Podesta? A short, stout man with a wide pink face and a crust of sandy hair with a mustache to match. He was wearing a Hawaiian shirt and trousers held up by a belt with a bronze bull's-head buckle studded with chips of turquoise. A sailor's cap slanted down over his wide forehead. All that was Gene Kellyish about him were his soft-soled tan dancing shoes. I flattened myself against a bedroom wall and watched him click his heels and offer Mern a box of fancy wrapped chocolates. If she'd been expecting Frankie, she didn't let on. She took the chocolates and asked how his ticker was after the hospital business.

"Ticker's fine. Ticker's great. No prob-lem-mae with the ole ticker," Sam said in the doorway, rapping on his heart. He admitted he shoulda called right away. He looked over Mern's shoulder and asked if he could come in. My mother stood aside. Removing his sailor's cap, Sam fell in behind Mern, his eyes fixed on her bum. In his buttery leather shoes, he floated over the floor like a man ten pounds lighter.

Mern led him into the living room, where he whistled at the fake jade dragon lamp. "Nice," he said, running his hands over the base. His fingers brushed across Grandma's pine chest. "I got an eye for the finer things in life," Sam said, taking in the rest of our place. "Just like my mama. She taught me."

"So. There's *nothing* the matter with you?" Mern said, getting back to the ticker issue.

"Ya know what they say in the navy? 'You can't keep a good man down.'" Mern smiled hesitantly. "Listen," Sam said, hiking up his trousers before settling on the couch. "You did a good deed. You saved me from a quick trip to the afterlife." He revealed that his stomach, not his heart, had caused the attack at Delrico's. "Acts up on me periodically," he said, rubbing his belly. "From eating in too many Tokyo slop joints. But, hey, it takes more than a little indigestion to stop a navy man."

Mern sat perched next to Sam on the couch, their knees touching. She blinked and smiled and nodded.

"Never thought I'd see the inside of an ambulance, at least stateside. But I'm not complaining. Wouldn't have had this opportunity otherwise."

"What opportunity?" Mern said. Sam pointed to the box of chocolates she was holding. "To say thank you, ma'am." Mern was about to tear open her gift when I decided to come out from hiding.

Sam glanced up and cat whistled. "Who's this? Dolores del Rio? You didn't tell me you had a movie star living with you."

I giggled.

Mern regarded me without enthusiasm. "This is Eunice."

"CC," I corrected.

"Nicknames are serious business," Sam said. His eyes were crystal blue, like the glaciers in *National Geographic*. "Come on over here, sugar," he said, patting his knees.

I went over and he took off his sailor's cap, swept back my bangs, and adjusted the cap on my head. "Got any beaus, Dolores del Rio?"

I shook my head.

"Son of a gun," Sam said. "If I were ten years younger..."

Mern had fallen silent, biting her lip. Sam threw me a humdinger of a smile. I was beginning to understand why she liked him.

"Wanna see something?" he said. I nodded. Sam rolled up his shirtsleeves. He had a tattoo in the middle of his arm, the name *Buddy* in block letters against a wavy American flag. "My brother Buddy," he said. "A genuine war hero." He rolled up the other sleeve. His skin was pale and freckled. The left-arm tattoo was of a woman in a grass skirt. When he flexed his bicep, her breasts bounced. *Hips Ahoy* was written across her belly. Heat crept up my neck. "Go ahead and touch her," Sam encouraged, and when I did, he flexed again. I laughed at his muscle popping like a Mexican jumping bean. "Betcha never saw anything like that," he said. He plucked the sailor's cap from my head and, zigzagging it in front of my face, produced from within the folds a small penknife with an ivory handle. I thought he might give me the penknife, but he put it back in his pocket.

Mern looked on sourly. "You are excused now, Eunice," she said. "Mr. Podesta has better things to do than entertain you." She put a finger on the grass-skirted lady. "Seen a lot of action, huh, Sam?"

Sam turned his hands over. "*Comme ci, comme ça.* I've been here and there. Depends on what you mean by 'action.'" He ran his tongue over his mustache. "But, hey! I'll tell ya, I've been a lot of places. A lot of places. Places you only dream about. I've seen things you wouldn't believe."

Mern appeared impressed. "Like what?"

"You name it, I've seen it." He closed his eyes for a minute. "Seen an iceberg so big it touched the clouds. Seen a man digging in the earth with a stick, routing out beetles and cramming them into his mouth. Seen another man chase a goat three times around his village so his wife would be free of the devil. I've seen the world, Mern. Turkey, Greece, Taiwan, Ind-jah! Brides with rubies in their nostrils. Seen it all, Mern." He rubbed the back of his neck, which looked a little raw from a new haircut. "But, hell, it was nothing compared to what my brother Buddy saw. Shot right out of his plane and fell like a comet." He hissed through his teeth, his hand dive-bombing into his lap. "This was in the Big War. Right before the end."

"Sorry," Mern said.

"Yeah, yeah," Sam said, rolling down his sleeves and fastening the cuffs. "That's life." There was an awkward silence. Outside a motor started up.

"But, hey! That's not why I'm here. I didn't come to talk about the past. No sirree. Bravery is why I'm here." Sam turned to me. "Do you know your mother is a fine woman? Not just any woman would escort a stranger to the hospital. She's the Good Samaritan and Ginger Rogers all packaged up into one fantastic doll."

The lines had a familiar ring, especially the "fantastic doll" part. James Cagney? Edward G. Robinson?

"I was just telling Eunice, 'It was in the stars for Sam and me to meet like that.' Which reminds me, what's your sign, Sam?"

"Sign of what?"

"When's your birthday?"

"August," Sam said.

Mern snapped her fingers. "We're both fire signs. What did I tell you?"

"You're an unusual woman, Mern."

"How do you mean? What kind of unusual?"

Sam considered. "I couldn't say exactly, Mern." He massaged his forehead for a minute. "You're rare, like...an Indianhead penny in a stack of Lincolns."

Mern tried to laugh. Being compared to a penny? She'd heard better lines from Alan Ladd. "Refreshments, anyone?" she said, and sauntered off to the kitchen on her white satin mules.

"Temperamental," Sam whispered when she left the room. "I know the type. They want to be appreciated. 'Handle with Care!' That's what ya gotta do."

Mern returned, carrying a tray with her idea of the royal treatment: Cokes, a carton of Neapolitan ice cream, a flask under a paper napkin. She'd ducked into the bathroom to reapply lipstick, rouge, and black liner around her eyelids. I'd forgotten she was so pretty.

Mern plunked the tray onto the chest and poured three glasses of Coke, spiking two with rum.

"Hey, none of that stuff for me," Sam said. "Puts holes in your liver. I just take a little Chianti or a Schlitz now and then."

Mern thought he was kidding. "Sailors and rum go together, like ducks and water."

"Yeah, well," he said, "not this sailor. Liquor turned my old man into a mean slob." Sam held up his glass. "But, listen, forget about my lousy father and the crazy past. To the future. To my Florence Nightingale. To the woman who saved my life."

"Oh get outta here," Mern said, lapping it up.

For a while they both forgot about me and talked about ambulances and freak accidents, Sam saying, "Remember the Lindbergh baby. Wasn't that something?" and Mern saying she was just a baby herself when it happened. Then Sam saying, "I bet you were one helluva cute baby, Mern, and I bet Dolores del Rio here was a knockout too," and this led Mern into my birth story, how they had to take me out with hooks. "Of course, they weren't really hooks," she confided, launching into the gruesome details once again, my face burning with pleasure and shame. When my mother finished, Sam stretched down a hand and touched my cheek. Mern's head jerked in my direction. "You still here?"

They got onto other stories about kidnappings, drownings, fires, and hatchet murders. The carton of ice cream sat in a puddle on the tray. Mern told one about a street cleaner who had swept gravel into his own eye and gone blind. Sam topped her with a tale about a baby who'd been eaten by an alligator in a Florida swimming pool. Mern gasped, pretending to be shocked. The height of the afternoon had passed and the fading light spilled across the floor. Mern uncrossed her legs and reached for a cigarette. "Call for Philip Moor-ris," she yodeled. Shaking out a Camel, she offered one to Sam. "I don't smoke American brands," he said, and pulled out a pouch from his back pocket and rolled two cigarettes, which he lit with a Ronson. He handed one to Mern. "Turkish tobacco. Once you try it, you'll never smoke anything else."

Mern let smoke drift out of her mouth, then sucked it up into her nose, a French inhale. "Tell me about yourself, Sam," she drawled, but before he could answer, she hit him with a slew of questions. Had he liked the navy? Where was he stationed? Not so slyly, she asked if there'd been a girl back home. "Nope, I was free as a bird. Mama was my best gal, my *only* gal back then."

"Come on. No wartime sweetheart?" Mern ribbed.

"I wasn't *in* the war," Sam said. "I was on a ship, sure. But Buddy was the war hero. Buddy saw action. Not me." His face pinkened.

The quiz went on. What was he doing in Wild Pea?

"Oh now that, *that*, is quite a story," Sam said, and Mern sat forward, expectant.

"I'm Dvorjek's numero uno guy. Ya wanna know what a produce manager does? He makes sure no customer gets a bruised banana or rotten tangerine." Mern stifled a yawn. "See, Mern, I call myself the 'produce police.' I check if the Idahos are grainy or the Big Boy beans are limp. I'm the one who sees that the ship is running smoothly." He made a smoothing-out gesture with his hand. He took care of things customers didn't notice unless they went wrong. Bulging cans of tuna, cabbages with worms. "Who do you think tests the brine in the pickle barrels, cuts the moldy edges off the cheddar, and fills the pans with homemade potato salad and slaw?"

"Sam, did you *always* want to be a grocery clerk when you grew up?" Mern said in her wickedly teasing Mernish way.

"As a matter of fact," Sam said, happy to have been asked, "my job requires a certain amount of savoir faire." Mern looked puzzled and scratched behind her ear. "Takes a kind of *sophistication*," Sam explained, "a person who knows what's what. Not one of those fly-by-night clerks who wouldn't know a kumquat from a persimmon."

My legs had fallen asleep. I got up and shook them out. Mern was mouthing, *Get out of here right now.* I shrugged. I wasn't bored. My mother was endlessly fascinating, kind of the way Frankenstein or the Wolf Man was fascinating: who was she now? Frankenstein in love!

"Come over here, Dolores."

I sidled over to Sam's side. He covered my ears with his hands, then shook my head as if it were a piggy bank. The final shazam brought forth a dime from each ear. Sam pressed the money into my hand and closed his fist over mine. It was a dumb trick, for babies, but I wasn't insulted. Sam won me over.

"If you want, I can teach it to you. An old parlor trick, is all."

"Sure," I said, reaching for his hand, "and I want to show you something." I pulled him up from the couch. Mern gripped Sam's other hand, and he staggered between us.

"I want to show him Eunice Turtle."

"Oh. The turtle," my mother said, dropping hold of Sam. "I saved the damn thing from being flushed down a toilet."

"You stole her from a hospital." Some nights I worried the parents of the dead child would track us down and take Eunice Turtle back.

Sam ran his tongue over his mustache. "Turtles are fine creatures, Dolores. Let's go have a look."

"Her name's Eunice Turtle," I said.

Sam considered a moment. "There couldn't be a more perfect name. Full speed ahead, *El Capitán*. Lead the way."

Mern let Sam out of her sight. "Don't take forever," she yelled as I slammed my door.

We knelt by my bed and Sam lifted Eunice Turtle from her box. "My oh my! Aren't you something," he said, cupping her lightly in his hand. Eunice Turtle peeped out to see what was going on, then pulled her head back into her shell.

"It's okay," I told her. "This is Sam."

Sam was practically a turtle expert. With his wide flat thumb, he stroked the patterned panels on Eunice Turtle's shell. "Turtles have been around for at least a hundred million years. They live everywhere on the globe. Every sailor's got a turtle story," he said.

In Asia he'd seen turtles worshipped like gods. A sailor once told him that the Indians believe turtles carry the dome of heaven, every star in the sky, under their shells. He looked up at me. "That's a damn sweet thing to believe, Dolores del Rio, and neither you nor I will ever know if it's true."

Sam held Eunice Turtle under the lamplight. As he bent over, I could see the lank strands on the top of his head, his rosy scalp. Gently he turned Eunice Turtle on her back. "This is called the *plastron*," he said, fingering her mustard-colored underside. "You're beautiful, all right, aren't you, Eunice Turtle?" He touched Eunice's back. *Carapace.*

He touched her sides. *Scutes.* I repeated the words. It was like naming new parts of myself. Sam thought Eunice Turtle was a red-eared slider because of the red patches on the sides of her head.

Sam put Eunice right-side up in my hand. "Eunice Turtle the red-eared slider," I said.

We sat on the edge of my bed, the evening darkness folding in around us. "This here turtle's going to need more than a shoebox and a cereal bowl full of water. She needs an aquarium. She needs to swim and use her leg muscles." I didn't have enough money for such a thing, I said. Mern thought a box and a cereal bowl were just fine. "Nah, they're not fine! Here," Sam said, pulling two dollars from a clip and pushing them into my hand. "This is between you and me. My contribution to Eunice Turtle's new abode. Make sure she gets a daily dose of sunshine. And don't forget about the aquarium." I thanked him and took the bills. I had more than three dollars now, counting Dupere's, plus some change from Mr. Tabachnik.

Sam set Eunice Turtle on the floor, and her head emerged slowly from the folds of her neck. She looked around with her dear, appealing face. She hadn't said a word, but I knew we'd talk as soon as Sam left. Mern had switched on the radio, and ballroom music filtered in from the living room. "I just poured us another drink," she yelled. "The ice is melting. Hurry up, Sam."

"Wanna see my Mickeys?" I said quickly.

"A tango's next," Mern called.

I removed my Mickey Mantle cards from under my pillow. The two Mickeys were the only cards I kept from the collection I'd started right after Lakeview/Oceanside. When I'd realized Dupere was gone for good, I'd thrown all my cards away except for the Mickeys. I believed Mickey Mantle was not just a great baseball player, but also a great person. I believed Mickey was fair and square and honest and most of all loyal, which was why on some nights, I laid those two Mickeys on my blankets and cried my eyes out to them.

"Those are sure swell," Sam said, admiring the picture of Mickey at bat.

I was going to be very sad if I never saw Sam Podesta again.

Mern let out a sharp whistle from the living room.

"Your mother's waiting," Sam said, and got up. In the doorway he clicked his heels and saluted. "Signing off now, Lieutenant. Hasta la vista. At ease." He threw his sailor cap across the room onto my bed. "You keep this one. I got others."

After the door closed, I put on the cap and took Eunice Turtle into bed and shut off my light. There were slow tunes on the airwaves. I heard Mern ask Sam if he wanted his necklace back. "It's yours, Mern," he said. Mern said, "You're a generous man, Sam Podesta. Your mother would be proud." They laughed and the ring of their easy happiness spoiled my stuck-on-Sam feelings. I tugged the brim of his sailor's cap over my ears, shut my eyes, and let their voices fade away.

"He's nice, isn't he?" I said to Eunice Turtle in the dark.

Yes, he is, Eunice Turtle said.

"Men aren't so bad, are they?" There was Mickey and Mr. Tabachnik; my father, of course; and Sam too. "We don't want a world without men, do we?" I said.

No, we do not, Eunice Turtle said.

In the morning, the kitchen drawers had been dumped out, old corks, empty matchbooks, limp rubber bands thrown away. The radio was playing show tunes. When Mern noticed me, she shut off the vacuum and spread her arms Ethel Merman style and mouthed, *"There's No Business Like Show Business."* Her hair was tied in a dishtowel, bunny ears up. Ignoring her theatrics, I went for the cornflakes. Trailing me into the kitchen, she belted out, *"Nowhere could you have that happy feeling when you are stealing that extra bow."*

"Quit it," I said.

She stuck out her tongue and bumped against my hips. "How's my little Moucheroo this morning?" What she really wanted to know was what I'd thought of Sam. "He's not Clark Gable, but whaddya think?" She pulled out a chair, sat down to interrogate. "He's got a sense of humor, eh?" she said. Friendly, eh? Not just the usual boring kind of loser? No small-town hick. She was no hick either, she said. So what if he wasn't exactly a dreamboat. She could do worse. She could do a lot worse. I said he knew an awful lot about turtles.

"Is that all you can say?!"

I couldn't express what I felt. Something didn't seem right about the two of them together.

"Forget I even asked your opinion," Mern said, shoving most of the spilled junk back into the drawers. She had to get to work. She was giving Annie a perm in the afternoon and then meeting Sam at Delrico's. She didn't ask about my plans. It was a Saturday, and I had the whole day, the whole summer ahead of me. From now until September, when I would return to school, the days would be nothing more than a string of empty rooms. I had no real friends. Who in the neighborhood could understand my life with Mern? I saw myself opening the door to one empty space, crossing through it to the door on the other side. I opened one door after another, on and on through the endless rooms, where there was not a single person or a stick of furniture or even a flower in a vase.

Mern was frowning at me. "What in the world is the matter with you? If you don't have your face in a book, you've got your head in the clouds." I pushed away my cornflakes. "Or you're sitting in a corner doodling. What's so interesting about that drawing pad of yours?"

I thought of how I sometimes snuck into my mother's room with the sketchpad Mr. Tabachnik had given me and drew pictures of her fluted perfume bottles, her satin mules beside an unmade bed. I was afraid if I showed her the drawings she'd think I was spying on her, so I only showed them to Eunice Turtle and Mr. T. "Nothing," I said.

That night I woke up to someone in my room. Everything was quiet except for the moths throwing themselves against the screen. A figure was peering through the blinds at the houses across the street. Moonlight licked the crown of his head, spilling down his neck to the ridge of his shoulders. He had on pointy cowboy boots with little heels.

"Dupere?" I whispered.

My father turned, his eyes searching for me among the bedcovers. *I've missed you, Bunny.*

I watched in a trance as my father stepped from the window and glided toward me, his body emitting a strange pinkish glow. I recognized the smell of his hair tonic, the scent of his aftershave, but there was something odd about the way he moved, the way the edges of his skin seemed to blur into the darkness. I sat up.

I've been lonely without my Bunny girl, my father said.

There was no reasonable explanation for how Frankie could be in my room, but I wasn't going to ask how he got there or where he'd come from or where he'd been. I wasn't even going to ask if he was real; he was real enough for me. He halted midstride and shook his head.

I'm worried about you, honey. This Podesta guy. What do you know about him? A sailor's got a gal in every port.

Wow. My father was jealous. I couldn't believe it. He sat down on my bed and took my hand. The words seemed to roar out of him, as if they were coming through a tunnel.

Please tell me you haven't fallen for this buffoon. You have to watch out for guys like Podesta. They can charm the scales off a snake. Frankie eased his long body next to mine, his eyes sending their fire into me.

Remember our little trip together? Remember the Ferris wheel?

I'd memorized every single moment of that night. In Technicolor. Starring Mr. Wonderful and His Sweetheart Kid. I laid my head on his chest.

I'm not happy, Bunny. I'm definitely not happy. I'm your flesh and blood. I resent another man in my house. I thought I could rely on you. He leaned over and brushed the hair off my forehead.

A father doesn't have to ask permission to kiss his princess, does he?

I shook my head.

Will you do something for me, Bunny? Convince your mother to get rid of Sam. Trust me on this.

My father closed his eyes and for a moment seemed to doze. I took his hand and placed it on my heart and watched his lips curl into a smile. I'd done it! All my hoping and praying had brought him back.

Chapter 6

Visitations

He was my secret. He came in the middle of the night. No one else could see him.

They won't believe you. They're blind, Bunny, but you're not blind.

It was bliss waking to Frankie, my beautiful father, sitting Indian style at the end of my bed.

We're not like them. We're a couple of gypsies. No one cheers me up the way you do, Bunny.

In the morning he was gone without a trace.

Even so, the things my daddy said to me demanded secrecy, and I took caution not to let something slip from my mouth. I couldn't look Mern in the eye, and I certainly couldn't have told her about Frankie's visits, but I needn't have worried: Mern was consumed with her own affairs, blabbing to everyone about her not-so-secret admirer who'd come a-courting full of razzle-dazzle and swanky gifts. And Sam, who might have picked up on something had he known me better, was likewise under the spell of love. "Guess who brings home the bacon these days!" my mother bragged to Annie, and it was true that food flowed from Dvorjek's shelves to our cupboard. Bing cherries, marzipan, Vienna sausages in a tin. "Ooh la la," my mother would say, as if she wasn't suspicious of foreign-looking items, the form of her gratitude running to sarcasm and taunts. Big cats flirted with growls and bites, and it crossed my mind that this was how Mern and Sam romanced.

One evening around six o'clock, Sam showed up in a Hawaiian

shirt blazing with fruit, and my mother couldn't resist running to the kitchen to pile bananas and grapes on her head. Shaking bags of pistachios like maracas, she bumped and shimmied her Carmen Miranda "Chica Chica Boom Chic" number, weaving around Sam until he yelled at her to quit it, but she'd already worked herself up. Bowing and smirking, she delivered her stupid Charlie Chan imitation: "Ah, so! So sol-lee, Mee-ster Pineapple!" and Sam's face turned beet red. His voice cracked, and for a split second his face contorted in anger. He took one giant step toward my mother, who I had to admit was funny but so mean—and was also one giant lesson in what kind of woman *not* to be. "That's some routine you got there, Mern baby," Sam said, calming himself.

"Ah, so, Mee-ster Pineapple," my mother peeped.

I held my breath. Sam wiped his nose with the back of his hand and glanced down at his shirt, then slowly back up at my mother. Their eyes met. Something like a smile quivered on Sam's lips. "Yeah, yeah. Pineapples. I get it." He did a little soft shoe, slapped a hand against his chest, and burst out singing, "*Yes, we have no bananas, we have-a no bananas today,*" sweeping my mother into his arms as they fox-trotted their way into her bedroom, and I was left wondering, *Is this love?*

Frankie said I had a fickle heart if I had room in it for two fathers. Someday, after I finished school, he'd take me away. Just the two of us.

We'll live in a caravan. We'll roam the world from sea to shining sea. Free as birds.

I brooded on my daddy's words as I brooded on my face, in car mirrors, shop windows, and puddles—a dark-haired girl with troubled eyes. Frankie was on a crusade to get rid of Sam and begged me to turn against him and to convince my mother to do the same. He told me I was special, his best gal, his only gal, and in an instant I forgave him everything, but I still refused to betray my new friend Sam.

Sam was with us most breakfasts and dinners. On weekends he did things like fix the broken toaster or replace the toilet seat. It was Sam who taught me how to hold a stalk of grass between my thumbs and make the blade whistle; Sam who taped my drawings to the fridge; Sam who spun tales about Sinbad and Aladdin; Sam who was full of wonders—sea ditties, how to tie a bowline and a double hitch. *I don't think you're listening to me, Bunny*, my daddy said, *and it's breaking my goddamn heart.* One evening he loped toward my bed, his shoulders hunched in a sad, new way. *You happy with this joker? What's he doing for you? I thought the son of a b would be gone by now.*

"Please don't call Sam a joker," I said.

Frankie slid in beside me. *Bunny. Bunny. I'm your own flesh and blood!* His arms went around me, and I had the feeling of falling through the darkness as I sank into his pillow-soft chest. *Stop worrying*, my father said. *Sweetheart, I'm on your side.*

In the middle of the week Sam came home with good news. Mr. Dvorjek asked him to turn the store into a first-class deli, "the likes of which Wild Pea has never seen." He'd raise his pay too. How much, Mern wanted to know. Sam waved her off. The real glory was that Dvorjek trusted him. "I don't mean to brag," Sam said, "but there isn't another person within two hundred miles as qualified as me." Mern was doing her rapt, fake-listening act, but I could see a streak of meanness moving in. "With my help, Dvorjek's will put Wild Pea on the map." He held up an imaginary banner: "From Dvorjek's to Your Table."

She stubbed out her cigarette and started in. "Sooooo. Should I call you Lord Coleslaw? Baron von Potato Salad?" She tipped her head and cackled.

Sam's chest flooded with air, but he held himself back. "Good food is like love, doll face, only it doesn't let you down like people sometimes do." Did she want to hear about his promotion or not? He, Sam Podesta, was going to cultivate people's palates, educate the masses. Teach them about real bread with real crust.

"Educate the masses?" Mern exploded, practically keeling over with laughter.

Sam snatched his cup of cold coffee from the pine chest and downed the remains in a gulp. "Laugh all you want, but just wait and see what happens."

Mern grabbed his forearm. "Hey, loosen up, mister!"

Sam jerked his arm away. "I'm plenty loose. Takes more than a little ribbing to get Sam Podesta's goat."

No one said anything for a second, and I imagined my father, pleased to see them arguing, flashing me a high sign.

One Saturday night in mid-September, Sam was coming over to cook a genuine Italian feast. *Hey Mambo! Mambo Italiano!* In preparation Mern had worked herself into another cleaning frenzy. Rolling her hair in a kerchief, Arthur Godfrey playing his ukulele on the radio, she chased dust mice from beneath beds. Old magazines, gluey nail polish, empty cold cream jars, worn-out powder puffs went into the garbage, and the wilted celery got tossed from the fridge.

At quarter past six, I spotted Sam on the walk wearing a tall white hat and a starched white jacket. He carried a box of groceries on his hip. Mr. Tabachnik was at the door before I could answer it.

"So what's with the fancy-schmantzy hat, Sam Podesta?" he said, helping Sam with the carton.

"The best chefs in the world wear them," Sam said.

Mr. Tabachnik hiked up his eyebrows in mock surprise. "Such a *best chef* is coming to my house?"

Sam reached into the cardboard box and handed Mr. Tabachnik a long twist of golden bread. "For my friend Tabachnik," Sam said.

Mr. Tabachnik ran the bread under his nose like a cigar. "When was the last time I had such a bread!" Were those tears in his eyes?

Mern was luxuriating in a sea of lilac-scented bubbles. She called from the tub, "I'm in here." The bathroom door was partly open, the scent of lilacs flooding the flat.

"My little tortellini!" Sam shouted.

"Mr. Sunshine," Mern shouted back.

"Mr. Sunshine, Mr. Sunshine," Sam repeated, looking down at himself. He was wearing an aquamarine shirt with suns and moons and red flying fish on it.

In the kitchen he unloaded groceries—olive oil, mushrooms, butter, two cans of Del Monte's stewed tomatoes, garlic, and onions. "Mern's going to think she's in Roma tonight," he said, unwrapping a wedge of cheese from its butcher paper. He held it to his nostrils. "Pièce de résistance! A fi-ne Par-mee-jhono."

It wasn't Sam's voice I heard suddenly; it was my father's. *Pièce de résistance, my foot. Watch this guy, Bunny. There's something fishy about him.* I looked around, stricken, but there was no Dupere. Just then, Mern started singing, "*I loves ya, Por-ghy.*"

Sam stopped searching in the carton for a cheese grater and chortled. "That Mern!" he said, brimming with admiration. He strode into the hallway and stood by the bathroom door and belted out, "*Bess, you is my woman now,*" then marched back into the kitchen and asked if we had candlesticks and any Dean Martin records.

"Oh, Eunice, honey," Mern called. "Come help me, will you?"

"Go, go, your mother needs you," Sam said, hustling me out.

Mother, I thought. Mern was never *mother.*

When I entered her room, Mern was in front of her mirror, pushing her nose from side to side to see if she had any blackheads. For the occasion she'd borrowed an evening dress from her friend Hattie. It was a soft lemony color with an off-the-shoulder bodice and nipped-in waist. She wanted to know what I thought she should do with her hair. Up? Or down? She let her curls tumble onto her shoulders. "Think Sam really loves me?" My mother wasn't as confident as she pretended.

"He's bonkers for you!" I said, but a look of anguish crossed her face.

"You can never be sure, Eunice, what a man is feeling. They're a different species from us and don't forget it."

When I went back into the kitchen, Sam was at the cutting board, dicing carrots. I asked him where he learned to cook. "In the US Navy, my girl," he said, searching in the carton for a garlic press. Did I know the best cooks in the world were men?

"It's true," Sam said, arranging several cloves of garlic in a line on the counter. He paused and glanced out the window. The giant peonies had come and gone, but the phlox stood up in spears of lavender and pink. "Actually, I taught myself to cook a long time before the navy." He smashed the garlic with the broadside of a knife; the room reeked. "See, my old man went on binges and would be gone for days.

Mama got the blues and wouldn't eat, so I started to cook for her. I wasn't much older than you." He tore a bag of spaghetti open with his teeth.

"Yeah, yeah," he said, setting aside the spaghetti and sweeping the garlic into a skillet, "when she couldn't get out of bed, I'd bring her a tray. I'd always fix it up nice, a plate of food and something extra, like a pretty pinecone." I saw the tray of meat loaf, applesauce, and a daisy. "Mama never hid the fact that my brother Buddy was her favorite, but I'm not ashamed to say I would've cooked for her even if she hated my guts."

He held his cigarette like a hoodlum, pinched between his thumb and forefinger, and took short deep puffs. "I lived with Mama and cooked for her again after Buddy was killed." He took another drag, rested the cigarette in an ashtray. The way he was slumped over the skillet, I thought he was going to cry. I felt like crying too.

"Yeah. Yeah, that was a real sad time." He asked me if I remembered how he'd said nicknames were serious business. I remembered. At the sink he filled a large pot with water, set it on the stove, then came over and touched my arm with his wet fingers. "The punks around the neighborhood used to call me Mama's Boy. Namby-Pamby Sammy. I got teased for taking care of her." His eyes sagged and most of his face looked naked and unprotected except for the mustache. Suddenly I was seeing another Sam Podesta. Six inches from me stood Namby-Pamby-Sammy Podesta, ten years old. I wanted to reach out and touch little Sammy's shoulder, reassure him he wasn't a failure. I asked if he got beat up. Sure he'd gotten beat up, he said. But then he'd gotten angry. The navy taught him to walk tall. "I'll let you in on a little secret. Most tough guys are only tough when they're standing shoulder to shoulder with their buddies, inhaling each other's sweat." Get one of them alone, they weren't so brave. Without warning, he pulled up his jacket. There was his belly, round and hard and pink as a beach ball. Not an ounce of flab. He punched himself with a fist.

"Feel this. Go ahead, CC. Try and hit me."

I ran my hand over his skin. I couldn't get over the sight of his belly.

Sam laughed—a mean, confident, bragging laugh, but I knew the meanness wasn't meant for me. He lowered his jacket, ironing it out with his sweaty palm. "But hey! Hey!" He smacked himself on the forehead. "What am I doing here, talking like a nincompoop?" He looked at his watch. "I've been blabbing so much, I'm going to have to do double time to get this meal finished." He placed a cheese grater over a bowl, rubbed the wedge of Parmesan over the metal. His freckled hands flew from countertop to carton to sink to skillet. "Sam Podesta was too classy a cook for the navy. I said to them I wouldn't cook no green potatoes and horse meat. 'I won't be held responsible,' I told them, 'if the ship's company gets the trots.' They knew who they were dealing with. They made me a gunner. I went from stuffing green peppers to stuffing bombs." I watched as he poured the pale threads of spaghetti into the pot.

I wanted to tell Sam how brave he'd been, but some part of me hung back. Instead, I asked him if he knew that Marco Polo discovered spaghetti in China and brought it back to Italy, but everyone thinks the Italians invented spaghetti. He knew. "And here's a little-known fact," he said. Marco Polo and his father, Nicolo, were sailors *and* gourmets, just like himself. "Speaking of fathers, do you want to tell me about yours?"

The breath caught in my throat. We hadn't talked about Frankie—not ever. Now I was afraid that if I twisted around, I'd see my daddy in the doorway, finger to his lips.

"He's a tough deal to talk about, huh?"

I stared at my feet.

"Yeah, he broke both your hearts. Left your mother when you were a baby. Not exactly a family man, was he? A deserter. You desert in the navy, you know what you get? A court-martial. The law on your ass—excuse my French." Sam opened a can of tomatoes and poured the contents into a saucepan. "You know what a man like your father is worth? Zero. Zip. Just like my old man. My old man had a million excuses. He worked in a slaughterhouse since he was a kid. His fingers got like claws after years of hauling carcasses and they gave him a lot of pain. That was his excuse for hitting the bottle and slugging anyone

58

who got in his way." Sam looked up and appraised me. "It's tough luck to have a lousy father. But I don't have to tell you, do I?"

The kitchen walls went blurry. *A deserter.*

Sam dropped down next to me and took my hands. "Me and my big mouth. I got no right to talk about your daddy that way. I never met the guy. The thing about me is, sometimes I get riled up." He raised my chin with a knuckle. "Forgive me, CC?" I nodded, my eyes stinging. Sam's strong arms went around my shoulders. He hugged me against his chest, rocking back and forth. I swallowed hard and hoped he wouldn't mention our fathers ever again. "It's okay, baby," he said, kissing the top of my head. "For a long time I woulda killed anyone who said a bad word about my daddy too." I wiped my eyes. Sam put out his palm for me to slap. Then we were back to preparing dinner.

"Ever eat these?" Sam said, spilling a handful of mushrooms out from a damp dishtowel. They resembled indecent parts of a dead person, and the thought of them going into the sauce was revolting. But when Sam dropped them into the smoking oil along with the garlic and green peppers, a surprisingly delicious aroma filled the room.

"Now," Sam said, holding out a purple onion. "What we have here is a mighty warrior. A mighty survivor of floods and droughts." He tweaked the onion's hairy nose. I imagined the onion in battle garb, like knights in my Classics Illustrated comics. A vegetable Joan of Arc! I started to laugh.

"What's going on in there?" Mern shouted from the bedroom. "Eunice, stop bothering Sam."

"She's helping me cook," Sam yelled back. He handed me a large wooden spoon and told me to stir while he poured another stream of thick red pulp into the hissing pan. "We haven't known each other very long, have we?" he said, dipping in a spoon to taste the sauce.

"Since July," I said. Two months.

"But we trust each other?"

I looked up from stirring and nodded.

"And we're friends?"

We were friends.

"Let's keep this conversation private, then, between friends, okay?"

"I can keep secrets," I said.

Sam smiled, resting his hand on my shoulder. "I bet you can. That's why I'm going to tell you what I'm going to tell you."

I kept my eyes on Sam, my heart swelling with pride.

"You see before you a man of the world..." He made a little bow. "I've had thrills and spills. But now, now I'm sick of traveling. Sick of living out of my duffel." He paused and took a deep breath. "What I'm trying to say is... *this* is what I want. A home. A family."

I blushed.

"I want to take care of you and your mother. I've had enough traveling. I want to settle down, want you to be my family." He walked over to the table and straightened the silverware. "See. Maybe this is my last chance. A guy gets to be a certain age..." He stopped himself, squared his shoulders, and looked directly at me. "I need your help. Let your mother know how happy it's going to make you to have Sam Podesta around. I'd do anything for your mother," Sam said. "She's got moxie. Guts." He went on and on describing some fabulous person who wasn't the Mern I knew. What he was getting at, he said, sprinkling oil and salt on slices of bread, is that women aren't made to live alone. Things happen. Things women don't know diddly about. Like busted pipes and carpenter ants. He brought his face close to mine and smiled. "Your mother's sacrificed for you, and now she needs someone she can rely on."

I couldn't name one thing my mother had sacrificed for me, but just as I was thinking this, my mother floated into the kitchen in her billowy yellow dress. Her skin was dewy from her bath and lightly sunburned, and she gave off a shine. Turning once, she modeled for us, teetering on a pair of strapless heels. She was makeup-free except for a summery lipstick, and her hair was loose. She wasn't glamorous in the sharp, bright way that red lipstick and eyebrow pencil and rouge made her. In Hattie's borrowed outfit, she appeared like a vision, soft and flowing and beautiful. She was herself, Mern, and also someone new.

"My fine woman!" Sam said, sailing across the kitchen floor to take her elbow and escort her to the table. The table looked festive. For a centerpiece, I'd wadded Kleenex to make carnations. There were two stubby candles, Sam's big wineglasses, and a red checked tablecloth—also Sam's.

Sam held the chair out for Mern while she spread her skirt and sat down smiling at me without a touch of sulk or misery or complaint on her face. I smiled back, fascinated. Once I was seated, Sam removed his jacket and chef's hat and came forward with the bowl of spaghetti, the platter of garlic bread, wine. *"Linguini con funghi,"* he said. *"Panne d'aioli. Chianti."* He sang out their names, standing beside us as we helped ourselves.

"A toast!" he said, settling himself in a chair. We raised our glasses, a bud of orange flame reflected in the ruby-colored wine. Thick red tomato sauce steamed over the spaghetti on the white plates. The slices of garlic bread, fried in oil and butter, were dusted with mint. All the odors mixed and mingled—lilac bubble bath, tomatoes and onions, garlic, the arriving darkness.

"A toast to two gorgeous dames," Sam said, his glass lifted. *"Votre santé, skoal."*

We clinked and I tasted a gulp of sour red wine. For a second, I allowed myself to imagine how it might be: more candlelight suppers, birthday parties. I saw the three of us playing Monopoly at the kitchen table, Sam teaching me magic tricks. Maybe we'd even get a dog.

Mern was quiet during the meal. She complimented Sam on his spaghetti and inquired after the name of the spice on the bread. Her cheeks were flushed, and her hair fell in easy waves around her face. She did not make one wisecrack or call me "kiddo" or sing in a fake Negro voice, *"I loves ya, Por-ghy."*

At the end of the meal, while Sam was setting before us paper cups filled with ice cream covered with slivered almonds, Mern began to cry. Big fat tears ran down her cheeks. She bowed her head and hid her face in her hands.

Sam was at her side in an instant. "What is it, Mern? What's the matter?"

As soon as she calmed down enough to speak, the tears started again.

Sam waited beside her, stroking her arm. "It's all right," he kept saying. "Whatever it is, it's all right."

Gesturing at the candles, the checked tablecloth, the wine, she sobbed, "I don't deserve this, not any of this. I don't!" She turned to Sam. "You're too good to me, Sam Podesta."

My mouth fell open. I couldn't believe what I was hearing.

Sam held my mother tight. "That's the dumbest thing I ever heard."

Mern sank her head into her hands. "But it's true!" she sobbed.

Sam stroked her hair, kissed a spot at the base of her neck. I thought he was going to say how she'd saved his life and he could never pay her back for that, but he said nothing of the kind. He knelt beside her and gently peeled her fingers away from her eyes, kissing away her tears.

Very softly, almost without making a sound, he said, "I know the feeling. I understand."

It wasn't over so quickly. The candles sputtered in their puddles of wax, the ice cream cups leaked a soppy cream, and my mother wept. She wept as though every sadness she'd ever known was crawling up her throat trying to get out. I felt my own throat clutch, my heart splinter into a thousand pieces. Mern was shivering so hard Sam sent me to get her pink cardigan from the bedroom, and when this didn't stop her shaking, he squeezed in next to her on the chair and wrapped his arms around her as if he himself were a fur cloak. Mern put her head on Sam's shoulder, their shadows merging, stretching across the table as one long shadow. A candlewick flickered and went out. We remained at the table until at last Mern stopped crying and blew her nose. In a thin, shaky voice, she said, "Jesus Moses! Where did those tears come from?" We all laughed with relief.

"Let's go outside and get some air," Sam suggested. "Whaddya say?" He went behind her and pulled her chair from the table. "Fall out, men," he said quietly. We rose from the table without speaking, without a second glance at the melting ice cream and crumpled napkins, Sam moving quickly to grip Mern's elbow, while I ran into my room to get Eunice Turtle. Mern had kicked off her strapless heels and looked like a gypsy dancer with her tousled hair and big sad eyes. Downstairs, Mr. Tabachnik was listening to Jack Benny, who was really Benny Kubelsky from *over there*. Sam held the door open and we filed out, Mern padding barefoot into the night.

The street was dark and the stars seemed very far away. We sat on the brick steps and gazed at the heavens.

"Do you think there are other planets out there with people on them?" Mern asked when our eyes had adjusted.

Sam hesitated before answering. "There's no way for a person to know, but I suppose there might be creatures like us living on other planets. They're probably looking down on us right now wondering how to tell us they're there."

"That's sad," Mern said.

Sam drew her close. Nah, it wasn't sad. Sooner or later, they'd make contact and share their knowledge. "Maybe they've figured out how to stop getting old."

That cheered Mern up. "I never thought of it that way," she said. She put her glasses on to see the stars better. She wasn't embarrassed if Sam saw her au naturel anymore. Sam smoothed her hair. His back looked so familiar next to Mern's it seemed he'd been with us always, as if we'd been a family forever. A car cruised down the street, its headlights skimming over our feet. Mern asked for a cigarette. Sam rolled two and handed her one.

"A sky like this reminds me of my first months at sea," Sam said.

We all glanced up instinctively. A streak with a long blue-green tail shot across the sky. Mern reached for Sam's hand. "Wow!" she said. "A shooter," Mern whispered. Sam kissed her fingers and held them to his cheek. She sighed and pointed to a bright twinkle low near the horizon and asked if it was Mars. Sam shrugged. She was an Aries, she said, and Mars was the ruler of her house. Sam shrugged again.

"I thought all you sailors knew about the stars," she said.

Sam laughed. "No, sirree. They don't teach astronomy to recruits."

"Speaking of stars," Mern said, and asked where Sam had gotten the silver cross necklace. "From an old lady in a black dress hawking them in a marketplace in Salonika. That's in Greece," he said. "I'd like to go to Greece someday. I've seen posters," Mern said wistfully. She asked if the necklace had brought him luck. "I think it was lucky that we were at Delrico's at the same time on the same night," she said. "Don't you?"

Sam took her hand out of her lap and stroked it, squinting up at the stars. "Lady Luck's a fickle dame, but she sure was with me that night. That night was the exception to the rule." He considered Mern's fingers for a minute, tracing the wrinkles on her knuckles. "Hey. Ya want another glass of wine? Coke for you, CC?"

While he was gone, a million more stars came out. "I wonder if he wants to marry me," Mern said.

"What about my father?" I asked.

Mern gave me a chilly look. "What about him?"

I said I didn't think a person was allowed to have two husbands.

"You can't," she said.

"Then how can you marry Sam?" I asked.

Mern grumbled something inaudible. Then Sam returned with our drinks. We watched the sky in silence for more comets.

"That's how my brother Buddy died. Like a goddamn shooting star," Sam said. He showed us with his hand how Buddy's plane dove right into the Sea of Japan. Mern took her glasses off and rested her head on Sam's shoulder. A spasm ran down her back, and Sam reached up to fasten the top button of her cardigan. There was a faint autumn chill coming on. No one was on the street. The trees were large and dark and silent.

"That's a horrible story about your brother," Mern said. "It's so tragic. It's worse than anything I've ever heard on *Guiding Light*."

Sam grunted. "This is real life I'm talking about, Mern. This is no soap opera."

"Oh, Sam," Mern said, her fingers creeping up his arm under the sleeve of his shirt. "I don't want to talk about sad things anymore. Okay?"

Sam drew her closer. "Righto, doll baby. But I ain't complaining. I got you now, don't I?"

Just before I slipped into bed, I kissed Eunice Turtle and asked her who she'd choose for a father, Frankie or Sam. *Sam, by a long shot*, she said, and that was all she said. I closed my eyes and made a wish. *Can it please be happily-ever-after now?*

Chapter 7

Our Hero

At seven-thirty in the morning, Mern was in the yard in her kimono shouting, "Geronimo!" and throwing tennis balls at a bunch of crows. During the night, dozens of birds had swooped in, choosing our catalpa for their convention. In his robe and slippers, Mr. Tabachnik was swatting the tree trunk with a broom. The pale and slender moon had not yet receded when my mother rushed into my room holding her ears and declaring we'd been invaded.

The day grew hot and sticky, the sun burned tiny mirrors onto the leaves, and the sound of crows filled every inch of space. By the time Sam got home, my mother was on the couch in dark glasses with an ice pack on her head. The ruckus, she said, was eating into her brain. "I'm calling the National Guard if you don't do something, Sam."

Sam stood under the catalpa with his arms crossed, staring up through the greenery. For fifteen minutes, he stood stock-still until a hush came over the birds. The sky deepened into a potent blue. One by one, the crows flew off, and quiet spread from the catalpa to the rest of the world. Mern prodded me with her elbow. "Our hero," she said, but the next day when the birds returned, Mern called Sam at work and told him to come over with a shotgun. Not long after, Sam arrived fuming. Look, he said, every time my mother called at work, Dvorjek gave him a dirty look. "He counts minutes in dollars. You're messing with our financial future, Mern." He eyed the tree, alive with the rustle of wings, then studied my mother, who was for drastic action. Shoot the birds or poison them. "You and me are as different as day and night on this situation. Should I grab a shotgun and shoot you if I don't like you?" His ears were valentine-red. "Ya can't win a war with Mother Nature, sweetheart."

My mother skirted away from his accusing finger and fled inside. "Don't get your bowels in an uproar, Sam," she yelled over her shoulder.

Sam spied me near the bushes, clutching Eunice Turtle. "Dolores del Rio! Mernie and me are just having a little discussion. Nothing to worry about." He yelled back at my mother, "Me in an uproar? I'm the most peaceful guy around. You're the dilly, Mernie. A real dilly." He sank his fists into his pockets and went back to see what he could do about the birds.

Upstairs, Mern was in the kitchen holding a glass of rum iced tea. "Don't you think Sam looks a little like Robert Mitchum when he's mad?" she said.

Later that evening, my mother said in a low, disapproving growl, "You couldn't get rid of a few birds!" Sam had failed in his mission, and now my mother was furious. Somehow she'd make him pay. She's ruthless, my father had said on his last visit. *But you're not like her. You're Daddy's girl. You're like my side of the family.* Which left me deeply curious about who his people were.

We ate our dinner in silence, our cutlery squeaking against the chatter of crows. Sam cleared our plates, and my mother went into her room and closed the door. The wind came in gusts, and the catalpa leaves shimmered against the violet sky. I took Eunice Turtle outside to watch Sam and Mr. Tabachnik shine a flashlight up into the tree's dark interior where the crows were shifting among the branches. Pretty soon Mern came out wearing her cardigan and carrying her smokes. She sat down next to me on the stoop.

Sam leaned a ladder against the tree and began to climb. "Careful," my mother cried out, addled by the birds and annoyed at Mr. Sunshine. When Sam was three-quarters of the way up, he stopped, opened the knapsack on his back, and fished out a multitude of shiny objects, fastening them one by one with wire to the branches. Catching a breeze, the spatulas and forks, tin cups and measuring spoons clanged against each other, tinkling like church bells. In a soft explosion of feathers, the crows lifted into the air and hurled themselves across the lawn and into the twilight. Mern stood up and cheered, and Sam threw her a V for victory sign. Mern and Sam were now nothing but accomplices, celebrating with knowing smiles. In my mind, I pictured how I would draw the moment and hold it forever without the before of the argument, the moment without its complications—only the wind billowing the catalpa and the pure line and upward soaring of crows.

"Who are you writing?" I asked Mern the following day. She was at the kitchen table hunched over her kitten stationery. "I'm writing Ma," she answered, "to tell her about Sam." "How can you write Grandma a letter? Grandma Sophie Sunny is dead!" Mern pushed back her chair and sucked on the nub of the pink eraser. "Ma always wanted me to be with a nice guy. I'm letting her know I am."

"But Grandma Sophie Sunny's not alive," I insisted.

"Not everything has to make sense, Eunice," my mother said. What did make sense, financial sense, she said, after filling two notepad pages to Grandma, was for Sam to move in. On September fifteenth his lease was up. Why should he sign another one? Why should they both pay rent? It had been a snap decision, the whole thing settled late last night while they were celebrating the departure of the crows. Even Mr. Tabachnik had approved. "You can't do better than Podesta," he'd told my mother.

"You're marrying Sam?" I asked, not at all sure what my booming heart was trying to tell me. My mind skipped to Dupere. What would I tell him? *You've betrayed me, Bunny*, he'd say.

"Not exactly," my mother said. She and Sam had an arrangement.

"You could have at least asked me," I said.

"How about showing a little more enthusiasm?" Mern put down the pen and rattled off a list of Sam's virtues. "He's good for me. He's a Somebody. Christ, he's a good provider *and* bon vivant!" She opened her arms. "Don't be a sourpuss. How about a congratulatory kiss for your old mammy?"

My old mammy! Who did she think she was? Peola's Negro mother in *Imitation of Life*? I took a step backward, but my mother threw her arms rapturously around me in a gesture so spontaneous and full of honest feelings it was unnerving. "Come on, Eunice, can't you be happy for me for once?" she said.

"I want to be. *I want to be*," I said, falling into her embrace.

Later, sprawled on Mr. Tabachnik's Persian rug, I concentrated on drawing the magical catalpa. Mr. Tabachnik sat in his maroon chair musing. "By me it's okay about your mama. I'm not such a stuffed shirt like she thinks. It's time already..."

I put down my pencil, laid my head on my arm. I couldn't make sense of my feelings.

"Cisskala, dumpling," Mr. Tabachnik said, "some things have to be faced. That no-good father of yours isn't coming back. Sam here wants to take care of you. He loves you like a daughter, like you were his own flesh and blood." He looked down at my drawing and shook his head. "You make pictures to remember, eh?" Something in his voice, something between a cough and a choke, caught my attention. I closed my pad and tucked the pencil behind my ear.

"So, you want to know a secret about crows?" Mr. Tabachnik said, leaning forward in his chair. "Once," he said in the most delicate tone, "*over there*, I ate crow." His whole body shuddered, and I could feel the horror go through him. "A person never forgets." He held out his tongue and displayed it as if it were a foreign object, then sank back into a cushion. "A tongue never forgets... the taste of crow." He closed his eyes. "Another thing I remember: *one crow sorrow, two crows joy; three crows a letter, four crows a boy; five crows silver, six crows gold; seven crows a secret never to be told.*" He had a strong singing voice that sounded surprisingly young. More rhymes formed in my head, and I sang, "*Eight crows diamonds, nine crows pearls; ten crows dreams that take you out of this world.*" Mr. Tabachnik blew into his big white hanky. "Very good. Excellent! You're turning into a poet, eh, Cisskala? A mystic, no less!"

That night Sam brought home my favorite treat—Jordan almonds—and placed the bag in my hand. "I hear your mother told you that we're gonna be a family." He stuck out his neck for a hug, but I stood without moving. I heard Frankie repeating, *Fickle heart*. Sam planted a hand on my shoulder, and I stiffened.

"Hey, what's wrong, Sailor?"

"You didn't ask me! You didn't ask my consent."

Sam reared back. "What?"

"About moving in with us, you could have asked me too. Don't I count?"

"Jeez, sweetheart," Sam said, rubbing his big knuckles over his chin. "You're right. I shoulda included you in the decision." He reached for my hands, which I let him have. "I'm asking you now." He got down on his knees. Did he have my permission to live in the house?

Of course he did. I loved Sam Podesta, *and* I loved my father. Did that make me a criminal? Or only a double agent working for love?

For the rest of the evening, I allowed myself to dream about our future. A turkey at Thanksgiving, at Christmas, a tree. There'd be family trips to the Grand Canyon and the capital of our country, where we'd visit the FBI building and see pictures of famous spies. The only problem was, when I closed my eyes, I saw Frankie's disappointed face. I had no one to tell. Even Mr. Tabachnik would not understand.

The following day, I put on my sailor hat, drew a turtle tattoo on the back of my hand, and went outside with Eunice Turtle to wait for Sam. I was going to help him move in. After I'd discovered a soft spot on Eunice Turtle's shell, Sam had advised sunbaths for her. "Vitamin D's the ticket," he said, but every time my fingers explored her mushy scute, my heart hammered out double doom. "You are the perfect friend, the best of the best, and I will love you forever," I told her, holding her close to my cheek.

Ditto, she said. *We're perfect mates.*

It was the last week of summer vacation, the last Saturday free of homework. Mr. T brought us bouquets of dahlias, big as plates. The roses were waiting to be clipped to a few thorny claws and tucked under burlap for the winter. Soon Eunice Turtle and I would again spend hours apart, something we acknowledged with deep regret. Mern came down the steps in her pink nylon uniform wearing large gold hoop earrings, a tribute to her new idol, Sophia Loren. "Grandma

Sophie Sunny's real happy about Sam," she said, eyeing the catalpa for a lingering crow. The tree swayed noiselessly in the wind.

"I wish I knew what I wanted," my mother sighed, giving me a quick, sad look. "If you want to know the truth, I haven't been sleeping so well. I keep thinking about your father. What if he shows up and Sam is here...?" Her voice trailed off. "*Que sera, sera,*" she said.

"I like your tattoo, Sailor," Sam said shortly after my mother had left. He pulled me up by the elbows and told me to fall in. *Company, march.* We started down the block—left, right, left, right—our feet in matching rhythm, our fingers entwined. Overhead the clouds twisted into gauzy angels. Sam had been renting a third-floor finished attic. The space was spare and filled with light: a daybed with the woolen blanket tucked smooth as a board, a pair of slip-on canvas shoes, toes lined up, by the footboard. For all Sam's talk about seeing the world, I'd half expected to find beaded curtains, Turkish slippers, pillows embroidered with gold, but his room was plain, except for the model airplanes hanging motionless in a wash of afternoon light.

"You like?" Sam said, walking over to the models.

They were perfect—the way I found shells and flowers and rocks perfect, like mysterious rooms waiting to be entered.

"I thought you'd like them. Model planes used to be a hobby of mine." Sam stood under one of the planes, the Red Baron, which hung between the Spirit of St. Louis and Amelia Earhart's Lockheed.

"But you never told me about them," I said, as if it were my right to know all his secrets.

Sam gave the Red Baron a spin. "I was planning to. I was waiting for the right moment." Sam got out a glass and poured me an orange Crush, after which he lit a cigarette. The smoke gathered like a cloud around the models suspended on their invisible wires.

"I wasn't interested in planes until Buddy died," Sam said. "You'd think a grown man wouldn't enjoy kid stuff, like model planes, but let me tell you, when I had the parts of that B-29 model in front of me, I felt closer to Buddy than I'd ever felt. When I worked on the models, I didn't feel hollow inside. In fact, building planes downright cured me of my grief. "

Crushing the butt of his cigarette under the tip of his shoe, he walked over to the refrigerator and took out a beer. Sam didn't often drink beer. The air felt dense with something I couldn't name—not love, but something heavy and unfamiliar with cold currents running through it.

"That plane over there," he said after a moment, "is a B-29. Buddy was flying one when he was shot down." Sam brought over a step stool and unfastened the B-29 from its wire, carried it to the table where I was sitting, and installed it in my hands. I remembered a movie about an American pilot who'd fallen in love with a beautiful Italian girl. "My Yahn-key," she called him.

"If I know Buddy, he was probably singing 'The Star-Spangled Banner' on his way down," Sam said. He lifted the model from my hands and flew it in a figure eight, making expert passes at the tip of my nose. We were supposed to be packing up, but Sam couldn't stop talking about Buddy. "Buddy Podesta was a genuine American hero. Only he didn't walk off a goddamn Hollywood set when he was finished. You tell me—how's a person supposed to believe in luck? Some Jap gets off scot-free while my brother gets incinerated inside his plane, and Mama dies of a broken heart. If things were fair, a hero like Buddy would be sitting here with us. I hate to say it, Sailor, but sometimes God stands behind the bullies."

This I knew was a dark truth.

Sam took my hand and looked into my eyes. "Life's a crap shoot, baby. All I know is that the past will kill you, if you let it."

This was the way things were. Sam would never stop feeling sad about Buddy, and I would never stop feeling sad about not having a daddy. You went on missing a person the rest of your life.

Sam walked over to a shirt hanging by the door and felt around for another pack of cigarettes. "Sorry for all the sour talk. I shouldn'ta got started." The phone rang and we both jumped. I thought it was Buddy calling from the beyond, but it was only Mern. What was keeping us? Sam glanced at his watch and whistled. "Time's flying," he said. We had to hustle. He dragged out a carton from under the daybed. Go ahead and rummage, he told me. He was going to the basement to clean out storage.

After he left, I got down on the floor. Inside the carton were books, a compass, a framed photograph of two boys, one I immediately recognized as Sam. The boys were in Boy Scout uniforms and standing by a tree, an arm thrown over the other's shoulder. I touched Sam's face, then Buddy's. I'd never had a brother or a sister and tried to imagine what it would be like to lose a brother. Eunice Turtle was the closest thing I had to a sister. I'd been pretending to myself that she was my sister, but I had no sister. My Eunice was and always would be a turtle.

I dropped the photograph back on the pile and got up. I wanted to go home. I wanted to tear down Sam's planes, stomp on them until they were broken into pieces. What a stupid hobby. Everything about Sam felt wrong. His big freckled hands, his beach ball belly. Did I want to see him every morning in his terry robe frying up bacon? Did I want to see his razor next to the sink? His stupid dancing shoes? I kicked his bedroom slippers under his bed.

I picked the photograph of the brothers out of the carton and curled up on the daybed with it pressed to my chest. The sun was beating through the windows: the close air, the planes hovering in silence made me extremely sleepy. I didn't know how long I'd been asleep when I felt Sam's hand was on my arm. Through half-opened lids, I saw BUDDY on Sam's arm and thought of Anne Frank, and Buddy's death, and Dupere wrapping me in his varsity jacket against the night's chill—how anything could happen in a lifetime.

Sam fished a cigarette from his pocket and lit it with a single match. "Didn't mean to get carried away about the war, sweetheart." He slipped his free hand around mine and squeezed. "I talk too much."

I sat up.

"Everybody's got a dream," he said. "Without a dream, you're a dead duck."

I nodded.

Sam glanced at the watch. "Your mother's going to wonder what happened to us." We hadn't even started to pack.

"So what," I said. Sam gazed at the photograph of himself and his brother. "You're absolutely right. So what!" He asked me if I wanted to hear one last story about Buddy. Sure, I said.

Buddy had been a remarkable boy. Handsome, smart, inventive. He had especially loved science. A single picture in a book one of Buddy's teachers had loaned him—Richard Halliburton's *Book of Marvels*—had made a big impression on him. It was a drawing of the Hanging Gardens of Babylon. "Buddy got this idea to plant a Garden of Eden right in our backyard," Sam said. "He planned on starting small, but eventually he wanted to plant all species of tree and flower." Birds would come. Butterflies. Even deer. Buddy ordered seeds from catalogues and made lists. Of course not everything grew. But Buddy didn't give up. He decided he would create a new fruit, a cross between a peach and a mango—a "pango," he'd call it. He wrote famous botanists and bought Petri dishes. "Mama said if he succeeded, she would invent a pie crust to go with the pango, and we'd all become rich and famous."

I imagined Buddy hunched over his tray of seedlings, a streak of dirt on his nose—a genius—hoping he'd win some big scientific prize. He didn't know he'd be dead in a few years. "What happened?" I asked.

Sam's lip trembled. He stared at the picture of his brother. "I'll tell you what happened. The war took Buddy, nineteen years old—shark food. No one got rich and famous. Mama passed away and for a long time, I stopped dreaming."

We walked home without saying much. It seemed like Buddy was walking along with us. Clouds of sparrows flew between the bushes. I wondered about the crows, if they had been a sign of something, but not something bad. I doubted Frankie had sent them.

Mern was waiting. "What have you two been up to?" she said. Where was all Sam's stuff? Sam said we'd been otherwise occupied, and when Mern raised a suspicious eyebrow, he said, "We got to talking, no big deal."

"What the hell were you talking about so many hours?" Mern said. "Things," Sam said, and winked at me.

We ate cold cuts for dinner and Sam didn't mention the planes or Buddy. I doubted Mern would have been interested in the Hanging Gardens of Babylon. Later, when I told her about the model planes, she said her living room wasn't going to be turned into an airport. They'd have to go into the basement with Sam's stuff.

The next day, Sunday, Sam returned to his apartment and didn't come back until after dark. He brought a carton into my room. I was going to get to keep the B-29 and a few of Buddy's books. While Sam tacked Buddy's plane above my bed so it was the last thing I'd see before going to sleep and the first thing I'd see in the morning, I opened the faded green cover of Buddy's favorite, the *Book of Marvels*, and looked at pictures of the world's wonders: the Empire State Building; Machu Picchu; Christophe's Citadel, owned by the black king of Haiti. The Taj Mahal. When Sam was finished hanging Buddy's plane, he reached into the carton and pulled out a book on magic. On the yellowing pages were drawings of men with curly mustaches doing card tricks. Some chapters were devoted to hat and scarf tricks, the construction of conjuring tables and parlor magic. "You'll like this one too," Sam said. Mern gave a fake cough in the doorway. "You two look like a couple of old librarians," she said, and time poured back in on us. Sam held out the book to her. "Not interested." She pushed up her glasses and walked away.

Sam kissed me and closed my door softly, and for a while there was only the racket of my heart and Eunice Turtle scuffling in her aquarium. Then even those noises evaporated, and I was the center of perfect silence.

Him or me? my father said in the middle of the night.

"Can't we talk about something else?" I said. What about all the things we were going to do after I finished school? What about going to the rodeo, what about buying my horse? "I'm tired tonight, Daddy. Do we have to talk?"

Bunny! You can't just shove me aside. I'm your flesh and blood. I'm your whole damn past and your future.

"Not tonight," I pleaded. "Please!" I turned away, but from the corner of my eye I saw the warm glow of his presence start to dissolve and grow sheerer and sheerer until the window behind him was outlined through his ribs. I felt an enormous sadness shoot through my chest, and my eyes burned with tears. It frightened me how much I loved him. I wanted to call him back from wherever he was going, but in a rush of knowledge I realized my daddy was a tricky, dangerous man, and I could never trust his love.

Chapter 8

Family

The Lovebirds they called themselves, but happiness made my mother squirm. Despite her good fortune in meeting Sam, my mother continued to be unimpressed with God. I was mistaken, she told me, if I thought God's will had anything to do with anything. God, if he existed, was deaf and crippled, just an old codger with hemorrhoids and cataracts, and he could barely make the world turn. It seemed her habitual pleasure to destroy expectations for the good. When President Eisenhower had a heart attack, my mother predicated the Russians would take advantage and hordes of communists would soon be at our door. She could not cut loose from the headlines that screamed prophecies she took as her personal fate. One morning in our shared bathroom, she issued another kind of warning: we came from a long line of piss-poor women, and if I thought I could escape the legacy, I'd better wise up.

Piss-poor. Legacy. "What are you talking about, Mern!" I turned to push past her, but she held my arm and stared into my eyes. Behind a mask of flaking Noxzema, I saw years of worry, irrational worry, which, I imagined, had only grown in rigor being a solo parent. Her words gave me pause, not because I thought they were true, but because for the first time I realized Mern hadn't been prepared for motherhood any more than I would be at seventeen. Fear, worry, and bitterness had gobbled up my mother's happiness—Mern whose absences and rants were beginning to make sense. I put my hand over her cold hand gripping my sleeve. In her wool socks and kimono, she seemed childlike, a kid in a masquerade, the Noxzema cracking into white bits that fell onto her chest. "Grandma Sophie Sunny took in laundry, Eunice. She sold greeting cards door-to-door. Sam's great, but who knows where love leads." She was about to say something else, but a small bird crashed into the bathroom window, and my mother, touching the smudge of bird blood, resumed her depressing perspective. "See. Just when you think you're sailing through clear air, you hit a glass wall."

For Thanksgiving we carried a bronzed turkey downstairs to Mr. Tabachnik's and ate parsnips and matzo ball soup. After dinner, Sam brought out a deck of cards and showed me how to do Buddy's signature trick—Cherchez La Femme. Buddy would have wanted Sam to teach it to me, Sam said. I practiced in my room until I was an expert, and then it was Christmas, and Sam and I walked over to Shafer's filling station to purchase a tree. "Next year I'll have a car and we'll drive out to the country and chop ourselves a winner," Sam said, but I couldn't see Mern in freezing temperatures, on a Christmas tree expedition, her feet trussed up in ugly boots. Besides, a lot could happen before next Christmas.

Bing Crosby crooned "White Christmas" as we strolled the avenues of cut trees, assessing their color and shape. The wind shoved its icy fingers under my sleeves, but I didn't mind. Sam couldn't get over the fact that Mern had never bought me a real tree. "A kid like you deserves more," he said, "and I aim to give you more." A single blue star shone brilliantly in the dim sky. "Hey, whatdya want for Christmas dinner, Lieutenant?" It was Sunday, lampposts and display windows had been decorated with pine branches and velvet bows, and we were on our way to Dvorjek's, which Sam was proud to show me. We walked along the empty main street, past the closed shops, down a side alley to a delivery area where the produce trucks unloaded. Sam reached into his pocket and jingled a ring of keys in front of a cellar door. "This is it," he said with reverence, as if we'd arrived at the Pearly Gates. Then we were underground, enclosed by cement walls and shelves stacked floor to ceiling with supplies.

"Hold on while I give us some light," Sam said, pulling strings down a center aisle.

The stockroom burst into fluorescence—kitchen supplies, toilet paper, a steel door against the back wall with a curved handle that gleamed like a slice of moon. *This* was Dvorjek's Market? I forced my mouth into a smile and tried not to show my disappointment. The dinginess of the place felt oppressive, clinging to the walls and floor and all the stuff, a sticky substance you couldn't wash off.

"Going to get us some dinner," Sam said, swinging open the freezer door. Frigid vapors swarmed our knees, and Sam disappeared into the maw. A minute later, he emerged carrying chops and a bracelet of frankfurters strung over his wrist. Uneasy feelings of stealing wiggled into my brain.

Upstairs, Sam did not switch on the lights. A muzzy grayness hovered over shelves of canned food, brooms and dustpans, bins emptied of cabbage and apples. In the corner, an encased deli section stood bereft of salamis and blocks of cheese. "It's gonna be grand when I'm finished with this place," Sam said, going behind the cash register to get a pencil. He placed the meat from the freezer on the scale, licked the tip of the pencil, and scribbled a note to himself. "To work in a place like this, a guy's got to know his Macintoshes from his Winesaps. Someday, ya never know, I may own the place." I thought of Buddy, and imagined a table bearing baskets of pangos, but I still couldn't see what Sam was so excited about.

"What do we want for Christmas dinner?" he said, wheeling around to survey the store. "Creamed corn?" Creamed corn, I agreed. He scooted over to a nearby shelf and lifted a can. What else? We shouted our favorites. Chocolate pudding. Mashed potatoes. Peanut butter cups. "Anything, *anything* you want," Sam gushed. I curled my fingers around a can of Hershey's syrup and hugged it to my chest. I remembered asking Eunice Turtle, "If God created the universe, who created God?"

Everything comes from hunger. Hunger created God, she'd answered. Hunger had nothing to do with what I was feeling, a wild desire to hold the weight of oranges, bricks of cheese, boxes of crackers in my arms. I leaped and pirouetted from shelf to shelf. Minestrone. Chicken noodle. Consommé. "Bravo, bravo!" Sam encouraged. Tipsy with daring, I stuffed my pockets with jawbreakers, licorice wheels, the sort of penny candy I usually scorned. A singsongy voice was telling me I never had to stop. And then I did—stop. My legs suddenly went stiff as poles. I teetered self-consciously, paralyzed to the spot. The joy ran out of me, and I was once again in Dvorjek's dreary store.

"We'd better go," I said, emptying the loot from my pockets onto a shelf behind some cans. Sam glanced at his watch. "Yeah, too bad we can't stay, but you know how your mother is. She'll be wondering what happened to us." I could just imagine if Sam brought Mern to Dvorjek's. Mern, big-haired and sassy, calling him *Mr. Pineapple, Mr. Tomato, Mr. Anchovy Paste.* She'd notice how the linoleum was pocked and faded, and mice lived in the brooms.

Sam buttoned my jacket, wrapped a scarf around my neck, and kissed the top of my head. We left through the cellar door and walked without speaking, Sam edgy, as if he'd been reading my private thoughts. In a store window I caught sight of myself—a strange-looking girl with dark hair and overbright eyes. The streets were quiet except for the soft tinkle of Christmas bells pinged by wind. We turned a corner, and Sam shifted the grocery carton to his other shoulder to better grip my hand. "Ya liked going to Dvorjek's with me? It's a special place, huh? I brought you 'cause you're special. You're my special star." He stopped and put his big face close to mine. I could smell tobacco and Wrigley's spearmint on his breath. "You know who I love?" I shook my head. "I love Eartha Kitt and Satchmo, Harry Truman, the man from Miz-ur-ah, and Eddie Arcaro, bless his pint-sized heart! And I love you." Sam swung my hand. "And Mernie too." We walked a bit farther without talking, our footsteps perishing into the silence, the black sky falling earthward between the stars. "Hey. You know what?" Sam said when we turned another corner. "We don't have to talk about what just happened at the store. We don't even have to talk about all the grocery loot we're bringing home." He shifted the carton of food onto his other shoulder and hooked his pinky around mine; we shook three times. I told him I wasn't a squealer. "You're the gen-u-ine ticket, sweetheart. A kid a guy can trust."

On Christmas Eve we decorated the tree with blue lights and strands of tinsel. At the last minute, Sam produced a blown-glass angel with flowing hair and scalloped wings from a nest of tissue paper. She'd belonged to Sam's great-grandmother. "This little gal's traveled everywhere with me," Sam said in his red vest, the tassel of his Santa hat dangling in his face. "We called her the Angel of Hope." He held the ornament on his palm for Mern and me to examine. She was about eight inches high, made of green-tinted glass. Between her slender fingers she held a tiny globe.

"She's so delicate," I said.

Sam nodded and said they didn't make them like this anymore. "Every Christmas the Angel of Hope had the place of honor on top of the Podesta tree." He climbed the step stool with his slippered feet to clip the angel onto our tree. "Of course, after Buddy was gone, Mama said the angel was a cruel joke, that our guardian angel had absconded to the other side of heaven, and the dirty rotten truth was, I also believed the angels had deserted us."

Mern held up her hand. "No Buddy talk tonight," she said.

"Yeah, you're right, Mern," Sam said, backing down the stool. "The past's over." He bent to retrieve tinsel that had fallen to the floor and shut out the lights. The Christmas tree was suffused with a smoky blue glow, and we breathed in its forest scent. Mern belched quietly in the dark. Outside the wind hooted, and snow crystals swirled by the windows. Mern squeezed my arm. In a hushed, reverent tone, she said, "I swear to God, Ma's around." The hairs went up on my neck. "I swear, Grandma Sophie Sunny's here. I can smell her. Do you, Eunice?" Her voice was awestruck and trembly.

I sat very still and felt distinct warmth on my skin, like when you enter a room where a fire has just gone out. Mern had been mentioning her mother a lot lately. She was under the influence of an article about a woman named Virginia Tighe in Pueblo, Colorado, who claimed to have been Bridey Murphy in a past life. Virginia remembered details of Bridey's childhood in County Cork, Ireland, a hundred years earlier, including kissing the Blarney Stone. After my mother read about Virginia, she became convinced she'd been someone else too. She dreamed Grandma Sophie Sunny was once a queen in Mesopotamia, which made her, Mern, of royal blood.

"'Mern Louise,' Ma's saying," my mother said, pitching her ear and listening with all her might. "'Thank the good Lord you are provided for and all your troubles have come to naught.'" My mother blinked at Sam and Sam smiled. "She's happy for me, Mr. Sunshine! I didn't fail her after all!"

I stared at the blue lights strung on our tree, at the Angel of Hope casting a double-sized shadow on the wall. Sam raised his glass. "Here's to the living and here's to the dead. They're not so far away after all!" We welcomed Ma, Buddy, and Mama Podesta, and I made a silent toast to my father, who existed somewhere between the living and the dead. Mern said she hoped Mr. Tabachnik would feel better soon. He'd been sick with a cold all week. Sam rose and sang, *"Silent night, ho-o-ly night."*

It is a holy night, I thought.

The next morning, the silhouette of the Christmas tree sprang into green magnificence under the dazzling sun. Icicles hung from the eaves, but there'd been no new accumulation of snow. Next to the tree was a cage on a stand covered with a plastic cape—turquoise with big white stars.

Sam pushed up the sleeves of his bathrobe. "Close your eyes, the both of you." Mern groaned and said she was too old for games. *"Close your eyes!"* Sam barked. We pressed our hands over our eyes. "Presto magico!" said Sam. We opened our eyes—a lime-green parakeet with a bright yellow head sat on a trapeze inside the cage.

"Jesus Moses!" Mern gasped. "A bird!"

"A beaut, isn't he?" Sam said.

Mern reached into her pocket for her glasses. I imagined she was wondering about the new satin mules and silver bracelet she'd hoped for. I myself was wondering how Sam had snuck the bird in and how he could have so miscalculated my mother's desires. Now he tapped on the bird's cage and called him a smart little fella. The bird splayed his wings and ducked his head under a raft of feathers.

Mern wrinkled her nose. "Something's the matter with it," she said, studying the creature hiding its head. "It doesn't like me."

Sam made a face. "You're crazy! He likes you just fine. He's taking a nap."

My mother wanted to know what the hell she was going to do with a parakeet. "They crap all over the place and spread germs." She turned to me—had I known about this project? I shrugged. She turned back to Sam. Could he get his money back? Tell the pet store the bird hadn't worked out? She dove for a handful of Raisinets and threw them into her mouth. This was our first real Christmas, but my mother always had to spoil things.

Sam convinced Mern to give the bird a trial week. My mother swore that if the bird didn't shape up, it was going to be fricassee. Outside, the winter sun was flat and lustrous, God's platinum wafer. The tapered Christmas bulbs were turned off, but the ropes of tinsel shone with a glassy brilliance. And there was the Angel of Hope, holding out her world.

Sam went off to the kitchen for a bottle of pink champagne. Returning, he popped the cork and poured the bubbly into paper cups. My mother stood up and toasted. Across the room, the parakeet jumped onto his wire bars and ran his beak back and forth, playing his cage like a xylophone. Mern tightened the sash of her kimono and sauntered over. "Pretty Boy, Pretty Boy. Prrr-e-tty Bo-y," she said. The bird cocked his head and initiated a series of eeks. Mern clapped her hands. "You cute thing. Say 'Mern.' Birdie say 'Mern. *Mern*'!" She stuck her face close to the bars and made little kissy sounds. The parakeet opened his beak and showed the nub of a tiny black tongue. Mern stumbled backward. "Uuugh. That's obscene," she said.

We hadn't opened our gifts yet. They were under the tree in elf wrap. I lifted the smaller package with my name on it and tore off the paper while Sam watched with pleasure. "For Eunice Turtle! She'll love them!" I said, turning over the ceramic castle with its turrets and tiny barred windows. The larger box contained a model airplane kit. On the cover was a picture of a man in flight coveralls and goggles standing in front of a biplane with wooden struts over the fuselage: Pilot Jack Knight, Pilot of the Night. "One tough hombre," Sam said. "You like?" Jack Knight had flown from New York to San Francisco, through storm and sleet, for the US Postal Service, with only a road map to guide him. I opened the box and smelled the raw balsa wood and imagined Sam and me in the basement assembling the pieces. Mern yawned dramatically. Pouring herself more bubbly, she waltzed around the living room, the sleeves of her kimono lifting and fluttering to the tune of "The Wayward Wind." She stopped in front of the bird. "What am I going to call you, you little devil?"

Sam jabbed me with his elbow. "See. She likes him."

We called out potential names: Johnny Ray. Nick for St. Nicholas. Valentino. The winner was Mr. Puccini. Mern said it was the most dignified, and Italians loved romance.

Soon Mern was bringing home library books on how to teach birds to talk. She left the radio playing so Mr. Puccini wouldn't be lonely, which was more than she'd done for me. When my mother wasn't home, I vied for Mr. Puccini's friendship, bribing him with thistle seed and dried apricots. I liked him plenty, but Eunice Turtle reigned far above. My mother bought Mr. Puccini a tiny red bell, a mirror, a cuttlebone, a plastic ball with a rattle inside. She taught him to step out onto her finger and cheep. She had discovered simple happiness.

Clouds smothered the sky in March. I walked to school in my new coat with a hood and toggle buttons, compliments of Sam Podesta. I wore knee socks and saddle shoes. We were learning about the Greek civilization. Our teacher, Mrs. Murray, told us stories about the gods and goddesses. The goddess I liked best was Artemis, who lived alone in the forest with her dogs and shot arrows at intruders. Sam and I put together Pilot Jack Knight's model plane. It now hung over my bed alongside Buddy's B-29. When it got a little warmer, Mern shut the windows, pulled the blinds, covered the mirrors with towels and let Mr. Puccini out. Occasionally he'd land on a ceiling fixture, and she'd run for the yardstick and have to sweet-talk him down. One time, when she'd left the bathroom door ajar, I saw Mr. Puccini on her shoulder, grooming strands of her hair while she peed. "The true lovebirds," Sam said, and they were.

By April Fool's Day, the bushes had blossomed into pale green fuzz. Underfoot, the earth was soft with rain. Sam attempted to keep our place spotless, so I tried not to track in mud, but Mern left trails of talc, cigarette ash, cold coffee in cups. Sam never complained. A cough had lodged in Mr. Tabachnik's chest and for a week he stayed indoors in his bathrobe, a muffler around his neck. It was Mern, not Sam, who cooked for him, barley broth and vegetable soup, big plaid thermoses full. She brought them down to his apartment along with old *Reader's Digest*s from Annie's and rubbed on Vicks VapoRub. In the middle of the week, I knocked on his door with my own offering of chocolate pudding. Long minutes passed before Mr. Tabachnik, rumpled and unshaven, thrust his head out the door. Ignoring me and my pudding, he squinted over my shoulder and spoke to an imaginary person. *Estherleh, Estherleh?* he called between labored breaths at the nothing and the no one that was there.

For the rest of the afternoon, I stayed in my room and read the letter from Richard Halliburton addressed to Dear Reader in the *Book of Marvels*. Richard Halliburton had dreamed of visiting the Wonders of the World, and I would be the first girl pilot to fly around the world. I'd wear goggles and a leather cap and fly over the earth in search of the Hanging Gardens of Babylon that King Nebuchadnezzar built for his lonely queen. I had started a sketch of my own Babylon, a place where orchids grew from the tops of gigantic pineapples and crazy-looking birds nested in date palm trees.

A late April snow produced big globby flakes that stuck to the windows like wet Kleenex, and Sam had to shovel the walk twice before noon. Schools and stores were closed. I put on my red galoshes and went outside into the blinding whiteness. Not even a dog print was in sight. Rainbows sparkled through the drifting flakes, and along the curb, the parked cars had become a chain of white elephants holding tails. Sweeping up a mittenful of glitter, I packed and sculpted until my snowball became a waist-high, winged stallion. But by then, the miracle and thrill of snow had evaporated. I was thinking about my father and all his broken promises, caravans and horses, and I kicked my little horse until his ribs splintered and his wings fell off.

That night my mother came into my room and apologized for all the mean things she'd ever done to me. She wanted to start over and erase the past. "What do you mean, 'start over'?" I said. "How come now?" She'd had a dream, she said, but she wouldn't tell me what the dream was. Only that it had frightened her. "I suppose even if you said yes, it wouldn't change anything, would it? The past can't be undone...?" Her hand crept under the blanket and searched for mine.

"You don't have to answer this now," she said. "Just consider that I'm asking."

When June came around, Sam and Mern celebrated the first anniversary of the day they met. Paper. *It's only a paper moon... But it wouldn't be make-believe, if you believed in me.* For the occasion, Mern cut bangs, put the rest of her hair into a ponytail, and said she was Debbie Reynolds. She gave Sam a subscription to a travel magazine. Someday they were going to travel, weren't they? "You betcha," Sam said. He presented her with a silver bracelet in a silver box. She deserved better than paper; he'd buy her diamonds if he could. Mern held out her hand, and Sam slipped the bangle on. Then she went over and opened Mr. Puccini's cage to show him what she'd got. Mr. Puccini flew out and pecked madly at the silver around her wrist.

The following Monday, not long after Mern left for work, I was crossing from my bedroom into the kitchen and saw Mr. Puccini's cage was open, and Mr. Puccini himself was hopping along the back of the couch. In a second, he could fly out the window, but how to get him back in his cage? A shadow came into the room, as if a black cloud had crossed the sun, and I lay down on the floor in the middle of it and whispered Mr. Puccini's name. He landed on my shoulder, then crept onto my wrist. I held him for a few seconds between my palms, a pulse jackhammering at the base of my neck, and felt his body, all softness and heat, his bones so fragile they might have been clay. I kissed the top of his head and put him back in his cage.

Two days later, his cage was left open again. I went from room to room terrified I'd find Mr. Puccini dead in the bathroom sink, his skull bashed in; he loved to attack the bird in the mirror. Mern's bedroom window was open. I stuck out my head and looked around. The sky was a pale blue sheet stretched tight without a ripple. Not a leaf stirred in the catalpa. Then I saw Mr. Puccini in the neighbor's shrubs, watching the world go by. "Mr. Puccini!" I yelled. For one second I saw him as he might have been in Babylon, his lime-green body flitting among the red hibiscus, the boldness of the sun in his eyes. When I looked again, Mr. Puccini was gone.

Chapter 9

The Proposal

There was no time for argument or blame. We formed a search party and set forth to hunt for Mr. Puccini, Mr. T posting himself at the front door in case the little birditchka returned.

I'd never seen my mother so motivated, or so distraught. She traipsed up and down the street, asking if she could inspect people's yards for a small green bird. Pointing and gesturing, she churned out explanations, unable to say *Puccini* without breaking down. God will find your bird for you, one woman said, and Mern might have done her serious damage if I hadn't hauled my mother away. We waded through thorns and hedges, mock orange bushes that left a blissful fragrance on our skin, through gardens where pink lilies still held the evening darkness in their throats. We searched from block to block, crawling into ornamental holly, ignoring barking dogs, shining our flashlights under eaves. Hour after hour, we searched in widening circles till the sky went from sharp blue to lavender to navy blue. The warmth vanished from the air, and my mother shivered, her eyes electric with fear. "Pre-tee Mr. Puccini, Pretty Boy," she called up into trees, but the trees remained silent, and with each failed attempt, my chest ached from holding my breath.

Her feet hurt, her knees hurt, hunger gnawed her belly, but she did not give up. She was a mother bear separated from her cub, or at least she had become one, and I was both proud of this new Mern and sad she'd been more smitten over Mr. Puccini than me. When she got too tired or defeated, she simply stopped, looked around bewildered and as wordless as a child, and reached for my hand, imploring me to lead the way. Her words rang with the certainty of the desperate—she *would* find Mr. Puccini—and shied away from the brutal truth.

Finally Sam had to shepherd us home. "It's over, sweetheart," he told Mern, his voice tender and grave. It was past eight and darkness was blurring the edges of fences and rooflines, but I saw the glint of tears in my mother's eyes. "He'll freeze out here," she whispered, thinking of other horrors. *Cats!*

"Ah, Mernie, forget it," Sam said, lacing his arms through ours. Mr. Puccini was happier being free. "Right this minute, he's probably winging his way to the Caribbean, headed for bee-u-tee-ful Havana nights."

My mother gave a cry and jerked her arm away. "Only a moron would joke at a time like this."

Scratched, dotted with pricks of blood, exhausted, and hoarse, we trekked home, as if from a battlefield upon which lay our former selves. That night Mern and I rocked and wept with great violence. I couldn't separate the emotions inside her from those inside me. "Oh, Eunice, Eunice," she said, gripping my wrist with her icy fingers, "tell me you'll never leave me," words that made my pulse skip while a shadow crossed over my heart. The depth of my mother's sorrow, I noted, was greater for Mr. Puccini than it had been for my father, anger being no part of this grief. Her sorrow left her dizzy and weakened and explained why she hadn't even asked how Mr. Puccini had gotten out.

Neither Sam nor I had the heart to tell Mern that she was the culprit; she'd been the cause of her bird's demise—all of this clear as day by recounting who'd left the flat last. Gallantly, Sam took the blame. Gallantly, he carried Mr. Puccini's cage into the basement so Mern wouldn't have to look at the motionless trapeze. Sorrow trumps anger, which was why in her state of mourning, my mother did not blast Sam. But someday she would. I had no doubt that in her hindbrain, one more strike was being leveled against Mr. Sunshine for his admitted negligence. All the rotten losses, all the merciless blows life had dished to my mother she saw now as culminating in the loss of her bird.

*　　*　　*

When it was clear Mr. Puccini had exited from our lives for good, Mern crawled into bed and refused to move, a haggard wraith of herself. Mr. Tabachnik sat by her side and commiserated. "From such a little fella such a big happiness bloomed." In bed, I wept with Eunice Turtle for those we'd lost, and for my mother's disconsolate soul. Weeks passed. One afternoon, Annie stopped by to try to reason with my mother, who had stopped going to work. Annie marched into her bedroom, extracting her from the rumpled sheets. She washed my mother's face and brushed her hair, and a less disheveled Mern stood chain-smoking in the living room, scanning the sunbaked day. Annie told her she'd better get a grip. "Besides, there's Eunice and Sam. They need you, too, Mern."

"I know, I know," my mother said, returning her gaze to the window, her voice drained of fight. Mr. Puccini had understood her better than any man, woman, or child, she said. He'd loved her unconditionally. "For all I know, we were married in a former life." My mother looked wistfully at the sky. Somewhere beyond the neighborhood, wide-open fields were calling to her; Mr. Puccini was singing her name! Maybe she was thinking of leaving too. I pictured her empty place at the breakfast table, but I couldn't really imagine a life without Mern. Before she left, Annie pulled me into her muscular embrace. My mother was having a little "episode," she said, and invited me to live with her, an offer I declined.

Meanwhile, Sam had done some research; my mother's condition had a name. "She's de-pressed," he stated. Everyone had a breaking point and my mother had just met hers. He'd seen it in the service, big bruisers who cried in their soup. Would she get over it? I wanted to know.

"Give her a week or two. Meantime, go easy. She's in a delicate state." I hadn't thought of my mother as *delicate*, but maybe it was true.

Mr. Tabachnik stated the problem another way: "With you, with your father, with Podesta, okay, she loves—this much." He spread his thumb and forefinger two inches, four inches. "To that birdie, she gave away her entire heart." His whole body shrugged. "But a person and an animal are not a match!"

For the next several weeks, my mother kept vigil on Mr. Puccini's corner on a hard wooden chair. Her kimono hung on her bony shoulders; her knuckles protruded under her skin. If she ate anything, it was gherkins from a jar. Sam heaped on the bacon and hash browns, but Mern refused them and went to bed early, and Sam disappeared into the basement to honk on his harmonica or jump rope till he was soaked with sweat. A few nights a week, he played pinochle with Mr. Tabachnik. I hid under the table sometimes, happy for male company, happy to eavesdrop on conversations about steelworkers, Rocky Graziano, and the Suez Canal.

The terrible thing about my mother's sadness was that she seemed to be sinking deeper and deeper into herself, a place I thought she'd never go, her silence almost a form of laziness, as if it were too much effort to speak. Summer was passing in a blur, and Sam said we had to take action before Mern went down the tubes. "I'm a specialist in sad women," he said. Hadn't he pulled Mama Podesta back from the brink after Buddy died? In short order, a whole new category of expensive gifts appeared—a pink Angora cowl-neck sweater, a pair of white kid gloves—gifts that were not from Dvorjek's but bought in nearby towns from stores with ritzy names. Mern bestowed upon Sam her weak, rationed smiles, but a wedge of interest opened up. Little by little, the gifts seemed to cheer her. And little by little, she began to ask for more: pearls displayed on a black velvet cushion, a topaz ring. Sam tried to make a joke. Who did she think he was, Henry Ford? But he worked longer hours to get her what she wanted, and our plans for after-dinner card trick lessons, our cooking adventures, our date to put together another model plane sadly collapsed.

I actually forgot about my father for entire days. When I did think about him, it struck me that he wasn't just jealous but cowardly and ungenerous. Sam was no enemy, and I did not have a fickle heart. If

Frankie visited me again, I made up my mind to confront him. Hadn't he run away from us, and wasn't he still running? Did he have any idea how awful and funny, how desperate and unpredictable love was?

He wasn't finished with me either because when I woke on a hot, moonless night and found him pacing, the first thing he said was, *You're all I've got, Bunny.* I twisted away when he tried to hold me in his arms. I hissed at him, "You're only a dream," but my daddy said I was making a mistake. *I don't want to lose you,* he said. *You're everything to me.* I felt his loneliness stretching out far into the future. I thought of Mern, haunted by loneliness, and it seemed the only thing my parents had in common was their loneliness. I couldn't imagine a world without Frankie, but I couldn't imagine Frankie in my world.

"I'm nothing to you," I said. I was nothing to him and Mern was nothing to him and nothing plus nothing equaled nothing. This was the truth.

My beautiful father. How he wept.

"Long story short," Sam said, "your mother's got an *inferiority complex.* She's felt deprived her whole life. Worthless on the inside. Losing Puccini was the last straw." I was putting together a cheesecake from a recipe torn from the *Wild Pea Times.* Granulated sugar. Three packs of cream cheese, softened. I listened to Sam while I cracked eggs into a bowl.

"According to this Freud, what your mother really wants can't be bought. Even diamonds and emeralds wouldn't make her happy."

Wrong, wrong, wrong! I thought. I poured a cup of sugar into the bowl and beat the sugar and eggs. Crush wafers into crumbs, add melted butter, and mix well. Press into a nine-inch springform pan to within one inch from the top.

"What your mother needs is someone who'll provide for her for the rest of her days, cherish her till kingdom come. Who'll give her another bambino or two. What makes a woman feel more loved than four little words: 'Will you marry me?' That's what every woman wants."

I let my head fall forward so I could think for a minute without Sam watching. Dr. Freud hadn't met Mern.

"Just between the two of us, I'm gonna pop the question tonight. Whaddya think?"

"It's hard to picture Mern a bride," I said honestly.

"Trust old Sammy on this." He placed his broad hands on the sides of my face. "Listen. I'm gonna take care of both of you, just like always, only now I'll be your honest-to-goodness pa. We'll go to court and fix it up."

He could never be my pa. It was too late. The very word was idiotic. Was it too late?

After dinner, after Sam and I cleaned up and he went off to change his clothes, I carried Eunice Turtle into the bathroom, dumped out the mucky stuff from the bottom of her aquarium, and replaced it with fresh gravel. She'd caught a cold and wheezed through her nostrils and wasn't her perky self. Sam warned of furtive bacteria and advised a thorough housecleaning. In homage to our mutual devotion, she held perfectly still, smiling, while I scrubbed off the invading microbes from her face and shell. But ten minutes later I was back in the bathroom sobbing into the blue bath towel, my head swarming with black thoughts. I was worried about Eunice Turtle. I was worried Sam's plan would backfire. I was worried over troubles that had no name, unconvinced Sam's love could change Mern into a happy wife. Her heart belonged to Frankie, but Frankie had walked off the edge of the world. Mern had to decide what she wanted. Maybe the thing about fate was that it was yours and yours alone, and nobody could rescue you from it.

At breakfast Mern gave me a blow-by-blow. "It was a real de-luxe setup, nice wine, moonlight, 'Love Is a Many-Splendored Thing' on the player." Sam had gotten on his knee and said the words—*Marry me, marry me, my fine woman.* My mother hadn't known what to say. Then she remembered Garbo in *Ninotchka* and offered her hand. It was a big decision, she had told him. She needed time. How much time? he'd pressed her. Days? Weeks? He told her he wanted to take care of us. He'd said no one could love her as much as he did. If she said no, she'd break his goddamn heart. "'Let's sleep on it. What's the rush?' I said to him. And, kiddo, I'm thinking, 'Mern the heartbreaker, Sam the brokenhearted.'" Mern pointed her finger at my chest. "Then Sam said, 'There is a rush. Your daughter needs a father.'"

"I have a father," I said, but Mern didn't hear me and carried on. "I can't marry Sam. He's too damn good—the man would iron my sheets if I asked him." Once she signed on the dotted line, she said, there'd be no turning back, not without lawyers and judges and a whole big legal mess. *Divorce!* The word jumped into my mind. I didn't recall hearing about any legal mess with Dupere. "Did you...?" Mern answered before I could get the words out. She'd never *actually* married my father. Sniffling a little, she pushed up her glasses and avoided my eyes. "No love, honor, and obey for Frankie." Apparently my father had persuaded Mern that romance was the glue that held them together and that marriage would drive them apart. A baby was no reason to pop a ring.

Mern toyed with a spit curl above her ear, monitoring my expression. My heart caromed behind my eyes, one monstrous beat at a time. My head was splitting. Maybe she shouldn't have told me, she said. "Don't make a big deal. He's still your father, flesh and blood." She was on her high horse now. Someday, she promised, I'd realize she'd saved me a lot of trouble by *not* marrying that bum. I didn't hear what else she said because I was thinking about strangling her. She'd driven away my father, and now she was driving away Sam. What right did she have to decide my future? Why did her life have to be my life? I'm like her moon, I thought. I'll always be in her orbit. I'll never be able to escape and have a life of my own. My mother ruled my days and nights, but I couldn't leave her, even though only a nitwit would stay.

Chapter 10

Doom

Did she want to become Mrs. Samuel Podesta or not? The decision was giving Mern migraines. Mr. Tabachnik actively campaigned for marriage. "In my humble opinion," he told her, "life is short, misery is long, and a man such as Sam Podesta won't come your way again." Annie was against the whole idea. "What do you really know about this guy?"

My mother sighed and studied the veins in her hands. "I'm getting old, Annie."

Annie held her ground. "There are better fish in the sea, Mern."

My mother responded that they weren't swimming these waters. A week later, she made an appointment to consult a psychic named Zerlina Janneke, formerly of the Spiritualist Church, reputed to converse with spirits beyond the range of hearing of dogs or bats. Sam was dead set against the idea, fortune-tellers being pure malarkey. No one could read the future, he said. There were no maps that indicated, "This way to your destiny." "Lemme tell you a story." He placed a Schlitz in her hand and led her to the couch.

"So Buddy takes his rabbit's foot from when he was a kid overseas. In every letter to Mama, he writes, 'Hey, Mama, don't worry. I got my lucky rabbit's foot.' Before he's shipped out to Saipan, he goes to some fortune-teller on Guam. Maybe she slips him a Mickey, but he comes out of her place thinking he's invincible. 'I'm golden,' he writes Ma. 'Those Japs can't lay a finger on me. I'll be home by Christmas.'"

Sam plugged a cigarette in his mouth and narrowed his eyes at my mother. "The old gook lady tells him he has the longest lifeline she's ever seen, puffs him up so when he's flying his B-29, he gets cocky because a dame with an accent filled him with a pile of crap. He takes some stupid risks. Do I have to spell it out, Mern?"

My mother drew in her chin and gave Sam a baited look.

Sam punched out the words. *"There is no grand plan,* sweetheart! There's good luck and there's bad luck—that's it!"

A second ticked by.

"That's one helluva sad story, Sam," my mother said, her finger drawing circles on the top of the beer can. "But what are you *really* afraid of? What do you think Mrs. Janneke will tell me?" Sam groaned in disgust.

The following Wednesday she got glitzed up to va-va-vavoom the spirits in a red skirt and dangly rhinestone earrings, her parting words, "Don't tell Sam!" After she was gone, the flat grew quiet, the kind of quiet that has something dangerous behind it. I went into the bathroom and stared at myself. A pinpoint of light that no one else could see shone in the center of my eyes, like my own private song. I read to Eunice Turtle from the *M* encyclopedia about the Mennonites and the first macaroni invented in Naples, Italy. Then I arranged Mern's nail polish from Apricot Ice to Tahitian Flame and Ajaxed the sink. Sam wasn't home, and I wasn't sure he was coming home. My mother returned a little after four, pale beneath ovals of rouge. She kicked off her sling-backs and collapsed on her bed. Following her into her room, I begged for information.

"She was fat!" my mother recalled with a look of absorption. "She wore a housedress printed with teakettles! Her hair was like cotton wool, white and fuzzy, and her eyes were pink. Pink! Can you imagine! And they wiggled!" I didn't care about all that. What had Mrs. Janneke said?

She told Mern not every spirit was cooperative. Just because it was dead didn't mean a spirit couldn't be stubborn and opinionated. Or dumb as a doorpost. Or outright cruel. Mern had been shocked. Mrs. Janneke said she'd try her best and ran her hands over Sam's underwear, items she'd requested because they carried Sam's "atomic charge." After a little while she said, "He's a volcano ready to blow, dear," and then concentrated harder. "This love feels lopsided, Mern dear." My mother's heart was flighty and unseasoned, in its youthful stage, while Sam . . . in two words: *unrequited love.*

My mother stopped talking, her mouth pursed as if she were turning over something difficult in her mind.

"Sam's too gaga, and I'm not gaga enough."

"Can't you get more gaga?"

My mother pushed up her glasses, her gaze drifting over the ceiling. "Mrs. Janneke said a figure from the past is knocking at my door."

After eight, Sam showed up without the usual groceries. He walked straight into Mern's bedroom demanding to know what Mrs. Janneke had said. He must have figured out she went without his blessing. "Forget Podesta because your ship's about to come in?" he yelled. Noiselessly I crept into the hallway holding Eunice Turtle against my cheek. My mother set her emery board on the night table and studied her nails.

"It's not going to work, Sam. It's not in the cards."

Sam made a whooping sound of pure outrage. The fight that ensued lasted hours, their voices rising in spirals of accusation and recrimination. During the height of name-calling, I couldn't listen any longer and flung myself down the staircase and into the darkness, my feet hardly touching the ground. I ran in circles around our house, outpacing even the throb of cicadas, my chest burning. The shrill voices fell away but I kept running, my sweat chilling in the cool night air. The next morning I woke with a terrible sore throat. I could not speak. An opaque brightness blurred my vision. I felt dizzy and weak. I heard Mr. Tabachnik say, "Dehydration." I heard Mern plead with Sam not to leave at a time like this. I heard Sam promise, "Podesta's in for the long haul."

Sometime later, Sam was sitting on my bed stroking my arm. His touch left lines of warmth on my skin. "I shoulda shut my big mouth last night—Mernie and me fighting like a couple of two-year-olds!" He shook his head sadly. "If I knew you were listening, I woulda stopped the brawling." He brought a glass of orange juice to my lips. "Watch, things'll get better around here. You'll be shipshape in no time."

His face implied otherwise. I knew he was lying. Some nameless entity had taken hold of me and would not let go. My body had turned against me, and I had strange dreams at night. Something mysterious was happening. Young Nathan Tabachnik chased his Esther around a willow tree by a wide river. The horse Dupere promised me galloped across a beach neighing my name. My father waved from a merry-go-round spinning on top of a cheap tourist motel. I was slipping far out with the tide, and no one could reach me, not even Sam.

My joints swelled, my temples burned, and my fingers were frozen sticks. The doctor was perplexed. I suffered constipation and vomiting, rashes and broken nails. Clara Barton my mother was not. She brought me grape Jell-O in a parfait glass, *Photoplay* and *Seventeen* from the shop, but her attention was skittish. It was Sam who knelt on the cold tile and held my forehead while I retched, Sam who applied salves to the rashes, ice to swollen joints. "I'd rather take care of Mern and you than anything else in the world," he said, and cut back his hours at work.

The illness imposed its own rhythms: sleep and wakefulness, the spike of fever and the languor that followed, recovery and relapse. I was living in a place where ordinary time did not exist. And yet time passed. I missed the beginning of school. A girl from my class dropped off homework assignments; they lingered on my desk and gathered dust. I reread *Jane Eyre* and wondered what Jane would do in my situation. *I felt resolved, in my desperation, to go to all lengths.* Sam gave me a set of colored pencils, and when I felt well enough, I sat by my window and drew the dwindling plumage on a giant maple. Mr. Tabachnik offered his compliments and matzo brei. "Right here in Wild Pea—our own CC Chagall!"

Six months into my ailment, I was beginning to feel a little stronger when Mern started complaining about changes on the home front: the imported cheeses, the pork chops, the thin-sliced Italian ham vanished from our table. Boxes tied with gold ribbons, silk nightgowns, bangle bracelets, Angora sweaters likewise disappeared. One day when the trees were bare and light fell between them clean as a knife, my mother appeared in her kimono and wool socks at my door. Sam was getting paid chicken-shit working short-shift, she said, while she was working her ass off at Annie's. If I weren't sick, Sam could go back full-time, and we'd be rolling in dough. I pulled the covers over my head and pretended to snore. "You won't sleep so well in the poorhouse, kiddo," my mother said. She went away and came back a few minutes later and apologized for blowing off steam.

"How *is* my little Moucheroo?" she asked.

I made room for her in my bed. There were so many things I wanted to say: what would happen to us if Sam left? Why wasn't she ever satisfied? She rested her head on my shoulder, the dye smell of the beauty shop in her hair. "I feel so old, Eunice. I feel like a broken-down mule. You might as well send me to the glue factory." Suddenly she was crying, her sobs soft barks against my skin. Once upon a time, she'd wanted to be a figure skater like Sonja Henie, or one of the Rockettes. "You're young, Mern! You're not even thirty-five!" I countered. My mother lifted her tear-streaked face. A hushed tenderness crept into her voice, and she clapped me to her chest. "You don't deserve what's happening to you, Eunice, being sick and all." Her naked affection terrified me. Love itself was gigantically terrifying, yet I wanted to remain in its slippery arms and had to warn myself to beware.

Rain stammered through March, delaying the bright relief of tulips and forsythia. On my birthday, Mr. Tabachnik presented me with one of my drawings framed, a graceful horse with wings climbing into the sky. Clucks of praise fell from his lips. Sam bought me a portable record player that closed like a hair dryer, and a vinyl, *Only You*. Mern washed and curled my hair. I still had a slight fever, but everyone tried to make it nice. Mern was spending longer hours at Annie's. Sometimes she came home smelling like cigarettes and liquor, shooing away the warmed-over meat loaf Sam held out on a plate. One night Mern told him, "If this is romance, romance stinks." Not long after, someone began calling our flat. When Sam picked up the phone, the person hung up. Sam yelled into the receiver, "Don't call again!" Then the phone calls stopped, and Mern went into another decline. No one could do anything right—not Sam or me, not even Mr. Tabachnik, Annie, or our reelected president, Dwight D. Eisenhower, who Mern said didn't give a hill of beans for working stiffs. But Eunice Turtle was steadfast. We talked about everything: fathers, mothers, Anne Frank and the Nazis, love and kissing, the atomic bomb.

I wondered if the person on the phone had been my father.

A few weeks after the phone calls stopped, my mother had a dream. In it, Grandma Sophie Sunny Polestar told her, "Mernie, you'd better make hay while the sun shines. You're not exactly a teenager anymore. It's over before you know it." The notion of marriage must have reentered Mern's head about this time, though it took her almost another eight months to finally decide to tie the knot. She hurried to that decision after Mr. Tabachnik's sister-in-law Bertha called long-distance from Brooklyn to say that Mr. Tabachnik's ex-wife, Esther, had drowned herself in the bathtub. "From what they did to her *over there*, she never got right," Bertha had told him. We'd all thought Esther died a long time ago, but at the dinner table that evening Mr. Tabachnik explained that though he hadn't seen Esther in years, she'd been alive and well, and the flame in his heart had never gone out. "So why'd you split up?" Mern asked, pouring whiskey for the adults. It was what I also wanted to know.

"I fell head over heels for my Estherleh and likewise her for me. But living together"—he turned up his palms—"we fought like cats and dogs."

My mother looked sharply at Sam, and Sam gazed knowingly at Mern. Mern raised her glass, as if willing the young Mr. Tabachnik to grow out of the old. "He still loves her! Isn't that something?" she said, elbowing Sam. She was impressed. Mr. T had loved Esther till the end and beyond.

In the morning, Mern said to Sam, "We're not getting any younger. Maybe we *should* get married!" They smooched at the kitchen sink. Mern grabbed a tea towel and paraded around with it on her hair while I banged a fork on the egg pot and Sam hummed "Here Comes the Bride."

It was going to be a June wedding in the backyard. The lilacs would just be fading, the roses coming into bloom. We'd set up card tables and serve wedding cake, three kinds of sherbet, petits fours, and champagne. There'd be a minister. Annie was the maid of honor, and Mr. Tabachnik held the dual honor of being best man and the father who gave the bride away. I'd walk down the aisle throwing carnations and marigolds.

Mern was all hopped up. She searched bridal magazines. Should her gown be satin or sateen? On her head a wreath of baby roses or a tiara of pearls? She bemoaned Grandma Sophie Sunny wasn't around in the flesh. "Ma would be so happy for me now," she said dreamily. Happy for *all* of us, I thought. A few days later, Sam borrowed a car and drove to the jeweler's in the next town to buy a ring. Mern said diamonds were boring. She much preferred what she got, a garnet set in fourteen-carat gold. She'd done her nails in platinum frost. "*Adios,* misery!" she said, flashing the garnet and her iridescent nails when Sam got home.

Shortly after Mern got the ring, I realized I was completely free of aches and rashes. I felt as though I'd been in hibernation while my body underwent a radical transformation that had left me cleansed and new. My shoes and blouses no longer fit. My clothes hung funny. My head seemed larger, my ears smaller, my eyes wider; I had ankles and calves instead of sticks. Mern said I was filling out. My first trip was to the drugstore to buy Mern a gift for the shower Annie was throwing, though Annie grumbled about the match. Mr. Warner, the druggist, came out from behind the counter in his white tunic and eyed my bosom, his lips hooked into a creepy smile. "You've become quite a young lady since I've seen you last." I edged away down the aisle, his sticky gaze on the back of my legs, and made for the aluminum storm door. That evening Sam caught me studying myself in the mirror. "Dolores del Rio! You're gonna break hearts."

The next day, Mern got up really grumpy, looking as if she'd eaten a rotten egg. My mother was one of those women who swallowed painkillers by the handful and still had cramps. At dinner she prodded her cutlet as if it were still alive. "Nerves," Sam said privately while we were doing the dishes, "nothing to worry about." But later I heard Mern groaning in the bathroom and saw Sam wrap her in a blanket and hurry her to bed, like a dazed child rescued from a cave. I snuck down the hallway toward her room, a bare foot skidding on something slippery by the bathroom door. I flipped the bathroom switch; the tub held three inches of pinkish water, the toilet smeared with blood. The shock was harsh and bright and violent. What had my mother done?

The following morning the bathroom sparkled, the mystery of the night before erased from existence. Mern, apparently recovered, had gone to work, but Sam sat with his thumbs pressed into his eyelids, his mug of coffee untouched. "Sweetheart," he said, and that was all. After he left, I devoted myself to reading the *Book of Marvels* to Eunice Turtle, but I couldn't concentrate; Mr. Halliburton's photographs looked fake. I went out and poked under the roses, searching for shiny beetles, wondering if all the wonders of the world were hoaxes.

At dinner, Sam set a plate of sweet-and-sour pork in front of my mother; she studied the syrupy chunks and pushed the plate away, the rift of silence between us thick enough to cut with a knife. Out of the corner of my eye, I looked Mern over, inch by inch, and found no evidence of injury. She was pale and sullen but nothing about her looked harmed. Later, when Sam came in to say good night, he tried to explain. "Your mother...," he began, his face more serious than I'd ever seen it. "She...We..." His words fell like heavy bricks. His skin was a deep shade of pink. I waited for him to say the word *dying*, but instead I heard the word *miscarriage*. A feeling of disbelief coursed through my body. Sam cupped his big warm hand on my skull. "Yeah, yeah. Rotten luck. But Mernie's gonna be fine."

The wedding was in two weeks. Saturday, a week before the wedding, the day before Annie's shower, a letter arrived from Mr. Dvorjek addressed to Samuel Podesta. Mern brought it into the kitchen and held it up to the light. "Hey, I think the old buzzard sent a wedding gift." She tore open the envelope. She read through the letter and went back to the first page. Then she sank into a chair and tossed the letter to me.

Sam had been fired. *During the two years of your employment, you were a good worker, a person I thought I could trust. So now I know you are no good!* The second and third pages of the letter contained a list of alleged stolen goods and the total cash amount Sam owed Dvorjek's, including money missing from the register. I was outraged. "It's not true! Mr. Dvorjek's lying. He thinks everyone's stealing from him. You said so yourself."

Mern was reading the letter a third time when Sam entered the kitchen, as if on cue, dripping puddles on the linoleum. We hadn't heard the rain begin. I looked out the kitchen window at the muddy green sky, and then at Mern, the letter hidden behind her back.

Sam regarded my mother. "What you got there?" Raindrops stood out on his arms and mustache. His left hand gripped a bunch of wilted daisies.

My mother straightened her shoulders with an energetic snap and slammed the letter on the table. "This!" The color had returned to her cheeks.

Sam stared at the letter without moving, dropping the daisies.

"How could you be so stupid!"

Sam licked his lips. *Take her on, Sam*, I silently coached. "What the hell are you talking about, Mern?" He pushed up his sleeves.

"You've been caught red-handed," my mother said, wicked mad.

Sam ran his palm over his scalp, looking from the letter to my mother and back. "I can explain. Do me a favor, huh? Let me explain."

"It's too late for explanations!" my mother said. "You should have thought about what you were doing earlier. We're supposed to get married in a week. These are supposed to be the best years of my life."

Sam's chest sank. He wiped his forehead with the back of his hand. "You're making a mountain out of a molehill, Mern." My mother turned to me. "Mark my words, Eunice. If a man lies to you once, he'll lie to you a hundred times."

Blood rose up Sam's neck, and he rocked a little with each word. "What the hell have I done to deserve that? Day after day I listened to you complain, 'If only I had this, if only I had that.' Whaddya expect me to do? Close my ears?"

"Did I ask you to steal? And what did you steal?" My mother seemed almost gleeful. "You stole hot dogs, Sam. Hot dogs, bananas, sauerkraut. That's really pathetic." She threw open her arms and wiggled them. "I'm not exactly covered in diamonds and pearls."

The refrigerator engine clicked off, and for a second we were sucked into the unnatural stillness until Sam sprang forward and slammed his fist on the table, causing Mern to jump.

"I did what I did for you, Mern. You wanted me to be a big shot. I shoulda aimed higher, huh, like Al Capone?"

My mother shot me a look from the corner of her eye. "I didn't ask you for a goddamn thing, Sam Podesta, least of all a baby." Sam and my mother glared at each other. I pictured the bloody bathroom. "How dare you bring that up...now," Sam said, pounding his chest. "If ya want to kill me, Mern, you're doing it." My mother glanced at me. "This is not for your ears, Eunice." I crossed my arms and refused to move.

My mother waved the letter again. "You didn't even know enough to cover your ass." *There are witnesses, not to be named.* "It'll take you a whole lifetime to pay this back." Sam patted himself for a cigarette, choosing his next words carefully so that they came out as a low, soothing song. "You got it all wrong, Mernie. Let's talk like rational people." He drew the smoke deep into his lungs, his chest expanding like the sides of a horse. "Here's what we'll do. We'll move and I'll open a restaurant." He scrawled the restaurant's name in the air: *Tratatoria Podesta.* "A little Fra Diablo. A little scampi and Alfredo. Whaddya think, sweetheart?" For an instant I saw Sam holding a tomato from Buddy's Garden of Eden, tables covered with white linen and gleaming wineglasses, a miracle.

"Forget it," my mother said, but I could see she was tempted. All she needed was a little more persuasion. I tugged at Sam's sleeve. "Convince her. Please!" Sam touched my arm. "You're what I've been living for, Sailor. You, your mother—a family." He turned to Mern. "How about it? We start over? I love ya more than all the tea in China."

Mern flexed her foot and admired her ankle, pretending she didn't hear, pretending her heart wasn't busted in a hundred places right that minute. Some people were color-blind but my mother was love-blind. She couldn't see love if her life depended on it.

Sam paced in a circle, scratching his head. "I don't understand you, Mern. Come on. Tell me what I have to do. Come on. Tell me."

"Mom!"

Mern stared at me; I'd never used that word before. Sam came over and tried to put his arm around me, but I backed away. I was shutting down, going into a deep freeze. "Sorry, angel. Sometimes, between a man and a woman...things happen." The ache in his voice matched my ache exactly. "See what you're doing?" he said to my mother. "You're not just hurting me. You're hurting the kid. Shame on you."

Mern sniffed. "Don't blame me. I'm not the betrayer."

But she *was* the betrayer. She must have known Sam was stealing. She knew and asked for more, and now she blamed him and pretended innocence. Sam was a proud man, and she'd defeated him. She'd defeated love.

Sam grabbed the daisies from the floor and threw them at my mother's face, a few wet, limp petals sticking to her cheeks. But my mother had turned to stone.

Later, I heard Sam's footsteps hurrying back and forth between the bedroom and bathroom. I took Eunice Turtle under the covers and we listened to Sam pack. The rain had eased off, and the sky was arched high and clear and dusted with stars. I knew I was in danger of flinging myself on Sam, begging him to take me along. I couldn't believe what was happening. It was like we'd been hit by a nuclear bomb, and my whole life had toppled. I waited for Sam and Mern to kiss and make up, for the truce signaled by their cooing, but there was nothing to be heard except the sounds of drawers opening, closing, a closet door shutting.

Sam came to my door and knocked softly. I didn't answer, didn't move. I could not bear to say good-bye. I heard him set down his duffel and take out his harmonica. He sang an old cowboy song with made up lyrics. *"From this home I surely am going. I will miss your bright eyes and dear smile."* The choke in his voice made my throat close with sorrow. *"Gone is the sunshine I've known."* The click of his heels faded down the hallway, and I pictured him in his sailor cap and leather dancing shoes, canvas bag slung over his shoulder, marching toward the horizon line. I put my head on my knees and listened to the silence for a very long time. In the morning I found a note wedged in my door: *Don't ever blame yourself, sugar. You're the absolute best. Try not to blame your mother either. I'll write when I have an address. You can keep Buddy's plane and books. Think of me sometimes, okay?*

The trouble was I loved Sam and didn't know how I was going to stop loving him. Trying to stop loving a person was like trying to stop your blood from flowing. It was like trying to hold your breath underwater for hours, which Eunice Turtle could do, but I could not.

Part Two

❧

Rose:
Via Sympathia

1958–1959

Chapter 11

Sorrow in the New World

A zillion times I said his name and then I stopped. Eunice Turtle issued a soft whistling sound, like from a tiny teakettle. *Sorrow in the New World*, she said.

In memory of S. Podesta, I tied a black kneesock around my arm, tore a rent in my collar like Mr. Tabachnik's Jewish people, and refused to speak to Mern. To cast evil back at her, I taped a picture of the Eye of Horus on my door, behind which my future paraded in a series of bleak newsreels. Against the sound of my mother's fingernails clicking off bums and losers, I plugged my ears. "I am a blithe spirit," she said on the phone to someone called Marion. "Mr. Podesta is mistaken if he thinks I will go to wrack and ruin over him."

"You'll thank me in the long run," she said.

"Do me a favor, Eunice. Get my smokes."

Everywhere Sam had been, he was not—the kitchen, dead and empty, not a single mustache hair left in the bathroom sink. Mern tossed his Earl Grey and melba toast, his Rapid Shave, but she kept the silver bangle, the silver cross, and her fake garnet engagement ring. Thank goodness I found one last treasured bit of evidence, a leather slipper stretched at the toe where Sam's bunion once throbbed.

I packed my pillowcase and went to live downstairs.

"That Sam Podesta loved you like a papa," Mr. Tabachnik said, letting me rail until my words thinned to croaks and I collapsed on the immaculate sheet tucked over the couch he'd made into a bed. Mr. Tabachnik held a hanky to my nose and commanded me to blow. The sun beat through the drapes, heightening the smell of overripe bananas, a smell that signaled comfort to my brain. "In war there are no winners," Mr. Tabachnik sighed, "so, between men and women, why should it be different? Love and suffering are like this, Cisskala." He crossed his pointer and middle fingers in front of my face. "Why should this be? Because a mischievous *pishadikeh* angel shoots an arrow, and the arrow doesn't kill you, but oy, the pain!" He rocked back and slammed a hand over his breast. "And that, my friend, is love!"

I could stay with him only a few days because family was family, and "from your mother there's no divorce." Meanwhile, Caruso would heal what ails. Mr. Tabachnik toddled over to the Victrola and slipped *Don Giovanni* out of its sleeve. If you believed in Caruso, you believed in life.

I slept on the couch, had bad dreams, and woke with the taste of dust in my mouth. I'd imagined Sam calling: *I can't live without you, doll face,* and Mern answering, *Come home, Mr. Sunshine. Come home.* But most likely Sam had reenlisted and was off to Lapland, or some place at the top of the world. Or he'd marry a quiet woman from Arkansas, and they'd sit on their porch shelling peas and laugh about his escape from crazy Mern.

"What's going to happen?" I asked Eunice Turtle.

I'm not a turtle that can tell the future, she said.

When three days were up, Mr. Tabachnik escorted me back to Mern.

My mother and I signaled each other with coughs and grunts. In silence we ate breakfast and dinner; in silence we scraped dishes and climbed into our separate beds. I saw the sluggish way she dragged herself up the stairs, saw her ragged cuticles, the lilac circles under her eyes. She'd let her hair go and dark roots were beginning to seep up like oil. Annie finally told her to saddle up her pony and move on. "You need a new outlook. Take a vacation. I'll give you a week with pay. Eunice can stay with me." My mother raised her foaming glass of brew. "To my generous friend, Annie," she toasted, but her unraveling continued. She took to slouchy socks, ratted hair, constant complaining, said she was too blue to brush her teeth. Resentment shifted the bones in her face. She'd given up becoming Katharine Hepburn or Ingrid Bergman and was only and forever Mern. She could not rise to the occasion because there was no occasion. This was her life, and there was no getting away from it.

But there was getting away. A month after Sam left, Mern decided we should move, just like that. Wild Pea was full of bad memories, my mother said, and why risk running into Sam? A friend of Annie's owned a beauty shop in a place called, of all things, Turtle Lake. It's not Shangri-La, Annie told her, but Shirlee could give her work. Before the war, the lake town had been a swanky resort; we'd rub up against a higher class of people. Annie'd miss us like the dickens, but she thought we ought to grab the bull by its horns. My mother became convinced that Turtle Lake was her last chance at happiness, and her mind burned a highway north. She had that whole American thing in her head—pull up your roots and start a new life. Manifest Destiny. Westward Ho. Maybe she'd meet a beer tycoon from Milwaukee. Or better yet, a sheik with his own plane; Aly Khan and Rita Hayworth were in the news. "What's to keep us here?" she said, tossing her nylons over her head. We'd go where the grass was greener. A rolling stone gathers no moss. Pack up your troubles in your old kit bag. *Gimme land lots of land under starry skies above.* At the Hollywood Cinema we'd seen the plot a million times: small-town girl dyes her hair, fixes her teeth, changes her name, and goes from being plain Jane to gorgeous babe who marries a handsome rich guy. By the end of August, at the start of the new school year, we'd be gone.

When it came time to say good-bye, Mr. Tabachnik prepared a banquet, but only Mern felt like celebrating, rattling on about Shirlee, her new boss at the Curl and Swirl, and about the legend of Turtle Lake. A Loch Ness–type monster lurked in its depths. Mr. Tabachnik smacked both his cheeks: "One meshuggener with a good story convinces a crowd." He brought out the corn and brisket, hot rolls and coleslaw and set them in front of my mother. "In your honor, and so you should remember Tabachnik, the old geezer who once upon a time you made feel like a prince." We held hands and said amen. After dinner Mr. Tabachnik took me aside and told me maybe Mern was making a mistake, but who was he to judge? On the Day of Judgment, only God was the judge. Right before we left, he pressed a small paper bag filled with seeds into my hand. "From my garden to your table. Next summer you'll eat one of my tomatoes, you'll think of me." Two bright tears balanced in the corner of his eyes. "Better yet, you'll pick up the phone and invite me to dinner, and we'll eat tomatoes together." He smoothed back my hair with a palsied hand. "Turtle Lake's not Siberia, Cisskala. It's in Wisconsin, the neighboring state."

Mern was on fire with the future, and we made a rapid departure. It was spectacular how she could so easily waltz away from the past. When it came time to leave, I lined up my precious things and chose what to take. Not Buddy's B-29 or Pilot Jack Knight, but Richard Halliburton's *Book of Marvels*. Sam's bedroom slipper; my Whitman's Sampler tin, which still contained the dollar my father gave me; and the Ferris wheel ticket stub. Colored pencils, drawing pad, Eunice Turtle supplies, Sam's sailor hat. Everything else would go into storage. Mern's eyes raced back and forth over our belongings; she touched the clasp of Grandma Sophie Sunny's chest. "It's not really valuable," she said, marking it for resale. I had the feeling she wanted to shed the old Mern, and Ma too. I was watching her molt.

Annie arranged for a driver, who arrived on our last day in Wild Pea in a beat-up Pontiac wearing red suspenders, his profile like a pterodactyl's. He introduced himself as Grunfelder. *Grunfelder!* I dared not look at Mern for fear we'd crack up. Grunfelder did not waste time; he grabbed our valises and hoisted them into the trunk. But before the last carton was squeezed in, Mern ground out her cigarette and ran back inside with me following. At her bedroom door, blindsided by tears, she sobbed, "I waited for your father...I waited and waited...I even bought new sheets and a pillow that one time." I thought she was going to throw herself on the floor in a fit, but instead she stood gripping the molding for a moment before fleeing downstairs and outside.

On the stoop, she called over her shoulder, "Mr. Puccini. You were the best friend I ever had."

Grunfelder held open the passenger door. My mother climbed in, spread the pleats of her purple skirt over her knees, primly crossed her ankles, and gazed straight ahead. She had on an embroidered peasant blouse, hoop earrings, and a silk scarf knotted around her neck, as if she were planning to spend the afternoon at a Mexican bullfight, where she'd drink red wine and throw her scarf into the ring. As we pulled away, Mr. Tabachnik stepped out from under the shade of the catalpa, his hair like floss, snowier than I remembered, his arm going back and forth like a windshield wiper.

In the backseat, I held Eunice Turtle's aquarium on my lap. With all my heart I would miss Mr. Tabachnik, but as we crossed the border, and the miles and miles of corn became open meadows, and then forest land, I fell into sort of a dream that pushed my sadness away. The flat earth rippled into hills and the hills grew rocky and thick with evergreens. I heard Grunfelder tell my mother that glaciers had carved out hundreds of lakes up north, "whole flowage systems," and I heard my mother harrumph and ask what kind of people lived in Turtle Lake.

We came down a steep curving hill, and the lake fanned out in front of us, smooth as a mirror, sun diamonds bouncing off its surface, the expanse of water prettily bordered by an arcade of trees. The main street curved in a horseshoe around to the east end of the lake. At the western end, not visible from town, was the dam. A boardwalk dotted with iron benches wove through the shore-hugging pines. Across the street was a general store, a restaurant with tables on a second-story balcony, a pharmacy, and several guesthouses showing vacancy signs.

"Quaint," my mother said, putting her hand over her eyes, craning her neck to see down the side streets lined with rustic cottages complete with flowerboxes and green shutters. My mother fumbled for her cigarettes and pulled a cardigan around her shoulders. "Is this all there is? No movies?"

Grunfelder eyed her with distaste.

"Where do people shop?"

"You mean milk and eggs?" Mr. Grunfelder asked.

Mern rolled her eyes. "Nail polish! Kotex! Playtex Living Bras!"

I flattened myself against the backseat and lowered my head. Grunfelder stared at my mother's lips, as if they were the devil's.

"Nick's got all that stuff," he said curtly.

Mern rummaged in her purse for our new address. "Take us to Oakwood Hill," she said, handing him the slip of paper.

The cottage Shirlee had rented for us was too cutesy-wootsy—braided rugs, embroidered tea towels, china spaniels on the mantle. Mern twirled around, knocking her front tooth with a knuckle. "We're going to be okay, aren't we? Jeez. What have I done, Eunice?" There was no Sam, and no Mr. Tabachnik to pat her hand. I would be the sole person to look into her eyes and see the bricked-over door with its final verdict of doom. The aquarium was growing heavy in my arms. I left Mern in the living room and went upstairs to the small bedroom. Outside, the weakening sunlight splashed through the trees, flushing out a single blue hydrangea bush. Where the bushes ended, the land rose in terraces up to a high ridge that touched the sky. I pulled Sam's cap out of my pack and put it on.

"What's the turtle word for *home*?" I asked Eunice Turtle.

Turtle, she said.

After she'd changed into her kimono, Mern called for me to keep her company. I climbed onto her bed, listening to a hidden bird in the bend of a branch. A fat, wet smell was unfurling through the screen. "It's just you and me, kiddo," my mother said, shuffling a deck of cards, "in this godforsaken place at the end of the world."

Later, I woke from a strange dream. I had a swollen foot and had to go to the doctor, only the doctor was Mr. Warner, the druggist, wearing his white tunic. He examined my misshapen foot. "You're a young lady now," he said. "We'll have to cut it out." He meant cut it *off*. In the morning, the air was ruinous with rain. I kicked off my sheet to examine my perfectly normal feet. I thought of Mern sitting on the toilet and a baby plopping out. Had she flushed it away? I went and got Eunice Turtle. "I love you I love you I love you," I said. She could barely crawl the length of my arm, and her lack of gusto alarmed me.

"Say something," I said.

I love you, too, Eunice, she said.

Turtle Lake was a ghost town with a single battered speedboat for rent, clay tennis courts overgrown with weeds, one restaurant, a bandstand, three churches, and two bars. The tourists, mainly retired business-men who liked to fish, brought their wives and children; the older women, according to Mern, insisted on hairstyles that went back to the days before women got the vote. At Shirlee's, my mother swept up piles of tight gray curls and put towels into the dryer. What had Annie been thinking? "There's nothing here but trees and more trees and that big cold lake and a whole dump of stars." Nick the Greek was Mern's salvation: "My savior," she said, upon discovering Mikonos Grocery. She came home one day at the end of the week with salty cheese, honey-filled pastries, and liquor bearing Cyrillic letters, and it was not lost on me that my mother might have found herself another Sam Podesta. Except Nick was happily married and fifty-four years old.

It turned into a wet September, the woods gray and slithery with sodden black leaves, the clouds shape-shifting through gaps in the branches, the wind surging and retreating like a tide. School started without me. I was too busy following trails left by hunters, trails of cigarette butts and spent plastic cartridges and abandoned campfires of charred stones where they'd heated cans of pork and beans. Some-times I sat on a log in front of a spent fire, chin on my fists, trying to imagine a life clean of civilization. It soothed me to imagine that one day I might learn to decode the messages the sun wrote upon tree trunks and frazzled grass and that when I lifted my nose, I'd know where the wind had been, what lost sea essences, what molecules of flower or fruit were wafting through its atmosphere. No one at Badger

High knew I was skipping school because no one knew of my existence: Mern had forgotten to mail in my forms. She was no fan of school or school authorities, and I found them one day before the start of the semester in the pocket of a borrowed sweater; she'd never even signed her name. I was no one to anyone, a nobody who lived nowhere—I was less than a ghost.

The leaves dwindled and the sky fell lower and darker each day. I followed where my eyes led me, up ravines and down verges into meadows where the last of the purple asters groped toward the waning light. My bones felt hollow and weightless, like the bones of birds, and I knew it wouldn't take much to open my arms and fly. If Mern caught me coming home wild-haired, my clothes stained with sap, if she found rocks in my pockets, nests of twig and string, sketches of big-eyed field mice and mallards in flight, she'd pout and warn me that normal girls my age had boyfriends, that normal girls used deodorant and brushed their hair a hundred strokes. She guessed I was playing hooky, but she had her own worries. "Don't I have enough problems? Don't be so self-centered, Eunice. With everything else I have to worry about, I don't need to worry about you getting lost!"

The only time she was really happy was after a visit to Nick the Greek's, where she drank the Elixir of Life, and Nick, uncurling her clenched fists, massaged her fingers and told her she was the best thing to come to Turtle Lake since indoor toilets. The shorter days grew cooler, the air transparent, filled with the last insects' song. Around Halloween, Mr. Tabachnik wrote us that he had new tenants, a German family named the Schultzes. "Nice people," he wrote. "Clean. You could eat off their floor." I sent him sketches of salamanders, a willow with its hair in the air. I wrote that I did not go down to the big lake very often. There were whitecaps now, and hundreds of gulls, and I was afraid one would swoop down for Eunice Turtle. To learn is also to forget, the events of one life crowding out the events of the next. In the ordinary newness of Turtle Lake, my lingering sorrows began to ebb away.

Mern and I were drifting into our private worlds, though some nights, unbidden, she'd turn to me on the couch, her teeth coated with

Hershey's Kisses. "I'm tired. Tell me a story." To keep my mother from tumbling down the well of despair, I entertained her with tales. I told her how the hunter Actaeon got caught spying on the goddess Artemis while she was taking a bath in the woods, and how she had punished him by turning him into a stag, unrecognizable to his own dogs, who then devoured him. I told her some snakes could swallow a pig twice their size. "Are you bullshitting me, Eunice?" she said. I shook my head. In Egypt, I said, so they wouldn't be hungry or lonely or poor in the afterlife, the pharaohs got buried with their favorite foods and pets. Then we talked about reincarnation. How many lives would you really want to have? My mother said she'd like to come back as Scarlett O'Hara and have a seventeen-inch waist. Temperamentally, Mern was not suited to distinguish between the fictional and the real.

One unusually warm day in November, I took Eunice Turtle on a new path that led to a marshy area hidden by willows and barkless trees studded with woodpecker holes, the water oozing decay. On a half-drowned log in the shallows I saw something move. "Eunice Turtle," I said, "there are turtles here." And then I had an idea. I would put Eunice Turtle into the water. If she swam back to me, we were meant to be together. If not, she was meant to be free. I felt I owed her that. I set her down and said, "Go ahead, Eunice," and watched her inch into the water. For a second or two she froze with her front claws submerged, her back two poised in the muck, and then she was off, swimming toward the silty depths. She swam in tiny circles, and then I couldn't see her anymore because she'd gone under, and I held my breath. I waited and waited. When her distinct face poked out from the boggy surface, I clapped and waved and shouted. When she reached shore, I dried her on my shirt and kissed her delicate little nose.

She said, *You knew I would.*

I said, "But I wanted you to have a choice."

During the last week of the month, when cold damp air rode in on the dusk and the stems of the oak leaves loosened their hold and fell to the ground, exposing to plain sight the old deer blind up on the ridge I'd discovered in September, Eunice Turtle began to fail.

"Eunice Turtle," I said. "What's happening to you?" The beautiful scales of her shell faded, and her skin, dry and scaly, grew sandy gray.

It's nothing to worry about, she said. *I'm changing.*

"I don't want you to change," I said. I felt like a truck had rolled over my chest. "Changing how? Changing why?"

It's not your fault, she said. *It's not a sickness.*

"What is it, then?"

It's a mystery, she said.

There were no vets in Turtle Lake, but I did what I could—meticulously cleaned her shell, grated carrots, pulverized dead flies, fed her bits of bread soaked in milk, but she grew steadily weaker and quieter. At night I listened to the wind in the trees, the soft tearing of the last leaves from their branches, the delicate tread of fox and deer, and I felt the tug of invisible life.

Soon we were speaking less—we seemed to have lost the need.

She died on a Wednesday. She went in peace, retracting into herself forever.

I spent hours holding her on my palm, calling to her, *Dearest Eunice Turtle. Please come out. Please!* watching for her head or a leg to emerge. I knocked on her shell. In desperation, I held her under the water faucet. I refused to give up hope. I could not accept that she was no longer there.

When it was almost evening, I suddenly knew what I had to do. I put Eunice Turtle in my shirt pocket and hurried to Turtle Lake, to a small cove we'd discovered with a white-pebbled beach. How light she had suddenly become in my hand. Who would have thought that in a creature so small, the weight of her living self was so tangible?

The lake was alive, mottled with silver ripples, swaying in its own bed. I took Eunice Turtle from my pocket. Only the tiniest specks of the red nail polish remained on her shell. I lifted her to my lips and kissed the place where our name had been written. "Eunice Turtle," I said. "Come back to me, if you can."

Mern cried when I told her, a fact that surprised me, but then sadness, I knew, was like any weather, coming and going at its own pleasing. I cried myself to sleep that night and then I stopped crying. I was finished crying. Eunice Turtle would not want me to mourn forever.

In the weeks that followed, I could not stop myself from wandering. I hiked long hours and did not know what I was looking for.

Chapter 12

Turtle Lake

Out of desperation, for a bit of festivity, my mother accepted Shirlee's Thanksgiving invitation. We arrived windblown in twin headscarves, bearing a collapsed Jell-O mold and a gift carton of mentholated cigarettes. Shirlee sat Mern between me and her mother, the balding Estelle, whose carrots had to be mashed and loaded onto a fork. When Shirlee's back was turned, Mern mouthed, *See what you have to look forward to, kiddo.* At home she flung off her fake mouton jacket and swore she would never subject us to an evening like that again. The next morning I called Mr. Tabachnik to wish him happy Thanksgiving and to tell him about Shirlee and Estelle. Mern hung around the phone pointing to her watch, yanking the receiver out of my hand to grill Mr. T about Sam: there was no news. Christmas we spent the day eating mounds of popcorn from an enamel pot and getting silly over knock-knock jokes, but all the knock-knocking in the world couldn't produce a Christmas tree crowned by the Angel of Hope. Six inches of snow had fallen in the last few days and eye-piercing sunlight leaped from drifts, the plows out early, winding their way up toward our neighborhood. I walked to the lake on New Year's Day to talk to Eunice Turtle, the cold air setting my teeth tingling. Snow flurried and skimmed the surface of the ground, accumulating on bare branches in perfect white lines. I strolled to the spot where Eunice Turtle and I had parted, slipping along the ice-banked shingle, making conversation with my dear dead friend. The chances of a truant officer finding me now were slim, I told her, and I admitted I was neither lonely nor bored. I told Eunice Turtle about Minette, the Romanian dressmaker across the road, who'd moved to Turtle Lake in its heyday in the employ of a wealthy widow and was teaching me the fine art of hemstitching. Minette was from *over there*, and I'd asked her if she'd known Nathan Tabachnik, but she smiled and said Europe was a big place. I liked to imagine them long ago, their bicycles colliding on the dusty road outside her village. They'd become sweethearts and resistance fighters and live in the forest with other partisans and be heroes after the war. On Valentine's Day, our mailbox was empty. Neither Mern nor I mentioned Sam. Mern's moods had gone from gray to black. She caught a cold, then twisted her ankle, the surrounding skin swelling like diseased fruit. I told Eunice Turtle I was hanging on by a nail.

A few days after St. Patrick's Day, Michael Todd's plane crashed into the Zuni Mountains of New Mexico: THE "LUCKY LIZ" CRASHES AT 9,000 FEET. ELIZABETH TAYLOR MOURNS THE DEATH OF HER HUSBAND MIKE TODD. TRAGIC ENDING TO A FAIRY-TALE LOVE.

My mother said, "The Man Upstairs plays with us, Eunice. Cat and mouse."

The bud-speckled trees fizzed into a soft green mist; the grass, beaten down from snow and rain, lost its mangy look; and small, chirpy birds bustled in the shrubs. By April Fool's Day, Mern's mood brightened. She put salt in the sugar bowl, laughing her head off when I heaped white crystals on my breakfast cereal and gagged on a spoonful—the first time she'd laughed in weeks. "Grow up," I told her despite my gratitude for her cheer. Mern stuck out her tongue. "You can't even take a little joke? Spring is sprung, the grass is riz. I wonder where the birdie is. The birdie's on the wing," she recited. "Come and give me a hug, Eunice." Her cheek smelled of Pond's Angel Face, a fragrance I could drown in if I let myself.

When the rains began late in April, the ground hadn't completely thawed. Water bounced off the earth and raced down the granite slopes into the streams and creeks that fed Turtle Lake. Mern bought a red and white field umbrella large enough to shelter five grown men.

When the weather continued, she bought a pair of fancy plastic rain booties and a secondhand Motorola console installed by Nick, a big lug of a guy with an even bigger voice. In no way was Nick as handsome as my father, but from a certain angle, with his wavy silver hair and olive skin, he was a dead ringer for Cesar Romero. Nick was no Sam Podesta either, and made little attempt to win me over. He knew his place and didn't push.

When I didn't feel like sketching or reading or watching clouds from the deer blind, I hung out with Minette, who'd lived in Paris. Minette always wore the same thing, a black smock topped by a round white collar stuck with two threaded needles. Her skirt was pencil straight and her nylons were seamed. She caught on right away that I was avoiding school and asked one day if I was lonely. "*Alors*, a young girl should have friends her own age." We were in her alcove under the dormer next to a pair of antique trunks when I told her I'd had a best friend but that friend had died and I didn't want any other friends. I said I didn't mind being alone; alone was what I preferred. Minette nodded as if she understood. "*C'est triste, très triste,*" she said solemnly, squeezing my hand with her cool, dry fingers. The wind sang like a pennywhistle through the patter of drizzle. "Maybe you travel one day. Maybe you see Paris and Rome." The greatest artists lived there. She didn't know, of course, that she was issuing an invitation to see my drawings, but the next time I visited her I brought some sketches along. She put on her wire-rim glasses and took the drawings from my hand. I watched her eyes, a dressmaker's expert eyes, carefully examine the connecting threads of pencil lines, and then heaving herself up with what I thought would be some perfunctory, bland words, she spoke a warning: "Take the gift seriously or the muse will persecute you, and you will be bereft."

With a flourish, she opened the smaller of the two trunks and held up a matching hat and muffler of Persian lamb. "From the St. Petersburg side. I recall nothing but an older woman in high-buttoned boots, hurrying along a train platform in a very dignified manner." She set the hat and cuff aside and lifted a dress the color of chicory flowers from the depths of the trunk. "My first creation," she sighed, flouncing the hem. "Like the sky over the Seine." Bright memories tripped off her tongue: beribboned shifts ordered by the portly Gertrude Stein for Alice B. Toklas. Helena Rubinstein's corsets edged in Maltese lace. "Next time I will teach you overstitching," she said, her composure restored. Why she'd left France, the names of her dead, the long agony of the war, the story of her real life sealed back into the trunks. She stood fanning herself, though it wasn't at all hot.

"*Vive les belles femmes,*" she said, raising a clenched fist.

The rain made things happen. A wooden bridge twenty miles north of Turtle Lake collapsed when several large trees, uprooted by storms, sailed downstream and smashed into wooden girdings. In another part of the state, a section of railroad tracks had been washed out, and the hogs in slatted cars waiting on a sideline caught pneumonia and died. I sat under a tarp in the old deer blind and tried to hear what the rain was saying. I imagined the hunter who'd sat here years ago, high above the valley, a .30-30 Winchester across his knees, a wad under his lip. He wouldn't have been thinking about messages in the rain; he would have been thinking about sausage he was going to make from deer meat. The rain kept on, day after day, and the message from the weather was that no one controls the universe; the universe controls us. It felt as if the tectonic plates were shifting under my feet, and I was required to be alert and prepared. I didn't know why. Mern said whatever I was going through, it was unattractive. I couldn't explain. But even if I could have explained, my mother would not have understood. I barely understood. I just knew I could see two worlds, the visible and the invisible, and how they were connected. I could see how the maze of deer trails running through the forest mimicked the streams' meanderings and how the curve of those streams mimicked the curve of the horse's haunches I was drawing, the horse climbing through clouds, his forelegs curving over the sun's halo as it arced up from behind the earth toward the mounded paths of starlight between the stars; how all these lines and curves pointed to something even more elaborate and fantastic, something nobody could ever describe, not even if she was the best mapmaker-astronomer-artist in the whole wide world.

Early in May I went to the barber's and got shorn, clipped up the neck and buzzed in front like a boy. I carried a green knapsack, a flashlight, a canteen, and a pennywhistle. I carried my sketchpad and pencils. I carried Eunice Turtle and Sam Podesta in my heart. I knew it was entirely possible to live in both worlds at the same time. My mother couldn't. She was drinking more, growing edgy and belligerent, puzzled and perturbed. "Okay, okay," she said one night. "I don't give a rat's ass about your hair. But there's something else, kiddo. You're not the Eunice you used to be."

Chapter 13

Higher Ground

Thunder billowed into the creases of my brain, and when I ran to the window, rain had already drenched the curtains and sill. Outside the air was black as smoke, the trees straining against an inland sea. Our lights blinked, and I heard Mern stop short on her way to the bathroom and curse. I was worried about her, again—the yellowish tinge to her eyelids, her hair teased to outrageous heights, her face smaller and more vulnerable under the platinum-streaked cone. A hush fell outside, a single slumbering interlude, and then hail started to ping against the roof. Mern slipped a leg through the zipper of her Curl and Swirl uniform.

"How 'bout moving to California," she said from my doorway, the sudden tempest moving off behind her.

"Where in California?" I said, giving myself permission to play along.

Mern looked at her stomach and sucked it in. "Venice Beach? Malibu."

The sky was polishing up from charcoal to soft gray. My mother smoothed the pink polyester over her hips and pulled up the zipper.

"Forget about California, Mern."

She blinked up at me, looking older than I remembered. "Greece, then," she said. "Definitely Greece."

The rain continued. Puddles tinctured with leaf rot had stretched into ponds. By late that week, some of Mern's customers complained of flooded basements, but we were spared because our cottage was built on higher ground. On the seventh day of the downpour, the roots of the pines circling the lake gave way and toppled into the water, leaving the shoreline bereft of their presence. Shirlee closed the Curl and Swirl, and Mern came home revved, her cheeks flushed from wind and excitement. Without removing her wet coat or rain-spotted glasses, she bushwhacked to the china cabinet, grabbed her favorite teacup, and beelined into the kitchen, where she shot back slugs of rum before shucking her dripping gear. Since yesterday with the spillways clogged, the water level in Turtle Lake had risen considerably and was nudging close to overflowing. Now some town councilman was on the TV, his bald head blurred by fuzz and static, saying an emergency team of engineers was on its way. Residents were advised to boil water and move important papers and belongings upstairs. So far, the councilman said, the dam was holding and prospects were good, but folks with friends or relatives outside the flood zone should evacuate immediately. If the situation worsened, local volunteers would evacuate those without transportation. Minette's nephew had already come for her, his Plymouth left running in the street.

Mern snapped off the TV. "I'm not sleeping on some cootie cot in a high school gymnasium surrounded by snoring strangers, Eunice, and that's that." My mother inspected her arms. I opened my mouth to argue, but she cut me off. "Look, Eunice. I've got goose bumps on my goose bumps. Now get my robe, will you?" She picked up a pack of cigarettes, took one, and held the pack out to me. I could hear the telltale thickening in her voice.

"You missed the point, Mern. We *have* to go," I said as quietly and soberly as possible, my stomach beginning to throb. "It's a bad idea to stay. A bad, stupid, insane idea." Just then the furnace clunked on, circulating warm, comforting air. Mern stubbed out her cigarette and asked what my problem was. I started to explain the danger of our situation, but she raised her hand.

"The Big Honcho in the sky is pissing on us day and night, Eunice. Get used to it!"

In the kitchen I filled a dozen empty Coke bottles with water, checked the furnace pilot light, took a supply of candy upstairs. I put on Sam's sailor cap and dug out my Whitman's tin. When the next round of thunder boomed and our scrappy little cottage rattled on its foundation, my mother called out, "Eunice! Keep me company." She was sitting up in bed clutching a bottle of booze and a bag of cheese curls. Rain hurled itself against the windowpanes; wind bleated through the walls. I ducked into my mother's bed and wove my legs through hers and listened to her suck the dye off M&M's. Just as I started to drift, she tickled my neck. "Remember the scene in *Elephant Walk* when the elephants stampede?" The movie had played in Wild Pea, and at the climax the elephants went on a rampage to destroy the mansion inside of which Elizabeth Taylor, looking her most exquisite, was trapped. "No one knows when disaster will strike," Mern said, slurring her consonants. "Or who will save you."

I shot bolt upright. So that was it: my mother was waiting for Robert Mitchum to tack by, for Bogey to steam up in his *African Queen*. No Rotary elder or pimply volunteer was going to rescue her while the wind whipped and groaned through the trees. When I confronted her, Mern said, "Don't be silly, Eunice." I couldn't bring myself to believe my mother was willing to risk my life or her own, but what does a daughter know for sure? She knows her name, her birthday, and if she's lucky, the names of her father and mother. She knows where she belongs and where she doesn't, eyes that like her, eyes that don't. She knows that love is just a label for a thousand different nameless feelings, a word like the words of love songs and about as real as the dead light thrown from dead stars. I dropped my argument, for the moment. "Tell me about my father," I whispered. "Something I've never heard before." My mother sighed, found her cigarettes, and sent a spiral of smoke toward the crack above our heads.

"Frankie loved me most when I was pregnant. He said I was the most beautiful pregnant woman he'd ever seen. 'A goddess,' he said." She put the cigarette to her lips and inhaled luxuriously; then she put it to my lips and I took a sputtering puff. "I *was* magnificent, hormones or something, my skin glowed like a pearl." She touched the back of her hand to my cheek. "He loved us both—then. The first thing he did when he came home from work was talk to you. He'd lead me to

---

the couch and lift my shirt and put his mouth to my belly button...
and he'd talk to you."

"What did he say?"

"I don't remember."

"Try."

"He used to make up names for you. Sometimes he called you
Rump Roast. 'How's the little Rump Roast coming along?' he'd say,
and pat my oven. Sometimes he called you 'Wappit.' Bunny Wappit."
A fork of lightning electrified the room; my father was moving toward
me out of the past, the heat of his face against my mother's belly, and
through her skin to me, his hot breath making the long passage down
the cord, magical ether from his lungs to my blood.

"Once upon a time," my mother said, "he loved me once, he loved
me twice, and then he left."

Someone was rapping on the door: the knocking stopped, then
began again. A man called out, "Anyone there?" Mern reached for her
glasses. I started out of bed, but she held my arm. "Don't go down
there, kiddo." I glared at her in silent accusation.

"I'm going," I said, and crept to the top of the stairs. The power
had gone out and a chill dampness clung to my skin. During the hour,
scummy water had seeped in under the door and was spreading at a
fast rate across the living room floor.

The beam of a flashlight circled across the walls, into corners,
under the chintz chairs. A face appeared in the bay window, a fat man
wearing a rain slicker and wide-brimmed hat, the strap cutting into
his double chin. I scooted down a few steps but not far enough for him
to see me, Mern on the landing, looming pasty-skinned, her hair in a
snarl. "Who is it?" she rasped, tying her robe.

"A man with a motorboat." I was afraid to see how high the water
was—high enough for a boat.

"Someone we know?" She slid down a step and hunched beside me
while he rapped on our window, cupped his hands to see in. "Hello?
Hello? Joe Anderson here. Part of the evacuation crew." The man
poled his aluminum craft from window to window, shining his light

into different rooms. He picked up a branch and threw it at an upstairs window. "Hey!" he yelled.

Mern covered my mouth with her hand. "Don't move, don't breathe. I told you I'm not going." She kept shaking her head while she held me hostage. "Christ, he's not wearing a uniform. I bet he's not even a Scout leader, let alone a fireman!" Spittle caught in the corner of her lips. The man waited another moment, evaluating the situation, then started his motor, his prow plowing a wake of bubbles and foam. My mother let go of my mouth and sighed, or maybe it was a little cry without tears. "Pissing on us day and night," she muttered.

I watched as she wove unsteadily across the landing, waiting until I heard her bedsprings succumb to the freight of her bones. Feeling slightly disoriented and unsettled, I went downstairs into the strange night.

Water the color of chewing tobacco, with slugs and other bloated unmentionables floating in it, eddied around my feet. While Mern, in deep communion with her bottle of rum, tossed in a tangle of sheets, I surveyed the landscape, monitoring for hopeful signs—the return of Joe Anderson in his motorboat or an angel carrying a bulrush to paint an X of blood on our door, or better yet, a dove with a green branch in its beak. Anything was possible on a night such as this. I should have made a plan—stockpiled blankets, food, and water under a tarp in the deer blind, prepared a warm nest for us to wait out the emergency. Now it was too late.

Or was it? I opened the front window and stuck my nose outside. The rain had eased off. A scent of rot wove through a sweeter smell, like a garden after it had been watered and the fumes of pesticides let loose. A vast water-world, spiked with stars and a naked moon with a trail of vapor racing over it, stretched as far as I could see, and only the vertical posts of trees marked real distance. The predawn quiet seemed to descend from some place just below the moon, forming a protective dome over everything, including the field of water, which made a soft chugging sound as it passed the window, a harmless glistening lake gliding through the woods and covering our lawn, the street, Minette's

yard. I stared at the water; it looked tame, almost welcoming, like soft
cotton batting or like another planet's fluid atmosphere, maybe waist-
deep. Of course I could do it! I could wade out with my flashlight and
some supplies, climb the hill behind the cottage, and flash SOS. I was
strong. I wouldn't let Mern and me drown. Breathless at the undertak-
ing, a little scared, I was nonetheless certain of success. *You taught me
good, Sam Podesta! Don't fight a riptide or current; let the current take
you; float on your back, rest.*

I changed into jeans, sneakers, sweatshirt, and nylon Windbreaker.
Sam's sailor hat. Mern was on her side, snoring raggedly, her arm
draped over the side of the bed. *Move!* I told myself. *Time's a-wasting.*
I threw on my knapsack, stashed my flashlight, and blew my stupid,
stubborn, hopeless mother a kiss. *Be right back, Mernie.*

What I hadn't accounted for was the penetrating chill. Though it was
June, the air was cool, the water near freezing. I hadn't accounted for
the ooze and slide under my feet, or the way my body swayed and
pivoted, struggling for balance without supports. I hadn't accounted
for the stinging smell or my eyes burning or how the puny beam of
my flashlight ended abruptly in impenetrable black. I swung the beam
right, left, straight on. Two steps forward, one step back, the water
at my knees, then hips, then, as the land sloped away, my waist, the
weight of it dragging on me like a wet parachute, the tips of my sneakers prodding for solid ground—a rock? A root? I slipped, swallowed
water, retched; something furry swam past, spiked fur and yellow
eyes; I screamed or thought I screamed and plodded on. And then,
just when I thought I had waded through the deepest part of the yard
and could curve around toward the back of the cottage and begin to
climb the hill, a rush of cold grabbed my ankles, catching and twirling me so that I fell onto my face, wet hair in my eyes and mouth, my
vision shrinking into slivers like a bad dream of sinking. Lungs afire,
choking with snot and water, I struggled to keep my head clear, to find
something to grab on to, but the current was alive and stronger. My
mind splattered with the humor of it—*this* was the monster of Tur-

tle Lake! A sick laugh started in my belly until the water rolled over me and my arms felt impossibly heavy, my sodden jeans, like the lead apron the dental technician threw over your stomach, my legs good as dead. I tried to stand, then tread water, but the monster was spinning me like a leaf, swirling me faster and faster through the woods to a place where there was nothing but trees. I pulled for air, forcing my ribs to expand against the pressure of water, but the flood was maniacal, without mind or strategy; the flood was simple and smart, determined in its own destination.

Three birch trees stood out in the gloom, three sisters, arms linked, as if expecting me. When I crashed into them, pain burst through my side like a bullet, a lucky bullet that shot adrenaline up my spine, giving me a burst of strength to claw up one of the trunks and fling myself to safety where two branches formed a V and made a seat. My head emptied of amazement, I conked out.

Chapter 14

Shelter in the New World

My rescuer's hands were warm and respectful. They examined my head like someone touching a feverish child and worked their way to my pulse and soft organs. Fingers with eyes and ears. With every inhalation, the pain wound its way deeper, as if a giant had stomped on my ribs. A soothing voice cut through the dizziness and confusion. "Easy does it." When I strained to focus, the face looking down at me broke up into pieces of light and dark. The voice came nearer, then went far away.

I heard the boat's motor before I opened my eyes a second time, my head rocking gently against the floor in the stern where I lay swaddled in a sleeping bag. My wet clothes had been removed and something soft and loose slipped over me. The pain in my head was dull and steady. My rescuer leaned forward from the bow and held a canteen against my lips, the liquid warm and sweet. A large dragonfly landed on the rim of the boat, and through its gauzy wings I could see the sun shimmer on water. When I twisted a certain way, the pain howled, and tears sprang to my eyes.

I slept, and when I woke again, the engine had been cut and tipped up out of the water, the boat hissing through the weeds. When I cracked my eyes, the light hurt. My legs were like fallen trees, dying but not dead. That my rescuer was a woman startled me. I'd assumed otherwise because of her size and the authority in her voice. Facing me on a wooden seat, a plaid hunter's cap and oilskin jacket stowed between two sturdy feet in waders, she rowed steadily into the afternoon sun. "You're safe now. Just rest." She spoke with confidence but sparingly, as if each word should be acknowledged for its own sake. Despite an aching head and bleary vision, I noted her strange beauty—the wild hair and a flat, wide face, her skin bronzed. Her gaze saw through you and addressed the inside part, her pale, upturned eyes like a Husky's. What happened? Where were we going? I couldn't find the words; the shivering was too intense. With a single consoling *shhh*, the woman set down her oars and crouched forward to tuck the blankets around my neck. Her hands swept my body in broad strokes, rousing the circulation and coming to rest like two warm doves over my heart. I closed my eyes and when I woke again, we were in a narrow passage bordered by cattails. "Can't use the motor again till we get out of the flowage. Too many weeds, too much muck," she said. The dip and pull of the oars calmed me. "A couple more hours and we'll be there." That I might be hallucinating this woman and her boat briefly crossed my mind; then exhaustion eclipsed all thought.

Through the delirium, memories flickered. Alone in our cottage, wrapped in a bedspread, Mern screamed my name. The image went blank and then I was propelling myself through the scummy water to reach her. During moments of lucidity, I knew something terrible had happened, but the sequence of events was all mixed up. When I slipped out of dreams, the woman was serenely rowing, slaking my agitation with sweet water and a lump of honey to suck. Sometime later I realized we weren't alone in the boat. Behind her, between her seat and the prow, a puppy, a fox, and a raccoon huddled together flank to wet flank, the odor of slime on their fur. "It'll be a little longer," she said. "There's a chop, and the wind's against us. I'll turn on the motor as soon as we're away from these weeds." A breeze whipped and tugged at her hair, and for a while, I watched the wind playing with it.

A darkness opened in my mind. I remembered: the bone-chill of the water and telling myself not to be afraid; the feeling of losing control;

the pressure of water building against my thighs, the current manageable but insistent. I had looked over my shoulder at our cottage. In the dark it was impossible to judge distance. How far had I gone? Wanting suddenly to go back to Mern, and just as suddenly the current's claws tightening around my legs. Who would save Mern alone in the house? I remembered the water surging up my thighs, my bottom going numb, as if I'd been sawed in half. Turning the last time, the glowing stub of Mern's cigarette in an upstairs window. My knees buckling before I got swept away.

Rose. I remembered my rescuer's name. And her saying she was a nurse.

"What happened to my mother?"

Rose reached out to stroke my cheek while her eyes addressed my panic. "Don't know, darling. I wondered if you were alone when I found you smashed into the tree, barely conscious. Didn't see anyone else around. Lucky thing I was navigating through Miner's Woods, not expecting to be picking up any humans that far from town, and then I heard you moaning. When I got to you, you were near gone, as ashen as those birches but willing yourself to hang on." With her bandana, she wiped away the goop of snot and tears sliding off my cheeks and then repositioned the bedroll under my neck.

"Someone's probably picked your mother up by now and brought her to one of the churches. Don't worry. We'll find her tomorrow, if you're okay to travel." We were on a slow river, its high banks congested with bushes growing acrobatically toward the sun. A mild wind spanked the boat. Rose pulled the cord on the motor; the engine sputtered and heavy molecules of gasoline sprayed into the air.

"I didn't want you to get lost in town in the shuffle, all those emergencies, every medic in the area with his hands full. So I took you with me and quit searching for anyone else."

In a moment of clarity, I saw Mern telling me how my father had loved her once, and what that love had done for her. *My skin glowed like pearl.* I started to bawl. I missed her. Rose reached down, her hand pressing my heart. "That's right. Cry all you want. It hurts."

*   *   *

She was taking me home to Honey Moon Point. She had her own little place. She was self-sufficient. Had some hives. A beekeeper. "A while ago, I caught a swarm and kept dividing it, and now I've got a flourishing colony. I do fine. Sell the honey and wax items in Liberty and other villages nearby. You'll see."

The river emptied out into a small bay guarded by tiers of evergreens, a place where either the world ended or began. A place forgotten by time. No one lived this far out, Rose said, except for her and a man called Lutie who'd followed the logging companies and now did trapping and hired out as a fishing guide. Rose and Lutie didn't have much contact, she said, except on occasion when they traded smoked fish and honey. "Takes a certain kind of spirit to live alone in the woods. Lutie and I understand each other."

At the far end of the bay, an inlet led to a pond surrounded by thickets. Rose steered west, hopping out of the boat when we hit the beach and dragging the skiff onto a strip of sand. I felt the jolt just as the puppy, his jaw anchored between two splint branches, whimpered, and the fox, with his bandaged leg, gave a heartbreaking yelp. Rose rolled up the sleeves of her flannel shirt, slid her strong arms under me, and carried me like a bride across the sand. I followed the clean line of her jaw up to an ear that held a tiny sparkling diamond. A crow flew out of a seam of light between some trees and landed on the trail ahead. Two more crows swooped past. "The welcoming committee," Rose said. I regarded the birds with a cautious eye. My bones felt tender, and the tiredness in me was sharp and disconcerting. Along the ground, shadows falling through the leaves danced over the twigs and stones, and I thought, *One day you're dreaming about your life, and the next day your life is a dream.*

The trail sloped and curved, the beach closing off behind us through the trees. Without stumbling, Rose stepped around rocks and depressions, as graceful as she was strong, shifting my weight in her arms so as not to jar my bones. She said little except, "Why'd you cut your hair?" The question seemed absurd given the circumstances. I remembered the day I got it clipped but I couldn't remember why.

"It's a good thing to know your own mind," Rose said.

We had come to a glade. At the edge where the light fled into the forest was a patched-together, dilapidated shack of blackened board, bits of moss, and newspaper stuck between the cracks. Rose set me down on my wobbly legs, her arm around my waist, my hand gripping her forearm. "You're going to be dizzy for a moment. Don't try to stand on your own. Lean on me till you get your wind." Her limbs were tan and muscled but delicate somehow, her ankles and wrists thin like Mern's, but not wimpy like my mother's. *Mern!*

"You got banged around plenty by that flood, but nothing's broken, I'm pretty sure. Try and walk but don't force it if you can't."

I glanced toward the shack and took a deep breath. The roof was a dismal tarpaper green. There were three front steps made of split logs, and above the door hung a wooden sign painted in large white letters that said PARADISE.

"This is where you live?"

She nodded. An elderly, roly-poly dog with bowed back legs and a long feathered tail bounded out from behind the structure. "Meet Aunt Francis," Rose said. I held out a hand, and the dog, circling us twice with happy barks, pushed his wet nose into my palm and licked.

"Don't let his scruffy looks fool you. He's part Rottie, the best watchdog I ever owned, but wouldn't harm a baby chick if it sat on his nose," Rose said. "Aunt Francis has the soul of a warrior, the mind of a genius, the appetite of a horse." She gave the dog an affectionate pat. "A time ago he belonged to a man named Elijah Wolf, who was reputed to be a great sage. One night Aunt Francis got into a tussle with a wild dog and Elijah thought Aunt Francis was a goner. So he laid Aunt Francis down in the grass, said a few prayers over him, then kissed the dog on the lips. The next morning Aunt Francis was fully healed. And not only that, but he also had become as wise as Elijah himself." Rose nuzzled Aunt Francis's belly with her boot. "Aunt Francis is cleverer than any freemason and twice as trustworthy."

Who was this woman? Where had I come to? I was sixteen years old, but if I let myself, I'd bawl like a baby. Mernie!

The shack was nicer inside than outside, one large room, fifteen by thirty feet, with a loft running the width of the narrower side. In corners, on shelves, were piles of geodes, or coppery stones snaked with green, or tiny mountains of milk-white river stones, or circles of shards as black as lava. There were bouquets of feathers—pure white feathers, peacock feathers with emerald eyes, the whole wing of a hawk tacked to the wall. There were tiny glass bottles filled with colored potions, clay pots out of which grew aromatic plants, split gourds containing seeds, cairns of shells, dried roots in bunches hanging from hooks on the ceiling, candles of various heights. Two lanterns hung near an ancient-looking cookstove. A rough-hewn table stood nearby. Across from the loft side was a rope bed and a wooden rocking chair.

Rose left me leaning against the door to throw some kindling into the small barrel stove. "We have to get you fed," she said. She took down a black pot, filled it with water from a jug, and added mushrooms and beans and herbs from what she called her *pharmacia* hanging from the rafters. Even in my exhausted, bruised state of mind, I knew I'd entered foreign territory. Plants, shells, feathers, bottles, dried herbs. A single bed, a rocker, a table and stove, a loft covered with a pallet. No photographs, no magazines, no record player. A hand-cranked radio. Lanterns, candles, cast-iron pans. Patchwork skirts of calico and velvet hung on hooks. Workmen's boots. Knives, twine, cords of rope. No clock, no calendar, no Cashmere Bouquet; no Revlon or Maybelline. Not a mirror in sight. No bathroom or shower; no curling iron; no crème rinse; no White Rain shampoo. The room was dark and cold and strange. It smelled of camphor and mint. I heard Mern's voice say, *Jesus H. Christ, kiddo, what did I tell you about taking rides from strangers!* The thought that I might never hear that voice again filled me with despair.

Rose studied me from across the room. "I can see you're frightened, but you needn't be. Everyone's life is a little surprising, a little unusual when you look inside it for the first time." Her lips closed, but her golden-gray eyes kept talking. They said, *Girl, I have stood where you are standing, in a stranger's strange world, and I have been afraid.* A geyser broke inside me and gushed forth. I pressed my face into the sleeve of my elbow and sobbed—Eunice in a sweater down to her knees and flannel underwear, crying like a baby. Rose's fingers rubbed a warm circle between my shoulders. And then we were outside again, and Rose was holding my elbows from behind, steadying me as I squatted and let hot pee stream from my body.

Chapter 15

I'm a Nurse

My mother was missing. In Rose's words, Turtle Lake had undergone a transformation: most everything not nailed down or of sizeable weight had been torn up or washed away. Sinks and mittens, bicycle wheels, water-chewed mattresses, books of all sizes, and garbage cans filled the crowns of trees. Ponds of standing water alternated with patches of bald, mud-glazed earth. A Red Cross volunteer handed out water-purification tablets and requests for blood. At a neighboring card table, someone else dispensed free venison jerky. Trees were down, Rose reported, along with telephone poles and power lines, the wire cables spitting like mating snakes. Everywhere debris piled up and stank, and everywhere crews in orange jackets as disoriented as everyone else worked to clear the streets and restore order. A slew of cats feasted on bloated mice.

Rose set out in her skiff after five days of tending my scalding diarrhea and mild concussion. I'd ingested water and my cure consisted of rice broth and medicinal teas and sleep. Even in my dotty state, I recognized Rose's kindness and knew she was on the side of life. But exhaustion was sadness in disguise; sadness was a maze with my mother at the center, and every thought led back to Mern. In my feverish dreams Mern was as real as the day I'd left her and equally present when I opened my eyes. Rose's conch shell to my ear, I heard her voice wavering through the static. *Kiddo, is that you?* I dreamed she picked up Rose's beaded moccasins that smelled vaguely of moose and snorted, *Out rescuing animals!* I hated that I missed my mother so much. I was racked by sorrow and guilt but tried to hide my feelings from Rose, who had the knack of reading my moods anyhow. When my belly cramped and stinky poop ran down my leg, I secretly called for Mern; when I woke disoriented under the rafters on my pallet of pine, I called for Mern. Anger chased away sadness and so I imagined my mother, safe and dry, exaggerating to a wide-eyed audience the perils she'd escaped, no mention of me, of course. If anything saved me from crumbling into a sentimental jerk, it was picturing Mern turning our tragedy into entertainment. Still, I would not forgive her if she was dead.

The day Rose left for Turtle Lake, eight miles south and east, I was strong enough to climb down the ladder from the loft and fix myself some oatmeal. After my days in bed, I was weak but restless and argued with myself not to be spooked by the radical strangeness of Rose's place. I ambled aimlessly among her collections, fingering the geodes and crystals, the long striped turkey feathers, and noticed a shotgun cradled in a bracket above Rose's headboard, its stillness like a sleeping crocodile, the quietest thing in the room. I supposed it was necessary to have a firearm if you lived in the woods, but it made me nervous, the gleaming barrel pointed at the door. After we saw *Rear Window*, Mern threatened to get a ladies' special with a mother-of-pearl handle, but that was different, a passing fancy like a lot of Mern's ideas.

I went outside, Aunt Francis snuffing at my heels. The trees were exhaling their pollens into the bright day; a sour perfume wafted off the pond. The fox and puppy were in their pen, a construction of slats and straw. Rose had saved a lot of animals—ducks with fishing hooks through their bills, coons that swallowed bottle tops, one-eyed gulls. Lutie sometimes brought her a mink pup or an eaglet with a broken wing, but many of the wounded inexplicably found their way to her. Once they were cured, they were set free. Rose had given me specific instructions on how to behave around injured animals: move calmly, quietly, predictably. Don't gawk or stare. Especially I was not to touch the fox, who had to stay wild. Human touch would tame him, make him forget he had the incisors of an omnivore, the cunning and single-purpose will to pounce on voles and shrews. From the loft window I'd seen Rose hoist the injured ones onto her lap and examine their tongues, gums, bellies, paws, the fox stretched like a pelt of fire across her knees. Some of the crows had been her patients, too, and had names: Vasco da Gama, Hester La Noire. Rose had rules about living right, which meant treating animals with respect. Life threw out provocations but we had choices, she said—we could be selfish bastards or we could care. We were all creatures of the same divine hand.

Our cottage in Turtle Lake had been abandoned, Rose reported when she returned, the shutters banging from their screws. Minette's place was vacant too. Rose checked for Mern at the VFW that had been turned into an emergency clinic, at churches and schools, at Nielsen's funeral parlor too. Shirlee was still at her cousin's up by Deerfoot Falls, and the Curl and Swirl was boarded up. Only one person named Bernice vaguely recalled seeing Mern—or someone who might have been Mern—draped in a horse blanket in the food line in the Mt. Olive church basement the morning after the flood. The woman Bernice thought might have been Mern had kept the weary flock of wayfarers from taking their misfortune too seriously by entertaining them with a chorus of "Bill Bailey Won't You Please Come Home?" Finally Rose visited the sheriff. Told him right off she was a nurse and was taking care of me, and the sheriff seemed relieved. He had his hands full with lost babies and lost grandpas and lost schnauzers, with scores of people stranded and no place to go. He took Rose's name, my name, and my mother's and said he'd get back to us. All this Rose told me in her patient, straight-shouldered, unblinking way. She had a strong feeling my mother was safe and would check again in town in not too long. Meanwhile I would stay with her.

I took comfort in the fact that I'd *tried* to get help the night of the flood, that I hadn't *really* abandoned my mother to the storm, and while I knew this was true, guilt had a way of breaking in and translating reality for its own use. Every day I fought an undertow of sadness. The logical thing to do, the most sensible plan, was to somehow find Grunfelder and ask him to drive me back to Illinois, to Wild Pea and Mr. Tabachnik, who would surely take me in. But my bus had pulled out of that station, and I couldn't see myself in my old hometown. I couldn't go back to being a relic of my former self, the ghosts of Mern and Frankie and Sam bowing from every corner.

At the end of the following week, Rose returned to Turtle Lake. Shirlee, too, had returned and was in the process of closing the Curl and Swirl for good. Business had been bad before the flood, she told Rose, but now it was sinking fast. "We discussed you," Rose told me. Shirlee had been concerned that Rose had sought her out to wheedle a handout for my care. Or worse, to ask Shirlee to take me in herself. But she hardly knew Mern, she told Rose. "We both agreed that if I consulted with the authorities, you'd be put into foster care." Rose dropped the potato she was peeling into a bowl, wiped her hands on her skirt, and looked at me hard. "And that just won't do, darling. No foster care. I'd feel like I was selling you into slavery." She cleared her throat and pulled an envelope from her skirt pocket. Rose always wore long, voluminous skirts, another of her oddities. Skirts didn't chafe, she said, didn't block the energy rising from the earth. Only she could say such a thing and not only make it sound reasonable, but also make the rest of us wonder why we wore jeans.

The envelope was addressed to me in Mern's loopy script.

"You might want to go outside and read this by yourself," Rose said.

I nodded. I wasn't foolish enough to think the letter was something good.

Kiddo, my mother wrote.

What was I supposed to do!!!! You took off and left me and I have no idea where you are??? You could have at least called. I guess you decided to run away but you picked a lousy time. Jeez. A flood!!! I tried to run away when I was fifteen but some stray mutt bit me on the ankle before I got to the bus station and I had to limp home. Did I ever tell you that story? Anyway, I contacted the police but they sure have their hands full with missing people. Okay. If that's the way you want it. I waited five days. Nick FINALLY decided to leave Klio, RELIEF, RELIEF, and we are on our way to the City of Angels. I feel bad about this, but listen, YOU LEFT FIRST. Remember that. You always did have an independent streak. I do not have bad feelings toward you even though you did leave me FIRST. I DO NOT. And I sure hope it's visee-versee. I guess that's all. I want you to be happy so please be happy.

S. W. A. K.

Love from Mern

P.S. I'll send more to Annie when I have it.

Four twenties had been stuffed in the envelope.

My grief was huge and immediate, the enormity of what had just happened breaking through the protective cocoon of shock. The drugged, dopey feeling of the previous weeks lifted and a new piercing awareness took over. I couldn't bear for even Rose to see my shame. I crumpled Mern's letter, stuffed the money in a pocket, and hustled on weakened legs to the pond. The temptation was to lose myself, to become anonymous, to be absorbed into the water's still surface or to run into the woods and turn into a tree among trees: to become anything but what I was now—a lost girl, a truly lost girl, a girl without a mother or father.

I collapsed onto the warm sand and lay panting, the sky, the clouds, the algae-gathering mallards indifferent to my presence. When I caught my breath, I read Mern's letter one last time before ripping it in half, then in half again until it was a handful of confetti. I watched the ink of my mother's handwriting smear and dissolve and the bits of paper sink into oblivion. Fine! I thought. I'm an orphan. I always felt like one anyway. I always figured Mern would dump me. If she didn't need me, I didn't need her. Fine!

That evening Rose mashed herbs and roots, steeped a tea, and climbed up into the loft without saying a word. A thumb under each eye, she wiped away my tears. It hurts and hurts and then it stops hurting, she promised, and I believed her because, so far, there hadn't been a single chink in her kindness. I looked into her face with its sharp angles and honeyed skin. "Are you like...a medicine woman?"

"Nope," she replied, unfazed. "I'm part Ohio River valley, part Everglade swamp, part Norwegian fjord with a little Creole thrown in. Hell, life teaches you the medicine you need to know."

It took a while but the grief worked its way through my intestines, and thanks to Rose got flushed out. Then I got good and angry, roused out of my mourning to whack trees with big sticks. I imagined my mother in a white Pontiac barreling toward a neon-blue ocean whose name meant peace in another language, the hairy arm of a Greek grocer warming her shoulder. I hadn't considered that Nick might have used the flood to pack his wife off to Chicago and abscond with my mother. I hadn't truly considered that beaches, bikinis, and coconut drinks might be closer to Mern's heart than I was. I could hear Mr. Tabachnik saying, "Cisskala, from such terrible trials good comes," and I sure hoped it was true. Sometimes I woke with my mouth dammed up, as if with glue. In a dream I carried a large gasping goldfish, its own mouth gaping in a silent scream. A voice in my head admonished, *Tell the truth, did you love your mother? Tell the truth, are you sad she's gone? Tell the truth, are you happier with Rose in Rose's house? Tell the truth, would you really go back? Tell the truth tell the truth tell the truth.*

The day after the dream, it was as though Rose had read my thoughts. "There's been something I've wanted to say to you," she said, setting a bowl of dough on the butcher block and coiling her loose hair on top of her head. "A person can't force forgiveness but they can welcome it." She went on to say that Mern had given me all she knew how to give and that resentment would poison me if I let it. Heat rose in my face. I opened my mouth to protest, but Rose held up her hand. "It's time to stop thinking of yourself as someone's little girl." The best way to get me unstuck from the past was to learn something new, she said, like how to string a rope bed, loop a pack harness, start a fire. She had a list of tasks.

I wasn't free to do as I pleased, but every day my breath came easier and my muscles thickened. After a long day of work, when I mounted the ladder to the loft, my mind was clear. One of the tasks I disliked the most was collecting eggs from the hens from hell. Marie, the smaller of the Rhode Island Reds, chased on my heels, her beak aimed like a spear. Pilfering chicken eggs was the art of stealing raised to the highest level. When the hens couldn't lay anymore, Rose said, they'd go into the pot, and when the pot was empty, she'd grind the bones and bury them under tomatoes. *Grind up their bones!* I imagined Mern mimicking Rose, bobbing her head in her demented Charlie Chan way. But I was getting used to Mern's comments about Rose and getting accustomed to Rose's ways. I may even have started speaking like Rose, her long *s*'s, the way she raised her eyes to the right before she said something serious. She had altered one of her skirts for me, and the next day I ditched my jeans and stepped into a circle of worn chambray, soft and fluid against my thighs. I found myself imitating how she walked—long, purposeful strides. I imitated the way she listened when she stepped outside, one ear tuned to heaven, one to earth. I was letting my hair grow.

We were all healing, the puppy, the fox, and me. The puppy had a line of shirred stitches up his jaw; the fox, a knee injury. To strengthen his leg muscles, Rose let the fox roam while she worked outside. While she was busy weeding or chopping wood, I noticed him meandering toward the hens that hung out under the honeysuckle, his dainty silhouette suave and gentlemanly, his legs sheathed in black stockings, his gorgeous bushy tail. I hadn't realized how much I missed the hours I used to spend sketching, the world issuing forth from my pencil tip, the magician's trick of transferring a ten-foot pine to a blank page. My fingers itched not only to draw the fox but also to stroke his silken ears, his coat of sooty flame. One day while he was trotting off, I hurried into the shack to get my pencil and pad, and when I couldn't find them, I set off to find any pencil and scrap of paper. In my distraction, I accidentally knocked over the orange crate next to Rose's bed. A leather diary tied with a velvet ribbon on which hung a baby's bracelet spilled out from one of the crate's inner shelves. I picked up the diary and ran my fingers over the coarse leather cover. The beads on the bracelet spelled out the name BELLE. For a second, I was tempted to force the lock and read Rose's private words, but I told myself the things I didn't know about Rose were things I was better off not knowing and put the diary back. The diary and name Belle stayed with me all that day, but by the time night came on, I forgot about them.

The weeks progressed. I tagged along behind Rose as she strode in her long skirts from shack to woodpile, to the outdoor pump with a bucket, to the puppy and the fox, to the garden and into the woods with a rucksack to collect herbs, a circle of chores that kept us busy till evening, our heels digging a path of half-moons in the dirt. I got used to the outdoor shower, a thick wooden bucket on a high platform rigged with a hose, and the Throne, a wooden seat with a toilet hole cut in the top. I now slept deep, dreamless nights. For whole days sunlight burned along the ridge of pine, bringing with it a fragile joy.

My true education began with learning about silence and what Rose called "soft eyes." According to Rose, if a person relaxed her eyes, she could see the world as it really was—not only trees and shoes and automobiles, but the spirit of these things. If you kept your eyelids lazy, you could witness a spirit's presence, its invisible comings and goings. One night after dinner, in the twilight before true darkness fell, Rose and I cut back through the bushes to the pond where she stopped to kneel and show me how the top of the ground cover had been nipped off. "Some animals mow, some mash, and some nibble," she said, naming which creatures did which. She pointed to twigs that had been broken by passing animals and to fallen logs that had been rubbed clean of their bark, and she knew whose belly had done the rubbing by looking at the tracks. "Everything's written down to read like in a book," she said, stooping to illustrate how to measure a paw print with my palm. We put our heads to the earth and studied the disturbances of stones. Dislodged pebbles had wet undersides. You could tell the size of the animal that had passed and where it was headed by the size and position of overturned stones. Shoulder to shoulder, I could smell the scent rising off the back of her neck and from her armpits, a scent not sweet and not brutish but pungent, not unlike the earth itself.

"If you get lost," she said, "nature supplies compasses." Flying squirrels chose hollows on the east side of a tree; the tips of pine pointed east; the plumes of goldenrod nodded to the north; frogs and water-birds nested on western shores. She led me to the beach where the skiff and her canoe were hidden and told me to sit on the sand with my legs crossed. Lowering herself next to me, she said, "You can't know what real silence is until you learn how to listen for it." She reached over and touched a finger to each of my eyelids. Signaling me to close them, she tied a cloth around my eyes and the world darkened several hues. "Now, just listen," she said, and I sent my ears out in all directions.

In this new dimension I began to sense what I had not been aware of before—the weight of my own body balanced on minuscule grains of granite and quartz, the skin between my neck and shoulder dusted with the cooling air. In front of me, the pond exerted its gravitational pull. Behind me, in the treetops, the leaves exhaled. A fish jumped, and I heard the measured music of ripples echo into infinity. An insect sirened by. Then silence moved in, or what seemed like silence, an immense glass dome without windows or doors.

"Open your ears," Rose whispered.

I strained more consciously toward the quiet, imagining my ears as big as an elephant's. A bird let out a single, high, sharp note, and the song entered my skull and rang with the clear sound of a flute. After that, the silence seemed to deepen, but only for a moment. A hundred different noises came clear, each with its own timbre. A wind sulked in the trees. The leaves brushed against each other like the rubbing of old ladies' undergarments. A series of clicking noises competed with the *ga-lug* of frogs and then more birdcalls. As soon as I attended to one sound, another erupted. There were sounds beneath the sounds—water rushing somewhere, or had the wind changed direction? I was busy naming everything I heard until I realized I'd forgotten about silence. Silence was the envelope in which all the other sounds were contained.

Rose touched my arm. "Not so easy, is it? When you've had more practice, you'll hear the presence of a fox in a sparrow's warning." A crimson sun was about to roll off the edge of the world. Rose unbraided the rope of her hair. "You're a good learner," she said, smiling. "I knew you would be." My heart swelled under her praise. *See, Mern!*

We built a fire on the beach. The driftwood crackled instantly into a fine yellow flame. Rose began to undress, her skirts collapsing around her ankles. She did not try to cover herself, her mounds and curves—hips, belly, and thighs—bronze and gleaming. I had never seen a naked woman except for Mern, whose breasts were tiddly and whose bones jutted out like a boy's. Rose's body reminded me of scoops of coffee ice cream, her breasts large and full, the skin around her nipples dark as blackberries.

"Come in," she said, sprinting toward the water. I could see the ladder of defined muscles holding her spine, the stone-smoothness of her buttocks, and I dropped my skirt. My own body was straight and spare in comparison, but it was a good body, long-limbed and agile. I was no husk after all.

We dove and chased each other, splashing and kicking, our bodies free and happy. Rose cupped her hands and called me over to come see what she'd caught, but when I looked into the privacy of her palms, she sassed and teased and squirted water at me. The full moon rose and arced across the sky, one minute a far-off disk, the next a huge ball hanging so close we could practically touch it. I stood in shallow water and stared. Everything under the moon's severe light—the pond, the surrounding trees, our arms, our chests and faces—had become silver. I'd never seen anything like it, as if we were about to be smashed by a fiery asteroid. Rose swam over and together we looked up, craning our heads to the moonlight. "It does make a person feel worshipful," she said. She looked like a queen, silver-gold haloing her head. Queen Rose.

"I've never been out when the moon is as bright as the sun," I said.

"Well, you won't forget it," Rose said.

I wanted the hours never to end, wished I never had to leave the water, but the evening's cool hand brushed my lips and across my shoulders and eventually I got out. We walked back through the piney woods, naked under blankets, and I felt close to Rose in a way I'd never felt close to anyone—an effortless kind of love. Before we reached the shack, she tugged at the bristly brown fringe growing at my nape and asked why I ever thought looking like a boy would help anything. She told me I should be proud of my hair and damn proud of my womanhood, and I felt her hand reach under my blanket and pinch my goose-pimpled butt.

Chapter 16

Swarming

In another life, I'd have a summer job at Annie's stuffing peroxide-streaked bibs and snarls of hair into the trash. In another life, Mern would be hatching plans to meet her dreamboat tycoon who'd buy her minks and My Sin. Where oh where was my mother now? *I love you. Mern, talk to me*, I whispered, exhorting her across the miles to let me know she cared. A whole lunar month and more, full moon to full moon, thirty notches on a Chinese oracle bone I'd lived with Rose and only slowly was I easing into ache-free days contained within sunrise and sunset, the unrolling hours mercifully ordered by chores. Only with the passing of time, with Rose's unceasing kindness and my acceptance of her kindness, was the extraordinary becoming ordinary, the past not disappeared but fading like old photographs. For the moment I was content not to dwell on the future. Besides, no matter how carefully you scanned the horizon, it barreled toward you unseen, shaping your destiny.

On a perfect August morning I was going into the woods to gather kindling and herbs. Wherever I went now, I tried to practice soft eyes and the wilderness skills Rose had taught me. As I hiked deeper into the forest, I noted that several species of birdsong were knit in a tight weave of music, and I stood for a moment trying to distinguish the flicker from the pine siskin from the hermit thrush. The sun bled cool and blue through the leaves of late summer, the locust pods and hickory nuts dreaming their future trees. Aunt Francis had been following me, but as I tramped farther into the underbrush, the dog vanished. The air had warmed up and I began to sweat. I took off Rose's tartan shirt and tied it around my waist. I was looking for the stiff, glossy wintergreen plant and wild ginseng. The forest floor was a tidy picture of evergreen needles, spongy moss, and fungi of fantastic shapes and hues, including the deadly *Amanita muscaria*, and I lost myself in the intricacies of shape and texture. The birdcalls had stopped, and as I slowed my pace, the only sound that came back to me was the magnified sound of my own breath.

I was resting against the trunk of an oak when I heard a cough, or what I thought was a cough. The noise did not repeat itself and had been so quick a vibration against my eardrum I wasn't sure I'd heard anything at all. And yet, I immediately wanted to leave and had to fight the urge to run away. Instead, sweat dripping down my neck, I decided to prove myself Rose's worthy apprentice and made myself stay and listen harder. Sunlight sprinkled from the trees, and I thought of Mr. Tabachnik hiding in the forbidding forests of Eastern Europe eating crows and sleeping under a blanket of dead leaves. I don't know how long I waited for the cough to repeat, but the silence now felt like the kind that watches you, ready to strike. I counted backward from a thousand, but before I reached the hundreds, I was charging through the undergrowth almost too distraught to find my way back.

When I broke into the clearing, I slowed down and composed my face. Hadn't Rose said, *Stop thinking of yourself as someone's little girl*? Hadn't she told me her job was to teach me to be self-sufficient? I caught my breath and threw back my shoulders. Rose was in the garden, absorbed in weeding, her hair kinked with perspiration. When she heard me, she glanced up.

"Everything okay?" she yelled, dropping the clump of dirt in her hand. She studied me, brows wrinkling.

I thought for a second about whether to tell her about the cough and how spooked I'd been but decided I would keep the incident to myself. I waved her a thumbs-up. I could feel Rose's eyes on my back, waiting for me to turn around and speak of what she must have sensed. But I hurried on, unsnapping my rucksack to unload the kindling into the wood box.

* * *

Secrets. Maybe they were necessary. They *were* necessary. Everyone had them. My secret was that I loved an animal, the fox, and was determined to win his affection. Not that there were any boys my age around to have crushes on, nor could I imagine myself attracted to a teenage boy, a boy with pimples or wisps of hair on his chin. The fox had a way of looking over his shoulder at me with an intense, flirty stare. The delicacy of his face, the slender lines of his body thrilled me, and though he might have sped away when I crept near, he merely tensed and froze until I could almost touch him, as though he *wanted* me to touch him, as though he, not I, were taking inventory of a different species. But if I came too close, in a blink he was gone. Rose said I was foolish to set my heart on winning the fox's loyalty—I'd only be frustrated, disappointed, but I was convinced I could lure him into being my friend and developed a plan.

The plan was to sit at a distance outside his pen while he was caged to let him get used to my movements and scent. When I started, the fox would hide in his burrow, but I persisted. I wore the same clothes every time and a red cap on my head, red to match his coat, for solidarity. I had to admit I had a strange and powerful infatuation with that animal. I don't know what I was thinking—that he'd become my pet? I couldn't deny the gnawing need I sometimes felt to run my fingers through his coat but had to be satisfied with sketching his nervous glances and thready whiskers and thumbprint shadows at the base of his ears. One day I dipped a finger into raspberry jam and offered the treasure through the slats of his pen. His tongue was quick on my skin, like a lash of dry ice, and my heart almost burst at the nearness to his unfailing beauty.

Of course I wondered if Rose knew, Rose knew everything, which made it doubly cruel when she told me one innocent afternoon a week later that she'd set the fox free.

"I don't understand," I said, a basket of oyster mushrooms spilling from my hands. I ran around the back of the shack and stood gaping at the empty pen.

"Where is he?" I demanded. Rose had just finished replacing a rotted step, and her fingers were flecked with bits of slimy wood pulp. She came around to where I was slumped against a tree. "You let him go without telling me! How could you?" I began to pace in a tight circle that got smaller and smaller until I stood at the center of it, huffing and shouting. "How could you!"

She passed her hand over her hair and started slowly and deliberately, studying my eyes. "There's a lesson here, a necessary lesson."

"That's what adults always say," I said. "Spare me."

Rose nodded again. "I'm not being mean, darling, just realistic. Wild animals need to go back to where they came from. That's a law of nature. Maybe I made a bad call on this one—I'm sorry—but the principle holds."

I was sick of her laws of nature, her stupid beliefs. I wondered if Rose had to choose between saving an animal or saving a human, who she'd choose. I knew she wasn't trying to purposely hurt me, but I had to swallow hard against the sting of tears.

Rose's face sagged. "A fox cannot possibly understand you or your motives. It is a creature that lives by instinct and is incapable of love." She inhaled and exhaled sharply. "You can't hold on to the things you love—I can promise you that. Don't make yourself miserable over this. Our fox isn't miserable."

Our fox?

Thunder rolled low and dull from the west. We both looked up into a vault of black clouds that was quickly bearing down on us. Rose turned away, as if she didn't want me to see her expression, then turned back again and came forward holding out her arms. "It hurts to love. I'm not going to baby you—it damn hurts. I told you that weeks ago." Large leaden raindrops splattered the ground, bringing with them a dusty summer odor, intimate and ruined. "We don't always get to say good-bye," Rose whispered.

I fell into the haven of her arms, feeling a little foolish, a little heartsick. She hugged me tight for a second, and we walked slowly back to the shack, letting the downpour cleanse us.

Rose was going to teach me how to be a beekeeper. She understood that the fox loomed large in my heart and that the bees wouldn't take his place, but they were possessors of uncanny powers, she said, and I would come to appreciate them once I lost my fear of being stung. Her honeys were capable of great architecture as spectacular in their own way, she said, as the pyramids or the Taj Mahal. Nothing man-made could rival the marvel of a honeycomb. For days she'd been explaining the complicated workings of hive society, enumerating the many virtues of the all-female worker bees that were incapable of reproducing but did just about everything else from gathering pollen to cleaning the hive. The females were the nurse bees, engineer bees, housekeepers, ladies-in-waiting to the queen. A few special male drones mated with the queen and died. The other males died, too, after a short and boring life. Each hive was a city with its own population and its own queen. Once the queen emerged from her cell, she stung the other queens-to-be to death.

Rose recited the hundred and one uses to which honey could be put. Honey and onion juice in equal proportions dripped in the eye for cataracts. Honey and cinnamon for a cough. Honey and black pepper for asthma. Honey on the scalp to smother lice. How did she learn all this honey stuff and about herbs and remedies? I wanted to know. We hadn't ever talked about her past, and now I was curious, and the leather diary with the baby bracelet attached flashed into my mind. Rose leaned the shovel she was holding against the side of the house, ran her hands over my head, and smoothed my hair. "Never mind the details about how I got to know what I know," she said. But for one thing, she'd been a nurse at migrant camps alongside some *real* healer ladies, and they'd taught her a thing or two.

She chose an August day when the sun was at its highest to introduce me to the honeybees. On overcast days the nectar wasn't running and the bees got grumpy. She did me up in a silly costume: white fluted bonnet with netting, a man's white shirt buttoned at the cuffs and neck, a pair of canvas work gloves. I was warned not to slap at the bees if they landed on me because their stingers ejected a chemical that excited the other bees, which would come swarming. Already I was hot and itchy in the stiff material and a little nervous too. Rose wore her usual clothes and not even a straw hat for protection.

"My honeys are judicial in their manner and have an exquisite sense of justice. They only sting when threatened." We'd taken the old logging road, the route Rose walked to Liberty come fall to sell her honey products at the fair. The last stands of timber and dense forest gave way to clear-cut areas, and at a fork we came to a footpath that veered from the logging road toward meadows that had grown up in the place of long-ago cabin settlements. A wind swept over the fields, the long grasses and purple star asters, the goldenrod and the last of the late lilies bobbing under its force. The beauty of the day wasn't lost on me, but my hands and feet were sweaty and my scalp itched terribly under the bee bonnet. I felt as if I were sweltering. "Look here," Rose said, stopping at a lily that once might have grown by a farmer's doorstep. She drew her fingernail down the lily's orange throat. Almost invisible lines led to a circle of crimson at the base of petals, to the heart of the flower and its nectaries, the stigma and anthers, where the bees feasted on pollen. Our eyes were mostly blind to what the bees saw, Rose said. They even performed a special dance-language on the floor of the hive to direct other forager bees to the honeyflow.

I stared into the heart of the lily and things miniature came into my head: moon-colored snails in pearly houses. Seahorses the size of a baby's thumb. Thumbelina herself in a walnut-shell bed. I thought how small our vision was and how much we missed. Rose and I walked on in silence, my bee veil flung back like that of a bride who'd just been kissed. After about ten minutes we came to another clear-cut area where black-and-orange-winged butterflies flew in fractured circles over the clover. It took me a moment to see the pale blue bee boxes among the ground cover.

There were eight such boxes and one of them was overturned, its broken wooden segments poking up powdery blue between the clover. Honeybees swarmed in pandemonium around the wrecked frames, dashing themselves at the ruined honeycomb. Rose marched into the field, her face immobile except for her eyes, which seemed to track in all directions at once. When she reached the toppled hive, she knelt and examined each section, running her fingers along the stone foundation from which the box had fallen. A hawk shrieked in circles over our heads, while I waited motionless in the shade of a hickory, watching a stream of bees loop around Rose. She held up splintered frames one by one, turning them over in her hands, sniffing them, sniffing her hands, and when she was finished with that, she snooped around the site, probably looking for tracks or scat. When she returned to me, her verdict was that some animal had messed with the bee box, though she couldn't find any trace of an animal. But then there was no telling what cleverness a hungry bear got into his head, or a raccoon for that matter. Something must have scared it off, though, or the animal would have overturned all the hives.

She squinted up at the sky as though the answer to this riddle were enfolded in the clouds. There was nothing to do except come back in the early evening, she said, when the swarm was sluggish, and catch the bees before they flew off. Her face was tight and unreadable. "Let's go," she said, and began walking so swiftly I had to run to keep up. Grasshoppers sprang out of our way as we plowed through the field, their fierce clicks drowned by the swarm that had split into two funnel clouds whirling over the wreckage. On the way back, I waited for Rose to say more but she stayed silent and walked on ahead, isolated in her thoughts. That night she was extremely quiet and sat in the rocker without rocking, one hand covering the other, watching twilight's blue gloss smudge to black. "Just pondering," was all she said.

Later, from the loft window, I saw Rose outside carrying a flashlight and heading for the pond. I stayed awake listening to the sounds of the night, whippoorwill and shaking aspens, the click of cicadas and the silence that coiled its way through everything. I had trouble falling asleep, and when I did, I saw Mern standing at a crossroad, bewildered and disheveled, holding an empty birdcage.

The next morning Rose surprised me by saying we'd be stopping by Lutie's before going to catch the swarm. She said she didn't really suspect him of mischief, but on occasion he'd gotten snookered on homemade rotgut and caused a ruckus.

The sky was a muted, pewter gray as we heaved the skiff into the water, the skep—an inverted basket of coiled straw with a hole at the bottom for the bees to enter and exit—in the stern. In a heartbeat we were cutting across the pond, the wind curving around my face, tinny-tasting, like water dredged up from a well. A pearly mist blurred the boundaries between land and water, loosening my tense thoughts, the light chop of the swells and smell of pine making it possible to momentarily forget anything worrisome. We headed southeast across Rose's pond in the direction of Turtle Lake, Rose holding the course through spanks of waves until we came to the mouth of the flowage, where she made a sharp right, due west, away from the southerly route we'd taken the night of the flood. As we entered a narrow channel that linked one lake to another, the softness of the air had begun to massage away the agitation in my belly. *Lutie*—a silly name.

At the end of the inlet, Rose steered us into a cove lined with a dense wall of fir whose doubles mirrored up from the surface of the lake. About a hundred yards from the skiff, veiled by trees, we saw smoke twisting into the air, and Rose killed the motor and started rowing to avoid the shelves of granite that ran into the water. "I'm going to get out to talk to Lutie, but why don't you stay in the boat until I make sure he's not soused." As we came around the point, Alfred Lutsen squatted on a spit of rock in front of his camp and waited. Rose maneuvered the craft into the shallows, and Lutie hopped down and grabbed our rope to draw us in, his movements spry and birdlike. Lutie was skinny in the chest with a big Adam's apple sticking out of his stringy neck. His face was drawn and complicated, his scraggly shoulder-length hair hanging in oily white strands. One of his eyes wandered while the other nabbed you with a pitiless stare.

Rose stepped out of the skiff and stood her full statuesque height in front of Lutie, a half head taller than he, making every inch count, and offered her hand. Lutie wiped his palm on his thigh before taking two of Rose's fingers in an obligatory shake.

"Trouble?" he said to Rose, securing our rope around a bush, his bad eye sliding over my face. He nodded hello but didn't speak. I could tell he wasn't dumb. My scalp tightened.

"Trouble is right, Lutie."

"Trouble how?"

"Someone or something's been messing with my hives."

"Messing how?"

"Knocked apart one. The hive's swarming."

Lutie rubbed his chin, looking down at his construction boots. "You thinking bear?"

I glanced at Lutie's grizzled face, then at his cabin of hewn logs set back on a rise, a shed with rusty tools and skins nailed to it, a chopping block with an ax sticking out of it, a neat pile of logs. When I looked at Lutie again through soft eyes, I saw a nice-looking boy, towheaded, quiet, the kind of boy who dreamed about being a park ranger or a mounted policeman, and I felt pity for the rank-smelling man.

"I'll come right to the point," Rose said. "You drinking swill and going on rampages?"

Lutie's head jerked back as if he'd been punched. "What would I be doing crazy stuff like that for?" The wound in his voice made me think he had a long acquaintance with false accusations.

Rose said, "Crazy, right! You're the only one who lives out here, knows about my bees."

"That don't mean shit, Rose." He narrowed his good eye at her, shoulders buckled forward. "Thought you'd have known better than to think I'd do wrong by you after all these years." His head dropped in a mournful way. I saw that friendship was no small thing for Lutie and that Rose had insulted him. Maybe he was the kind of kid who got blamed for things his whole life, and he lived in the woods and had no friends because he was ugly, squint-eyed, and poor.

Rose said she meant no disrespect, but there was no taking back the insult before a witness—me—so I squared my shoulders and stepped out of the boat next to Rose. To ease his hurt feelings, I asked Lutie what Boston Blackie might have asked. "Have you seen anyone suspicious, Lutie?"

Lutie ran his tongue over his dry lips and, whether out of shyness or bad manners, didn't ask my name, who I belonged to, just answered, "Nothing here to see."

Rose draped an arm around my shoulder.

Lutie said, "I'd tell you, Rose."

Rose raised an eyebrow, then pointed to the woodpile. "You selling firewood these days?"

Lutie twisted around as if he needed to see what was stacked in his yard to answer. "Yup. Got customers. A few."

Rose nodded. "Fishing good? Done any trapping?"

"Not much," Lutie said.

"Not the same as it used to be in the northwoods."

"Everything changes, Rose. You know that." His eye skittered over to me, but he didn't say anything more. A cindery, burnt-toast smell rode off his clothes. He untied our rope and watched us push off without waving. None of us waved. At the last moment Lutie yelled out that he'd keep his eyes open for trouble.

When we were out of sight of his camp, I asked Rose if Lutie was telling the truth. "He's telling the truth," she said. I asked how she could tell he was telling the truth, and she said Lutie would have never stayed around for the neighborly small talk if he'd been lying. Wouldn't have been able to stand that much observation. Sometimes people just did crazy things for no reason, she said. Loneliness moves in and takes over, but even if Lutie had never been a lover of the opposite sex, he was generous to living things, bees included.

"Lutie is probably a private misbehaver, not a public one," she added.

"How can you tell if someone is lying?" I asked. I was thinking about my father. Mern was a fabricator, but my father might have been an honest-to-goodness liar. *Lakeview, Oceanside—what's the difference?* A light rain was falling, but in the distance the clouds were edged in shocking pink. We were going back the way we'd come to Rose's pond to a path that led to the hives. My feet were cold and my back was tired from sitting hunched on a bench in the stern, but we had to get the swarm before it flew off.

"Lying's an interesting subject," Rose said. "I made a study once of how to tell if a man was lying to you. Maybe I'll tell you about it someday. I can give you a few hints to keep in mind, though. You're old enough."

I smiled self-consciously and ran my fingers through my raggedy hair.

"Rule one, don't look into a man's eyes if you're looking for the truth, and rule two, don't look at his mouth either, especially don't look at his mouth. Looking at a man's lips is a sure road to perdition." She laughed and bent forward, rocking the boat, and smacked my knee. "That must be some cracker ancestor in me talking."

"So...what else?" I asked, taking up the joke.

"Watch his hands," Rose said. "How deep is he stuffing them into his pockets? The deeper the fist, the bigger the lie. And look to see which way his feet are pointing—toward you or toward the door? Are his shoulders aimed at the exit? Hold on..." She cut the motor and the skiff bobbed toward shore. Rose took up an oar and back-paddled through the reeds, jumping out into the knee-high water to tow us around floating deadwood and onto a small crescent of sand. From there we'd take the trail inland to the bees. There was no more mention of men or lying or bears or Lutie.

She carried the lightweight skep in her arms. The drizzle had stopped and sunlight painted broad stripes between the trees. The moss on the forest floor had deepened into a livid green. An animal scent poured from our bodies, and I smelled myself among the duff and ferns. I'd slipped on the bee bonnet and white shirt and gloves. We walked up a slope to an old pine plantation, wound our way to the edge of the field, and stood for a moment looking at the blue bee boxes. Rose set down the skep and put a hand on my arm, then walked ahead of me like a lion, wild mane over her shoulders.

The swarm, a pulsing black heart, dangled from a branch at the edge of the field. As we came closer, its roar grew insistent, each grain of sound rubbing against my skin. Every atom of space seemed alive with the bees' electric mania.

A song rolled out from deep in Rose's chest, a French song I couldn't understand, low and sweet and promising. The honeybees scrambled over each other, a mass of gyrating bodies at the core of which was a rosette of bees—and in its center, the queen. Their mother, and the hive's future.

Rose produced a small jar of honey from her pocket and, rolling up her sleeves, slathered her arms, chest, face, and hands. Moving slowly toward the bees, she threw back her head and sang her French song in a pure, clear voice. Bees began to detach themselves from the roost, settling on Rose's arms, crawling onto her neck and hands, some braceleting her wrists, more bees unwinding in ribbons and orbiting her head, flakes of yellow pollen raining on her hair. Bees skated over her cheeks and lips, a whole island molding itself to her back. Rose stopped singing and a higher roar arose from the bees. At last, the solitary queen separated from the cluster. Rose raised her bee-encrusted arms and signaled her welcome. Turning west, where the sky was not yet a distillation of dying sun, Rose, covered with the sheen of a thousand wings, retraced her steps through the field to the skep, a figure consumed by dark fire.

Chapter 17

No One Knows

We built a new tongue-and-groove bee box with boards and galvanized nails on a worktable in the yard. The swarm would happily follow their queen to the new hive, Rose said. They couldn't survive without her. We worked five days on the project, starting after breakfast, shoulders touching, the scent of wood shavings and glue mixing with the smell of our sweat. My talent with tools pleased Rose: I could handle the hand drill, the carpenter's angle; I could hammer a nail with one stroke. I carried Rose's praise with me all day and repeated her words to myself at night. The days were shorter, and I missed my mother less. I missed my mother less but wondered about her more. Was she happy with Nick? Would I ever see her again? How much did she miss me? *Did* she *really* miss me? Some nights I composed letters: *If we ever meet again, I guess we'll probably forgive each other.* To my father I wrote: *I could never say when I was younger how much I loved you and how much you disappointed me.* Long after the words evaporated, images of my parents burned in my head. That's when I made lists: five great things about living with Rose. Four things I miss most. Ten ideas for a new name. I'd get caught up in the distraction until my brain flipped a switch and the memories returned.

We performed the resettlement of the hive at the tail end of summer when the first frost crystals shone in the morning mud. A few brilliant maples flagged the changing season, the blueberries gone, and gone, too, the wild strawberries and the eerily beseeching call of the loons. Rose transferred the bee queen, sluggish from the night's chill, into the new bee box, the remaining hive members ejecting themselves in a pulsing throng through the skep's narrow hole.

Upholstered in my bee costume at a safe distance, I watched Rose open with her bare hands the square lid of the new hive and entice the queen and her attendants onto the frames inside, her courage never failing to leave me a little unsettled, a little breathless. A few stray bees escaped from the mob, and Rose held out her hand, offering her honey-coated palm. Rose the tamer of bees! How did a person get to be like her?

When the transfer of the swarm from the skep to the new bee box was accomplished and the cover slid into its groove, Rose and I went by skiff to the landing and walked the dirt path to the field. After we set the new hive among the other boxes, Rose spread a bedroll and we celebrated the return of the rescued swarm to the bee colony. Rose stretched out on the coarse wool, her arms folded under her head. The sky was a torn, broken blue. "Beautiful, isn't it?" she said. The meadow, dusted with sparkly light, was picture-book pretty. I pulled off my bee bonnet and sank to my knees next to Rose. A few golden leaves spun in the air, defying gravity.

"It's like magic here."

"*Is* magical," Rose said, closing her eyes.

"Except for the bear!"

Rose turned on her side and twisted one of my newly grown curls around her finger. "Don't worry about that bear. He won't come again. I suspect the honeys gave him a lesson stinging his paws and nose."

I laughed, imagining a cartoon bear tearing off with an army of bees charging after him. "I'm not as afraid of bees anymore," I said. I just wasn't. When I thought of a bee now, its striped body and fragile wings, it seemed incomprehensible and embarrassing to have been frightened by such a creature. "Are you ever afraid?" I asked Rose. Everyone was afraid of something.

Rose was looking straight at me, but her gaze had turned inward, as though she were shuffling through snapshots to pull out one to share with me. "We moved around a lot when I was a kid. The thing I was most afraid of was snakes. I'd found a rattler once curled up in a sunny corner of my room, and my daddy had to come and chop its head off with a hoe." Sunlight fell in a swath on Rose's cheeks, and she covered her eyes with a forearm and yawned.

"I can tell you one thing. What you are most afraid of is never the thing to be most feared. I've since made friends with all kinds of snakes. Lots of creatures have bad reputations they don't deserve." She opened her eyes and lifted her head to study me. "What about you? What are you afraid of?"

I thought for a moment. "Polio and murderers," I said, feeling a little foolish stating the obvious, and a little superstitious that naming my fears would bring them on.

Rose touched a finger to my nose, tapping it once for reassurance. "Poliomyelitis is a serious killer. No polio here in the woods." I had a fleeting image from a movie of a girl in an iron lung. I remembered wondering how the girl peed inside the contraption. "I've seen some bad epidemics in my day," Rose said. "When I worked at the migrant camps, infections were rampant. Terrible places. I was part of a team. Olive Rikkers was the other nurse. We visited each place twice a month. One camp had an outbreak of polio that ran through it like the scourge. That was right before I moved to Joplin, Missouri." Her chest heaved, and she stopped speaking and sat up, tossing her hair with a quick flick of her neck, something jerky and tense in her movement. "Never mind. It's not worth looking into," she said, squinting at the sky, but not like she was reading the weather. I sat up, alert, wondering why her mood had just changed. I looked up and saw no threatening clouds. Around us the field and forest were as serene as they had been a moment before. "We should be heading back soon," she said, whisking the blanket from under us.

Not worth looking into. A door had been closed, maybe locked. The celebratory feeling had drained away. At the landing, Rose untied the skiff and did not speak the entire ride back, something unnamable hovering inside her silence. "I forgot to collect eggs today," I said above the purr of the motor, not sure if she heard or cared. She sat in the stern, steering the boat, her face dotted with spray. "Tomorrow, then, Eunice," she said.

*   *   *

Fall's unmistakable chill rose up from the earth. The full moon waned and the Harvest Moon arrived with the last ripening tomatoes, and every day our stack of wood to split grew larger. Aunt Francis developed kidney problems and a white muzzle; the puppy, now alpha dog, slept at the foot of Rose's bed. We fell into a whirlwind of activity but Rose did not seem like herself. She was forgetful, preoccupied. I watched to see if she was eating okay, sleeping okay, and she was, but I couldn't help feeling that when we stood side by side extracting honey from the combs and sealing it in sterilized jars, or when we boiled herbs for tinctures to sell at the street fair in Liberty, Rose's mind was elsewhere. I thought it might be fun to go to the fair with Rose; I even fantasized I would run into my mother, if she hadn't really fled with Nick or become part of a mariachi band in Mexico. Maybe she'd have let her hair go natural and become a waitress in a small town like Liberty. But meeting Mern in Liberty wasn't an issue because Rose didn't invite me to go with her.

I had plenty to do while she was gone. We were building a stockade fence around the garden, a little late in the season, but not too late to save the frost crops like cabbage and broccoli from marauding woodchucks and deer. We used young popple, each sapling to be dragged from the woods and sawed to the exact six-foot measure, one end shaved to a point like a beaver log. The dragging and the sawing to size were my job, the ax-blade shaving, Rose's. Recently I'd taken to whittling pieces of driftwood the pond spit out, and with a few flicks of a knife, I carved them into some semblance of a horse or fox.

I pretended I wasn't disappointed when I waved good-bye as she poled the skiff away from the shore, just as I pretended I hadn't noticed her distraction. After she left, I walked along the shore with Aunt Francis and the puppy kicking up stones to throw in the water. A splash startled up a great blue heron from a snag it had been attacking, and I watched it disappear above the tree line. The bird didn't like intrusion any more than Rose did. No one would live alone in the woods like Rose if they needed company. It made me wonder, how many people had Rose loved, and how many had she lost to sorrow or to relief? Where had she lived, and who were her people? On what beach had she found the conch, where had she traveled, where had she gathered geodes and gem rocks? And before that, who had named her, who had comforted her, why was she living alone in the middle of nowhere? Who was she to me, and who was I to her? What did I know about Rose? What did I know for sure?

When she returned, the stars had already jumped solidly into the evening sky. At the sound of the outboard, the dogs trampled each other down the path to the water to greet her. They were used to the odor of her body at the end of the day when she leaned down to fill their bowls, accustomed to our quiet dinner afterward when they curled beneath the table at our feet. "Lots of sales," Rose said, lifting the empty crates from the hull and throwing a tarp over the boat. Folks buying up the honey faster than she could take their coins. Her hair smelled of tobacco smoke and her voice sounded barricaded. The black night was hurrying down, blotting out even the darkest trees, and she said not a word about why she was so late.

I'd lit all the lanterns, so I could see when she stepped inside and unhooked her nappy wool cloak that her eyes lingered on the shotgun above her bed. "I miscalculated," she said. "I miscalculated and misjudged and I am ashamed of my mistake."

The hair on my arms stood up. "What happened?"

"I thought my ex was in jail, but he isn't. He's living outside Liberty and he's been watching us." She shook her head twice like she couldn't get over something. "I misread everything," she said.

I went around lighting more candles and put on water to boil, picked up the eyedropper bottle of nervine tonic and placed a few drops under my tongue. I'd never seen Rose so drawn. She sat at the table running her fingers through her hair.

"I thought I could choose the time to tell you this," she said. "I won't glamorize it."

My heart was thumping. The kettle began to whistle, and I made Rose a cup of mint tea and set it in front of her. She smiled weakly, her hands cupping the hot mug, though it wasn't cold in the room.

"What happened? I don't understand. Why is he watching us?"

"It's a long story." Tears glistened in her eyes. "I should have guessed he was around. I should have been protecting you."

"I don't understand what I have to do with anything."

Rose studied her palms. She laughed in an awful way. "He thinks you're my daughter. He thinks I had a second child."

"A second?"

Rose nodded. Her hand shook when she sipped her tea.

I told Rose I didn't know what she was talking about and reached out for her. She shook her head as if to clear it and stared at my fingers on her wrist.

Ruben had been her patient; she'd sewn up his knife wound at one of the migrant camps years ago. "There were always fights among the pickers. Lots of violence. And Ruben drank." She hadn't gone looking for trouble but trouble had found her. "Love is in no way orderly, even under the best circumstances. And some people, they're like gods. Or maybe planets. They influence us even when we think we are free of them." She and Ruben ended up living together in Wisconsin picking crops. Belle was born on a snowy February afternoon. Belle had the translucent skin of Rose's Norwegian ancestors and Ruben's deep-sea eyes.

Rose got up from the table, walked to the window, and stared out at the blackness. My mind raced to put everything together.

"Ruben was up in Two Harbors working for the mining people, coming home every other weekend. We rented a handyman's special west of Sturgeon Bay. Ruben traveled several hours down the shore of Lake Superior plus the whole northern width of Wisconsin to get home. When I worked night shifts at the county hospital, Belle slept at a kindly neighbor's—Ingrid Untermeyer. Belle called her Untee.

"There was a fire. An electrical fire caused by frayed wiring. It wasn't anyone's fault, really. Belle and Ingrid and Ingrid's two cats died in the fire." Belle had been three years old.

Rose dropped into a chair and struck her fist on the table. The

The Conditions of Love

table jumped. Rose struck harder, and tea sprayed out of her mug and fell in droplets on the varnished surface. I was in tears now, glued to my seat.

"Shattered," she said. "You can't imagine how shattered I was."

It was proof of her love for me that Rose opened her fist, her hand reaching for mine. Our fingers gripped, tightened, released, and crept toward each other's again.

"Ruben blamed me. Why had I left Belle with an old lady? And in an unsafe house? He quit work after the fire and retreated inside himself, shutting me and everyone else out, as if Belle's death belonged only to him. He wanted to bar me from Belle's funeral he hated me so much."

Belle was buried in a cemetery outside town up on a hill. Rose went and Ruben held her hand. He cried on her shoulder. When the coffin was lowered, he fell to his knees and swore to Belle he'd make it up to her.

I forced myself to keep breathing. A lot of pictures came into my head: Rose on the night of the fire, sobbing in front of steaming rubble. Ruben grinding his forehead into Belle's grave. Why had I thought Rose was different from other women, wiser, stronger, invincible to dangerous men? Charming and dangerous men like my father.

Ruben had come to Liberty to get back together with Rose, to start again. Whether he knew it or not, Rose said, she was his one connection to Belle, and Belle was his connection to life. "He hadn't planned on discovering you while he was here," Rose said. "He wanted me to himself and here you were, so-called evidence of my love for another man and my abandonment of him and Belle." Her face hardened. Over a beer she'd tried to convince Ruben I wasn't her child by birth, but she could see him thinking: Why trust Rose? Why walk through that door again? Her eyes looked sunken, the rims red and shiny. She gazed at her cold cup of tea and shook her head once more.

I could feel the pressure of a real cry behind my eyes. What was I doing here, in Rose's house, in Rose's skirts, in Rose's care? I felt sorry for Rose and sorry for Belle and sorry for myself. I felt like an outsider.

"You know you're a lovely young woman?" Rose said softly. "How

167

old are you now, barely sixteen? That's old enough to know some things, important things about men and women. If there's any good that comes out of this situation, it's that you know a little more about life now." Rose got up and said she was going out to think for a while. "Ruben's a crazy, ruined man. He honestly believes I had another baby after Belle. That I could love another child after Belle."

I climbed up to the loft, lay down on my fresh pallet, and fell asleep without thinking. It was as though my mind had actually zipped outside my body and did not want to be reached. In the morning, Rose was already up and out, and everything she'd told me the night before seemed impossible and unreal. But when I went to collect eggs, I imagined that if I glanced around at just the right moment, I'd see Ruben peeking from behind a bush, determined to slice open our lives.

What does a daughter know? What does a daughter know for sure? A daughter knows about contradictions. Rose had said, "Contradictions are ours to grapple with, the things that make sense and the things that don't." Snow in the desert, birds that were once gilled fish under the sea. The deaf that made music, the blind with vivid dreams. A daughter knows about contradictions. She believes in her mother's secret life because she has discovered her own. I wasn't Rose's daughter, and yet I was. An impossible contradiction.

There was more. There was Belle. Rose wanted to show me. She placed the diary on her pillow and the baby bracelet beside it. Rose had written poems to Belle. She read them to me. *This cold night, When the timbers lean, Toward a distant moon.* And songs: *Your mouth at my breast, Little Wonder. Ten tiny fingers, ten tiny toes.* The last poem she'd written was dated four months ago, none since I'd arrived. We scrunched up against the pillows, bits of paper—love notes to her dead child—fluttering from between the yellowing pages of the diary. I asked no questions. At one point Rose said, "I know Belle would have loved you." The thought of it saddened and honored me. The room grew dark around us. We could hear the mice scrabbling in the cupboards,

Aunt Francis wheezing in his sleep. After a little while, I got up and made a fire in the barrel stove. The new oak logs gave off an acrid tang. Rose didn't move. "I never knew how talkative grief is," she said.

I began to keep to myself, polite, courteous, dutiful. Birds play call and response, and that's how I was with Rose, the real conversations shadows between the words. For a week Rose let me be, but it was impossible to pretend some change in our relationship had not occurred. One evening after Rose had been working on shingling the roof all day, and I'd worn myself out making lists—would I become a seamstress like Minette and study painting at night? Go to Paris or head west to work on a ranch? Marry a cowboy?—Rose opened the door and said, "Quit daydreaming and come here." In the cool evening air, she seized me by the elbows and led me to the pond. Every few seconds, new stars winked into existence, the sky an account of plenitude beyond imagining. We sat on the cold sand, lonely and together, the distance between points of starlight no more than the distance between a thumb and forefinger. The ringed moon radiated pale fire. When Rose began to speak, it was as though Ruben had never tinkered with our world.

"When you lose a child, you look at other people's children and think, 'Why is this one alive and not mine?' You take inventory, tally up your sins. Are you the world's worst sinner to receive such punishment? Accidents, their arbitrariness, are a humiliating blow. We think we can protect those we love and we can't." I shifted my weight and damp sand splashed up my skirt. The moon went behind a cloud, and Rose searched for my hand. "I'm not so foolish to think one child replaces another. Never! But you're like my flesh and blood now, and whatever else you are thinking, add to your thoughts that Rose will not desert you."

My breath came in little puffs but I was determined not to cry. I wanted to throw myself on Rose and kiss her face and neck and pull her up by the wrists and waltz with her along the beach, leaving a weave of our footprints in the sand. I wanted us to dash into the icy pond singing "Hallelujah." I'd waited all my life to hear those words.

Rose seemed to have lost her voice for a moment, and we sat and gazed at the sky packed with stars. When Rose resumed speaking, her voice sounded hushed against the lapping water.

"Have you ever stood on a bridge and watched a river rush past below?" I nodded. "You've seen how the current snatches things, sweeps them downstream, and when you run to the other side of the bridge, they're spinning away?"

I closed my eyes and saw a child's toy boat disappearing in an eddy.

"What I'm trying to say is that the bridge is an in-between place, and that's where you are now. You're bound to cross over the bridge and move on because life is change. But for now, honey, for now, we are here. And we are thriving."

The end of our pleasure arrived on a day we were at the beach scraping the old red paint off the hull of the skiff so we could seal her with new, waterproof varnish. Rose had taken a break from the shoulder-tiring work and was sitting on a log, sunning her knees and drinking from her canteen. I'd meandered along the water's edge, searching for interesting pieces of driftwood or pretty stones. A whole season seemed to be gathering its forces to come alive and show itself spectacularly for a day or a week before it made way for winter. The pond twinkled with curls of sunlight, and the breeze that had been mild and warm earlier in the day turned chilly. I walked on a bit farther, noticing how the beach was being overtaken by tufts of wild grass and sedges. Something told me to turn around.

Rose had gone back to scraping the skiff and was curved over the boat, sleeves rolled up, and I could see from where I was standing her scowl of concentration and determination to finish the job in the forceful way she plied the scraper. The wind picked up and spun a few rosy maple leaves along the ground. My shirt billowed and I had the sensation of tremendous lightness, as if I could fly. I stopped walking and twirled, arms raised, skirt flaring.

When I stopped twirling, my head was spinning, which made me unsure that what I was seeing was real. Behind Rose's back and inland from the beach, exactly where the shack was located, a column of smoke rose into the sky, losing its shape as it drifted out over the water. I did not comprehend at once, though the smell was unmistakable. Rose noticed it, too, and dropped her tool to pivot and look up to where the cloud had originated, the greasy plumes billowing above the shack. I had already started running toward her as she put her hands around her mouth and shouted my name.

We couldn't get near enough to do much. Flames encircled the outer wood siding—metallic red, deep orange, mustard yellow tinged with blue, like feathers from some exotic bird, the wind sucking them higher and higher into the fierce white haze. The smoke made us choke, and my skin felt as if it were being fried, the hairs on my arms and legs standing straight up. Rose's new roof was bubbling tar, the smell sharp and vile and nauseating. Rose was shouting at me to cover my face with my skirt and keep it covered. She had a bucket and was throwing loose dirt on the flames as fast as she could, her turquoise scarf a mask over her nose. I looked around frantically for the dogs, but neither was in sight. "Get the shovel from the garden," she yelled, seeing me freeze in a panic. "We'll try to smother it." I ran, my eyes full of cinders.

We worked for what seemed like hours digging a trench to keep the fire from spreading. The walls of the shack had exploded outward, sending chunks of burning lumber into the air. Miraculously, the weather came to our aid: the wind stopped and the sky thickened, unleashing a drenching rain. When it was over, sunlight gushed through cloud chinks and mist rose from the smoking rubble. Rose warned me not to go near the steaming boards because there were likely to be hot spots buried beneath. A part of the roof had collapsed and balanced precariously on beams too thick to have burned through. A charred sink and the stove hulked among the ruins. The butt of Rose's J. C. Higgins peeked from under one of the stove's iron burners.

Every inch of my body reeked of smoke, a stink I thought I'd never get rid of, nor the soot under my nails, nor the taste on my tongue, nor the grit coating the back of my throat. I was scratched and bleeding, my palms singed. Rose had a bruise under her eye, and a good portion of the hair surrounding her face was sizzled to wisps.

Reeling from exhaustion, we dragged old army blankets from the shed, which had been scorched but not burned, and wrapped ourselves in them, sheltering under an oak. His name hung between us, a terrible fact. I imagined Ruben sneaking through the forest, laughing as he threw the burning torch or whatever he had used. "Why did he?" I finally asked. Rose held my hand without speaking for several minutes. "I don't know if we'll ever know," she said at last, gripping my hand more tightly. When sleep crept near, I resisted and resisted until finally my vision warped and I let go of Rose's hand. The sky came down at me from all directions, the stars disappearing behind my lids.

The next morning we grimly went through the wreckage, shoveling, raking, sifting, making piles. I was in a stupor, trying to think of something good. Most of our iron cookware survived, dented and blackened but perfectly usable. It was amazing the bits and pieces that did not burn. Somewhere I had read that burned soil was rich in minerals and that new forests thrived where lightning struck. How long would it take for saplings to root here where we had lived and where the last of my precious keepsakes, Sam's sailor cap and necklace, were buried? It soothed me to imagine a cavernous space inside the earth where missing or lost valuables—the cracked teapots, broken dolls, torn photos, bronzed baby shoes, dead turtles—made their habitation, a place where all our losses came to rest. I was not sure the dead lived among these things, but I was perfectly willing to suppose that they did or that they at least stopped in, as if visiting a ghostly pawnshop, to retrieve what had once, through misfortune or error, been surrendered.

Rose took my hand and led me to the garden, where she crouched to examine a seared stalk that had once been a tomato plant. "We can save enough seeds for next year," she said. A slight wind pushed at the underside of leaves. The common calls of birds rang out robustly as if no calamity had occurred. I started to hyperventilate, and Rose told me to breathe into my hands. When I quieted, she pulled me down on my knees, and we gave thanks we were alive. The dogs were missing, but the hens had escaped uninjured. The honeybees were flourishing, and the shed was intact. There was lumber to build anew. We said if we found Ruben, we'd put glowing embers in his fists and make him walk barefoot over crushed glass; we'd let him bleed and burn and then we'd beat him with a broom till his brains fell out. Later, Rose changed her mind. "He's ill. That's the only explanation. He's ill in the head. I'm going to find him and see he gets help. But I will never let him hurt you again."

The next day I looked up and saw a tall man advancing out of the sooty woods, his features partially hidden under the wide brim of a felt hat. He had on a khaki uniform with stiff creases down the legs and heavy black boots. His long arms and legs swung out from his body like a toy soldier's. Rose was sorting out suitable boards for rebuilding. I yelled to Rose that someone was here.

The man came within speaking distance, stood with his hands pushed deep into his trouser pockets, and glanced around. "Where's Rose? Looks like you've had some trouble here, miss. Anyone hurt?" I shook my head. "Well, that's a piece of luck." He studied me for a moment. He seemed naturally soft-spoken, almost shy. Just then, Rose came out of the bushes.

"I saw the smoke from the observation tower. Didn't look too bad, but I thought I'd better pay a visit," the man said. He took off his hat and rubbed the flat of his hand over his scalp. "Glad it didn't spread, Rose, but an incident like this is going to get the Johnston Lumber people worried. I'm mighty glad no one was injured . . ." He picked up a blackened, twisted piece of metal. "But I am going to have to report this."

"This was no forest fire, McGregor," Rose said, cutting through his politeness, "and I'm no threat to anyone's lumber."

The man said, "You've been a fine tenant, Rose, but you know the agreement. Johnston Lumber owns the timber rights. You get to stay so long as there's no trouble." He cleared his throat. "It's never sat easy with me, you alone here and all." He looked at her intently. "How'd this happen?"

I could see Rose deciding what to say. "Candle-making," she told him. "Pan of wax caught fire. The whole place went up."

The man turned to me. "You must have been scared?"

"Uh-huh," I said, blushing.

"The lumber folks have been waiting for any excuse to get you off their property, Rose. The Forest Service wants the land back under federal control, so they're not going to be interested in defending you against the Johnston claim. If I were you, I'd think real hard about relocating." He glanced around. "Tough luck. Is there anything I can do?"

Rose held his gaze for a good long minute and nodded. "Make it so we can stay."

A few days later Ranger Bob returned with a heavyset man dressed in a double-breasted suit too hot for the weather. In one hand he carried a large leather briefcase. His other hand fanned his face with a gray fedora. He was Johnston Lumber's lawyer. He'd done some research on Rose and come to make a report.

He asked us a lot of questions and poked around the remains. Johnston Lumber cannot afford to take chances, he said. Did we know how much money was lost to fires every year? He extracted a sheaf of papers from his briefcase and scanned them with a finger. "I have information here that says Ruben Scully, your common-law husband and father to a daughter, now deceased, lives nearby and has some assault charges against him. Does Mr. Scully have anything to do with this fire?"

I saw Rose's shoulders roll back and her face turn to stone. She held herself very erect and shook her frizzled head.

"So he hasn't been around here?" The lawyer scrutinized her boldly. "You stated in the report a few days ago that the fire started while you were candle-making, but I must tell you, we are not so naive. You've heard of the term *domestic violence*?" He paused for effect. "We suspect arson here." The lawyer looked down at his elegant shoes and said with distaste, "Your relationship with your ex-boyfriend is none of our business, but he is a proven risk. Madam. Do you suspect he set the fire?"

Rose stood even straighter. "My God! Can't this wait? Can't you see we have our hands full?"

The lawyer pursed his lips and turned his attention to me, and I froze under his glare. "Please tell us the truth, young lady."

My mind went blank, but the lawyer pressed on. Where were my parents? What was I doing with Rose? I closed my eyes and tried to remember, but it was as though I actually couldn't remember. My whole body was vibrating. Ranger Bob stepped in and touched my shoulder. "You aren't a runaway, are you?" I shook my head. My parents were gone with the wind, I said. Rose was my only family. After the two men left, a single question burned in my head. Why had Rose covered for Ruben?

"Love's deluded loyalty," she said when I asked her that night. "And because of Belle."

Misfortune was in the air. The next morning, we made a fire at the beach. Rose marched straight to the pond and walked in, clothes and all, her skirts floating up around her like extravagant petals. She smelled of sweat and smoke and desecration. Coming out of the water, she lost her balance and clutched my arm as if all her strength had left her. She said she would make this up to me, then pulled me against her chest and cried without making a sound. The sun was high and pale, and in the west, a faint moon was visible. When she stumbled a second time getting up from the fire, my heart lurched. Was she dizzy with hunger? We'd eaten nothing but boiled cattail stalks, hackberries, and one lone egg. A mourning dove began to coo, its song matching exactly the grave blue stillness that had settled over us.

The matter of our separation came via Ranger Bob McGregor. On a charitable impulse, he brought two bags of groceries, sweatshirts, and sneakers and apologized for being the bearer of bad news. Johnston Lumber wanted Rose off their land pronto; I would be put under the jurisdiction of Social Services. Someone in some agency had done her homework; they'd tried to locate Mern and couldn't. Until she was found, Social Services was sending me into foster care in Vieuxville, a town three times the size of Liberty, twelve miles due west of Rose, and a long zigzag from Wild Pea toward the Mississippi.

It hadn't occurred to me that anyone still considered me a child or that people who neither knew me nor wanted to know me could decide my future. *Good luck finding Mern*, I thought. She was probably in Hollywood by now, her name changed to Zadie Lalabridgetta.

I had been working on a story about my origins: I was Rose's niece, Lily, the daughter of her dead sister, acrobat extraordinaire, who had died in the great Hartford circus fire.

"It's out of my hands," Ranger Bob said.

Later, I lay beside a sleeping Rose, shivering. What if they did locate Mern? They'd find her in someplace like Kansas City, not Hollywood, waiting tables or working in a bank. She'd have let her hair and eyebrows grow back in, become respectable and brunette. When I tried to imagine what it would be like to live with her again, I couldn't see myself putting up with moldy food and outrageous moods or having to listen to the old grievances about my father. The rest of the night I spent worrying and arguing with myself. I concluded that either they'd never find Mern and I'd get to stay with Rose, or they'd find Mern and I'd be shipped back. I could not contemplate leaving Rose.

"I've decided," Rose said before sun-up the next morning. "Here is Our Plan. You will go to Vieuxville and I will follow you. I will get a job and earn us some money and then we will leave."

I shook her shoulders. "No! We have to leave right now! Together!" In the wisest chamber of my heart, I knew Rose would be destroyed living in any town. Like the fox, she wasn't meant to be tamed.

She peeled my fingers from her shoulders and told me to calm down. She was going to do it right this time. She wasn't going to lose another child. She would take care of me, good care, till I was ready to be on my own. With her thumb and index finger pressed together as if holding a needle, she stitched us heart to heart.

That night in a dream, I saw the bees swarming across the sky and woke up thinking about home. Where was it? Home! I finally had one, though it was nothing as solid as even a house of wax: it was a ramshackle construction made of atoms of love. How had I not recognized this before? Mites furrowed a home in the waxy secretions of Aunt Francis's ears, and with patient loving abidance, the dog housed their work. The carrot seedlings on the sill had swelled microscopically toward distant stars and the adoring stars sent back their galactic light. Two ants lugged fish scales across acres of floorboards. In the dirt beneath us, maggots digested the ancient bones of elk. And all this violent seething, riotous simmering, this charging and recharging, this energy exchange, was love. I had only half understood! Love was constantly working change with its terrible, precise force. Love leaped and roiled, rammed against itself, entered and exited, bloomed, died, and was reborn in things. In us! I closed my eyes and saw the sleek head of a mallard among the cattails, the golden-eyed frog. And what would they become but seed and spawn? I felt the breath lock in my throat. I saw how the maple rocker had once been the Tree of Knowledge, once a winged seedling traveling on a cloudbank, and how the clay in the clay pots had once been mere particles of silica and feldspar. My breath faltered. A new image of my mother rose up in my mind, a big head on a narrow neck. She was a child, wide blue eyes unblinking at the future. She was looking for me.

Chapter 18

Lonely Girl

The boy driving the Social Services van had the reddish skin of an acne sufferer. Earl was his name. Sullenly Earl slid open the van door and waited, jiggling his leg. People who did not know Rose or me, people who worked for the state and did not care to know us, had ordered our separation. I took one look at Earl's pocked skin, his stripped-down surliness, and thought, *I am going to live in a place called Sadness.*

When it came time to separate, I couldn't let go of Rose's hand. "Be brave," she said soberly, and shook loose of my embrace. "It's only for a little while." Yellow leaves were drifting down over the ash and mud that marked our ruin. Looking at the devastation made me sick. "When will I see you again?" I said, searching Rose's eyes and finding my own sorrow reflected. "Soon," she whispered, "very soon." She'd developed a cough that made her cheeks look flushed despite the pallor of her skin. The puppy came and licked my hand and I knelt to kiss his head. In the driver's seat, Earl was revving the engine. I slid into the backseat. Rose leaned in and tightened the hood of my sweatshirt. "It's getting cool," she said, and quickly planted another kiss on my cheek before closing the door and backing away. I struggled for a smile. Earl threw the van into gear. His nape was dotted with soft-looking scabs and the vehicle smelled of cheesy, unwashed socks. Rose blew kisses, her face shrinking among the shadows as the van lurched over the uneven ground.

The money Mern sent me, which I kept under my pallet, had burned, but Rose's metal safe had survived the fire. She had some savings, bee money, and the last days we were together we'd begun to make plans. Foster care for a short while. But when we had enough money for bus tickets, we'd take off. We could go north or south but would have to cross a border to be free of the authorities. If we went south, we'd stay with her friend Constanza, who lived near Nogales and sold tin crosses to tourists. Rose and I would sell earrings and crucifixes to the tourists too. We'd find a place of our own and live simply—a goat, a few chickens. Bees. If we went north, to Canada, there'd be as much wilderness as we wanted, and we wouldn't have to worry about bandits, only frostbite and starvation. We'd get jobs in a mill or a cannery. I'd paint landscapes; we'd breed dogs.

We were traveling down unfamiliar roads, bog land overrun with tamarack and spruce. Earl sped up around bends, watching in the rearview to see how scared he could make me. "Cretin," I said. Swerving to the shoulder, he threatened to leave me to the wolves. After what seemed like hours, the countryside turned residential. Sidewalks. Lawnmowers. Traffic lights. Dogs chained to trees. Which made me particularly sad. We'd found Aunt Francis the day after the fire. He seemed to be sleeping on his side, but his face was blanketed with flies: done in by smoke inhalation, Rose concluded. Earl turned left onto an elm-lined street that seemed vaguely familiar—clapboard houses, clipped yew bushes, tricycles in the driveway. It was as if I'd been wrenched from one life and redeposited into a former one, Rip Van Winkle coming awake in the same place a hundred years later. A woman in Bermuda shorts pushed a pram to a stop sign, and I half expected to see Mern trot up behind her, waving and calling my name. Vieuxville was laid out in a grid, the north–south streets named after presidents, the east–west ones named for trees. Main Street cut the grid down the middle, ending in a vacated train depot, abandoned fields on either side. The van cruised by a bakery, a shoe repair shop, and a greasy-windowed café called the Lorraine, pulling up to a brown brick building with two large display windows overhung by green awnings. WEDENBACH'S FIVE & DIME was printed in white letters on the canvas. Earl shifted to neutral at the curb, and I studied my new home. I was supposed to feel grateful I hadn't been thrown into an orphanage, dispatched to live among the damaged and forsaken, or abandoned and left to tramp around in a sordid kind of daze, like the beautiful Paulette Goddard in *Kitty*, but I only felt numb.

Earl jumped out and opened my door. His discolored teeth and pitted cheeks told the story of his own sorry foster-care life. "Good luck, retard. You'll need it," he said. I was unable look him in the eye for fear of seeing my own self-pity, but nonetheless, I acknowledged our mutual predicament. "Good luck yourself, cretin."

A man and a woman and a little girl clinging to her mother's skirt had just come out of the five-and-dime. The girl was dressed in a pink dress with smocking over the bodice and a big bow in the back, the kind of dress that I'd longed for when I was the girl's age but that now made me itchy and claustrophobic. Earl had driven off, and I was alone at the edge of the abyss, the enemy advancing.

"We've been expecting you," the woman said, stepping forward to speak for the family, introducing herself as Phyllis Wedenbach and her husband, Marcus. She was a short, pear-shaped woman in a white smock with a big round collar. Her hair was the color of potato skins, coiffed in a tight pageboy, a style Mern referred to as "the kielbasa." For a moment, we stood staring at each other, and I had the most basic, primitive feeling of doom as she ran her eyes over me, clicking her tongue, shaking her head. She said she knew I'd lost everything, *everything*, in the fire and declared me "a poor homeless thing," just the sort of project I assumed she liked.

"We're your new family and we shall look after you, dear," she said, her voice so dishonestly sentimental and gooey nice, it made me want to gag. I kept my face blank. Her husband rushed forward and asked if I was hungry. "Later, dear," Phyllis said. It wasn't nearly dinnertime. "A snack, then," Marcus said, cupping my elbow to lead me from the curb. Maybe it was the red bow tie and the armbands pushing up his sleeves, or his fat, jolly face, but he reminded me of a bandleader at a picnic. The little girl snatched up her mother's hand. She was pretty in a nervous, high-strung way and alarmingly thin. "Aurora, say hello to our new guest," Phyllis said. Inside the store, the fourth member of the family had crawled into one of the display windows and was plastering his nose, palms, and tongue against the glass, leaving clouds of condensation and snail trails of saliva. "Tooty! Come out of there," Phyllis cried. By the time we entered the store, Tooty had scrambled from the window and was hiding his face in the pleats of his father's trousers. He had beguiling dark eyes, calf eyes, and lovely dark curls. Marcus ruffled his son's hair.

"Tooty, this is Eunice," Marcus said.

Tooty raised his head to examine me, his hand drawing a rock the size of a half-dollar from his jumper pocket. "Wock Peeple," he said.

"Rock People," Marcus interpreted. Tooty had a collection.

"Very nice, Tooty," I said.

Aurora tugged on my sleeve. "Tooty's almost four, and he's naughty. I'm older, and I'm not naughty."

I saw how it would be. Division in the ranks.

The dark wood paneling, the ceiling fans fitted with brass trimmings, the aisles of merchandise—school supplies, notions, electrical cords and lightbulbs, bird food, aquariums—had a strangely soothing effect. Soothing, but also agitating. I saw Mern having a spree, smelling the Jergens lotion, dabbing Jungle Gardenia behind her ears. Where was she? Where was my mother? I shifted my gaze. At the rear of the store was a soda fountain with red leatherette stools parked under a marble counter. To the right of the fountain area were stairs that connected the store to the living quarters. Phyllis led our loose formation up the narrow staircase to a cramped alcove at the end of the hallway, a room blossoming into pink with the switch of a light. On the walls, columns of posies alternated with stripes two shades brighter than the candy-pink bedspread. A lamp with a pink tasseled shade, a pink plastic tissue box, and a ceramic ballerina in a pink tutu decorated the dresser. Even the air smelled revoltingly pink. Phyllis slipped off her Hush Puppies and made herself comfortable on the bed, arranging herself like royalty against the pillows, her bowling-pin-shaped legs ending in oddly dainty feet.

"Every girl dreams of her own bedroom. I know I did when I was

growing up," she said, smoothing her hair and waiting for my appre-
ciative smile. I looked away. The pink room was a lie. The pink room
did not project cheerfulness; the pink room was a prettied-up jail I
quickly converted into a bower of green: walls the green of Luna moth
wings, ceiling the green of the first, damp summer stars.

Phyllis stopped smiling, her vocal cords tightening. "It's very satis-
fying to help a youngster come up in the world. We still get Christmas
cards from some of our girls. They write to tell us that if it hadn't been
for us..." Her hand went around her throat and her eyelids fluttered. I
was her eighth foster child. Her voice lowered, rattling with emotion.
She leaned over, woman-to-woman. They were, she confided, an older
couple, she and Marcus. They'd tried and failed to have babies, tried
and failed until Aurora, then Tooty. Marcus appeared in the doorway and stood stroking the molding as if it were a trophy. Phyllis shut
up and readjusted her skirt.

Marcus's voice boomed, "Eunice. Make yourself at home." He'd
been raised in these very rooms, he said. Tomorrow he'd tell me the
history of Wedenbach's. His grandfather Caesar had built the store.
Caesar had bought the big brass register downstairs with his first prof-
its. Phyllis puffed out her cheeks and waved him away. A girl my age
wasn't interested in hearing about old Caesar Wedenbach and all that
ancient history, and why didn't Marcus just go do his business so us
girls could get to know each other? "Eunice is a modern girl, aren't
you, Eunice?" I raised my eyebrows and said nothing. Marcus bowed
and disappeared, but not before handing me a gift, a small brown
diary with a key attached. Phyllis pinched the diary from my hands,
got off the bed, opened a dresser drawer, and set it inside. There'd be
time for diaries later. She handed me a worn nightgown covered in val-
entines. From another drawer she withdrew a Ban-Lon twin set, not
pink, thank goodness; thick white socks; and a scratchy cotton slip
that might have belonged to a nun.

"It must have been frightening to lose your mother and then be
carried into the wilds by a hermitess," she said, fluffing the pillows in
their floral shams. "I'm all ears when you're ready." A spray of droplets
flew from her lips. I hated her pity. The last thing she said before clos-

ing the door was that she presumed I knew about being a woman. "Certain items clog the sewer system and under no condition—no condition—should you flush anything but toilet paper down the toilet." When the afternoon light began to fade, Marcus came to check if I was okay. He brought a piece of apple pie and a glass of milk. I went back downstairs with him to learn about the business of glacé cherries and parfait spoons and which nozzle shot out butterscotch and which spurted chocolate syrup. He spit on a corner of his apron and polished the stainless-steel surfaces and pointed out the tubs of simple syrups— raspberry, cherry, pineapple, and lemon lime, the mason jars filled with mashed fruits, the container of pecans, the ice cream cabinet. Lifting his apron higher, he showed me Caesar's watch hanging from a fob. I saw he loved old-timey things. There had been sawdust on the floor in the old days, he said, running his hand over the ancient, pale green Hamilton Beach malt machine. His own father had let the business run down, but he, Marcus, was like his grandfather, a proud Rotarian and member of the Kiwanis Club. I heard Sam Podesta in Marcus's boast, but glancing around at the gingham potholders, the ladies' long underwear, the moth-eaten Daniel Boone caps, I knew that this was exactly the kind of life Mern had tried to warn me about, the kind of life Sam would have provided: Rotarian picnics, Ed Sullivan, and gin rummy on Sunday nights. *Normal! Who wants to be normal, kiddo?* Fate had flung me into the bosom of the Wedenbach home, but surely fate did not intend for me to stay. Rose would come, and meanwhile I made up my mind to reject, heart and soul, my imprisonment.

That night the wind blew unspeakable omens into my ears. It had been months since I'd bathed in water not heated on a stove or slept on a mattress with clean sheets, and yet I sweated and tossed on my new bed and prayed for liberation.

At breakfast Aurora sang "On the Good Ship Lollipop," making little Shirley circles with her palms. Tooty watched over his bowl of cornflakes filled with enough milk to sink a tugboat. He ate with one hand clutching a Rock People. The day teetered between sunny and gray.

After breakfast, Phyllis handed me a list of chores—not that I was to be her housekeeper, no, no—but in the basement she introduced me to the washer and dryer, showed me where she kept the detergent, and how to clean the lint filter. She asked if I knew the difference between bleach and bluing; then she pulled down the ironing board and illustrated the proper way to iron a man's shirt, back and front panels first. She showed me the standing freezer stocked with fruit pies and half a cow and told me that a good wife knew the tricks and turns about flaky crusts and cuts of beef and getting stains out of diapers. She was here to teach me the arts of domesticity, she said, licking a finger to smooth down my unruly eyebrows. My hair needed to be pruned, too, she said. Well, what could one expect? I'd been living in the woods like a savage.

The next day, carrying laundry up from the basement, I caught Phyllis hunched over the sink stuffing green peppers, the telephone jammed in the crook of her neck. The kitchen was a small bright room, the walls papered in orange roosters nesting in broccoli trees. A philodendron plant had been trained to climb a wire above the sink. I stopped when I heard Phyllis mention the name of my new school. An interrogation was under way. The person on the phone was pressing Phyllis for details. Something about foster care regulations. Phyllis grimaced and stared into the mouthpiece. Who was this? She repeated the name: Ruoy Esor? The hair on my neck shot up; I did a quick translation. *Your Rose.* Phyllis replaced the receiver into its cradle and declared someone was up to monkey business. What kind of name was Ruoy Esor?

I floated through the remainder of the day awaiting Rose to claim me. *Adios, Senora Phyllis. Rose is on her way.* Good-bye pink room, hello freedom. A bit later, Marcus asked me to help him redecorate the display windows. If Phyllis had told him about the fishy phone call, he didn't let on. We set aside the cardboard back-to-school girl carrying her plaid lunchbox and wearing black and white saddle shoes, and framed the window with rust and mustard colored leaves. Marcus commented on my eye for color and arrangement and asked me to paint a Halloween scene, handing me jars of acrylics in primary colors.

And so for an hour I lost myself in a pleasure-trance of concentration, almost giddy with the thick and tawdry glide of paint on glass, its smell harsh and sweet and alcoholic, like Mern's rum. When I finished the mural of pumpkin-headed witches with ruby shoes, my neck and shoulders ached. I was sure what I'd painted was juvenile and silly, but Marcus oodled out praise. The sun had disappeared in a splash of orange, and my thoughts returned to Rose, but it wasn't until after I tucked Tooty and Aurora into bed that worry wedged itself into my brain. Maybe Phyllis had had Rose arrested. Maybe a car had hit her. She'd lived in the woods so long, maybe she'd forgotten how to cross streets.

After a week, she finally contacted me. I answered the house phone upstairs while Marcus and Phyllis were downstairs in the shop and heard a stilted voice that said she had to talk quickly because we were being watched. "Meet me at the old depot on Sunday morning when they're at church. Be careful!" We made quick plans. I hung up, happy as a maniac.

According to what Marcus had told me, in Grandpa Caesar's heyday when the quarries were still running, the train depot had been the grandest building in town, all gables and filigrees and wrought-iron benches. There had been a tulip garden, a stone fountain of leaping fish. On Sunday, my nerves jumping with excitement at the prospect of seeing Rose, I moaned to Phyllis about cramps, and she let me stay in bed with a hot water bottle while the family went off to church. The world was about to come right again, and as I hurried along a circuitous route to the depot, I felt fearless and tough and undefeated.

When I reached the railroad station, I paused on the cobbled platform to catch my breath. Across from the tracks were a large overgrown field, a tumbled-down barn, and a silo. The tracks ran east and west into a hazy distance. I imagined them stretching across vast plains, winding round and round mountains, spanning bridges to reach the sea. My future was out there, shining and unknowable; happiness fluttered inside me. The sun beat on the cinders between the rails, but as I turned to face the depot, my happiness shriveled. Cracked and grimy, its windows covered with cobwebs, the place was a shambles. Dried leaves, dead flies, a red mitten had lodged in the corners of the doorway; weeds had sprung up around the foundation. With my shirtsleeve, I wiped a patch on a window. Inside, a disheveled woman sat on a bench with her hands in her lap talking to herself. Her hair was frizzled and she wore ill-fitting men's clothes. The woman lifted her head, and the cold, queasy sensation in the pit of my stomach vanished. It was Rose in disguise! When she saw me, she opened her arms and smiled. In an instant we were waltzing around the depot, knocking into a schedule board covered with mildewed notices and walls on which tramps had peed. "What are you wearing?" I said, tugging at her sweater. She was dressed in coveralls, men's clodhopper shoes, and a green cardigan sweater that hung on her bones. Her hair was an untidy nest. She was almost unrecognizable.

"Work clothes," she said, pulling out a box of raisins from her pocket and pouring some into my hand. She told me it hadn't been easy finding lodging or a job. She'd forgotten about things like cash in advance and Social Security. Yesterday she'd convinced George Klinke to hire her at his laundry. She had a job loading the machines. One of the other workers, a woman named Nellie, had sneered at her when she'd come into the shop, declaring that she wouldn't work "with no gypsy," but George Klinke was desperate for help and hired Rose on condition that she wear different clothes. Nellie was an ignoramus, I said, like Phyllis Wedenbach, who wanted me to get baptized and renamed "Grace."

"We don't belong here," Rose said, slitting her eyes. "We're not like them."

I nodded vigorously. I had to start school soon and it was going to be horrible, I said. It wouldn't be for long, she said. All in all, the Wedenbachs were pretty decent, I said. I liked Marcus, and Tooty reminded me of something far away in myself I'd almost lost. Aurora needed a good friend and herbs for her blood. Rose kissed the tips of each of my fingers. Her lips felt cold. It was getting frosty. We went outside and stood on the railroad platform facing into a northerly wind that brought with it a smell of dry earth and creosote. The tracks were a coppery ladder fallen from the sky. Rose put her hand on my shoulder, and we looked up. It wasn't yet midday, but a sliver of moon was just visible through the blue. "Where do you think the bees went?" I asked. In a solemn ritual of farewell, we had gone to the bee colony. Rose had taken apart each bee box and with a light touch swept her fingers over the brood chambers where the queens laid their larvae and over the waxy cells plump with honey where thousands of workers crawled. Several times she swept the combs with her fingers so that the confused insects at last *zizzed* into the air, circling Rose's head twice before departing for the forest.

Now the wind off the plains pushed into us, and Rose's mouth moved against my ear. "We can't know where the bees have gone but do not doubt they have refuge."

When the bell rang, I waited until everyone else went inside, and then I walked up the front steps and entered Badger High School. It was like entering a cage that had been hosed down and sanitized for a new set of animals, though the old odors stank beneath the Pine-Sol. A girl in a blue sweater smiled at me, but when I didn't smile back, she pretended she'd been smiling at a person behind me. A bell rang. Doors sprang open and students disgorged from their classrooms. A male teacher in a crisp white shirt ordered them to stop running. I slouched behind a trophy case to make myself smaller until the commotion died down. Another bell rang and the classroom doors closed. Bells, I thought. We might as well be cattle.

I found the principal's office and went in. A woman was cranking a mimeograph machine. She had purple stains on her fingers. "Yes?" she said, putting on the glasses that hung from a chain around her neck. I straightened my backbone. "Eunice Polestar," I said. "Social Services."

The woman thought for a minute before excusing herself and disappearing behind a plastic partition marked PRINCIPAL. She returned carrying a packet and some books. "Good luck, Eunice," she said, as if she was really rooting for me. I took the books and left. I'd been placed in a homeroom, given a class schedule and a locker full of books, but I wasn't interested in the school. I was a swan among pigeons. I walked down the corridor with my head erect. For the rest of the day I took my place at the scarred desks and ignored the flitter and giggles around me. After the last bell of the day, I waited in the girls' bathroom until the halls cleared and went to my locker. I was thinking about what I would tell Rose about the day. Someone tapped on the locker next to mine. It was a teacher I'd seen earlier, Mr. Dodd, the hall monitor. I thought I was going to get yelled at, but when I looked into his face, I saw my error. He gave me a slow smile that started with a dimple in his chin.

"I saw you come out of the bathroom. You weren't smoking, were you?" he asked, bending forward to sniff my hair.

"I don't smoke," I said.

There was a little hollow between the twin peaks of his upper lip where the razor had missed and where a few dark hairs grew. I kept my eyes on those hairs. It was like seeing a secret spot in the middle of his face, which gave me the feeling I had something of an advantage on him. The nearness of his body made me breathless.

"Really?" he said, laughing, and sniffed my hair again, his head buzzing my neck. He smelled manly, of leather and soap. "Looks to me like you were hiding in the girls' bathroom."

I glanced up and down the empty corridor. Every single locker had a padlock except mine. Was Mr. Dodd flirting? I couldn't tell for sure. Wistfully, I thought of Mern, who could have decoded this situation in a snap.

"I wasn't hiding," I lied.

"I've never seen you before. What's your name?" Mr. Dodd asked.

I was aware that his arm was still braced against the adjacent locker, barring my way.

"Gabriella."

A locker slammed in another hallway. Mr. Dodd turned to see if someone was coming, lowering his arm quickly. The back of his head was black and glossy, like a cat's back.

"Gabriella?" he said. "No kidding? Are you lost, Gabriella?" He glanced at my breasts.

"I have to leave right now," I said.

Mr. Dodd laughed. He was even better-looking when he laughed. "A girl with guts," he said. "I like you, Gabriella."

He said this in such a charming way that I suddenly felt embarrassed for having been gruff. I remembered Mern imitating Marilyn Monroe's walk. "It's more like gliding than walking," she'd said. She was coaching me right now. *Show him who you are, kiddo.* I turned and sauntered off, loose at the hips, butt held high and tight. Mr. Dodd's eyes burned into me until I rounded the corner, and then the heat of his gaze evaporated like water on a hot skillet. I liked a man's eyes on me. I liked it a lot.

Once I was outside and past the school grounds, my cheeks stopped burning. I regarded the elms forming graceful arches above the street. I couldn't wait to discuss Mr. Dodd with Rose. I was filled with questions about men in general, and Mr. Dodd in particular. How come Mr. Dodd attracted and disgusted me? What was he up to? Everything I knew about men came from the movies, which was probably why Mern had dragged us to the Hollywood Cinema, why she'd dished out our much-needed cash for film after film; we were getting an education. The movies taught you everything you needed to know about life and men. Bad men turned good women bad. A good woman saved bad men. Bad men went to war and turned brave and good and came home and apologized for treating their women badly. Men who were good from the start died in battle. Easy women got thrown away. What Rhett said to Scarlett—*I don't give a damn*—was a death sentence.

I didn't want to go directly back to the Wedenbachs', so I set off for Klinke's Laundry. The sky was a high blue. A mild wind carried along the smell of wood fires and leaf mold, scents of the changing season. Klinke's was a few blocks away on a treeless street, sandwiched between Ned's News and Tobacco and a liquor store with a stuffed monkey in the window, its arm around a dusty bottle of gin. Next door, Rose was sorting soiled clothes. She'd probably been on her feet for hours, trudging from the washer to the dryer, bending and lifting, lifting and bending. Or perhaps she'd been standing for hours in the same position over the presser, raising and lowering its metal arm. She had come to Vieuxville because of me, but she could have stayed in the woods. She could have gone anywhere but instead chose me. I strode down an alley to Klinke's service entrance, thought of knocking to get her attention, but I didn't want to get her in trouble. Near the Dumpster, yellow jackets were attacking a squashed juice carton. I crouched against the wall and listened to their feverish plunder and hoped Rose would come out for a break. People passed along the sidewalk, but only a man walking a black dog looked down the alley and noticed me. I waited and waited, afraid I'd missed her. After a while, I went back to the Wedenbachs', walking as slowly as possible, unable to stop thinking about how we were going to get away from Vieuxville.

That night in bed, while I thought about leaving, my body kept remembering Mr. Dodd's hostage-taking smile and the tight sensation I'd felt down below. I imagined saying to him, *I'm different from the others.* And he would say, *Call me Mike.*

I did not see Mr. Dodd all the next day. I asked someone what he taught and was told geography. Apparently he was passionate about the cataclysmic formation of mountain ranges, about earthquakes and fault zones. In each of my classes I sat stiffly in my seat and did not talk. My mind wandered. In biology class I learned I could look forward to dissecting a frog, which would be the prelude to dissecting a fetal pig. Soon, in English class, I would have to memorize Hamlet's "To be or not to be" speech. After my last class, I hid in the girls' room again until the corridor was empty. If Mr. Dodd knew anything about women, he'd wait for me.

He was pretending to read something on a bulletin board. The sight of him made me slightly dizzy. I walked up and he turned slowly, studying me with a kind of transparent leer. "I did some research on you, Gabriella-Eunice. Foster care, right? They put you back a grade, huh?" I did not like the sarcasm in his voice or the crude way he said my name. Did he think because I didn't have parents he could treat me any way he wanted?

"You won't see me around here much longer, so don't get your hopes up." My answer took him by surprise. The next words poured out. "I'm royalty, actually. My mother was the most famous bareback circus rider in all of Europe. She rode Bengal tigers, not horses. Once, she performed in Outer Mongolia, where a famous Buddhist monk came to chant holy words while she was in the ring. He believed my mother was an incarnation of a goddess who would bestow greatness on his monastery. Everywhere she went, her admirers threw roses and garnets and amethysts at her feet." I took a deep breath. "My father was a sword swallower who once dined with the king of Sweden. My real, real, real name is Magdalene, and I, too, am destined for great things." I looked Mr. Dodd straight in the eye. "You may not believe any of this, Mr. Dodd, but that is your loss. I am not who you think I am." I paused. "And now I have to go."

Crushing my notebook against my chest, I walked past the basketball trophies and out the front door and heard him exhale a loud, "Jeez."

Where had all those words about my mother and father come from? I started to smile, then laughed. Maybe Mern *had* joined a circus. Maybe that was as close to Hollywood as she'd gotten. I almost bumped into a girl in pigtails playing hopscotch. She'd been balancing on one foot, the other up in the air as she leaned over to pick up her stone. I'll never be that young again, I thought. I never *was* that young.

There was nothing easy about having to wait for days to talk to Rose. I kept company with my loneliness and otherwise tried to pass the time with Tooty and Aurora. One morning I made them chocolate pudding for breakfast, and Aurora, puzzled and delighted by my breaking the rules, asked if I was going to stay. Later I took them outside and named all the trees in the yard. I ran their hands up and down the trunks and showed them how different the bark was on each, whorled or smooth, shaggy with drops of resin. As different as each of our faces, I said. I proclaimed that beetles and bugs lived under the bark. Tooty put his nose to the trunk of one tree and squinted into the crevices. I said some beetles wore armor like the knights in one of his storybooks. I said the scalloped oak moth's wings matched the pattern of oak bark exactly. All living creatures have a way of protecting themselves, I said.

That's just how it is. Tooty listened, his expression rapt with wonderment. Never too early to learn you're kin to everything on earth, I said. I explained how, to seek water, the roots of a tree reach out farther than its branches and showed this by spreading my feet as wide as I could and lifting my arms straight up. Tooty and Aurora imitated me, and when I began to twirl, they followed, until the three of us were twirling like dervishes. When we fell down laughing, Phyllis pounded on the window for us to come in.

Every night I wrote in the diary Marcus had given me. I wrote: *I snubbed Mr. Dodd and now he's latched on to a girl named Suzanne. What a creep!* I wrote: *I dreamed about my mother. She had a new baby that cried all the time. She stuck it in a drawer but it wouldn't stop crying.* I wrote: *Phyllis wants me to be someone she can dress up and order around.* I figured Rose's silence meant she was planning our Big Escape.

I did not have to work at the soda fountain every day, which was a relief since I was a new item in town and with quite a history; people had lots of questions. I supposed it was natural for them to be curious, but I told different stories depending on my mood or the manner of the questioner. After school I helped Marcus unpack bags of candy corn for Halloween and put up pumpkin cutouts in the window. Phyllis was sewing Tooty's and Aurora's costumes, Captain Hook and Little Bo Peep, respectively. Marcus said the store had to be decorated weeks in advance of a holiday to give customers plenty of time to shop. What was left of Mr. Dodd in my mind was not really about him. It was about kissing and what happened to your tongue and your teeth. It was about what you might say when you were alone with a man. When I tried to imagine what Mr. Dodd and I would have said to each other after the kissing stopped, I saw we would have had a real problem. Several mornings later, at school, I opened my locker and found a note from Rose in the pocket of my jacket asking me to meet her at five o'clock at the train depot. How and when she'd slipped the note into my pocket, I did not know, but nothing was beyond her.

After school I gave Tooty and Aurora their snacks, made fresh pots of coffee at the soda fountain, and told Phyllis I needed a book at the library. Perry Como was on the radio singing "Round and Round."

The Conditions of Love

Phyllis glanced at her watch and told me to be back in an hour. I took a different route to the depot, past a construction site that seemed to have started overnight. The jackhammers were still going full blast. They were putting up an office building for dentists. "Quality people," Phyllis had said.

When I got to the depot, it was empty. I went over to the ticket window and peered into the office. Behind the huge rolltop, a visor dangled from a peg. Above the desk was a liver-colored circle of paint where a clock once hung. I walked over to one of the benches and ran my fingers along its wooden arm. Outside in the old tulip garden, two goldfinches pulled at the silky down of a thistle. Where was Rose? My impatience was driving me nuts. It was unthinkable that she might not come. I went to the front window and rubbed a circle on the dirty glass. In the changing light, the tracks reflected the peculiar russet-green color of the sky. I sank into one of the benches and made myself concentrate on something real, something concrete—the knuckles of my left hand. I could smell the old soil under the depot floor and it smelled of the grave.

I came back to myself when I heard Rose's footsteps and the depot door creaking on its hinges. "Here I am," she said, looking frailer and more fatigued than I'd ever seen her. Against the yellowish cast of her skin, two blush spots stood out on her cheeks. She had wrapped herself in the overlarge green cardigan, which draped over her bones like the hide of a sick horse over its ribs. But her eyes were bright and full of mischief, and immediately I rushed to greet her. She started to laugh, then to cough and put her hands over her mouth to stop herself.

"I hate being apart from you," I said, bursting to tell her how much like her I was—an outcast who did not fit in anywhere. I grabbed her arm and blabbed about Phyllis and the horrid Pink Room, of Phyllis's intention of turning me into a proper girl. I said a customer named Mrs. Nesbit had held my hands and prayed for me and asked if I would consider a life in Christ, which made Rose smile and stroke my cheek.

"I know, I know," she said. Her skin had lost its luster. Her chapped hands no longer smelled of earth and honey but of laundry detergent and bleach. "They're going to try to tame us or shoot us," she said,

193

drawing her cardigan around my shoulders. A damp chill rose from the cement floor through our soles up into our bones. My feelings were all tangled, like worms in a bucket. I felt tears coming on. "That's right," Rose said, wiping a drop with her fingertip. "Let the Nile overflow." I had not yet mentioned Mr. Dodd, and Rose, picking up the scent of withheld information, asked what else was troubling me. "Start at the beginning," she said, and immediately I let loose the sharp, painful, lonely, tender feelings thrashing inside. I told her I hadn't known if Mr. Dodd had been flirting or mocking me, hadn't known how to act. I admitted I'd liked his attention but his tone enraged me. I told her that the nearness of his body made mine weak, that my body had a mind of its own. That I wanted to be looked at and admired contrary to my own will. "What's wrong with me, Rose?" I began to pound my thighs.

Rose grabbed my hands. "Don't torment yourself. The secret provinces of your heart are preparing for love."

"It's insanity!" I bellowed.

Rose laughed, and then coughed into her fist. "All right! Insanity. But don't worry. This Mr. Dodd is only a complication, not a disease. You'll outgrow him."

"I wish you could wave a wand and get us out of here right now," I said sulkily.

Rose fingered the top button of her sweater. It was getting colder, a glassy and brittle cold. Rose withdrew a cigarette lighter from a pocket in her coveralls. The top snapped back and with the flick of a thumb, a blue flame leaped up. We sat on the wooden bench in the cold violet-gray dusk and watched the flame burn steadily. "We're heat-seeking creatures, moths to the candle," she said, clicking the lighter on and off.

I put my hand on her arm. "You're not over Ruben, are you?" Lights were going on in the houses beyond the depot, the faint blue glare of a television set visible in more than one.

"Ruben! That mad bull and his misshapen love! But I do bless what sprang from his loins."

Belle. The Beautiful.

Rose pulled me to my feet. "But your Mr. Dodd is no lover of you or anyone else. Stay away from him." She looked at me with great seriousness, then out the window into the coming darkness. "Klinke's Laundry pays me on Fridays," Rose said, and counted on my fingers how many paychecks we'd need until we could afford bus tickets. A string of twinkling stars appeared above the highest branches. Up there lay the course of our future. I trusted that Rose could be guided by the faintest emanations of stars.

It was time to leave. I was already late and Phyllis would be annoyed. I followed Rose out to the platform. The night smelled of something so ancient it could no longer be identified. A low moon was scattering ivory pellets along the ground. Rose told me not to worry about school or Mr. Dodd or anything else. "Don't trouble yourself. I'll consult my guides," she said, and threw her head back in the old way, convincing me she could still summon the spirits at her command.

Part Three

❧

Fox:
Coniunctio

1959–1961

Chapter 19

Fox

A raw afternoon, the purple sky lowering, touching earth, thunder arriving in long drum rolls—a freak autumn storm. Phyllis was unpacking dust mops. The ceiling lights blinked, and she asked me to shut the windows upstairs. Already water was cascading from the gutters. Just then, the bells chimed. A man entered, sweeping away the blue gloom of the downpour, the harsh weather beaten back by his presence. I was behind the soda fountain washing the last parfait glass and felt the air go electric before I looked up, the soapy stem slipping from my fingers.

I compared every man to my father, my beautiful Frankie, and most paled in comparison but not this one. His effect on Phyllis was probably the effect he had on most women: she dropped her armload of mops, tugged at the elastic of her bra, resettled her bosom, and hustled to greet him. Marcus advanced from the register, offering his hand. The man hadn't seen me yet at the back of the store behind the marble counter, and I hunched deeper into the shadows. A siren went by. The men shook hands. Something solid banged against the display window, and the three of them turned to watch the awnings billow and buck.

The man ran his hand over the back of his dense, wavy hair. His head was large and noble, like the head on a coin, his body slender but muscular, with large hands and feet and broad shoulders. He was oddly dressed in thick wool trousers and heavy knit socks, a white scarf thrown dashingly around his neck. Water beaded on the rough yarn of his sweater. I wondered if he might be a Scotsman or a Macedonian— he looked so unlike the other farmers. And there was something else: he seemed weirdly familiar, but in a way I couldn't pin down.

Across the street, shoppers huddled in doorways. The baker, Meisner, stood with his little terrier under his arm, scowling at the battling clouds. The wind picked up and punched at the brick walls, and above us Tooty started to wail. Feet scampered across the upstairs floorboards, and the door near the soda fountain smashed open. Tooty raced headlong into his father's legs. Phyllis feigned chirpy laughter while scolding, "Oh, for goodness' sake, Tooty. It's only the wind."

The man's brow furrowed. He peered around so that he finally noticed me with a blink of astonishment, his gaze touching my face fleetingly, then again, with more interest and curiosity. I clutched the rim of the sink, trying to compose myself and stop the tremor in my breath. A branch crashed onto the roof. Tooty screamed, and I jumped. Marcus knelt beside the boy and patted his head. Aurora had snuck downstairs and stopped short of the tall stranger to shyly smile at her toes. The man observed the children with polite concern. I studied the swirl of ice cream floating in the basin of a dirty tub. Now the man was sauntering toward me, and the dilemma was whether or not I should look up. I could feel him inspecting me, willing me to meet his glance, but I was stunned, as if a bolt of lightning had paralyzed me to the spot. I knew how Mern would handle the situation. But Rose?

He stopped at the end of the aisle, and I ordered myself to act unrattled. I opened the cold-water faucet and wrung the dishrag under its icy stream until my hands went blue, then ran the cloth over a jar of Horlicks, the syrup nozzles, the valve for carbonated water. I lined up the saucers of chopped walnuts and pecans, counted out coffee filters, wiped the jar of marshmallow fluff. The glazed doughnuts on the cake plate gave off a tantalizing smell, and suddenly I wanted to cram them into my mouth, ravenous for their sugary intoxication. I thought, *Eunice, you've been in the woods too long!* I stole a glance. Phyllis had overtaken the man and was chattering at him, while the man stared boldly in my direction. Phyllis followed his gaze, her face reddening. "Eunice, please take the children upstairs and give them their baths, *now.*"

I had no choice. I came out from behind the marble counter, my heart crashing so loudly I thought everyone could hear. Outside, the traffic was returning, the streetlamps turned on. The sky shone lustrous gray, like wet rubber. If I were brave, I thought, I'd grab this man's hand and run into the street to escape. I approached the children, my fingernails digging into my palms. Phyllis was shooing us upstairs. Go. Go! I dragged my feet, but when I got within speaking distance, I realized he was older than I thought, at least thirty. For an instant, I felt relieved. But the mere nod of his head sent my heart fluttering. The children scampered to my side, and I gripped their hands. It was almost dinnertime, the day ending. Marcus stood at the sidelines near the bolts of oilcloth, holding a pencil stub, waiting to write down the man's order. I fled with the children.

Tooty crawled up the stairs like a baby, Aurora twiddling behind on her tiptoes. She was practicing her ballet. What had I wanted to be when I was her age? she asked. I couldn't remember. I could hardly remember my name. I got the kids into the bathroom, lathered up the Palmolive, and washed their hands and faces. Aurora prodded my lip with a finger and asked why I didn't wear lipstick like her mommy. I tried to explain about the injustices foisted onto little girls in the name of beauty, remembering what Sam had told me once about Chinese concubines, their bound feet as gnarled as famine potatoes. I held on to Aurora's thin shoulders. "Forget what I said. You're just a kid. You ought to be practicing cartwheels, not worrying about girl stuff." Her face fell into a pained expression, her eyes welling as if she'd been rebuked. I lied to her and said my very own mother had told me that some girls needed lipstick, but she and I were gorgeous without it.

"Mommy says you don't have a mother because you're an orphan," Aurora pronounced.

"You have that backward," I said, "but anyway, I do have a mother. She's curing lepers in Hawaii."

When I went back downstairs, the man was examining a teakettle with a black Bakelite handle. He put the teakettle on his huge palm and weighed it, the fingers of his other hand grazing the curved handle in a slow stroke. I struggled to keep my face blank. Every move he made seemed to be especially for me, a sexy little show no one else would notice or understand. But then I thought, *I'm imagining this,* because he was completely ignoring me. I took up the can of BAB-O and immersed myself in scouring the sink. I couldn't catch my breath. My knees were shaking. Get a grip, I thought. Before I could decide what I intended, the man replaced the kettle on the shelf and slipped out of the store.

Marcus shoved the pencil stub behind his ear and scratched his forehead. Phyllis stood in the brown dusk with her hands on her hips, shaking her head. "He's a strange one," she said.

"I thought you liked Fox," Marcus said, going to the door to shut off the streetlight and bolt the lock.

"I didn't say I didn't! I just said he was strange."

Marcus knew better than to pursue the conversation.

Phyllis walked down the notions aisle toward the soda fountain, straightening price clips as she went. "Eunice, your mouth is open. You'll catch flies," she said as she passed. Marcus locked the register and picked up the green account book to take upstairs. The rain had stopped, but water dripped from the awning. I hugged myself and shivered. The man's name was Fox. *Fox!*

Over meat loaf and mashed potatoes the next evening, Phyllis ran on about Aurora and the local photographer's Miss Cutie Miss Photo Contest. Marcus put down his fork and rubbed his napkin over his lips. Around the table everyone fell silent. Tooty picked up his paper napkin, held it over his face like a curtain, and in a high nasally voice, asked if he could be in the contest too. "Absolutely not!" Phyllis said. Boys couldn't be in beauty contests. Aurora kept her head down and scraped the prongs of her fork across the daisied tablecloth. *I'm in a battle zone*, I thought.

Marcus set his big-knuckled, ruddy hands on either side of his plate. "I don't want our Aurora in that contest either," he said.

Phyllis said, "Let's discuss it later," but we knew she'd already won.

While we were clearing the table, Phyllis switched on the radio. Johnny Mathis was singing, *"And I say to myself, it's wonderful, won-derful."* I closed my eyes and took deep breaths. The words seemed uncannily to have been written for me. When the song ended, I was staring at miniature roosters climbing the kitchen walls. The philodendron was lividly green. At the window fluffing her pageboy, Phyllis gazed into the oncoming dark. Marcus was scratching away in his ledger, his feet shuffling in and out of felt slippers. The skin on his heels was dry and cracked. I imagined he climbed into bed next to Phyllis, his naked, flaking feet tucked between her plump pink ones. The Wedenbachs weren't that old, but life passed so quickly! Had they once been slim and attractive? Had they once kissed with parted lips? I was seized by despair. When Phyllis left the kitchen, I hung behind Marcus's shoulder until he finished adding a column and asked if *he* came into the five-and-dime often.

Marcus knew immediately who I meant and gave me a patient smile.

I tried to act casual. "Just curious," I said, and asked why Phyllis had called him strange.

"Ah!" Marcus said, leaning back in his chair. "Any man who's not married by the time he's thirty is strange to Phyllis."

"He's not married?"

"The facts are"—Marcus counted off on his fingers—"Fox is a fine farmer, raises sheep on his place. He's a good businessman. He's trustworthy with money. Pays his bills on time. Lives alone, except for seasonal help, and as far as I can tell, keeps himself clean and upstanding. Some people in town gossip about him, mostly the women. More than one of them have tried to win him with pies or casseroles brought out to his place." Marcus encouraged me to laugh with him at such foolhardy women. "The ladies can't stand to see a good man get away." Marcus pushed his chair away from the table and stood up. "But don't go getting any crushes. We can't have a lovesick young woman around here." He rested his eyes on me for a minute, and I saw a shadow of concern behind his lightheartedness. "What I have to say about Fox is...he's a loner. He has his own ways, doesn't like other people interfering." Marcus held up his hand again and counted off another round. "A loner is someone who doesn't join the town traffic committee. He isn't interested in the volunteer fire department, though he'd help in an emergency. He doesn't come to the Christmas Sing." He held up his fist, four fingers curled inward. "Loners aren't exactly the family type either." He pulled in his thumb. There was no malice or judgment in his voice. "The other thing about a loner is that he's an unknown quantity. He never shows his cards."

Fox was mystery. Beautiful mystery.

That night when I climbed between the sheets, I felt altered. A full moon hung above the trees, fluorescent against the black sky. My eyes kept misting up under my lashes. I'd never known such longing. I sat up in bed and put on my light. The pink shade sent out a sunset glow. I wrote in my diary: *It is a mistake to think he will love me. Am I asking for trouble?* I tore out a blank page from the back and wrote: *Please let him love me.* I folded the paper into quarters, stuffed it under the mattress, and fell asleep wishing I had a sister who knew about love under unusual circumstances.

It was on a Wednesday when I looked up and saw Fox coming toward me down the central aisle. He was wearing the same heavy wool sweater, breeches, and boots. He walked swiftly, like a man crossing against the light. My hands began to shake, and I knocked over a jar of crushed pineapple, which I mopped frantically with my apron. There were several other customers in the store but none at the soda fountain.

Then he was at the counter. There was a rich, complicated animal smell rising off his clothes. His eyes were cinnamon brown, a black band circling the irises, his face weather-whipped and glowing. Coppery hair.

He sat on a stool at the counter, and I could hardly speak. I finished wiping the marble and turned to wring out my apron over the sink.

"I'd like some coffee, please," he said.

I'd begun to swab at the counter with a fresh dishcloth.

"Do you take cream and sugar?" I asked. I was afraid Marcus would see something was amiss and come over. He was across the store, cutting rope for a lady customer.

"Both. Two teaspoons of each."

I bent to get the cream from the refrigerator. He motioned for me to pour the sugar for him. "Two teaspoons, please," he repeated.

I stirred the coffee.

"Yes," he said, and pointed to the cream.

I picked up the little cow-shaped pitcher and poured a thin ribbon of cream from its mouth onto the spoon and stirred it into his coffee. Then, without thinking, I licked the spoon clean and placed it beside the mug.

Fox picked up the spoon and examined it. "The Turks like their coffee dark and sweet," he said, "but without cream. I couldn't do without cream."

I said, "You're not from around here." His voice had an unusual inflection.

He crossed his arms and studied me. "No, I'm not from around here. You're not either."

"I'm not from anywhere," I said.

He smiled and sipped his coffee. "Good," he said. "Anonymity suits us both." When I asked him what he meant, he just laughed and sipped his coffee. I said I was at Wedenbach's because my aunt couldn't afford to keep me anymore, and now I was working to support us both. He said, "You're just like a girl in a fairy tale—no parents and at the mercy of a poor old auntie."

His laugh rushed into me, straight into my blood. He asked for more coffee.

I went to the pot and refilled his cup. The aroma of coffee was the most delicious thing I'd ever smelled. I came back to him and slowly, meticulously poured his cream and sugar. It made me dizzy to watch how the streaks of cream blended into the black liquid as I stirred.

Our heads were very close.

He said, "There are sparks of electricity shooting from your hair, do you know? Ultramarine sparks."

Chapter 20

Salaam, Shalom

My mother always said, Never, never, *never* let a man know you love him. "Once the chase is up, kiddo, they run for cover." But it was too late for me; I was under a spell—consumed, sickened, elated. My life shrank to pacing, pouting, brooding, dreaming—my body, an idiocy of nerves. At night I scalded in the tub until Phyllis rapped on the door demanding to know if I was still alive. When my period arrived, I examined the menstrual blood, thick with unused cells. *Someday this blood will nourish a baby.* The pages of my diary filled with a single prayer: *Please let Fox love me.*

I did not tell Rose. How could I betray the woman who saved my life? What excuse could I give for my divided affections—or was it my affliction? A crush on an older man. How juvenile and stupid and Hollywood! How could I tell Rose I no longer relished the thought of our escape to Canada or Mexico, Jersey or Tennessee, or wherever we'd alight, that I wanted to be with Fox? She wouldn't be scandalized; she'd be hurt, wounded in a way she might not say or show but that would deepen in time, and time was already attacking her from the treacherous depths. A friend of one of Rose's friends owned a café in the Northwest, a small coastal town where, if we wanted, we could wait tables or help with the baking. Eager, counting her dollars, Rose was gearing up for us to leave in a few weeks.

Some nights I dreamed us back in the woods, saw in that forest of marvels the strangely fleshy purple spathes of jack-in-the-pulpit or frog princes bearing gold-rimmed eyes. I missed the songs that night spawned, missed waking purified by the sun. Here, on Mondays I marched off to detested school, its dusty green corridors and metal staircases, the sound of lockers slamming, girls with Breck hair. Here was Phyllis, never mean but always poking her nose into my business; here was the pink cage of my room, scheduled bathroom hours, Hanes saggy underwear. Here was misery and loneliness, but also, consolingly, Tooty's sweet face. And Fox. Daydreaming, I conjured two separate destinies: Rose and Fox.

Several days a week, I helped in the five-and-dime on a sort of "leave of absence" from Badger High; it wasn't a suspension, but a negotiated treaty between Phyllis and the school superintendent, a work-study plan advantageous to the Wedenbachs. This suited me fine. Rose and I met when we could at the old depot, but we had to be cautious. We had to sneak. If the day wasn't too chilly, we walked the abandoned tracks far out into the countryside, Rose pulling her raggy cardigan across her chest, striding headlong into the wind, clouds of cindery dust chasing our heels. The russet fire of the dying leaves reminded us of the season's end, but we tried not to dwell on the end of anything, only our journey forward. What surprised me was that Rose didn't guess about Fox, didn't read my lovelorn blahs. Maybe, like me, she was in suspended motion between the past and future, and maybe she knew more than she let on; maybe my secret crush had erected an invisible wall, one she could feel but not yet name. It would be Rose's way to wait until I was ready to explain, and besides, the news about her was not good. Almost overnight her powers had diminished, her face drawn into harsh lines, her eyes watchful and suspicious. It wasn't just that she was getting steadily thinner or that she was shabbily dressed, but she'd developed a bad cough, and when I tried to convince her to see a doctor, she waved me off. She couldn't treat herself without her *pharmacia*, and being without access to herbs and roots, I decided laughter would be her cure. So I invented a game to chase off the damp humors: *Two years from now I will be; five years from today you will be...* That's how it started, and then we'd whup each other at wild creations. *I will be living in a tree house in Katmandu. You'll be living in Las Vegas and driving Elvis's two-tone Coupe de Ville. I'll be painting the famous tulip gardens in Amsterdam. You'll be a bareback rider for the famous Brazilian circus, Circo Luna, and called the Magnificent Queen Rose.*

The sad thing was, one by one, the things that sustained Rose had vanished: her home, her dog, her bees; Ruben and Belle, long gone; and now me, in a way, deserting her, too, at least in my heart. And sometimes I could feel her sorrow reach out for me like a hand in the dark, and though I hated myself for it, I had the impulse to turn away. Late one afternoon Rose arrived at the depot cradling an orange tabby she'd unearthed from the bottom of a Klinke's laundry bin under a mess of linen and striped oxfords. The tabby was a scraggly, feral-looking thing, but he submitted to swabs of hydrogen peroxide and now slept on her pillow and ate from her plate. For the first time in weeks, she laughed her old laugh, and even her cough's ominous rattle had subsided.

The day after Rose introduced me to the tabby, Fox stopped in at Wedenbach's, made a quick purchase, and left. I was stung. That night I went over everything I'd ever said to him, afraid somehow I'd caused offense. I thought how cruel and senseless love was and swore to give it up. Two days later, he paid another visit. This time he dallied among screwdrivers, scrutinized mollies and an iron bracket, and I was suspicious. He appeared disinterested, but I felt him monitoring my every move. My hands shook sorting the silverware. My breasts ached. I scurried off into the basement to get some clean dishrags, and when I returned, Fox was leaning against the edge of the soda fountain. I shut the basement door, ducked under the wooden arm of the counter, and slapped down the dishrags. Heat swarmed to my cheeks. Across the room Phyllis was holding a carton of fish food against her chest, looking as if she'd gotten up from a chair too quickly. She'd probably like to go feel herself up in the bathroom right now, I thought.

He reached out and touched my hand, probing the bone at my wrist a moment too long. Up close, worry lines rayed around his eyes and mouth, a grown man's silence behind his lips.

"Coffee. Please."

Against my will, I fingered the cuff of his sweater, the wool fibers, like prickly fur. His body went still, and I quickly pulled my hand away. Something was about to happen, but it wouldn't be something crude or coarse. Fox was a gentleman.

"Don't be scared," he said, lowering his voice. "Friends?"

I nodded.

He took my hand and lined up our palms and said I had large hands for a girl, said he was glad I didn't wear nail polish, that red nail polish reminded him of Lady Macbeth. He looked to see if I knew what he meant.

"Murderess," I said.

"Inspiratrix," he corrected. His hands were gigantic compared to mine, calloused, nicked and weathered, but the fingers themselves were elegant, slender, and curved up at the end, like a pianist's.

"Would you like to see some magic? Watch." He grabbed a spoon and balanced the handle like a seesaw on the tip of his forefinger. He could bend the spoon in half by merely concentrating, he said. I blew a rude noise through my lips and said that was impossible, but what was impossible was to keep myself from grinning. He laughed.

"Mind over matter," he said, and flipped the spoon into the air, catching it in his upturned palm. I liked the way he was teasing but formal, mannered but flirting. I felt like a guest at his party, someone he wanted to entertain.

"Maybe I'll show you some other time," he said quite suddenly, startling me with the abrupt change of his mood. Something had died quietly in the moment, his face masking any emotion that might give me a hint about what. I watched as he laid the spoon beside his cup, thanked me for the coffee, put some coins on the counter, and, pivoting gracefully, left the store. That night the rain was steady and insistent, comforting in its monotony. I tore ravenously at the rough peel of an orange I brought to my room, devouring it section by section without being the least bit hungry. Before I fell asleep, I remembered a tale about a beautiful seal that fell in love with a human and forfeited her sealskin so she could be his bride. After a while, she missed her wildness and pined to go back to her own, but it was too late—her husband had thrown away her skin, and the seal-woman had to stay landlocked forever. The seal's desperation squeezed my heart. Tears dribbled from my eyes and I thought of the yearning in my mother's voice, heard her singing somewhere in the vast universe, *Give me land lots of land under starry skies above, DON'T FENCE ME IN.*

The next night, while I was setting the dinner table, Phyllis sidled over. "What in the world do you and Fox talk about?" She was trying to sound casual, but her voice had a decidedly aggressive edge.

"Nothing special."

"I wasn't born yesterday, Eunice," she said.

I set down the plate I'd been hugging. "I haven't done anything wrong."

Tooty, who'd been banging together pieces of cutlery, squeaked, "Don't be mad at Eunice, Mama."

I reached out to him. "It's okay, monkey." My defender.

"Oh for goodness' sake, Tooty. This is girl talk," Phyllis said.

Defeated, Tooty sucked a spoon. After a minute, Phyllis returned to her subject. "You probably haven't done anything wrong, but I worry about you, Eunice. A girl with your background. I don't suppose anyone's ever sat down with you and told you the facts of life." Her voice husky with confidentiality. Being a foster parent was a heavy burden, she said, one she and Marcus had taken on willingly, but I had a responsibility to them too. "You understand what I'm talking about, don't you?" She had moved over to the sink and was decapitating the green hair from a bunch of carrots with a single twist.

"I guess."

She spoke quickly, in a hissed whisper. I was making a fool of myself. She didn't blame *him*. Men had appetites they couldn't control, and I was going to get hurt if I wasn't careful. It was her job, hers and Marcus's, to teach me about the ways of the world, because how could I know anything about anything if I'd had no upbringing, really. Poor thing.

When she finished her rant, she breathed deeply with relief and I almost felt sorry for her.

"All right, then. Come over here and help me chop," she said. She selected an onion from a basket. "When I was your age, I would have loved to have had an older woman to confide in. I had no one—we didn't talk about *those* things." She stopped to wipe teardrops with the back of her hand. I thought she was going to tell me her life story, but downstairs the cash register pinged loudly, and Phyllis straightened as if rapped on the shoulders and glanced toward the doorway. "Marcus, finishing accounts," she said. Then she remembered the uncooked chicken and scooted to the bird, plunging her hand into its chest cavity, drawing out the slithery liver and gizzard, spreading its legs under the faucet while cold water ran out its neck. "I'm trying to understand you, Eunice. I'm trying to be your friend. All I can say is..." Marcus was coming up the stairs. "We've opened our home to you, Eunice. We trust you. You know what a scandal would do to our reputation?"

I bowed my head and let her talk. I thought, *My body is alive, swift and graceful, a cresting river, and what is Phyllis? A lumpen thing. A fat rutabaga with a woody stem.*

I tried to be jokey when I told Fox what Phyllis had said. I imagined he'd laugh with me at her expense, but he didn't. "She has a point. Some men can't be trusted." I couldn't tell whether he was including himself. It was a Saturday afternoon. Phyllis was at the beauty shop and Marcus had a Rotary meeting. The days were colder, dark when I woke up, dark again before supper. I'd had a vivid dream about Fox, a dream so real I was sure it was a sign. I decided to tell Fox, to bring him closer by sharing something private.

"We were in a sunlit doorway," I began. Then in a grape arbor near a body of water. The water was churning, like the sea, only it wasn't the sea. Black, choppy waves. "Then I was sitting on a glider swing in a garden. The sun was out again. The delphiniums were a deep violet blue. You were in a bathing suit, teasing me, but I didn't want to go swimming. I wanted to stay in the sun. I was afraid of the water. I was afraid you were going to insist."

We were sitting on stools at the soda fountain. Fox listened with his head bent to one side, his eyes downcast, not focused on anything, swinging an empty coffee cup by the handle. When I finished speaking, he raised his eyes, and they were filled with sadness. I was surprised, and sorry I told him.

"It's just a dream," he said.

I decided he was sad because the dream reminded him of a happier time, maybe his childhood. I wished I could put my head on his shoulder and make him happy again.

"A silly dream," I said. "Dreams don't mean anything, for Pete's sake."

He drew a deep sigh and nodded. Seeing that he'd hurt my feelings, he said that dreams were like paintings, rich with images, and I was like a painter. The world left its impression on my inner eyes. He said artists saw visions where other people saw only empty space.

I said I knew what he meant. He looked at me. "Really? How so?" I said I'd drawn a lot when I was a kid. What did I like to draw most? he asked. I thought for a moment. "It wasn't like that," I said, but I didn't know how to explain. Then I saw what it was.

"Certain things asked to be sketched. It was like I'd come across a lost family member, and first I didn't recognize them, but then I did. And then I'd want to be in their company and hold their hand and notice everything about them I'd missed for years."

Fox was silent for a long time. He picked up my hand and ran his thumb over each of my fingers. He'd painted once himself, he said.

"What did you paint?" I asked.

He arched his neck and stared at the ceiling. It wasn't worth talking about, he said, disappearing into his cloak of anonymity.

I said, "Maybe you could paint again someday?"

He put a hand on my shoulder, the tips of his fingers hot through my shirt. "Who are you?" he whispered. "Where does a girl like you get her ideas from?"

"Secret sources," I said.

He released me and laughed. Phyllis came through the door, her hair all smoothed and lacquered, and she stopped short, staring. As if I were a swami, I closed my eyes, pressed my palms together, and spoke another part of my dream. "I see a girl and a boy chasing yellow but-terflies through a row of purple cabbages."

I did not say, *This world is a glass egg and inside it is turbulent water.*

The day after Halloween, Chuck Sobowski called to say Aurora had won the Miss Cutie Miss Photo Contest. Tooty had a jealous tantrum and drew on the bathroom wall with one of Phyllis's lipsticks. I found Tooty hiding in the bathroom vanity and lifted him out and rinsed away his snot and tears. "I don't blame you one bit," I whispered. He placed a finger on my lips, the woe vanishing from his face. "Kish, kish, kish, Tooty," I said, kissing his cheeks and nose. The following afternoon I hurried off to the depot, but Rose wasn't there as we'd planned. I waited awhile, and then found a note behind the teller's cage saying she'd be gone for a bit, but it did not explain where she went or why. The train station felt drafty and full of ghosts. Maybe Rose knew why my attentions had strayed, or maybe she didn't. Maybe she was giving me some breathing room before we left. It was hard to know lately what she was up to. But the guilt and relief I now felt was quiet and warm and tender and brought me to tears. I worried about Rose. I loved her and worried about her. *We'll be on our way soon. Kiss the old life good-bye,* she had written.

November was a dreary month, the foretaste of snow without its tem-porary glitter. Marcus and I changed the window display from jack-o'-lanterns and skeletons to turkeys dressed in pilgrim hats and buckle shoes. Boxes of Christmas tinsel and candy canes waited in the base-ment. Fox brought in a book with a dark red cover and a thin, black, satin ribbon bookmark. The cloth binding smelled vaguely of vanilla and cloves. "I own more books than you could read in twenty years," he said, carefully opening the cover. Most farmers didn't have an extra second to read, but Fox was different. "Reading is something we have in common," I told him.

I ran my fingers over the embossed title. *German Expressionism.* The fly page bore an inscription in blue ink, which Fox flipped past quickly, saying the book had belonged to his uncle Matthew. This was the first time Fox had mentioned family. Matthew had taught him a great deal about appreciating art. Appreciating life. He stared down at a painting of a sorrowful Christ. His smile faded.

"When you were a painter?"

His head jerked up. "Did I tell you that? That was a long, long time ago." He began to flip through pages again. I waited for him to say more, but he didn't. We both kept our histories to ourselves.

"Here," he said, and placed the book in my hands, my elbows sagging under its weight. I gazed at the painting. A spotted fawn was bedded down behind some tree stumps. The second deer stood with its back to the viewer and seemed to be guarding the smaller one.

"This painting reminds me of you," Fox said. A moment later, he added, "And me." I could see that it was important to him that I liked the painting and that the book was a more significant present than candy or flowers.

"The painter's name was Franz Marc. He died at Verdun during the First World War. He was very young." Fox lifted the tome from my hands and thumbed past several pages. I stayed silent while Fox spoke gravely, the repressed excitement in his voice seeping under my skin.

"These painters weren't interested in painting beautiful surfaces. Marc, in particular, believed animals were purer than humans. What do you think of this one?" He slid the book back into my hands. A horse gazed out over a cliff at a body of water. The horse was a horse, but it was human. You could feel how human it was. How intent and dreamy. You could almost feel its mind working.

Fox bent over my shoulder and placed a finger on the horse's flank. "If I said, 'Marc sees the spirit in nature,' would you know what I mean?"

The answer came to me without my having to think. "The horse knows everything. The horse is very wise. The cliffs are very wise too. The river is very wise. They're all speaking to each other. Something is about to happen."

Fox gazed at me for a long moment, his face growing softer and softer, making his handsomeness less intimidating, less foreign. There was a look in his eyes.

"Has anyone ever painted you?"

"What?"

Fox shook his head. "Nothing. Nothing. Forget it." He stopped speaking and placed the satin bookmark along the spine of the page and closed the book. "Here. You can keep it for a while." There was a purple bruise under one of his fingernails.

"Won't you tell me what you just said?" I'd heard him, but I wanted to hear him ask me again.

"There's nothing to tell," he said, abruptly annoyed.

I felt struck. Everything was spoiled. The painting didn't matter. The book, the present, didn't matter.

Phyllis came up from the basement carrying a carton of laundry detergent. "Fox!" she cried. "Hello. Hello!" Marcus climbed out of the display window, a rag in his hand. Fox stared at Phyllis as if he didn't recognize her, as if he suddenly didn't know where he was. She stepped out of a rectangle of sunlight and again yodeled his name. I closed the book and held it against my chest, its cloth cover rough under my fingertips.

Fox opened his mouth as if he were about to say something. He tapped the book once with a finger, turned, and walked past Phyllis and Marcus, nodding to each respectively. And then he was out the door, without having bought anything, without giving me a decent good-bye.

"What happened, Eunice?" Phyllis demanded.

"Nothing," I replied. "Nothing at all." But I was wondering the same thing.

The sky was ashen when I woke several mornings later. Frost covered the lower windowpanes. I tiptoed to the window and scratched a valentine and put FOX inside it. Then I rubbed out his name, my brain endlessly replaying how he'd left the store the other day. It seemed now that he might never come back. I plodded to the mirror and tried to see myself as Fox saw me, piling my hair on top of my head, shaking it loose around my ears. I sucked in my breath and turned to view my profile. Small breasts. Nice neck. My shoulders were very straight. I pushed my face close to the mirror and studied myself. I remembered seeing my miniature self reflected in Fox's pupils. Is this what *he* saw? A shiver went down my legs. My bare feet on the floorboards were bluish white with the cold. I was getting Mern's bunions.

I crept back to my bed, kneeling by the dust ruffle to retrieve the art book, which Fox let me keep. Most of the paintings were disturbing. I came to another painting by Franz Marc. It was called *The Fate of the Animals*. It was one of the more terrifying paintings. Beautiful and terrifying, the world exploding, everything shattered—darkness and light, flesh and nonflesh. In the upper left, I could just make out the vibrant green heads of wild horses, their jaws unhinged in silent screams. At the bottom of the painting, a purple boar froze in terror. At the very center, a large blue deer had thrown back its head, the long blue throat completely exposed.

In the kitchen, Aurora was nipping at a banana like a small terrier. She was still in her nightie. Tooty was trying to gouge holes with his spoon into the cherrywood table. Outside, sleet had begun to fall.

"Hi, monkeys," I said, forcing a gaiety I didn't feel.

Tooty raised his head and waved his weapon. Phyllis was rushing around, slamming the refrigerator, mumbling about a shipment due in. There'd been a run on turkey basters and frilled toothpicks. "Aurora, go wash that banana off your hands," she said. Her hair was sleep-pasted against the back of her head; something womanly in her was going unused. Aurora hopped down from her chair. I took her hand to get her changed.

"Eunice, wait," Phyllis, said. "There's something we need to talk about."

I braced myself for another grilling about Fox.

"Rose is missing," she said.

"What do you mean?" Terror ripped through me. I glanced at the calendar. It was almost three weeks since I'd seen her. Was that possible?

Phyllis was terse with the details. Rose was missing from work.

George Klinke called her rooming house, but she wasn't there either. The landlady said she didn't bother about her boarders' comings and goings as long as they were paid up. Rose didn't owe her a cent.

My first thought was, *Rose knows about Fox and left without me*, but that didn't make sense. Rose would fight for me. I knew she would. "There must be a mistake," I said. Cold panic washed through my veins.

"Do you know where she is?" Phyllis said.

I shook my head.

"Well, she's probably run off. Her kind always does. Bites the hand that feeds it," Phyllis said.

It was impossible for Rose to be missing. She was like the moon in the midday sky—you simply had to know where to look to find her. An hour later, I ran to Klinke's to ask if she'd returned, then to Rose's boarding house, where the landlady came to the door in an apron, holding a headless fish by the tail, then to the depot, which was an empty tomb. I ran across town to the banks of Lost River, frozen leaves under my feet, half expecting to see Rose waving from a skiff. The river itself looked angry, frothing over a tumble of rocks, swirling up against the banks. I went to all the places I thought Rose might be, and when I finally gave up and returned to the store, I was sweaty and exhausted, and Marcus, noting my distress, poured me a ginger ale and instructed me to bathe and change my clothes. I toyed with the idea that maybe this was the best solution—Rose charting her own destiny, leaving me to mine, but one love did not replace another: Fox could never replace Rose.

Later, Marcus asked me to help him take inventory. He knew I needed to keep busy. In the basement he opened a large carton with his X-ACTO, and we counted out skeins of wool, packages of clothes-line, jars of Elmer's glue. Rose was probably off scouting out the territory, searching for habitable caves, exploring abandoned barns and wooded back acres. Or else she'd gone to buy us bus tickets, her dollars secured under an improvised turban, like golden eggs hidden under that magical goose.

Back upstairs, I was on a step stool dusting the *Enjoy Coca-Cola* advertisement when I heard a *plonk* that sounded like a bird hitting the window. I turned, expecting to see a mash of brains on the glass. The sun had broken through a mantel of opaline clouds and was sending out feeble spears of light. A figure with her hands cupped around her eyes peered into the dark interior of the store. It was Rose. She was wearing sunglasses, a fedora, and an oversized man's coat. She looked crazy and dangerous. I jumped off the stool, my rag left dangling over the Coca-Cola girl's smiling face. Marcus had gone down to the basement to bring up more stock, and Phyllis was upstairs fixing dinner.

By the time I got to the door, Rose had disappeared. I looked up and down the street. A man was coming out of DiSalvo's Shoe Repair carrying a pair of brown wingtips. He got into his red Ford and drove away. Down the block, the florist, Mr. Choles, was rolling up his awning. Five large crows emerged out of nowhere and landed on the telephone wires, their eyes riveted on Wedenbach's and then on me. I was standing alone on the sidewalk, shivering in my thin pullover. One of the crows snapped its head back and forth, back and forth, cawing loudly. The other crows joined in. The one who'd started the cawing stopped, spread its wings, and jumped into the sky. I followed.

At the end of the block, we turned in the direction of the depot. The crows hovered just ahead of me, alighting on a branch if I got out of breath. Turning another corner, I caught a glimpse of an old man behind a window sitting in his bathrobe by a radio. His teeth were in a glass on the sill. *Loneliness is as common as acorns*, I thought.

When we reached the depot, the crows flew up into an oak tree and sat on parallel branches, like trained birds on a ladder. The sky gleamed yellow gray, a northern sea. Between the tracks the railroad cinders appeared wet in the raw dusk. A coolness rushed up between the rails. I knew Rose would be in the depot when I opened the door.

She looked terrible. Her skin had a sickly cast, though the hollows beneath her cheeks were flushed. She'd lost more weight. She held out her hands. I felt exuberant, afraid, relieved, worried.

"Sick and tired of this town, darling girl. Time for us to pack our bags."

"Now? What's happened?"

"We're finished here. We're not going to favor this town with our presence any longer."

"Where have you been?"

She swept away my question with one arm.

"Where will we go?" I asked.

"Oh, someplace where the rain is so sweet the bees drink it for honey," she said. "We're off to find the old glory."

"But . . . I'm not ready."

Rose removed her sunglasses and stared at me. "But?" she said, raising her eyebrows in perfect arches. "Not ready? For Rose?"

"But" is the meanest word in the English language, I thought.

She came up close, coughing. "Am I misunderstanding you? Have we not been planning to leave since the moment Welfare dragged you here? Are we not a tribe? *Whither thou goest.*" Her eyes locked onto mine. It used to be that Rose could enter my head and read my every thought.

"It's Tooty," I said, breaking away. "I can't leave him so suddenly."

"Nonsense," she said.

"Phyllis doesn't care a hoot about him," I continued.

"That child has a mother, a father, and a big sister. For better or worse, they're his and he's theirs. You're an extra helping of pie." Rose pushed back the fedora and wiped her forehead. "Besides, love has more staying power than you credit. You won't be lost to Tooty— you're the good dream he can have again and again. That's part of the Conditions of Love."

"The Conditions of Love," I said numbly.

"Okay, then," she said, walking over to a bench.

I regarded her unbalanced gait. "Has something happened to your hip?"

"Not a thing," she said, rubbing it. Her face looked clammy.

She gripped the brim of her fedora in both hands and pulled it down over her scalp. "Now. Come sit by me while I tell you our plans."

I went and sat down next to her.

"In two days, we'll be heading west, across the Big Muddy. I've got money for us till we get to Nester's Cove out by the Pacific. Paulette will be waiting for us at the café with jobs."

What could I say? I glanced outside at the platform. The silent rails stretched to the horizon and our future pulling us forward. Or was it the past that pushed us onward? Ruben Scully, Belle the Beautiful. Mern. Dupere.

"Trust me," Rose said, her eyes incandescently bright.

"In two days?" I asked.

Rose held up two fingers.

"Thanksgiving?"

She nodded. The Wedenbachs were going to Phyllis's cousin's house. I was to pretend I was sick.

"We'll meet here. When the moon comes up. Watch for the moon." Her cough started up again and bent her in half. Her fedora fell into her lap. Underneath the hat, her unwashed hair was wound in an old lady's bun. There were more gray streaks in it than I remembered. How old was she really? I reached to pat her back.

"Fine. Fine," she croaked, pushing away my hand. Her spasm had stopped. She spat something into a hanky, wiped her nose and tearing eyes. "I'm all right," she said, and waited until her breathing settled and her voice sank into the depth of her chest. She leaned over and whispered, "Maybe Queen Rose of the Circo Luna will join us."

I smiled and gave her the V-for-victory sign.

"À bientôt, then," she said, and blew a kiss off her palm.

"Arrivederci," I whispered.

"Salaam, darling girl. Shalom."

Chapter 21

The Fate of Animals

Later that night, while I buttoned Aurora's pajamas, she planted a bashful kiss on my forehead. I finished the top button, let her climb onto my lap, and sang, *"Come and sit by my side, if you love me,"* and my longing for Sam threatened to pull me under. Tooty clambered onto my other knee, and I encircled them in my arms. They were like baby animals, these two, clawless, breakable, still covered with fine, pale fuzz. Who would stand up for Tooty when I was gone, or teach Aurora that early beauty couldn't be counted on? How do you explain to a child, "Sorry. Can't stay. My life is calling."

At daybreak, wet flakes fell from a broken sky. Tomorrow was Thanksgiving and our countdown for Operation Departure had begun. Judging from the growing accumulation, we might not be able to leave until the snow stopped, and I prayed for a blizzard. By the time I got dressed, Tooty was at the window chanting, "Snowman, snowman, snowman." The plows had come through, creating waist-high snowbanks. I swept Tooty up in an exultant swirl.

Downstairs, Marcus was cracking a roll of pennies into the cash register. Phyllis was pouring water into the coffee urns, the smell of pumpkin pie and cinnamon buns wafting in from the bakery next door. I hoped no one would notice my puffy eyes, but Phyllis caught my arm as I passed and inspected my face. "Getting a cold? Your eyes look glassy." I shrugged her off just as two ladies stomped in, exclaiming about the early snow, and happily filled their baskets with scouring powder and cocktail napkins. I asked one if the buses were running. "Not yet, dear," she said.

I was folding dishtowels when a police car, flashing its red beacon, pulled up. Phyllis rushed to the door, her face pasty with concern. A short, bulky officer in an orange poncho slid from the driver's seat and tromped over the pile of snow at the curb. Inside, he doffed his police cap, nodded to everyone, his cap squeezed in a fist over his chest.

"What's the trouble, Dennis?" Marcus said, going over. "Storm keeping you busy?" Phyllis marched to the window and cupped her hand around her eyes. "My goodness, Dennis. Shut off your beacon. We don't need a spectacle in front of the store."

The officer smiled regretfully. "Highway guys got the roads under control, Marcus." He drew a breath and stood taller, turning to me. "I got Rose Mecredez in the squad car asking for you. Do you know her?"

I peered out through the streaked glass at the erect figure in the backseat, and my heart lurched. "What did she do?" I squeaked out.

Dennis whistled through his teeth and wagged his head. Decked out in skirts fashioned from the drapes of her rooming house, she'd invaded Klinke's Laundry and demanded fifty dollars in back pay from George, the owner, accusing him of paying his workers slave wages. George had thought she was one of those union organizers, a pinko in disguise. "But then she told Klinke she needed the money because she and her daughter, Belle"—Dennis aimed his finger at me—"had pressing business." Dennis gave a flummoxed shrug, stared down at his overshoes, and scratched his head. "When George started to argue, Miss Mecredez had a coughing fit. That was when he called us." Officer Dennis now looked from Marcus to me to Phyllis and back to Marcus again. "That cough—could be pneumonia, flu. Who knows, maybe TB. She's one sick lady."

A great fatigue descended on me. I knew the truth when I heard it. Rose was dying. Moving into town had killed her.

Officer Dennis continued, but I wasn't really listening. "She's not making much sense. Could be she's had a stroke. We got to get her checked out."

Phyllis said unhelpfully, "Lesions in the brain."

Cold spread from the pit of my stomach. "Where are you taking her?" I whispered.

"To the station. To question her and get her some medical attention. If it turns out she's unbalanced"—he pointed a finger to his temple and made little circles—"we get a head doc." He glanced at his overshoes again. "But listen, I don't want to take up more of your time. I came by because she started ranting about her daughter, Belle, and she insisted Belle worked here."

Phyllis wove her arm through mine. "This girl's name is not Belle."

"That's what I thought," Dennis said.

A snowplow scraped by. Marcus scowled. "For God's sake, bring her in. It's freezing out there." Marcus draped his arm around my shoulders and drew me to his side. Nothing had prepared me for this, not my father disappearing, not even Mern absconding with Nick. Rose whittled down to a crazy lady.

In a slow-moving dream, her long, barbarously tousled hair dotted with lacy snowflakes, Rose heaved herself out of the police vehicle and teetered on the snowy walk before gathering up her skirts—forest-green drapery material dotted with crimson pomegranates—and shoving off Officer Dennis's helping hand. She strode toward the door in work boots fit for a lumberjack. My panic eased. Rose was playing a prank! The whole thing was a ruse! Rose was stubbornly refusing to accept the conditions of her exile.

I didn't have a chance to think through the logic. As soon as she stepped inside, the sad truth shone from her highly flushed cheeks and fierce but unfocused eyes. The truth rose from the sourness of her body, the way she looked through me while looking at me, the dance her eyes did between here and some other place. She came straight at me.

"Are you ready?" she said, and held out her hand. "Why are you crying? Rose is here."

"Do you know who I am?"

She smiled and nodded affirmatively. "Of course I know who you are. I haven't lost my marbles!"

"But what's happened to you? Where have you been? I was worried."

Something caught in her throat, and she doubled over in a spasm—a muffled rumble of packed muck deep in her lungs. I gripped her hand and my fingers came away damp. She needed care. I could feel my fear kicking in, blood shunted from my limbs to my swollen heart.

Marcus returned with a glass of water. Rose drank several sips and recovered herself. I looked to see if the person peering out was the Rose I knew. Rose stared into each of my eyes. She swept back my hair and clamped my face between hot hands.

"I saved you, didn't I? Heard you calling from miles and miles away and got up from the chair in that old man's room where I was doing night duty as a practical nurse. I went right outside and tried to listen with my whole body." Her lower lip trembled, and she licked her dry lips. "Clear as day I heard you, and here you are. Alive."

She stroked my hair. I buried my head on her shoulder and let her. I didn't care who was watching. For those seconds, we were alone together. I knew how much I loved her. Would always love her. Terror was love threatened.

Rose doubled over again, throwing me from her arms, and Marcus stepped in to enclose me against his chest, shielding my face from the view. When Rose straightened, a tiny red star, a broken vessel, bloomed in her left eye. Phyllis and the officer snaked their arms around Rose's waist and flanked her to the door. She was dripping with sweat, her wild hair matted to her temples, but she turned and gazed over her shoulder at me and something deep and true and unspoken ran between us.

Eunice, I mouthed, and her face glowed with happiness and she stopped struggling.

"We'll see that your Rose gets good treatment," Officer Dennis said. "I got a grandmother myself and I got sympathy for you. Chances are, Klinke won't press charges. If she's contagious, she'll be going over to the sanatorium in Wesley County. They'll fix her up dandy."

When she was gone, I stared out the window at the snow falling silently across the darkened storefronts. I felt certain Rose had known about Fox and had trusted I would not desert her for him. She wanted for me what she desired for herself: to live on the wing, to cross invisible meridians, to travel guided by the cold fire of stars. I couldn't think about Rose being put away. I wept for the time that had run out, for the time that was gone, for the time that was coming.

Phyllis came over and tried to comfort me with some nonsense about "for the best." She wondered how in the world a person got that way. I did not deign to respond.

Marcus locked the cash register and shook his head. "She's been through lean times, poor thing."

"She is not a 'poor thing,'" I raged, and flew off down the aisles, snatching bottles of nail polish, boxes of Carter's Little Pills, shower hooks, multicolored toothbrushes, roach traps, paisley bandanas and dashing them to the floor. "Who cares about *things*," I shrieked, "when a person like Rose is being destroyed!"

Later, Phyllis knocked on my door and I told her to go away. Marcus knocked, and I said I did not want to talk. I opened my diary. An unaddressed letter to Sam Podesta fell out.

I wrote: *Dear, dear Rose. Why didn't you tell me!*

I wrote: *Dear Rose. I should have realized you were sick and done something about it.*

I saw her on a cot in a long row of cots, among the wasted and dying. I'd seen Garbo in *Camille*. *Please take the medicine they give you because tuberculosis is a serious disease.*

I could not finish the letter. I got off the bed and went to the dresser and stared at myself. When I left the Wedenbachs', I would pack my diary and nothing else. The clothes Phyllis had bought for me I would bequeath to the next foster girl. Temporary accommodations.

I picked up my pen again and wrote. *Today, the most terrible thing has happened.* And then I couldn't stop writing. I wrote so rapidly my fingers sweated and the pen got slippery. I wrote all about Rose, starting with the flood, then about Ruben and the fire, then about our move to Vieuxville, our meetings at the depot, our plans to leave. I wrote for a long time without stopping. The words zoomed out of me. My hand could hardly keep up. When I finally stopped, I reread what I'd written. It was as though I wasn't writing about myself; it was like seeing a movie run backward with someone else name Eunice as the star.

Before I put my diary away, I began a list of my fears. I was going to have to conquer them one by one.

1. Being alone in the world.
2. Being alone with no place to live.
3. Nightmares.
   a. I'm in trouble and I have no voice.
   b. I'm in trouble and the phone is dead.
   c. I miss a train and I'm stranded.
   d. Rats and bats.

My fingers ached. I'd been writing for hours, my shoulders burning as if they'd carried an elephant. I got up to pee, but in the bathroom, I bent over the toilet and threw up, waited a minute, retched again, then splashed icy water on my face until my teeth tingled. As I passed the children's room, Aurora was sitting up in the dark, her gold-white hair rayed out in angel wisps.

"What are you doing up so late?" I whispered, peering in at her pinched, white face.

"Was that your mommy?" she whispered back. "Did the policeman take your mommy away?" She and Tooty had been sitting on the stairs and had seen the whole sorry affair.

Was that lady a bad person? she wanted to know. Why had the policeman taken her away? Was I sad? Why was I crying in the bathroom?

"Oh, Aurora," I said, taking her in my arms.

I told her that the woman was my auntie Rose. The policeman was driving her to the hospital because she was sick and needed to see a doctor and the doctor would give her medicine to make her better. A car moved down Main Street like a rush of wind, its headlights throwing bars of light over Tooty's head. He lay twisted on his side as if he'd fallen from a great height. I had an urge to kneel at his side and kiss the bottom of his bare foot.

Aurora picked up my hand and inspected it. "Is your auntie Rose coming back?"

"Of course she's coming back," I said, "when she's all healed up.

We'll have a big party with ice cream and balloons." Aurora bit her lip. She didn't believe a word of it. Worry had made her wary. She would never have fallen for Sam Podesta's trick of pulling nickels out of ears.

The next day, Thanksgiving, Phyllis kept insisting I come to Cousin Betty's. She didn't want to leave me alone and tried to tempt me with promises of homemade ice cream and sausage stuffing, but I could not be persuaded. Clucking and sighing, she let me be and pulled out her curlers. Several minutes later, the Wedenbachs were assembled downstairs in their good woolen overcoats. When the door closed behind them, I felt frightened. I was not a Wedenbach and never would be. Tooty and Aurora were Wedenbachs. Maybe they needed me now, but in a few years, I told myself, Tooty would be in love with his grade school teacher, and Aurora would be bribing little boys to kiss her with Bazooka gum. I didn't belong with the Wedenbachs. I didn't belong with Mern either, but even if you despised your family, you couldn't ever separate yourself from them. They were a part of you: the cleft in your chin, the bunion on your big toe, the dogtooth that showed when you smiled. Mern was with me no matter where I went. So was Rose.

Chapter 22

The Farm

Phyllis said, "What possesses a woman to live like that in the woods? And then following you here. She was just inviting trouble!"

Possesses. Like that. Trouble. Phyllis spread her fat bottom on the side of my bed where I lay curled like a fetus, and there was no escaping her stupidity.

"Not that I don't pity her. But honestly! Dennis said they found a mangy cat and a blind possum in her room. Dried weeds hanging from lightbulbs." She pointed to the light fixture and shook her head. "Imagine!"

I rolled onto my other side, away from her. "Was her pet squid in the toilet?" When my sarcasm broke down, there was only sadness.

Keen on showing the virtues of sympathy, Phyllis wielded her hand like a windshield wiper across my back. "You're tired, still absorbing the news. It is sad what's happened to her."

Her. These days even a smidgen of kindness made me teary, but I was unwilling to cry and concede to Phyllis's false intimacy and bit my tongue against the overflow. Rose: sentenced to the county sanatorium, her scratch test for TB swollen to a pink, infectious lump. And on that very day, a cat, not Rose's cat but some other stray, run over in front of the store, the driver braking for a second, scratching his head as if pondering an unanswerable question, then driving off. The florist, Mr. Choles, had stepped into the road with a broom and cleaned up the mess, but the threads of bad luck were weaving a tighter net. I'd pounded up the staircase and vomited.

Phyllis's hand retreated from my cold shoulder. "I'm not the enemy. We're good people, Eunice." She swallowed, sniffed, waited, rear-

228

ranged her perch on the mattress edge. "Always remember we've tried to do well by you." Another pause. "And the children adore you, dear."

I closed my eyes, opened them, shut them again. Outside, the Thanksgiving gale had left packed gray mounds at the end of driveways and treacherous ice slicks when the temperature fell. The sky as we knew it had drifted off to southern climes and been replaced by a vaporous gray murk. Because of drifting snow, Rose and I would not have been able to leave on the day we'd planned, and not the next day either, which didn't matter now anyway.

"Maybe you'll hear from your real mother! What's her name—Alverna? Maybe Alverna is looking for you right now. Wouldn't that be something!" I let Phyllis tackle my limp hand and swing it back and forth, staunching a single teardrop that dared to splash from my eyes.

"What are you thinking?" she asked when I'd been silent for a beat too long.

Though I wouldn't say it, I was thinking of all those years she and Marcus were trying to make babies and couldn't, and I wondered if she'd had miscarriages, or infants who died after birth, or both, and how it probably wasn't easy to raise foster children and have them leave. I scooted my hips a little closer to hers.

I was thinking about the fantastic wishes and hopes we dream for the future, and then *poof!* how that future goes awry. I could feel myself getting all mushy-slushy in an urgent, restless way, and I didn't want to cry. I was no weeper! I sat up and hugged my knees.

"We would have been gone by now. Rose and I had it all planned." Phyllis gulped.

"We were going to live in a log cabin next to a mountain on the edge of a cliff overlooking the Pacific Ocean. We were going to raise Labrador pups and roses."

"I don't believe you," Phyllis sniffed, but I could tell she half did, which only encouraged me. I tightened my arms around my shins and rocked.

"Rose knows witchcraft, she honestly does. But she doesn't practice the bad kind. She can make things happen, though, like she was going to make our trip happen." I was starting to believe what I said. "Only then she got sick."

Phyllis got up, smoothing out her smock, distraught by my words. Hurt feelings crimped her eyes: she had failed to civilize me, and now both of us were failures. She started walking away. Regret washed over me, and I suddenly missed her fat, warm backside against my hip, the way she'd called me "dear."

"It's not your fault," I said, quiet as a prayer, and if I could have unburdened my brain of its funneling thoughts and leaps, if I could have told Phyllis about Mern and Sam and my father, if I could have laid my head on her broad chest...but the consoling image soured and dissolved.

Phyllis ran her thumb across the tips of her fingers, her face sagging into doughy jowls. "No, it's not my fault," she said, and instead of leaving, she walked slowly to the window. "Things happen, don't they?" The wind dove up under the eaves and jounced the metal. Phyllis rested her head against the glass. "I ran away once, over a boy named John O'Neil. I didn't get far. When my papa caught me, he beat me with a hairbrush and, 'to starve the devils out of me,' wouldn't let me eat anything but bread and water for days." She turned and pinched a roll of fat around her middle. "I wasn't always like this. I was slender and pretty too."

The room was dark, the cold world stationed outside. I could see the young Phyllis, her generous mouth and large, luminous eyes.

"I believe you," I said.

Phyllis snapped out of her repose, pulled the cuffs of her smock, and straightened her shoulders. "We're going to bingo tonight. Would you like to come?" When I declined, she said, "Well, then, I'm glad we had this little chat. I'm sure we understand each other now."

Sunday, while the rest of the family decorated the Christmas tree in the display window, I gathered my diary and a few things I'd bought, put them into a shopping bag, and went from room to room to say my good-byes. In the doorway of the children's bedroom, I took in the twin maple beds, the balding teddy on Tooty's pillow, Aurora's ballet slippers set primly by the side of her bed, the winning photo of Aurora as Miss Cutie Miss, Tooty's village of Rock People and memorized the sweet, yeasty odor of their bodies that lingered in the air. I switched on the carousel night-light that played Brahms, the masterpiece tinkling a few seconds before I hustled out and down the staircase, down the second flight into the basement, and out the cellar delivery door into the alley. What dumbstruck expressions might arise on any of the Wedenbachs' faces when they found me gone, I dared not contemplate.

The side streets of Vieuxville crackled with cold December. No one spoke to me; no one noticed the girl in jeans and sneakers carrying a shopping bag. At the edge of town, the houses grew farther apart, separated by weed-filled lots and wizened fruit trees displaying their shriveled fruit. I walked on, fingering Fox's address in my pocket, aware of being alone but no longer feeling lonely. After a mile or so, I stuck out my thumb and an auctioneer called the Colonel, his face halved by a sandy handlebar mustache, pulled over. The countryside dipped and rolled as his truck labored up a hill, then descended through a boggy area of tamaracks and alders, the gold-leafed willows catching the last strings of sunlight. "Thought I knew all the farms around here," the Colonel said, glancing back and forth across the road. "Not the best tillable land. Bet your farmer bought his property for a song. Can't make much off of it, I'd say."

Fox's farm was on an isolated road. I had the Colonel drop me off at the bottom of a gravel drive that sloped up toward the house. The farm itself wasn't visible, but sheep bells and bleating rang out in the distance. A dog gave a series of quick, piercing barks, then stopped. I unhooked the cattle gate, my knees buckling with nerves, and walked the short distance to the farmhouse, kicking pebbles into my shoes. The animals had gone silent, as if honoring the whispery purr of wind.

In the diminishing light, the place appeared vacated. A fence with a spring-latched gate separated the house yard from the barnyard. Between islands of snow, the trodden lawn shone with bare packed soil. The farmhouse, framed by towering evergreen, was unassuming, common, ornamented with a wide front porch and not much else. I walked around the side of the house, past a hedge of lilacs to the outbuildings—a woodshed, a larger structure that had a tractor parked in front of it, and up a slight grade, a peaked barn. A scythe with a blade like a slice of moon leaned against the back door. Fox's mud boots stood next to it. The boots seemed friendly.

The dog showed himself first, low to the ground, less a dog than a primitive hunter, his ice-blue eyes fixed on prey. Fox appeared a minute behind him in a lumber jacket, the sleeves rolled up. They'd come from the barn. Fox's hair was ticked with hay; a dirty towel hung over his shoulders. He ordered Richard the dog to sit.

"You?" he said, staring at my shopping bag.

"Me!" I could hardly breathe but searched for a line from a movie, trying for Mae West's husky voice. "I'm no angel."

"Look," Fox said, unamused, "I can't talk right now. One of my ewes is lambing out of season. She's in trouble." He was all business, no flirtation in his voice. He pulled the towel streaked with blood from his neck and wiped his hands. But I didn't care about the ewe. I was waiting for some kind of fuse to ignite. I needed to believe some sparks still existed. I needed to know if it was over between us.

"I'll leave," I said, without moving.

Fox scowled and rubbed his thumb over his lip. "I didn't say that. But, look, I have an emergency here. Have you ever seen an animal give birth?"

I shook my head. "I've been around animals, though. I could help."

"Look," Fox said, returning to me, adopting an expression of impatience. "Katrina's in the barn. I can't leave her. If you want to stay, go in the back door." He pointed to some steps. "In the mudroom, you'll find boots, work gloves, and a jacket you can wear." To my relief, he smiled, a long, genuine smile. "You're not dressed very warmly, are you?" he said, pinching my sweater between his fingers. I looked down at the loosely woven knit, glad he was taking an interest.

"Leave your shopping bag in the house. I'll put you to work."

"I'm not afraid of work," I said.

He was walking away. "Hurry," he said.

*   *   *

I did not spend one unnecessary second in the house, but my immediate impression was one of order. The dishes had been washed and stacked on a drain board; the worn linoleum was clean of crumbs. A pair of wire reading glasses sat folded on a stack of books. Sharpened pencils and a clean notepad were laid out next to the books. I found Fox's jacket and boots. The rubber flapped around my calves as I ran, exhilarated, across the path between the back of the house and the barn, almost losing my balance on the narrow river of ice threading the passage. The moon only faintly revealed itself, a silver half-disk shifting through clouds.

With a big heave, the heavy-planked barn door slid along its track, and then I was inside a cavernous space, the barn's interior vaulting skyward, last light falling in splinters through chinks in the boards. The air was heavy with a mash of mildew and urine, hay mixed with some mineral smell. Blood. Toward the middle of the barn stood rusted stanchions, the stalls like cells without doors.

Fox was in the birthing pen, a small enclosed area, about four by five, reinforced with slatted sides. A workman's trouble light cast a hazy yellow circle over Fox and Katrina, who lay on her side on a pillow of hay, panting, wheezing, heaving, foam at her lip. Even in the poor light, her tongue looked a deep purple color, almost black. A space heater, its coils glowing orange-red, drew off the bone-chilling dampness of the limestone foundation.

"She's having a difficult time," Fox said when he heard the pen open. "She hasn't made much progress. I'm going to have to help her." He removed his hands from her flanks and rose on one knee to turn and look at me. Katrina tried unsuccessfully to twist her upper body to see who had just entered, but her body writhed and thumped as she rode a contraction, and her head fell backward into the hay. The air held a tang of something acid and bitter but not disgusting, not rank or decayed.

Mucus dribbled from between the ewe's hind legs, the thickened tissue red and swollen. "Go and wash your hands and all the way up your arms," Fox said. "There's a tap in the back. Use the brown soap."

I did as I was told, hay dust making me sneeze as I trooped to the sink at the far end of the barn, away from the lambing pen, next to a makeshift bedroom, a cot covered with a cotton print spread and a crate table. A steel razor peeked from a cup by the faucets. Drying my hands, I heard Katrina's grunts, and by the time I got back to the pen, Fox was anointing his hands with baby oil, crooning to Katrina as if to a distraught child: "You've done this before, my girl. Come on, now, be a good girl." At the next contraction, he knelt between her legs, one arm disappearing into her body as she strained against it, her bleats, wheezy and urgent, with panic trapped inside. I felt sick. "Will it be much longer?" I asked. How much longer could it last—Katrina's confused body flapping in pain? "All right, easy now. Easy, girl," Fox coached, too busy to consider my question.

I squatted by Katrina's face, trying to read her eyes. "Katrina, Kat-er-in-a," I sang. Fox waited for the next contraction to pass, then spoke quickly: the lamb was trying to get down the birth canal but was jammed in at an odd angle. "Shoulders too big. One leg tucked up under the body." He withdrew his arm, coated with goo, and sat back on his heels. Bits of hay and dirt lodged in the creases along his neck. Wind and sun had burnished his skin, but there were serious shadows under his eyes. Katrina convulsed in a contraction, and Fox was again between her legs catching the small hoof poking out from the pelvic opening, grasping the slick appendage and giving two hard pulls, his neck muscles rigid with the strain: the lamb was stuck.

"They're both tiring," he said, rocking back onto his bottom again. We watched the tiny hoof emerge from the horribly bashed-up vagina: emerge, retreat, sucked back up into its mother's womb. Fox's hand slithered inside. Katrina flared her lips and twisted her head to stare at her own rear end, and when the hoof appeared again, Fox gave a furious yank. Katrina's entire torso jerked upward, and Fox pulled again and brought forth a leg and shoulder, sweat breaking out on his forehead, his words accelerating with the birth. "Good girl, good girl. Don't quit."

With his other arm he reached for a small hacksaw I had not seen nearby, and in a few strokes—a monstrous sawing sound—he severed the lamb's front limb at the shoulder and threw it in a pile of hay. Immediately he pushed the lamb back up the birth canal, repositioned it with a twist, and delivered a creature in a milky sac no bigger than a wild hare.

Moving quickly, cautiously, talking to himself, sweet-talking to Katrina, his steps soundless on the straw, he placed the birthed lamb in a pile of towels, folded the towels over the creature's muzzle, and held them as a red stain soaked through the cotton.

A cry rose in my throat.

"Katrina wouldn't have let it nurse. She would have butted it away." Fox said this without apology and set the clump of towels outside the pen, returning to Katrina to disinfect and iodine this and that part. The towels lay next to the hacksaw on the barn floor, the blood already changing from bright red to black. There was no movement under them. None.

Fox saw me looking. "A dead lamb isn't a catastrophe," he said. "Especially if it's deformed. The ewe doesn't care, and she can have others." I glanced at Katrina's expressionless face, which bore no evidence of any human feeling, the strange yellow eyes with their strange horizontal pupils, and I felt revulsion, something I'd never felt about any of Rose's animals. A vision of the little fox swam toward me, how we'd flirted and teased, and I thought of Rose and how she would be waiting for me now. My heart gave a little squeeze. I longed to help her escape from the sanatorium, but she needed their medicine. She needed more than the love I could give her.

Fox was rolling down his shirtsleeves. "Listen, you should know this. Death happens all the time on a farm. You get used to it."

As if in concert, bleats from the pasture raised in pitch. How long had the sheep needed attention? Babies whining. "It's time for their feeding," Fox explained. The weariness around his eyes looked deeper than fatigue, more permanent. He cut the twine on a bale of hay and spread it around Katrina. "Stay with her while I feed the others. It won't take long." Come get him if Katrina seemed in trouble, he said.

"Trouble," I repeated, trying my best not to let my own need show. Now that the birth was over, he'd soon be asking me questions. Why had I come? *If he lets me stay,* I thought, *I'll change his life.*

Fox stooped to pick up the hacksaw and the dead lamb in the towels, which he held against his chest like a papoose. "Be good company for Katrina while I dispose of this," he said, his mind surfacing from the ewe for a moment to take me in. "You'll be okay?" I looked into Katrina's dull eyes.

"Fine," I said, and pushed some straw into a mound to sit upon. Fox opened the barn door, and Richard bounded in, chasing two hens who'd flown down from their roosts to quarrel over globs of placenta. Fox shooed the dog out into the night. Richard was an obedient hound, but for some reason I didn't like him.

"Go ahead," I said. "I'll wait here with Katrina until you get back." *He's testing me,* I thought. *He wants to know if I can handle his world.*

When the barn door rolled shut, I was enclosed in the dark with the sound of my breath. Beyond the wooden walls, Fox was calling in the sheep. "Come on, girls. Come on, now." An old tune came into my head. *Hey nonny nonny nonny. Hey nonny nonny no.* It was just a tune and didn't mean anything, but I couldn't stop singing it. I sang it to myself and to Katrina. Nonny nonny. Hey nonny nonny no. The stillness deepened. Katrina did not blink. Her tail twitched once; that was all.

When I awoke, Fox was in the loft forking hay, his arms swinging rhythmically in an arc, his shadow mimicking his actions. The hay fell down the chute, landing in soft *thunks*. Fox had spread a blanket over me. I threw it off and picked at the straw in my hair. My lungs felt heavy. Two barn swallows—or were they bats?—whizzed under the rafters, something panicky in their flight.

Fox's silhouette stopped moving. *Katrina the ewe must be dead,* I thought. *It's so quiet.* But I saw, in the sunless light, the pale hump of her rib cage rising and falling. Fox climbed backward down the ladder. He was freshly shaven, his wet hair combed straight back. He'd changed his shirt.

"You must have been very tired," he said, offering his hand to help me up. It was the most natural thing in the world that in my weariness and disorientation, I should slip my arms around Fox's waist and kiss him. His hand came up to brace my neck so that I couldn't look away, but he did not kiss me back. He swept a finger over my lips, his eyes a dark opacity. I stood on tiptoe not knowing what I was going to do but doing it anyway, no holding back, tired of holding back, tired of obedience to anything but the impossible, staggering urge to forget everything and feel the wet silkiness of his lips against my lips.

And then the heels of his palms were on my shoulders and he was pushing me away.

"Whoa!" he said.

I felt slapped, knocked down by shame and humiliation. "Please?" I said. When he didn't answer: "I hate you." I could smell his sweat on me, his animal smell. *I have become an animal*, I thought. *I have an animal's appetite.* I could track Fox like a bloodhound now, pick him out blindfolded in a room of a hundred men.

His eyes were shrouded and grave. He pushed me away but held on to my shoulders. "You don't know what you're doing," he said. And, more kindly, "You're not thinking. Something happened to you. But this won't settle it, whatever it is."

"What do you know?" I spat.

"I know it's been a trying afternoon. I know you're exhausted. You can tell me about why you left the Wedenbachs' tomorrow."

I wanted to say, *Remember when you told me I had sparks in my hair?* The moon shone through the high loft window with a terrible silver glow that seemed to break apart on the barn floor. I shut my eyes against such dangerous signs.

"You haven't eaten," he said.

"I don't care about eating. What's going to happen?" It was a big, wide-open question.

"I'm going to feed you—that's what's going to happen." He took my arm and fondled the protruding bone on the outside of my wrist. "Little ulna," he said. Katrina erupted in a snore, and we laughed.

"How come you know so much about bones?"

"I studied anatomy."

"When?"

"When I studied art." Moonlight cut his face into colorless geometric shapes. "That's enough questions." He took my face in his hands and kissed my nose.

I moved to press against him again, but he put his hand on my chest to stop me. "No," he said, but I could tell he wasn't completely sure of himself. A bird stitched through the barn's high lightless dome, a strand of hay in its beak. "There's a fable about why swallows have clipped tails, but I can't recall it now," Fox muttered.

My mouth tasted of tin. *Do you want me or not?* I thought.

"I wasn't a serious artist," he said. "I lived that life before you were even born." He laughed in a sad sort of way. I didn't like being reminded of my age.

"I'm the proverbial cat with nine lives. I'm on my tenth life right now," he said, and laughed again.

We left the sleeping Katrina on her clean hay, then closed in the chickens to roost.

Outside, Fox placed a hand on the small of my back, its warmth like lavish praise. At the machine shed, he stopped to point out the Dipper, the Hunter, the Dog Star, Venus in the northern sky, starlight raking through our hair. I recalled the nights by the pond, Rose calling out the constellations, and the pain of her absence sprang alive. The sky swelled and stretched and deepened as I peered up into infinity, and I told myself I was no longer that Eunice. I had closed a door and walked away. *This is what a snake must feel at the first splitting of its old skin*, I thought.

Chapter 23

The Troublesome Body

He held open the back door, handing me the plastic slop buckets carried in from the yard. We rinsed them in the utility sink, stacked them in a corner, hung our jackets on pegs. My new life!

Fox rolled up his sleeves and washed with a bar of strong-smelling soap. When he finished, he levered his head beneath the faucet and drank from the running stream. "Thirsty?" he asked, and I drank icy well water from his palms. Every action implied a hidden meaning: the way he examined his fingers, scrubbing each nail with a hard-bristled brush; the way a single droplet of water clung to his eyelash; the way well water tasted from the cup of his hands. There was something dreamlike and unreal about the slowness of each moment, a dream I was inside of and outside of, watching. Nothing was as I had expected, and yet the unfolding moments seemed destined, as if a script had been written and we were playing our roles.

"Did you bring warmer clothes?" Fox asked, glancing at my shopping bag.

"Only what I'm wearing." Baggy brown sweater. Blue jeans. White socks.

Fox searched through the bench under the pegs and found a pair of bedroom slippers, flannel with broken backs, and put them into my hand. His face looked happier now, more relaxed, and I tried to guess what he was thinking. He touched my cheek with the back of his hand, but our eyes skirted away, and I struggled not to show what I was really feeling.

"I have a few things to finish up." He pointed to a battery charger on the top shelf of the mudroom. A truck needed recharging. "Be back shortly," he said, and carried the battery charger outside. I watched him veer toward the machine shed, a stiff westerly wind grabbing at his hair, and I thought maybe the bad and scary things from my past could be buried here on Fox's farm along with Katrina's dead lamb.

The kitchen smelled of coffee grounds, old dog, and old house, stale cooking oil and chimney smoke imprinted in its walls. The linoleum's forgettable pattern was spotted by time; the plaid wallpaper barely covered cracks in the plaster. An old-fashioned stove was fitted with iron grates crouching over the burners like fat spiders. Here, a screwdriver with a see-through red handle; there, a spindle holding receipts. Fox's wire rims. I unfolded the stems, hooked them over my ears, and studied the magnified creases in my hand, then, still wearing his spectacles, rummaged through his pile of books: sheep management, a biography of Abraham Lincoln, a small book of poetry, the binding coming unglued. The book fell open to a page marked by a crisp maple leaf. *Weep not, child, Weep not, my darling, With these kisses let me remove your tears.*

"What have you found there?" Fox said, making me jump.

I slammed the book and put it down as if I'd been caught reading his mail. The tips of my fingers were white. Fox kept his house stone-cold.

He came over, trailing a vapor of crankcase oil and winter cold, and picked up the book. "Did you learn Whitman in school?" The mention of school made my skin prickle. I wished he'd stop referring to my age. "Probably they teach the patriotic Whitman. 'O Captain! My Captain!' or 'When Lilacs Last in the Dooryard Bloom'd'? The other Whitman is dangerous." He opened the book and read, his voice not teacherly but deeply hypnotic. *"The sleepers are very beautiful as they lie unclothed."*

When he finished, something unnamable had been stripped away from his face, the lines on his forehead and around his eyes relaxing. "Whitman the lover," he said, but before I had the chance to respond, he slipped into the pantry and returned with a glass of amber liquor and a small picnic of crackers and smoked ham wrapped in a red linen napkin. I realized I was starving.

"I read poetry," he said, "to find the truth I didn't know I needed to know." Holding the whiskey to his chest and closing his eyes, he quoted: *"All goes onward and outward... and nothing collapses, and to die is different from what any one supposed, and luckier."*

"Beautiful, isn't it? And what if it were true?" There was a catch in his voice, which he cleared with a little cough. I almost told him then about Mr. Tabachnik, who'd taught me to love books and who used to say, "Cisskala, books are maps. Wherever you want to go, a book can take you." What would Mr. Tabachnik say about Fox and me? *What's a grown man doing with a little girliechek like you?*

I followed Fox out of the kitchen and into the dining room, where a series of watercolors of brightly plumed birds in thin black frames hung on the wall facing the windows. A fieldstone fireplace dominated the living room. Next to it stood a wooden elephant encrusted with bits of colored glass and carrying a tray on its back. There were more paintings, small, dark landscapes. A disturbing picture of a tiny, pale swimmer easily unnoticed, lost among turbulent waves. All were done by Fox, I assumed.

"It's late, but not too late for a fire," Fox said, wadding newspaper.

I looked around. Bookcases lined two of the three walls. Fox excused himself and returned with kindling, breaking the larger branches over his knee.

"What are you smiling about?" he asked.

"It's a secret," I said, lighthearted, aware of a keen sense of rightness about being with Fox.

"Secrets already!" He struck a match, and the newspaper exploded into flame. "I have to warn you, I don't like secrets." Fox handed me a cracker, watching as I ground the wheat and oversalty ham to a paste. "Take some," he said, and held the glass of whiskey to my lips, the fumes harsh and bracing, rushing up my nostrils. I took a sip. Straight whiskey tasted nothing like Mern's rum and Cokes. I laid my head against the back of the couch, daring to let myself dream of touching him, the threat and temptation. Evening's deep blue saturated the walls. Fox drank some whiskey, and with his other hand reached to finger my hair.

The room looked unearthly beautiful, the jeweled elephant lit by the fire, the dance of shadows across the wall. My eyelids grew heavy. A stone rolled away, and I tumbled into sleep's weightless chamber, but seconds later, the peace was interrupted. I sat bolt upright, knocking the crackers and ham to the floor. The lamb had come to me, hunching its way forward on three legs, dragging its bloody eviscerated shoulder, demanding a reason.

"Why did you kill the lamb?"

Fox reached for the whiskey glass and drank a long draught, considering my alarmed face. He spoke calmly, each word weighed out to reassure. "I killed the lamb out of respect."

"Respect!"

"A crippled lamb, a crippled anything, wouldn't last a day around here." He swirled what was left of the whiskey.

"Yes, but you killed it!"

"I had a purpose. To save the ewe. Katrina would have died from a difficult labor."

"But how can you act as if nothing happened?" How many times had he done the same thing? With a mallet to the skull, an injection in a vein?

He held up the glass and drank the last dregs. "I'm not unfeeling, but I am practical. Every farmer has to be. The damaged don't survive. Period. Law of nature."

"You're heartless," I said. What I was really thinking was that Rose would have saved the lamb. She'd have fashioned an artificial leg and nursed it herself. All the things I loved about her flooded into my mind. I was seeing a side of Fox I didn't like.

"I told you, you'll get used to it," he repeated, irritated.

I tried to gauge what he meant by "you'll get used to it." Did that mean I could stay? I rose unsteadily and paced in front of the fireplace, my mind fuzzy and disturbed. Living with Fox might not be perfect after all. I needed a cigarette. Despite being Mern's daughter, I didn't smoke, but now I craved tobacco. "I'd like a cigarette, please, if you have one."

My question broke the ice, and Fox laughed. "Mine are probably stale." He went into the kitchen and I heard him opening drawers. He returned with a pack of Chesterfields, lit one, and handed it to me. I held it stylishly to my lips.

"Listen, you weren't wrong to come here," he said, gentle again. "You can stay tonight. I'll call Marcus later to explain." He looked tired, the glimmer of stubble on his chin. "Are you enjoying that cigarette?" He nodded at the cylindrical ash about to drop on the floor. My hand started to shake and the ash collapsed into the waiting ashtray of his hand. He took what was left of the cigarette and threw it in the fire. He had not said *I'll call Marcus later and make arrangements to take you back.*

A burst of air in one of the logs made us both start. Fox got up to stamp out the spray of embers on the floor and bank the fire for the night. The living room grew gloomy and cold. "You must be sleepy," he said. The evening was ending and he'd not attempted a single kiss. What was the problem? What was holding him back?

"Watch your step," he said at the bottom of the stairs. "These have a steep rise." The treads were uncarpeted, the banister rickety; each rise had a metal lip.

The top of the stairs opened to a small landing, big enough for a table and lamp and four doors. One door led to a bathroom, one to Fox's room, one to a spare bedroom Fox used for storage, and the last to the room I would sleep in, his study. He opened the door. An iron-framed bed painted white was pushed against the wall: more shelves with more books, a leather reading chair, a small desk, and a night table. "Go in," he said. "I'll get you something to sleep in." A draft flowed from under the window sashes. He left me standing in the middle of the room, reentering an instant later with a man's pajama top, striped cotton, wrinkled but clean. He handed it to me.

"Thank you," I said, with formality.

He wouldn't wake me in the morning. I was to help myself to breakfast; both of us were tense and polite.

"Would you please leave on a hall light?" I asked, realizing the moment I said it how childish I sounded, and waved him away. He opened a drawer in the night table and handed me a flashlight.

"Hope this will do," he said.

"Sure," I replied, and walked across the room to sit on the bed. The mattress was thin, the bedsprings loose. It sagged in the middle.

"Do you need anything else? I'm not used to houseguests."

I remembered what Marcus had said about Fox being a loner.

With one quick movement, I stood up, unzipped my dungarees, stepped out of them. I began to remove my blouse, my fingers fumbling with the flat buttons.

"You know nothing about this," Fox said roughly. "Stop it!"

I continued unbuttoning. It wasn't fair of him to just close me in a room and act as though he didn't care.

"I don't want to hurt you," he said, but nonetheless, he marched over to grab my hands, crushing them in his fist.

Anger shot through my body.

"Good God, girl! You're a bundle of conflicting emotions. You don't know what you want or need. You think this is about sex"—he gave a sardonic laugh—"or maybe about love, but your feelings are all mixed up and contradictory and, well, adolescent! You're still a child."

"You don't know anything about me! I am not a child. I *want* to be with you." Who had put his tongue to the spoon I had licked? Who had fondled a teakettle? "Is it never going to happen?"

He pushed my hands away, more in annoyance than disgust. "You've seen too many movies."

"It's never going to happen, then?" I whispered. I felt miserable.

"Good Lord," he said. "Stop asking me."

He walked out and slammed the door.

I sat alone in the leather chair. I'd ruined everything. How could I stay? I got up and peered into the night, my face floating in the darkened glass. I saw my eyes, as round and blank as moonstones, my mouth in a grimace. I remembered my shopping bag in the kitchen with my diary inside and went downstairs to retrieve it. Fox had stepped outside, the light on in his workshop.

In the living room, I ran my fingers over the spines of books. Art books with smooth, shiny pages. History books. Books on plants and birds. I pulled a blue cloth-covered book off a shelf and opened it randomly. Poems. A line marked by a red check. *One man loved the pilgrim soul in you.* I read the whole poem. Another love poem! I shut the book and shoved it back on the shelf as if it were on fire. So many things not to feel, not to touch. Men were a test of your bravery. Was I brave enough to love Fox? Was I brave enough to walk out onto a frozen pond and see how close I could come to open water? I mounted the stairs, and as I passed the bathroom, I saw Fox's green toothbrush on the lip of the sink. I set down my bag and ran my thumb over its splayed bristles. In the mirror, I watched myself raise the toothbrush to my mouth. Open my lips. Put the toothbrush inside.

That night I told Rose about Fox. I told her I was safe and that I missed her like crazy and that somehow we would be together again, though I wasn't sure how. *Please take care of yourself and get better,* I said, forcing myself not to picture Rose in a hospital room or shuffling along a cafeteria line. The night was quiet, and I felt her listening to me. I wasn't used to praying but that night and every night thereafter, I prayed Rose could hear me. I kept her a secret in my heart, a private grief.

Chapter 24

Orchard in Winter

Outsider. Not exactly the word Phyllis had used; *outsider* was Fox's word. Phyllis had responded to his call the night before with a controlled chilliness meant to convey the severing of her affection for me. "As far as Marcus and I are concerned, Eunice has broken her pledge to us and can't be trusted. Since she is almost seventeen, she is free to go." They would not make a hassle. Phyllis went on: It wasn't as though I was from around there, "one of their own," one of Pastor Karl's church orphans or an unwanted change-of-life baby from some poor, overburdened Catholic family, the usual candidates for foster care. I was like Rose—a stranger, a strange stranger, an outsider.

"Do you want to go back?" Fox asked. I shook my head. "Do you have regrets?" I shook my head again, the ache of losing Rose and Tooty and Aurora at the same time all jumbled up and roiling through me. Morning light spilled onto the blond trestle table under which my toes would not stop tapping. Fox put on his glasses and studied me over the rims. "Hmmm. What are we going to do now?" I shrugged. "You look less fraught this morning, by the way." Surprised gratitude must have popped out on my face because Fox dropped his reserve and said, "Don't be embarrassed. You're an unexpected pleasure at my breakfast table." I blushed and studied the freckles scattered among the gingery hair on his forearms. He ran a finger over the worry lines above my brow. "You don't believe me?" And because he said this, I did believe. My voice rose to a question mark. "I guess that's settled, then?" I'd intended to sound stronger, more assured, but with creeping astonishment, realized I hadn't thought about money or what I'd do on a farm. My leatherette pouch held a single twenty-dollar bill.

"Here's what I suggest," Fox said.

I lifted my eyes.

"You said you've worked with animals?"

I nodded.

"Okay, then. I'm going to hire you. I could use someone to do chores, see to the feedings and such. I've got a big overhaul to do on my John Deere, and the smaller tractor needs work, too, and I could use help." He paused to sip his coffee, monitoring my expression. "What do you think? I usually hire the Pulmacher boys around lambing time, but you could be their stand-in."

I stared down at my bowl of oatmeal, into which Fox had dropped a pat of melting butter.

"I'd pay you, of course. We'd come to agreeable terms." In the bright morning light his age showed, his creased skin like a stone with many lives, many surfaces: he interested me. I didn't imagine I was being wooed.

"I won't take advantage of you, if that's what you're worried about." He picked up my spoon and handed it to me, indicating the oatmeal was getting cold. "But don't you take advantage of me. I won't coddle you, and I don't tolerate slouches. Farming is serious business." He crossed his arms, his lower lip puffed out in a stern pout. I couldn't resist grinning.

"All right. Deal! For now. I'll put you to work. Starting with these breakfast dishes." He glanced out the windows dripping with melting frost; the wet trees shone as if polished. "And just so you know," he said a little stiffly, "the animals always come first."

"Right!" I said, and bit into my toast, fighting the show of happiness that wanted to burst through my pores.

Gladly he let me take on the cooking since his culinary skills, he said, were pagan. On the stove sat his unwashed fry pan, pungent with bacon grease. In went the sausages, in went the eggs, the pan barely wiped afterward. I'll learn to bake, I thought, envisioning steaming, honey-colored buns, cakes decorated with real violets and turrets of whipped cream. I would delight and astonish Fox in ways he'd never been delighted or astonished, the fantasy punctured only slightly when he began to impose rules. Don't put trash paper in the fireplace. Don't leave gates unlatched. Don't go into his workshop. Don't touch his tools or machinery. Don't answer the phone or collect the mail or go into his room. Along with the rules, there were warnings—about Raj the rambunctious ram, coyotes in the back pasture, the rickety loft ladder—and stinginess concerning soap, string, toilet paper, and hot water.

I settled in, settled into both Fox's ways and the old farmhouse, a structure with its own past, its legacy of families and their ghosts. The latter I did not go looking for, not in the attic or basement, nor did I try to peek into Fox's room. Maybe I was afraid of what I'd find, or not find, a revelation of the ordinary more disappointing than some shameful secret. Fox was chock-full of secrets but so was I, and if he retreated into the cave of himself, reading in his chair by the fire at night or climbing the stairs early—farmer's hours—so did I. I kept to my round of chores, waking at dawn to the breathtaking cold, the sun smoking rosy red into the violet sky, out to the barn to collect the eggs, stopping to break the scrim of ice that formed December mornings on the water troughs. Accustomed to my presence, the sheep encircled me like schoolchildren, crushing their muzzles into my thighs. Even the high-strung Katrina came around.

Of course, I knew more about animals than I admitted, and I guarded the source of my knowledge, cautious not to show how much I knew. Fox enjoyed being my instructor, and so I let him, listening attentively while he explained my new responsibilities, things I was already an expert at like splitting wood, stacking logs, building a fire, taking eggs from under a hen. I couldn't imagine how to explain Rose to Fox or that he'd believe me if I did. It seemed necessary to keep Fox and Rose separate, the secret of one love not bleeding into the secret of the other. Besides, Rose was too large in my mind to fit into a sentence or a paragraph, too large to explain in an hour, or a day; trying to explain about her would have been like trying to paint a landscape with a single boar's hair. She was a private part of me I wasn't ready to give away. Every time I thought of her, my heart hurt, but Rose herself was my model. "Sometimes love hurts," she'd said. "And sometimes we just have to feel the sorrow." Love hurt a lot of times, it seemed to me, but once you knew that, it was already too late.

I wondered if Fox was waiting for me to tell him about my past in my own good time, or it might have been that he did not want to be asked about his background and so didn't encourage me, but in either case, he did not push.

A few times while I was cleaning, I came upon sketches Fox had done. On the back of old bills, on pieces of brown wrapping paper, one inside the cover of a sheep magazine, I'd find my face or body in profile drawn in quick, bold lines. They were good sketches, better than good. Underneath one of them—me stretching with my arms open on the back step in what I must have thought was a private moment—Fox had drawn a small turquoise bird in flight. *Sparrow,* he'd written and the lines from the Yeats poem: *Someone loved the pilgrim soul in you.* The feeling of being observed was both creepy and flattering, and that night I wrote in my diary: *Do I have a pilgrim soul?*

During the week before Christmas, I found a dead cardinal in the snow, miraculously untouched by rodents or weather, a holly-red male bird with a black face mask, its beak slightly open, as if it had died in the act of cracking a seed. Two minuscule worms slithered from an eye socket. I knelt and cradled the bird in my hand, its body light as smoke. Later, I told Fox, describing how I'd come upon the cardinal, a bright red flower blooming out of season. He wrapped his listening in the seriousness of a witness to a painful tale and, when I finished, looked at me in a way that made me feel uncomfortable.

"Don't romanticize. Death is not a flower. It's death," he said, and my happiness crumbled. There was nothing to argue about since what he'd said was true enough, and so I let his comment pass. But maybe he felt guilty he'd spoken so bluntly because his voice softened. "Come on. I want to show you something," and he led me into the living room. He ran his fingers over several books, pulling out one large volume of illustrations, then two smaller books. *The Peterson Field Guide to Birds of North America*. Audubon. Dürer. "Sit," he said, and opened all three books.

Audubon and Peterson were basically illustrators, he said, and showed me brightly colored, gorgeously detailed but lifeless pictures of cardinals drawn with a scientific eye. *Cardinalis cardinalis*. He turned to Dürer's etching of a hawk, a study of the bird in great detail, a specific hawk with a specific curve to its beak and a particular look in its eye—particular, but also the essence of hawkness.

"See the difference?"

He flipped back to the *Peterson Field Guide*. "If you draw only what your eyes tell you, you get this kind of picture." He jabbed at a random illustration of a gull, flat and inanimate, like a trading card. "Look," he said, and went to the shelves again, pulling down another book and opening to a painting by Vincent van Gogh called *Crows Over Wheat Field*. I thought immediately the image was part of a dream, the fields of wheat charged with a furious energy and plowed by a hurricane of sunlight ravaging in its brilliance, though no sun was visible, the light having a force like wind. Another storm was just coming or going, a brooding presence at the sides of the painting. Above, in a whirlstorm of dark clouds, crows were fleeing into deep space. Compared to the rest of the painting, they were small black shreds. I felt suddenly unreal, as if I'd once stood in that very wheat field watching crows fly into the storm, as if I'd once inhabited van Gogh's dream and was imprisoned in it. With this feeling came a sense of dread. Fox was watching me closely.

"Quite a painting," he said, his finger tracing the path of the crows off the canvas. "It may have been one of van Gogh's last."

"Last" had a dust-of-heaven ring to it. I was sorry I'd mentioned the dead cardinal and tried to change the subject. It was almost Christmas. "Will we cut a tree soon?" I asked cheerfully, but Fox wouldn't let go, his fingers drumming the page, his attention returning to the fleeing black wings.

"There's something here beyond technique, even beyond the elementals of line, light, color, form. What a great artist captures. The eternal spirit that dwells in things. *Shen*. The Chinese word for it." He closed his eyes. "The spirit that lives on."

I thought at once of something I'd read a long time ago. *Matter cannot be created or destroyed.* And I saw the vacant hot dog stand at Lakeview/Oceanside shuttered for the night, and my father tossing bits of bread into the big lake's sprawling waves, the smell of his hair tonic, and the ride on his shoulders back to the train station under the salt of stars.

"What are we talking about?" I said, pulling away. "We're not talking about paintings!" His body radiated a fierce heat. Had he shot crows as a boy? The soft clanging of sheep bells drifted in.

Fox gazed at me now with genuine surprise. One of the books slipped from the couch. He closed the book on his lap. "That's enough of my melancholy for tonight." He shelved the books, removed the ironwork screen from the fireplace, and piled on logs, holding the struck match a moment too long. Back at the couch, he said, "Sometimes I get carried away."

Bluish flames encircled the larger logs and a lovely smell of pine spread throughout the room. His lips were cracked, dark red under the thin skin. His words were slow. My cardinal, the *Field Guide* had reminded him.

"Every summer," he said, "a friend and I would spend hours roaming meadows and woods with our nets and field glasses, a magnifying glass, and our *Peterson Guides*. When you're ten years old and set free in the woods, life is a fantastic mystery."

"Who was your friend?"

"What?"

"Are you an only child? No brothers or sisters?"

Fox seemed confused, and then annoyed. Something about cousins. Uncle Matthew. A house in the country. It seemed he wanted to get somewhere, and I was interrupting; he was the boy caught off guard climbing over a chain-link fence, a boy dangling a leg through a neighbor's window. Or was I wrong?

"Look, I'm sure my nostalgia is boring." He stood up and went to the window to the right of the fireplace that looked out onto the front yard. A river of firelight shimmered down one side of his body. "It's getting late. My childhood can't be very interesting to you." In a few paces he was at the fireplace again, lifting the iron shovel from its hook, smashing the smoldering logs to orange embers.

A few days before Christmas, I fell on the prong of a pitchfork in the hayloft and punctured my leg. Fox heard me scream and came running from the machine shed wearing his welding goggles. More alarmed than the accident warranted, he raced with me in his arms into the house, skipping two stairs at a time into the tile-bright bathroom, where he laid me on a rug and, hair falling over his face, pulled off my bloody jeans, too distressed to linger on my near-naked state. The wound was in the fleshy part of my calf, bloody but not deep, and even I, who sought his attention could see he was overreacting. There was a real touch of anger in his voice when he said, "You shouldn't have been up there by yourself. I shouldn't have let you."

Later, after insisting on giving me a tetanus shot, something he injected the sheep with yearly, he brought up a bowl of mutton stew with large lumps of potatoes, cold milk in a glass, and a cookie, and placed the tray on my lap. When I refused to eat—I wasn't hungry— he looked at me with sudden impatience and said in no uncertain terms that he was a farmer, not a nursemaid. The next couple of days he was alternately devoted and demanding. Solicitous and distant. Anything, it seemed, could tip him one way or the other. What he couldn't see was how confusing his behavior was, and how anxious I was to please him.

The day before Christmas Eve, a day of bright sun in an opaque sky, Fox asked if I would pose for him. I wouldn't have to do anything special except hold still for a while, and he promised not to make me too uncomfortable. It was early morning and the wind held the taste of a winter night in its mouth, cutting around the corners of the house and barn, biting into my bones. Already a soft, puttylike scab was knitting over my sore, and I'd lost my limp.

Yes, I wanted to. Yes, a hundred times yes, I wanted to model for

Fox. I sped through my chores, my mind straying to the hours after sunset. How would he pose me? What would I wear? While Fox fence-mended out in the back acres, I passed the interminable afternoon concentrating on his Christmas present, a lariat fashioned from a pair of rawhide laces I'd found in a drawer. Every few minutes I laid aside the half-finished braid and ran to examine myself in the bathroom mirror. The prospect of posing encouraged my vanity, and now, in anticipation of our evening session, I brushed my hair until it crackled with static, bending over to make sure I got the neck fuzz, twisting my head from side to side and miming seductive looks. Did I really have good bones?

By late in the afternoon, a galactic blackness wrapped itself around the house. The sheep had parked themselves near the barn, a blanket of rough wool thrown over the sleeping landscape. When I went out to close in the chickens, the frigid air was too hurtful to breathe. By dinnertime, my perfect fantasy of the evening ahead had collapsed and it now occurred to me that the entire venture might fail. I might fail. At dinnertime, Fox stamped in, ruddy with cold. He seemed to have forgotten our date, until I was clearing the dishes and he grabbed my wrist and said, "You don't have to do this." I knew he did not mean the dishes.

He set his drawing pad and pencils on the elephant's tray in the living room. The elephant smiled triumphantly, its teak trunk rising up to trumpet, its eyes gleaming like keyholes with red lights shining behind them.

"Come along," Fox said, and placed me in a straight-back chair parallel to the fireplace, my hands spread on my thighs. He set a goose-neck lamp that shot out a cylinder of intense blue-white light above and behind me. The shadows of my hands crept down my knees.

I said, "No one has ever drawn me before." Bashfulness made my voice almost inaudible. Soundlessly, he opened the top buttons of my shirt, his shirt, the plaid flannel I'd adopted, spreading the collar, then reached in to touch the flushed skin over my collarbones, his heated fingers infecting me.

Legs extended, chin down, he hardly changed his position. As he drew me, I studied him, the way he ratcheted up his mouth on one side when he concentrated. His arm moved in large broad strokes across the paper, and from my chair I gathered evidence of his square thumbs and the crooked pinky like a hook on his left hand, the pert tip of his boot flexed in the air. Coppery stubble emphasized his strong jaw. He was growing a beard for the winter...My work was silent, entirely composed in my head, but Fox moaned or let out little animal sounds, neither of which were meant to engage conversation. They were like random notes from his soul. I heard myself squeak in the chair. I heard myself inhale deeply when my thigh began to twitch from the discomfort of the hard wood under my seat and the hot, itchy gooseneck light shining over my shoulders. Fox was drawing very rapidly, smudging with the side of his thumb, obliged not to stop even for a sip of water.

Finally he stopped and bit the end of the charcoal pencil, his slitted eyes looking at me, studying what he'd done. I could see he was disappointed. The skin around his eyes sagged, his fervor spent. I got up to stretch.

Fox stood up, too, and turned the pad over on the couch. It slipped to the floor and we both stared at the gray cardboard backing.

"Can I see what you've drawn?"

"No. It's not finished."

"That's okay."

He didn't answer.

I was determined to see his picture of me. I wanted to see how he saw me. The pad was between us on the floor. I walked over and flipped open the pages. There were several sketches, but they weren't of me; they were of another young woman who slightly resembled me. I didn't know what to say. I looked up at Fox, confused. I felt morbidly cold, as if everything that gave off heat in that house had suddenly died.

I knelt down to the picture to examine it more intensely and saw a closer resemblance. Maybe it was me after all, a girl in a chair, a fireplace behind her, hands on her thighs. There were fine cross-hatchings that raised her cheekbones to the light. Her eyes seemed to be gazing at far-off stars.

"I don't think it's me," I said, and glanced at the sketches again.

"I told you, it's not finished. Besides, I haven't drawn in years. I'm rusty. Don't take the drawings too seriously." He picked up the pad from the floor and placed it high up on one of the bookshelves.

That's that, I thought. I was sorry.

Fox walked over to the gooseneck lamp and unplugged it. The room grew a shade darker. The furnace kicked on. The farmhouse made lonesome, wind-driven noises. Fox waited in silence for me to leave the room first.

The next morning, Christmas Eve, an armada of low-bellied clouds sat on the horizon, their rims like beaten tin. The sky made me think of a picture in one of Fox's art books, *Mary on Her Flight into Egypt*. This was her day, and here I was with a shepherd. It was still quite early when I thought of something I could do to make it a real holiday. I saw the kitchen shimmering and spotless, boughs on the table, a fudge-bottom pie waiting on a dollied tray.

I went downstairs in Fox's pajama top, my bare legs pale and straight as saplings. Fox was in the mudroom putting on boots that left maggoty pieces of dirt wherever he walked. He was dressed like a poor country squire: worn woolens, high argyle socks. No coveralls or baseball cap. No tin of Red Man in his back pocket.

"It's almost Christmas," I said.

"Almost Christmas," he answered. Sheep were bleating in the yard. "I'll be in the workshop most of the day." He nodded toward the door.

I was planning the chocolate pie in my head, real whipped cream. After he'd gone, I went to the window and followed the slope of his shoulders as he crossed the frozen track to the barn. He'd picked up the scythe in his other hand and was swinging at dead weeds.

Once he was out of sight, I turned my appetite toward brightness, toward sparkling linoleum and porcelain surfaces. Toward scouring powder and lemon oil, toward the particulars that women see and men find a waste of time, dead flies on the mullions, gummy roach traps under sinks. In the mudroom I stopped to bury my nose in Fox's sweater, slipped my foot in and out of his old boots. In the basement I found old wallpaper and lined the kitchen shelves. When

I was finished, I put my hands on my hips and surveyed my accomplishment. The ceramic mugs sat in a neat row, bottoms up, handles pointing in the same direction. Fräuleins all over the world were busy cleaning their houses today. Next I started on the pantry, the small sunless room off the kitchen. I opened the step stool that hung nearby and began to clear the shelves that ran up to the ceiling. A flecked canning pot, large sieve, economy-sized boxes of graham crackers, sacks of rice and beans. Fox bought in bulk, cheap. I saw us driving to a grocery store and together filling a cart. Each item would hold a secret meaning: the breakfast cereal, a symbol of our morning appetites, hearty after a night of love; the bar of Ivory, a shared bath.

I was going to scrub every grimy shelf in the pantry. I filled a pail with Spic and Span and wet a sponge. In an opened bag of flour, I found mealy bugs. The box of granulated sugar was hard as a brick. Behind a can of lima beans sat a jar of homemade jam. Dust had accumulated on the inner rim of the lid. A faded label bordered with tiny yellow ducks said: *From the Kitchen of Marie: Strawberry Preserves.* Who was Marie? A woman in a starched shirtwaist on Fox's doorstep with desperation in her eyes? I saw myself, wicked, in a red peignoir, opening Fox's front door.

I shoved Marie's treasure to the back of the highest shelf. Preserved fruit had gotten her nowhere. Nowhere at all. A honey-colored dusk was settling in and I had to hurry if I was going to make a dessert. I put a defrosted onion pie into the oven, heated water for the potatoes, and whizzed through the cabinets like a washerwoman. Where had I gotten the notion to arouse Fox with a bleached sink? Certainly not from Mern or Rose.

I threw out an empty jar of peanut butter that had a brown crust at the bottom. In another cabinet I found a pile of old dirt-flecked, fingerprinted calendars with Fox's writing on them. I threw them out.

Wedged between the back wall and the bottom of the cabinet was a warped photograph that must have fallen out of one of the old calendars. A boy of about ten with a flop of hair over his forehead was lying on his stomach in long grass, chin propped in his hands.

A younger girl with straight dark brows sat in the saddle of his back. Behind them, to the right, arced in a white waterfall were branches of a flowering spirea, a hint of a lilac, lilies, delphiniums. In the corner, the edge of a glider swing. All of it looked vaguely familiar.

It appeared that the boy and girl might have recently been horsing around. The boy's white shirt was coming out of his pants, his hair scrambled. He stared straight into the camera, smiling boldly. His smile showed a lot of teeth, but his eyes were quiet and serious, as if he knew right then, as the camera clicked, that he'd keep this photograph for the rest of his life.

The girl had bony knees and thin legs that stuck out like a grasshopper's under her flimsy cotton shift. Her feet were bare. Something must have distracted her at the exact second the picture was snapped because her head was averted and she had a surprised look in her eyes. Someone must have heard them laughing and stepped outside to take their picture.

I was sure the boy was Fox. I thought I'd seen the girl before as well. I held the picture close. There were cabbages gone wild at the right edge of the picture frame. I studied the girl. Her hair fell in long dark sheets that covered her ears. I felt I knew her, although not her name. I closed my eyes to remember, but no name came to me. I imagined that just before the photo was taken, the girl had performed three perfect cartwheels and was very proud of herself. She had an acrobat's wiry body. In the act of tumbling, her dress had flown over her head and the boy, seated Indian-fashion in the nearby grass, noted the flash of white panties, watching closely as her arms and legs turned into luminous spokes of a wheel. After the cartwheels, she'd hopped onto his back, nudging him to rise with gentle heel-kicks, her head thrown back as he galloped around in circles for her. She was not afraid of flinging her arms out in space, of twirling and showing her underpants. She incited him with throttles and horsewhipping. The two of them had collapsed in giggles, rolling away from each other, then toward each other. She threatened to make him into a horse again, and she sat herself on his back. At that moment, someone arrived to take their picture.

I turned the snapshot over. In neat, womanly script, their names were given. *Iris and Christopher. Finch Cottage, May*... the rest of the date blurred.

So Fox's name was Christopher. Christopher Fox.

I don't know how long I stood in the pantry staring at the photograph before I put it back where I found it, pulled the string to the pantry bulb, and walked into the kitchen. The photo of Fox as a young boy had brought him intimately close, as if I'd observed him looking at himself in the mirror. Now I had a strong desire to know everything about him.

A single line of bulky clouds stretched over the horizon into the creeping darkness. I wouldn't have time to bake, but at least we could have the little redskin potatoes drenched in butter and the onion and cheese pie hot from the oven. I took a sharp knife from the kitchen and went out to cut boughs for the table, wondering if Fox would ever hold me in his arms and take off my clothes. The air was very still, the surrounding ranks of evergreens erect and solemn. When I came back into the house and began to set out plates, I heard Fox whistling outside. His workshop light was off. He was filling the troughs. I remembered the dishtowel on my head and whipped it off and went to splash water on my face. I would have given anything for a few dabs of Mern's Jungle Gardenia.

Fox came inside and kicked off his boots. "Damned cutter bar," he said. "A bolt's broken off." His voice was hearty, content. There were red patches on his cheeks from the cold. Fox was a tinkerer; he enjoyed taking the guts out of one thing and putting them into another. I'd seen the cutter bar sitting on a tarp in front of Fox's workshop. Its teeth were curved and sharp enough to tear apart a rhinoceros. The size and ferocity of the farm machinery humbled me. The John Deere tractor stood almost as high as a man but was a hundred times more powerful. Its treads pulverized anything beneath them. Even their names humbled me: drill press, welding gun, auger, baler, sickle.

Fox stuck his head under the faucet of the utility sink and washed himself. "What's for dinner?" he asked, padding across the kitchen in his socks. I had no plot in my head except that my holiday tidying up would be noticed. I stood with my fingers laced in anticipation.

"No coffee?" Fox said, rattling the empty percolator.

I bit my lip, waiting for him to comment on the gleaming counters. The metal toaster that shone like a silver loaf. I felt like Olivia de Havilland playing the good twin in *The Dark Mirror*, the model of sweet domesticity.

Fox had his back to me and was thumbing through some bills. He'd emptied his pocket of a Phillips screwdriver, links of chain, some penny nails. He had his mind on important things. Farm things.

I cleared my throat. "Merry Christmas, Fox. I gave the downstairs a good cleaning today. I papered the kitchen shelves, see, see." I knew he hadn't gotten me a gift, but I told myself it didn't matter. He wasn't a believer; that was all. I opened a cabinet next to the sink. "And I cleaned out the pantry..."

He stopped shuffling the bills and stared at me critically. He put down the bills and walked silently into the mudroom again, stuck his head in, inspected it, and strode past me, through the kitchen into the pantry. He was displeased about something. What?

"What did you throw out?" he asked.

"Flour," I answered, too confused to say anything but the truth. "It had bugs in it."

"I don't remember giving you permission to throw anything out."

"The bugs were disgusting," I said. I pictured them becoming beetles, hideous brown beetles that would fly out of the ripped bag and choke the kitchen with their frantic wings.

"What else did you get rid of?" he asked.

I tried to think. "An empty jar of peanut butter. Unusable sugar." I remembered the calendars. "Old calendars." I started to say that the calendars had been from years ago, but Fox was already on me.

"Old calendars from the pantry?" he said, and when I said yes, he spun around in a temper and slammed the closest kitchen cabinet door.

"Dammit," he said. "I hope they're not ruined."

He told me those calendars had year-to-year farm records on them, and he asked me where they were. When I said I'd put that bag of trash out in the cans behind the house, he ordered me to go get them.

A cool white ease came into me. "I'm not your slave," I said.

"What?" Fox cupped his ear as if he hadn't heard.

"I'm not your slave."

He started to laugh. "You little idiot," he said.

Maybe I would get him his calendars, and maybe I wouldn't.

"All right. Let's stop playing games. Go get the calendars and then we'll have our Christmas supper."

I strolled past him with my head high, tears smarting my eyes. How do you argue with someone you love? With someone you want to love you? In the mudroom, I sat on the bench and slowly pulled on a pair of boots. Fox followed me, standing in the doorway with his arms folded over his chest. I thought maybe he wanted to apologize and didn't know how and stalled for a moment.

"Are you going to get the calendars?" he asked.

I turned away from him and removed a field jacket from its peg and didn't answer. My anger felt clear and beautiful, exactly like the sharp crescent moon that had forced its way out of the clouds. "You don't know who you're dealing with," I said.

I left him in the doorway with a worried expression on his face.

Outside, the bare trees cast long black shadows. The thin curve of moon was now ringed by haze. In its wavering light, the ground shifted between water and earth. Without thinking, I walked swiftly across the yard to the gate, through the gate, into the barnyard, away from the house where Fox was waiting. I repeated to myself, *You are not a prisoner here. You can leave anytime you want. Let him wait. Let him worry and fume.* As I passed through the first field, the flock arose from its slumber and fled to a far corner. Alerted to a disturbance, Richard came after me, and I ordered him off.

I began to run diagonally across one field into another, over stiles, my breath flying in front of me like a clan of white moths. The land rose and fell under my shoes, the sound of my feet, the sound of blood pounding in my ear. The tips of my fingers tingled with the damp cold.

The tingling prodded me to run faster. The almost-healed wound in my calf began to throb. I worried about meeting up with Raj the ram but remembered he was penned in a field near the barn.

Then it was snowing. Airy, dry flakes. Six-pointed stars. Filaments of ice that clung to my hair and eyelashes, a film of crystal and glitter. In very short order, the dark sky disappeared and snow poured down in blinding sheets, obliterating all landmarks, and I could not see where I was going. I did not know where I was. Somewhere on the back acres, I assumed. After a couple minutes, I stopped running to orient myself.

In the near distance, I saw the outline of shapes in a field. I ran in their direction. Soon I found myself standing in an abandoned orchard among trees so gnarled and elegantly hunched they might have been arthritic ballerinas. Snow swirled around their trunks in candy-cane stripes. Their branches drooped with their heavy winter burden. I followed a deep furrow that divided the orchard and led to a small clearing with a shed in the middle. The boards of the shed were mossy and rotted with age, the wooden planks soft gray and furred by the elements. Snow was beginning to form drifts on the side facing the wind, but the way to the hinged door was navigable.

As I held the door open, I was able to see into the interior darkness. Against one wall were two narrow ladders. Next to the ladders were bushel baskets and work gloves made of some soft material, now partly decayed. The winy smell of rotten apples rose to my nostrils. In one of the corners I saw a pile of canvas tarps.

Wind and cold jabbed their fists into the small of my back. My legs felt stiff and numb. Even the chill darkness of the shed felt more welcoming than the storm outside. I stepped inside and quickly spread a tarp over the ground, wrapped myself in another, and sat with my back against a wall. Drafts of icy air blasted through the chinks. I curled into a tighter ball. There was my breath, the steady, wispy shreds of it, and the persistent *psh-psh-psh* of snow falling on the roof. I sat for some time, fighting the heaviness of my eyelids and the numbness in my body that was a kind of no-sleep sleep.

Then Rose was leaning over me, touching my shoulder. "Darling girl! Don't you fall asleep. You'll freeze out here." She was herself, dressed in heavy skirts and a dove-colored buckskin shirt with tiny turquoise buttons. Her skin was tan and smooth, her hair milky white, flowing down her back in turbulent waves that made me think of the Arctic Sea. I reached out to hug her just as I heard Fox in the distance shouting my name.

"He's calling for you," she said. We listened as the sound of his voice came closer. Something passed over us just then, something with wide black wings. "Go," she said, and nudged the small of my back.

We stood together and walked out of the shelter. The snow had stopped, but a few crystalline flakes floated like feathers from the trees. The sky was a rich blue velvet sprinkled with stars. I stood in wonder at the orchard, its splayed, earthward-pointing branches, some sheathed in ice, winking and tinkling, as if they'd been hung with glass chimes.

My dungarees were frozen stiff and I was painfully cold. Rose wiped under my eyes with a corner of her skirt and kissed me on the forehead. "Keep going, darling girl," she said. "Keep going until you meet your own true self face-to-face, and when you do, give that sweet girl a big kiss from Rose." She turned and strolled off between the rows of ancient apple trees, disappearing into a misty pink halo of snow.

Fox's call came again. Richard was with him. I could hear the dog's emphatic barks. I stared in the direction of Rose's disappearance. The apple trees seemed to have moved closer together, leaving no path through the orchard. The pink glow was gone. "I love you, Rose," I said, and blew two kisses into the sky.

Now Fox was in the neighboring field. He'd emerged from the woods between pastures, rustling through low brush, shaking the snow off the forked branches of the sumac. The beam of his flashlight was roving over the ground, and when it found me crossing over a stile, he yelled, "There you are," and blinked the light on and off.

A rifle was slung over his right shoulder. When he reached me, he threw the rifle to the ground and wrapped me in his tweed coat and hugged me to his chest. "Thank God," he said, the alarm in his eyes readable. Beside him, Richard's labored breathing slowed. "You're all right, then?" Fox asked.

I huddled against him and shivered. "Cold," I said. My tongue couldn't form more than one word at a time.

"You've been gone for hours. You could have froze," he said, warming my hands with his breath, rubbing them between his own.

I knew I'd behaved badly in an important way.

"It's a good thing you're young and healthy," he said. He scanned my face, his own stripped of anger. The rifle lay at our feet in the snow. Fox picked it up and dusted it off and put it back over his shoulder. I wondered vaguely what he'd been thinking he'd have to shoot.

"Come on," he said, and reached for my hand, which I willingly put into his. He whistled for Richard, who'd gone off again and now raced back from a black chute of darkness between some bushes. We retraced Fox's tracks. "I hope you're finished with running away," he said. "It's a very childish thing to do. You might have got frostbite, you know." He squeezed my hand. "We'll have a good look at you when we reach the house."

Our shoes creaked with cold. The new-growth spindly poplars shone silver gray, the color of paper wasps' nests. I felt like a guest in a new country, travel-weary and slightly dazed.

Fox did all the talking, a cautionary tale about runaway sheep.

"Sometimes a ewe will get caught in the fence. She'll bleat all night but it won't do her any good. I'm too far to hear and Richard stays with the flock. If there are pack dogs around, they'll come and butcher her. If it's cold enough, she'll freeze to death." I thought it was gruesome that he told me about the dogs.

"It's been a long night," he said. He looked tired. I let him hug me to his side, ice crystals clinging to the nubs of his sweater. "I don't know what to do with you," he said.

I glanced up at him. I couldn't tell if he'd said it in jest. I started to hum the French song he liked to play on the phonograph, "Je Ne Regrette Rien." Fox laughed. I liked making him laugh.

It was much shorter getting back to the house. We walked down the broad dirt tractor lane, and as we approached the lights of the house and barn, the darkness of the night gave way to the harsh, artificial light. Fox stopped walking and placed a hand behind my neck.

"Promise me you won't ever do that again. Not ever." Fox held my hand to his cheek and pressed it to his lips. I thought, if my mother hadn't refused to be rescued the night of the flood, and if Rose hadn't found me hanging in a tree, and if Belle hadn't died and her dying hadn't made Ruben crazy with revenge, and if Ruben hadn't burned Rose's shack, then I might not have met Fox. Maybe fate was always ahead of us, throwing crumbs for us to follow.

The cold air was fragrant with resins and the possibility of more snow. Entering the farmhouse, I swore to myself I'd never ask Fox if he loved me, even though I knew I would never be able to stop loving him. Even though I knew I was going to suffer.

Fox ran the bath. In the big farm bathroom I sat on the toilet seat, my teeth chattering, my muscles pulling closer to their bones. Steam rose from the tub while Fox swished the water, testing its temperature on his wrist, like a nurse. He undressed me like a child, not glancing directly at my body but concentrating on buttons and zippers as if they were complicated machines, coaching me with his *good girl, good girl* when I untangled an arm from a sleeve. I'd heard him talk to Katrina the ewe in that voice, coaxing and kindly, all patience and love, which might have sounded condescending to others, but to me it was how he spoke love.

When I was completely undressed, he helped me into the old claw-foot tub, holding my hand for balance. My body was so cold—too cold for self-consciousness—my skin turned bright pink. "You'll be warm soon enough," Fox said, rolling up his sleeves. "Now sit down like a good girl, will you, so I can wash your back." I became aware of my nakedness, my slim body under the water, its dark weedy patch. I sank deeper into the tub.

He lifted me up gently and, starting at my nape, made slow sudsy circles with a washcloth, kissing my shoulders, lifting each arm to dip into the shallow cave beneath. He sang, in his rich baritone, about a fair lassie named Annie McGee. I sank into the extravagance of his voice, the warmth of the bath, the lovely buoyancy of my limbs. The water in the bath began to cool.

"Castor and Pollux," he said, anointing the twin dimples at the base of my spine, and when I opened my mouth to say, "Merry Christmas," the mention of the stars reminding me, he leaned forward and crushed my mouth with his.

I put my arms around his neck and pulled him down to me.

"See what you're doing," he said, laughing, pointing to his shirt. "You're getting me all wet." He kissed me a second time, parting my mouth with his tongue.

I slid forward to meet him.

He lowered his mouth to my breasts, his large head lost in the blue shadow of my body.

He carried me from the tub wrapped in a large towel, laid me on the bathroom rug, and quickly undressed himself. His body was gold and rose and cream. Ivory at the center where there was no farmer's tan, a V of sandy hair between his nipples, nipples like a woman's, but paler and flatter. Another line of hair, closer to the copper tones on his head, led straight from his belly to his rosy penis. His legs were straight with pronounced kneecaps ridged by prominent muscles. His thighs were lean and long, his calves covered by curly golden hair.

He knelt between my legs and kissed me. A high, wide throbbing began deep in my belly.

Raising my legs over his shoulders, he guided himself in, entering gradually, his controlled nudges driving my wetness, a surprise, an overflowing, and then there was no inside or outside, only wet, slippery, salty, lushness driven by a taut urgency, and at the center of my brain, a brilliant light. He placed his hands flat on the floor alongside my hips, arched his back. We plunged, a thousand silver-blue flashbulbs flashing, and I grabbed his hair. I was slipping away from myself, ascending into a diamond-bright hugeness, a clear, dazzling space that was and was not my body, that contracted and expanded, that had jagged edges brushing against me, painful, exquisitely jagged edges. Before I became a body without vision, I caught a glimpse of Fox, his head thrown back, his teeth bared, like a dying, slaughtered animal.

He did not roll off me right away. His sperm ran down my legs. Our hearts were perfectly aligned, beating like two red flags in the wind. Something snagged had been freed. Something caught in a net, released. I didn't mind the trickle of blood, the swollen pain down below. Nothing this important, I thought, was without pain.

Later, we slept. In my room, in the white iron-frame bed.

Later, much later, I woke up and smiled to myself and whispered into Fox's ear, "Again?"

Chapter 25

Sparrow

The first time. And then again, before the sun was up.

Slowly the second time, like the slowness of a new creation, a different story than the old creation in which God made the universe one, two, three. Our god—Fox's and mine—marveled for eons over the beauty of his creations. Our god took his time enjoying awe.

There was the wonder of rapturous sensations, contradictory and compelling, their final authority over me, the wonder of being two Eunices, one enthralled, the other cataloging her pleasure, as if some part was a turbulent wind contained within a vast, calmer atmosphere. The wonder of all those sly, enfolded places, of our bodies, tarnished and gleaming, rubies, iron, salt, and bone.

There was the wonder of Fox. The whiteness of his scalp along the part, his cowlick with its counterclockwise swirl. His jelly drying on my thigh. Our slippery skin. Slippery things of the sea: we became iridescent fish matching exactly the translucence in which we swam, the sleekness of our bodies echoing the sleekness of the water.

After that night I knew I was enough. And, being satisfied I was enough, I was willing after that night to dedicate myself to loving Fox, the high voltage of sex my conversion and deliverance. I saw myself coupled to him, uncoupled from the Child Eunice, her immature misgivings and the rooms of her past. For all things ordinary and teenage, I felt nothing but disdain: I'd been initiated. A man loved me.

I'd never had anything in common with other girls, their piano lessons, dancing lessons, their canopied beds, girls whose mothers taught them only sluts chew gum and smoke in public, girls who gave tight-lipped good-night kisses and saved the rest. And now my difference was confirmed; now my body improvised desire, seized its own order, took charge. I couldn't help wondering what my mother would think about Fox, what, eons ago, she'd imagined for my future when a nurse put a swaddled bundle into her arms. Maybe I was programmed from birth to follow her example, because now I felt in my guts the same kind of staggering yearning she had for my father, the way it ruled everything and no other man would do.

On Christmas Day, Fox and I stayed lassoed together—chores, meals, bathing, even the steam of our breath braiding in the air. Snow was predicted. I wanted to prove to him that despite my delicate frame, I could heave an ax like a logger; I wanted to prove I was capable. The slope between the house and woodshed had compacted into a frozen bluish crust, and we walked mindfully on its slick surface to the chopping block, Fox steering my elbow and voicing misgivings. Fox knew nothing of my life with Rose and reluctantly stood off to the side in the quiet cold, hands clasped behind his back, warning me to watch out for my feet. I took a wide-legged stance, split the log neatly down the middle with one whack, and bowed. I couldn't quite persuade myself I was lying to Fox; I was just hiding some elemental facts.

At dusk, a barred owl hooted from a nearby spruce, and we stepped onto the front porch to locate its hiding place. When the bird hooted again, Fox cupped his hands around his mouth and returned the call. In a minute came the echo, a hoarser, more haunting cry. Snow spackled the branches, white with the faintest veining of blue, hoarfrost tipping the weeds in the ditches and the lawn like a frozen sea.

"Are you superstitious?" Fox asked.

I shrugged, his derisive tone preempting my answer. I didn't know what I believed.

"But I suppose you throw salt over your shoulder?"

"I don't go wishing on four-leaf clovers, if that's what you mean." I scooped snow from the railing, made a little snowball, and threw it into the yard, hoping to end the conversation. The cold pinched Fox's face and made him look drawn.

"There's no way to control what happens, you know. We can't seem to accept how helpless we are." His fingers massaged the joints of the other hand. "We're not even as smart as birds."

"True," I said, hugging myself, "but not everything that looks silly is silly." I'd begun to shiver, and Fox drew me to the warmth of his side.

"I've gotten on my high horse, haven't I?" he said.

I nodded.

"A farmer's dead in his shoes if he depends on luck." He stood behind me and crossed his arms over my waist. The night belonged to the owl.

Then it was the New Year: 1960. To celebrate the new decade, Fox brought up a dark green bottle from the basement, his homemade dandelion brew, and presented me with a blank ledger he'd unearthed to use as a new diary. The first thing I wrote in it was: *New Decade. New Year. New me!* I drew a picture of us in a swooning embrace.

January brought more snow, enough to keep us shoveling. Fox fastened the plow to the small tractor and cleared the cow lane up to the pastures. We brought in wood, closed the chickens in the barn, stayed vigilant for stray sheep. But it wasn't long before a viper wind blew in from the north, bringing with it flat, mercury-colored clouds sunk like stepping stones in a sky that almost touched our heads. January, the month of Janus, the two-faced Roman god. More than ever I felt myself split into parts. One Eunice was indolent, full of lust, and might, in the middle of an afternoon while Fox was out, fill the clawfoot tub and luxuriate, half hoping Fox would find her and take her to bed, half hoping he wouldn't. The other Eunice was careful, modest, attentive. Fox was proud of her. She wrote long, questioning letters to herself. When she thought about her past, about Rose and Mern and Sam, Mr. Tabachnik and her father, the pain was less searing, more like a piece of buried shrapnel that ached only if touched.

Fox left the farm on brief excursions for provisions and supplies. I was never told where he was going or invited along. He returned with cider, tins of sardines, sacks of feed. The unspoken agreement between us was that I would not leave the farm or go out in public with him. The restrictions didn't feel like restrictions at first; I'd found refuge. Why leave? Why even challenge Fox's reasoning that a man his age and a young woman were a forbidden duo and an object of scorn? I suspected he feared I would be taken from him. Maybe both of us had a hunch that we were together on borrowed time.

As the weeks passed, my acquiescence became a restlessness that at times edged into despair, thrashing through my days and stamping on my sleep. One night, while I was tromping Fox at rummy, I asked if I could go to the farmer's co-op with him, though I knew it was against the "rules," a breach of the invisible circle he'd drawn around me. His face went tight.

"Maybe some other time," he said.

"I'll stay in the truck. No one will see me."

"I don't want to argue."

"But why not!"

He pushed his chair away from the table and went upstairs. Rather than pursuing, I sat quietly and let the sting melt away, because, after all, Fox loved me and wasn't love possessive?

The next morning, shoved under my door was a fine-lined pencil drawing of my hand, with its protruding wrist bone and narrow fingernails, holding a fan of playing cards, as delicately sketched as a botanist's fern. Fox had written a message: *I've come to care about you very much, Sparrow.* And under his name for me he'd drawn the little insignia, a small bird in flight.

During the bleakest winter afternoons, I daydreamed about meadows of buttercups, the summer alfalfa fields a lush violet-green over which jubilant bees would compose their symphonies. In the orchard, the apples would swell to perfection while the small plot of corn would shoot out its silken tassels, the avenues of stalks becoming habitable shelter for raiding deer. I imagined moving through time like a figure on a calendar, season lifting unto season, the rhythmic cycle of the months reliable and beyond control. Outside, the sun had vanished behind an opaque sky, the snow a permanent crust, slippery and treacherous, the frozen trees cracking like bones. Some mornings I felt a deep unwillingness to rise and forge my way to the barn. I found myself worrying when it got dark and Fox was late. I wanted to cleave to him, folded against his back like a pair of wings. When there was no creature to be tended, Fox would build a fire and read me Shakespeare's sonnets. Homer, Pliny, St. Francis. Kandinsky's theories on art. Once or twice, he mentioned that he'd like to sketch me again, but nothing came of it, though I was willing. I sensed a flipside to his impulse, a tentativeness that was not indifference but something else, something like fear, and I wondered if he was afraid to test the artist in himself.

In February the sky took on the look of mottled sea glass. One day there'd be snowdrifts angled up against the foundation, and the next day the sun would rule an entirely blue sky. I was peeling potatoes for a stew one evening when Fox came into the kitchen and asked if I'd be willing to pose later. There was something sweet and vulnerable in his eyes that tore at me, flattered and honored me. I wiped my hands on my apron and gave him a kiss.

He brought out a white slip of the sheerest cotton, carried in his outstretched arms in its original crinkled tissue paper. It was an old-fashioned thing of beauty, hand-stitched, with an edging of lace and a tiny satin rosebud where it scooped between my breasts, a slip Minette might have made in Paris that must have belonged to Fox's mother or aunt. He smoothed it over my upraised arms and placed me on a chair in front of the fireplace with my hands on my knees and drew me from different vantage points, looking up at me from the floor or from behind my chair. After he finished a sketch, he muttered new instructions: "hands in your lap, head turned left." Or he posed me holding a book, staring into the fire, or on my side on the couch, knees curled up with my hands under my cheek, as if I were sleeping. He was working so feverishly, I wondered if he was really seeing me, the real me, or just some object he was composing on the paper. Hours must have passed, and when the session ended, we were exhausted. My hair had fallen over my eyes, and Fox leaned forward to push it back and kiss my forehead. I asked if I could see the sketches, but he shook his head and returned to carefully folding the slip back into the tissue wrapping. He thanked me again and said good night.

By the end of February, a marrow-chilling dampness set in, the melting snow puddling in ruts that turned the high yellow of animal urine. Beneath the snow, the earth was dung-brown and slurry. I made my twice-daily rounds to the water tanks to hack away ice and thought of the orange-breasted warblers sunning themselves in Mexico, ruby-throated hummingbirds settling along tropical marshes. When Rose wandered into my thoughts, I would get teary and have to send her away.

The pregnant ewes were due in a month and Fox was working on enlarging a lambing shed off the side of the barn. If it was a wet spring, we had to be prepared to keep the sheep warm and dry. The fences needed to be checked for warps and holes, the posts checked for sturdiness and rot. The old hay, which had lost its nutritional value, had to be cleared from the loft. We would spread it in the lambing shed as an underlayer of bedding for the ewes. March brought a bout of constant drizzle. In another month, poplars would sprout silver white buds, and goldfinches would dart between thistle and sumac. On the distant hills a light haze of growth would rise through the earth's surface, the green threads pushed up by something dark and heavy, something that pushed life ahead of itself and would not stop. Though it was early, Fox took the big tractor into the fields to disk the heavy black soil. We were hurrying to prepare for lambing. I was learning about acidosis, impacted rumen, the importance of good flora in the four stomachs of a ewe. We checked the flock for broken teeth, inspected hooves for bumble rot, examined beneath their tails for maggots or flies. Fox was meticulous about keeping his flock clean. The pregnant ewes were treated like queens now. They especially loved the treats we doled out on a limited basis: last year's windfall apples, molasses. We were a team, Fox and I. One afternoon, up in the hayloft, the far corner stacked three high with sour-smelling, mildewing bales, Fox pulled down a baling hook the size of a man's arm from the wall and showed me how to grab the bales and slide them along the floor to the chute. I had to clear the floor for new hay. Each bale weighed about sixty pounds and was bound in sisal twine that left fibers in your fingers if you grabbed it the wrong way.

"When you're finished up here, get the barrow and cart the bales to the other side of the barn and stack them against the eastern wall, then sweep up the place." He reached into his back pocket for an extra pair of work gloves and told me to button my jacket and shirt cuffs too. "Chaff gets in every place," he said. He was curt and bossy. *He has no right to speak to me this way!* I thought. I have licked salt from this man's neck. I have watched dreams flash under his eyelids. I have seen him almost betray himself with tears.

Fox climbed backward down the ladder. I stared at the steel hook, recalling a movie I'd seen with Mern, *The Best Years of Our Lives*, starring Fredric March and Myrna Loy and a real soldier who'd come home with metal hooks, just like the baling hook, at the end of his arms. I was wasting my life with a man who was going to work me to the bone, a man who never let me off the farm. I decided to take a break, and kicked at one of the hay bales before descending the ladder. In the makeshift bedroom at the other end of the barn, I found the radio and brought it back upstairs. I couldn't locate a station until I heard the voice of Mo the disk jockey asking for requests "for all you guys and gals, gents and dolls." For Susie and Don, Angela and Tony. "Here's one for the birthday girl, Naomi, a request from her secret admirer." "Sixteen Candles" came on. I sat on a bale and listened and let myself wonder about Naomi and her boyfriend. Only for a second was I reduced to a grudging ache at the base of my spine. Only for a second did I feel an irrepressible yearning. I'd never been Naomi's kind of sixteen. The clowning voice of Mo the disk jockey returned, and I shut off the radio and got to work.

Later, I entered the empty house and hung up my jacket in the mudroom. I couldn't breathe deeply enough. My heart felt like a sprung clock, the hands going haywire around the dial. The next day

I asked Fox again if I could go with him to the farmer's co-op. I'd gotten all the bales down the chute. I'd worked hard. I deserved this reward. We were outside, near the back steps. It was nearly lunchtime, and Fox had not left yet. He was crouched with a flashlight inspecting Richard's ear, brooding on the pink skin inside.

"Why would you want to go to the co-op?" he said, as if I'd asked to go to the moon. "There's nothing at the co-op but seeds and grain and a lot of old farmers shooting the breeze. It's not a place for a young girl."

"Why can't I go with you? Why do I have to have a reason?" I knew I was making it worse for myself.

"We've been through this before. We can't be seen together. It's as simple as that."

"I won't even go in with you. I'll duck down if someone comes out. I just want to get out. Please?"

He snapped off the flashlight and flipped up the collar of his lumber jacket around his neck. "Let it be, Eunice," he said. Blood flowed to my cheeks. Something frightened and mute in myself pushed up inside me. I pushed it down.

Fox did not go to the co-op that day. In the evening he cooked dinner for me and brought it up on a white tray set with a cloth napkin. I had my period, cramps. He'd made a special omelet with finely chopped onion and ham. A feast. While I ate, he sat at the end of the iron bed and kneaded my soles and apologized for losing his temper. He asked if I was unhappy on the farm. I said I wasn't. *Unhappy* wasn't the right word. I looked for a way to say "I love you but I'm lonely."

It was raining delicately. Fox poured milk from a red clay pitcher into a tall blue glass and handed it to me. There was a chain of bubbles near the top. After lambing, Fox said, we'd go someplace for an afternoon. He said farm life wasn't easy, but he'd never promised anything different. He spoke with his other voice, the soft, contrite, sexual one. He said the animals had to come first. He couldn't leave the pregnant ewes. He hadn't intended to hurt my feelings. After the lambs were weaned, he'd take me to a movie or maybe to one of the carnivals with rides and games that came around in the summer.

He lifted my left foot and kissed the arch. Would I like that?

I nodded.

When I finished eating, he took the tray downstairs, brought in a damp washcloth, and wiped my hands and face. Sometimes I liked it when he treated me like a child. He asked if I was feeling better.

I said I was.

He lay down next to me, lifted my shirt, and pressed his cheek to my belly. I felt him grow hard against my thigh. He said he wanted me, but he knew I wasn't feeling well.

"Wait," he said, and left the room.

He returned holding a beautiful dress over his arm made of georgette the color of ripe plums with ruffled, short-capped sleeves and a flared skirt. Ivory buttons ran down from the square neckline. Fox laid the dress over my body. It weighed almost nothing, a fairy costume.

"For your birthday," he said.

I'd almost forgotten my birthday was a week away. It was a simple but stunning dress, not like any I'd seen, a dress worn by a girl in a straw hat under lemon trees by the Mediterranean Sea. Fox began to undo the buttons, his fingers trembling, and asked if I'd like to try it on. I eased off the bed, and he dropped the hem over my head, the heat of his palms bleeding through the fabric. I caught a scent of lilacs, or lily of the valley, the musty dregs of fragrance in an old perfume bottle. Fox stepped back to admire me, and I twirled for his approval. The bodice was a bit tight but not uncomfortable. I twirled again.

"It suits you," Fox said, his face an open field of love.

I ran my hands over my waist. "This belongs with the slip?"

A quick ascent of Fox's head: yes. I rubbed the flounced skirt between my fingers. Minette had taught me about fine tailoring and fine silks; the slip and the dress were old, but expensive and in good shape.

"They belonged to someone you knew?"

Fox's response was puzzling. His smile evaporated along with his enthusiasm; even the air around him went still. I felt a rift between us, but before I could sputter anything else, he said the original owner of the dress wasn't important: did I like it? He seemed unnerved and unprepared for my obvious question.

"Oh yes!" I said, aware of the honor he was bestowing on me and guessing that he'd given me the present on impulse. "I'll treasure it."

He made a reserved bow of acknowledgment, punctuated by a sad, forced smile. I twirled one more time, hoping to regain the spirit of celebration, but something grudging clung to the dress that forced a somber respect.

Chapter 26

The Death of Raj

A handsome blond boy stood on the back step—Colin Andersen—long and lean in cowboy boots and faded jeans, sun-streaked hair, eyes the color of huckleberries. He'd come to cart away the carcass of Raj the ram.

The animal had gotten his horn caught in the fence trapping him. Things like this happened all the time on farms, but Fox blamed himself, although nothing short of constant vigilance could have prevented the accident. It was April, lambing season, a sleepless thirty days spent ferrying towels and scissors, tagging ears, docking tails, weighing, recording, burying; days of stingy sun, the wind making slow loops around the fields, nights of standing alone in the kitchen too tired to change smelly clothes, downing squares of orange cheese and stale bread; nights I was stabbed by loneliness and sick unto death of worrying about retained placentas or prolapsed innards. In abbreviated sentences, Fox and I exchanged updates on a lamb's diarrhea, which runt might get pushed from the creep feeder or which had a chill. I was so weary of sheep that when Fox found Raj the last week in April, the animal's tongue black and stiff as leather, I wasn't sorry. No more would I have to fear Raj's malevolent gaze, the bulk of him crashing against the fence, his single calcified horn that looked ready to pierce or pulverize me.

And here now was Colin Andersen in the first light on the last day of the month when the sky finally cheered us with solid blue; Colin Andersen knocking on the back door and Fox saying to me, "I'll take care of this," trying to surreptitiously push me out of sight so that

Colin would not catch a glimpse and spread the word of Fox's young companion.

In the yard the two men joined hands in a brief shake, Fox standing apart to point east to Raj's field. Colin nodded, and they walked to the back of a beat-up ambulance sprayed black. Fox peered through the smoky glass, measuring the cab's width. Colin pulled out a cigarette, and, as if sensing someone watching, turned, his eyes sweeping the kitchen windows. I ducked behind the curtain, a tingle in my spine. Really, what could I say to a boy like Colin? *Take me for a ride in your truck? Let's go dancing? Buy me a beer?*

When I looked again, the ambulance was bumping up the tractor road, Fox in the passenger seat. I went to the pantry and grabbed the whiskey bottle, unscrewed the cap, and poured sweet fire down my throat, the molten sensation creating a new appetite. I glanced around at the eight-quart flecked canning pot, canisters of sugar and flour, sacks of rice, and without thinking opened a drawer and took out the oversized work scissors. I hooked my fingers through the black handles, power flowing from the cold steel loops up my arm. Holding the bottle in one hand, I walked from the pantry through the alcove, where the phone sat like a stuffed raven, snapping the blades open-shut, open-shut, pleasure and whiskey heat a reckless duo for snuffing out pain.

In my room, I laid the plum dress on my bed and stared. What did it want? It wanted something. Maybe it wanted me to tell it how beautiful it still was, or maybe it wanted to be updated, altered, modernized. The scissors grew hot, then cold in my hand. I considered a slit up the side, or a sleeveless improvement. Slim-hipped Colin Andersen evaporated into a mirage, a momentary column of golden boy flesh sighted through the kitchen window, a trick of the eye, and like any trick, quickly over. No longer was it possible for me to be someone's teenage love. All the Colins in the world would always and only be like brothers now. I could teach them how to kiss a girl, how to stroke her neck, what nice things to say, but who I was would be incomprehensible to them, a snarl of complexities.

The dress wavered, its edges blurring into the green quilt. A dress as fragile as spun sugar. A dress that made me think of Carole Lombard or Claudette Colbert. Or just someone's old dress. I was getting silly with booze.

I hung it back in the closet, flopped onto my bed, languidly searched around for my drawing tools, and began to sketch: the scissors, open-bladed on my pillow; a maple branch arching toward the sky—the dull lead of my pencil flowing over the lined paper in loose, effortless lines. I thought I heard the back door screen whine shut and Fox calling. I smiled to myself and did not answer. I heard him again at the foot of the stairs, but nothing in me was willing to stop and answer: my drawing hand felt charged with knowledge. Then he was in the doorway, for how long, I didn't know. The tip of the eraser in my mouth, I was pondering what I'd drawn, fatigue and alcohol clobbering my brain. Fox was staring at the whiskey bottle on its side on the floor, three-quarters empty.

"Oops," I said, and giggled.

Fox swooped down, grabbed the bottle by the neck, and held it up to the light. "I see you were thirsty."

I giggled again, but when he did not move closer, did not smile, my breathing apparatus lurched.

Fox held up the bottle again. "What's this about?"

I couldn't tell him because I didn't know. Then the words shot out of my mouth. "I'm in love with Colin Andersen."

The impact of what I said was almost nothing, but it was not nothing. For a split second, Fox's shoulders heaved and his gaze fell to the floor, a smear of anger in his eyes when he said, jokingly, "Shall I call Colin back to take you as well as Raj?"

I wanted to laugh him off, but his face blurred, the room fuzzing out of focus.

"It can be done, you know. I can call Colin right now, if you like." He set the whiskey bottle on my nightstand, sweeping the table's surface with a finger. I couldn't tell if he was kidding around. Whiskey splashed up my throat and giggles gasped into hiccups, then tears.

"Do you want to get rid of me?" I'd done a lot of weeping lately; a click into place of a certain memory, and my throat filled with unspeakable names.

"That depends," Fox said. "Are you going to drink my whiskey again?"

I felt frightened, exposed for the child I still was. A pretend adult.

"You're free to go, Eunice. You're free to go anywhere on the planet, if you like." He started to leave the room. I picked up my ledger and threw it at him. A corner hit him between the shoulders, and the ledger bounced to the floor. He stood motionless for a moment, then knelt to retrieve it.

"Can I see?" he said, holding the book by its spine. I nodded, and he turned the pages slowly, studying the drawings, skipping over the written sections, a murmur of "ahhs" or "hmmms" punctuating his concentration. I watched in the quiet heat of my disgrace.

He came and sat beside me. "You have talent, you know. You're unskilled and awkward, but you have a good eye and capture the aliveness in things. I can teach you how to work with form and composition..."

My clarity returned with his nearness, the smell that was only his—his fingers on my wrist, tapping.

And in my mind, this was when it began and how it began. So commenced our almost nightly sessions, after dinner, after chores, the mild spring dusk of May scented with dying hyacinth and lilac, and me, mounting the stairs already in a trance, the here and now about to be dismantled when I slipped on the dress, the dress that spoke of some urgent necessity, something somber and dangerous in the weave of its silk.

Into the living room, the failing sun making a ruby sea of the carpet, the elephant's tusks gleaming, Fox brought his drawing pad, pencils, charcoal.

"How should I pose?"

"I want you moving, not stiff."

"But how—"

He hummed a tango. I threw my head back, and my arms flew over my head. Fox opened his pad. I kicked out my heels.

"That's right. Keep moving," he said. I snapped my fingers and stamped. He drew me dancing with my neck arched, mouth open, laughing. He drew me crouching, ready to spring, the dress pulled up over my thighs, and my sex, in the darkening room, violet-black.

Afterward, he showed me what he had drawn and spoke professorially about grids and perspective: don't *think* what you see, just *see*. The figure was no longer ambiguous, no longer a girl who resembled me but was not me. I saw how he loved me in the images he drew, giving me back myself in the curve of my arm, or my eyes deep in shadow, questioning but haughty, a girl aware of her power but still a girl. Later, he would explain what he'd had in mind, why he'd chosen to include such and such or leave out something else. Instructions on point of view, lighting, smudge, and shadow. He was a wonderful teacher—knowledgeable, patient, able to point out my talents without inflating them, able to criticize without offending. Able to inspire but not dictate. When he was finished showing and explaining, he placed the stick of charcoal in my hand, rising to take the stage. "Your turn."

Chapter 27

The Arcade of Wonders

Leaf mold damp in the woods, perfume of fading blossoms. Apple. Hawthorn. Fox stopping midstride to shove his hands into his trouser pockets to tell me I was unfathomable, sulky one minute, cooperative the next. I had been daydreaming, distracted by the moths flinging themselves against the machine-shed light.

The insult stung. I spun around to face Fox, my mouth open in protest.

"I'm a grown man, Sparrow. I have a farm to run. I don't have time for your moods." A little smile to soften what he said that showed the recent chip in his front tooth where a winch had smacked his mouth. I started to move ahead on the path, considering the accusation, smarting at the injustice, but also knowing very well I was sometimes unpredictable even to myself.

I stopped and waited for Fox to catch up. "If I seem a little crazy sometimes," I said, groping for just the right tone, not complaining but not denying either, "it's because I haven't talked to a single person besides you since Thanksgiving."

Now it was Fox's turn to consider the situation. He glanced down at his feet, then up at the moon shuffling through the branches. "You're absolutely right! You deserve some fun." A carnival was coming to Gleason over the weekend. Would I like to go? He'd trust Richard to scare off any predators.

Even a small-town carnival sounded glamorous, and I threw my arms around Fox's waist and besieged him with questions. Would there be a fortune-teller? A Ferris wheel? The minute I said "Ferris wheel," it was impossible not to think of my father. Fox was too astute to miss the crack in my voice, the flinch that must have swept my face, but too gentlemanly to pressure me when he asked what was wrong and I said, "Oh, I just remembered something from a long time ago," rearranging my face to show a proper smile. And I *was* happy. But that night in a dream, my father stood in the center of a circus ring wearing a red ringmaster's jacket, slapping a whip against his thigh and calling out acts that never appeared, not a single one. In the next ring a horse with sawed-off legs plopped onto its belly and a voice said, *It ought to be shot*. I woke dazed with foreboding. Fox was out, and I padded into the garden and pulled weeds until the sun was fully up. The rest of the day I stayed fastidiously busy trying to forget the dream. We ate our dinner—fried egg sandwiches and coleslaw—in silence, Fox studying me throughout the meal. When we finished, he said, "You don't seem very enthusiastic about the carnival tonight. Still want to go?" I took a sip of water, trying to compose what I should say. He'd think my dream was silly, and I couldn't explain the gloomy feeling that still hounded me, but I said yes.

"Good," Fox said, returning my smile above his tented fingers.

The sky was the color of diluted iodine, scarlet bands streaking across the west. Fox, strikingly handsome, all bronze-skinned and starched white–shirted, escorted me to the pickup, opening the door and kissing me on the forehead as I leaned back against the vinyl seat, the gearshift thrust up like a baton between us. I'd done my hair in a French twist, the epitome of sophisticated dos, held in place with paper clips. Fox had said I looked elegant, and I felt elegant sitting next to him in his old Chevy pickup as we jounced along on rough roads. He told the story of Cecilia Gallerani, the model for Leonardo da Vinci's *Lady with an Ermine*, who had posed with a white weasel in her lap, and said he was going to paint me in oils wearing the dress, sitting on a stile with a lamb instead of baby Jesus in my lap. As we crested a hill, he downshifted and the truck backfired and we both laughed. He shifted again as he changed the subject—nights like tonight reminded him of the lake where he'd spent summers as a boy and learned about birds and

butterflies and fish. He looked surprised when I said I remembered—
Uncle Matthew, who'd given him the field guides? Right! There'd
been a spring-fed stream near the cottage. "I'd lie on my belly for hours
below the falls and watch for the trout." The word *trout* prompted him
to turn to me as if he'd just recalled something disturbing, the truck
swerving into the empty opposite lane. "Can you swim?" he asked,
realigning the wheel. I assured him I was a good swimmer and his
shoulders relaxed, but the question struck me as odd. He continued
talking about his summers as if the question had never been asked.
The road had leveled out, and we passed a market with a gas pump out
front bearing the logo of the flying red horse. At the town limits, we
saw the first handbills taped to lampposts. Over the laughing mouth
of the Fat Lady, the endless cavity of her open mouth, her candy-red
lips beckoning vampirishly, ran the words FRANCA'S CARNIVAL. On a
quiet, elm-shaded street we passed a brick school with darkened windows where two bicycles leaned against a wall. A sense of peace spread
through me. Ahead, the sky had a soft, pastel glow. At a four-way stop,
we heard music and turned left. The music grew louder.

Fox pulled onto a chalky lot among vehicles parked helter-skelter
in crooked avenues. Colored lights infused the area with an orange
haze like the inside of a cloud at sunset. Fox cut the engine, and
then we were out breathing the popcorn-scented air, crickets leaping
against our legs. Families with small children streamed out through
the entrance. Fox pointed to his left. "You can hardly see it from here,
but there's a limestone quarry over there." I looked where he was pointing: behind a high chain-link fence, two silvery mountains of crushed
stone broke into the twilight. The quarry had been an illegal swimming hole, Fox said, but was boarded up now because of accidents.
We had entered the glare and commotion of the midway and were
engulfed by the bustle of farmers in Wranglers and suspenders, their
wives with overheated splotchy faces and baggy cheeks, shapeless in
housedresses, girls too young to have babies shushing fussy infants—
all of them jabbering and ugly, ugly and tawdry, the carnival nothing
like I'd expected, nothing like the grandness of Lakeview/Oceanside.

To avoid a little boy's soiling my dress with his teetering cone of cotton candy, I stepped around a heap of garbage bags and almost tripped. A boy my age was hurrying around a corner and knocked into me just as I regained my balance. "Sorry," he muttered. His sweetheart, small and perfect in black ballet flats and a crisp sleeveless blouse, the collar turned up, a cinch belt emphasizing her doll-like waist, was waiting for him by the hot dog concession. Her fingertips brushed idly over her full skirt as she gazed at me in pure condescension, a heavy silver ID bracelet around her thin wrist. I glanced down at myself in the sick glare of a rotating pink spotlight—white sneakers, thick white socks crumpled around my ankles, my dress hanging frumpily below my knees—and froze in humiliation. The girl slid the ID bracelet up and down her arm, her smirk changing to astonishment when Fox asked if I was okay, lifted the hair at the back of my neck, and planted a kiss. I pointed to the shooting gallery three booths down and said loudly, "Win me something," already reinterpreting what had just happened. Why should I envy her? She was jealous because I had Fox.

Metal seals moved along a track painted with bright blue artificial waves, each seal balancing a different colored ball on its nose. A man held out a rifle. "Everyone's a winner. Win something for the lovely lady." His hair was black and oily, his sallow skin made greener by colored lights. Fox put down a quarter, took up the rifle, and fired four shots. Two seals flipped over. I'd willed happiness to return and it had. The man told Fox to pick a prize and brought down a display arm wearing a black suede glove and stacked with cheap silver and gold bracelets. I picked a bracelet with charms—a gold heart with a red gemstone in the center, a cat with tiny yellow jewel eyes, and a shamrock with an emerald chip in one lobe. It was dark now. Darkest over the quarry, where there were no lights, only a welter of ice-blue stars.

We made our way to the carousel, where a heavyset man in a back brace was working the levers at the center of the ride, a spider monkey with a hooked tail on his left shoulder. The painted horses, narrow-flanked with elaborately carved headdresses and scalloped manes, bobbed up and down on their poles. Next to them, large-breasted mermaids with scaled green tails, the paint flaked and ruined, and angels with round blind eyes and enormous wings, invited riders onto their backs. The carousel man yanked a lever and the huge wheel under the platform slowed, the last chords of the music dragging through the air as if the orchestra were falling asleep over its instruments. The monkey jumped down from the man's shoulder into the gearbox, out of sight, an ankle manacle sprouting a long chain attaching him to his owner. The girl with the ID bracelet and her boyfriend were threading their way from the inner circle of horses in our direction. There was something raw and beautiful and tacky about her, her pale pink lipstick thick as paste. Her sharp blue eyes stared into mine, then dissected every detail of my outfit until the hair piled on my head felt as heavy as cement. Her attention shifted from me to Fox and back again, as she tried to figure out what we meant to each other. I wanted badly to go home now but slipped my arm through the crook of Fox's elbow, shaking my charm bracelet at her unfriendly eyes.

The Flying Saucer: an eight-armed contraption with spinning disks attached at the end of each arm. Fox lifted the safety bar, and we lowered ourselves into the bucket seats. The disks spun; the stars blurred. "Hang on! Hang on!" Fox shouted as we whooped around again, the dizzying rush of adrenaline hitting our brains. I loved the breeze raking my hair, loved how I felt shaken loose from myself, the bones in my skeleton shifting in shock while Fox pretended to cower against me, his face slashed with bands of orange and blue light. Toward the end of the ride, he covered my eyes with his hand and I reciprocated, and for the final minute we whipped through space, blinding each other in exalted terror.

Afterward, my legs shook. Fox was damp under the arms. We walked to the far end of the midway, our fingers clasped, breathing hard from the thrill. We were together in a new way in the outside world. It hadn't been clear to me before tonight how much Fox had been holding himself back, holding himself in, guarding himself except in those moments when he fell asleep next to me, his ear against my heart, one hand loosely uncurled like a child's on my chest.

At the other end of the midway, we came to a series of long trailers and a red-and-white-striped tent roped off by a corded sash, THE ARCADE OF WONDERS stenciled above the entrance flap. People milled around the now-empty front stage, their faces lit by punches of neon. Voices trickled from inside the tent, a scratchy version of Cancan sifting through the canvas. Handbills for the acts were stapled to a billboard nearby. Siamese calves, an albino piglet, and the human acts: "Darnell the Dog Man," a V of hair growing right down past the bridge of his nose. "Selma, the Adipose Venus" with her three enormous shelves of stomach and dainty feet crossed at the ankles in buckled pumps, her eyelids lacquered a deadly mineral green. Selma smiled as if she could show you a thing or two. Another poster displayed "Joseph/Josephine, the Hermaphrodite," one eye kohled, Egyptian-style, the other as unadorned as a plumber's. The heat of excitement had collected on my skin and the back of my dress stuck in the dip of my spine, a faint fragrance of lilac wafting from the material. Fox had been studying another poster, the corners of his mouth turned down. I went over and put my arms around his waist to read over his shoulder.

"Hermes, Le Savant de la Musique."

Fox shook his head at the Hermes poster. "Putting freaks on display turns my stomach," he said. The fine print noted that Hermes had come straight from Vienna. He knew Schubert, Chopin, and Gershwin by heart and had memorized thousands of songs. Yell out your favorite, and he'll play it on a mouth organ, without hands. "Stump Le Savant," the poster said. Hermes was paralyzed from the neck down.

A man zipping his fly slumped out from behind a generator truck and glanced at us, his lips sputtering something unintelligible, then wobbled off. When I looked around, other derelicts loitered among the shadows, multiplying as the night progressed. Fox kept his eyes on the man's back until he was out of sight. "This sleazy area is no place for you," he said, taking my arm. "Let's go." I brushed him off and pointed to the wooden platform. A person dressed as Uncle Sam now sat behind a table arranging rolls of tickets. "I want to go in," I said. I wasn't trying to be contrary; I just wanted to *see*. The side flap opened and clusters of people sauntered out, mostly men, mostly snickering, but some families too. "How can it be so bad if kids can go in? It's all a joke anyway, isn't it? I mean, it's not real?" I thought Selma's stomachs were made of foam rubber.

"Who knows if it's real," Fox said. "That's not the point. The point is civilized people don't laugh at nature's mistakes."

I turned on him. "Aren't you the one who told me that teaching someone to draw is teaching them to *see*? I want to *see* with my own eyes what's inside the tent, Fox." I might have been pushing too hard for something I knew nothing about, and Fox might have been right: how did I know I wouldn't feel degraded the minute I joined the gawking crowd? But I had fifty cents in coins in my shoe and impatience won.

"You can wait here," I said, and walked off in the direction of the tent.

"I don't like it when you act so headstrong," Fox called after me. I handed a coin to Uncle Sam, who smiled, exhibiting a single, dazzling gold tooth. "The miraculous, the bee-zar. The miraculous. The bee-zar. Step into the Arcade of Wonders," he said. Miracles. Wonders. Fabulous Freaks.

I entered an atmosphere sick with human odors and tobacco fog. For a second, I considered plowing my way out, but I saw that Fox had followed me, and I was determined not to give in. The acts, divided by curtains, went on simultaneously, and from behind each partition came different music, different talkers. People tumbled from one show to another, nudging and shoving, congealed into one big human mass that pinned me, propelling me along with its force.

Joseph/Josephine. On a makeshift stage surrounded by dull red velvet curtains, a person with a divided body modeled his oddity. One shaved, shapely leg and bare foot with painted toenails mocked the other in cowboy boots and pants running up to his waist. One side of his bowed lips bore Revlon's reddest hue, the cheek above it theatrically rouged, a greasy blue lid and fake lashes almost hidden by his Veronica Lake do. The other side where he'd grown a furry little Hitler mustache was as ordinary as pie.

The spotlight flashed blue, then gold, while Joseph/Josephine waited for his audience to settle. Someone shouted, "It's a trick. He's just a girl!" Joseph/Josephine aimed a finger at the man and pretended to shoot, spun around, unbuttoned his shirt, and let it drop, his arms held out like Jesus Christ on the cross. The audience gasped. Every patch of skin from the back of his neck to his waist was tattooed. The Tree of Knowledge rose in a brown column up the knobs of his spine, leafing out forest-green across his shoulders. Adam and Eve faced each other in astonishment under his wing bones. A turquoise snake oozed down from a branch over Eve's head. Joseph/Josephine stood for a minute while we took in the spectacle, then with his back still to the audience, wrapped his arms around himself, his own hands caressing his own shoulders, his own hand at his hairline stroking his own neck, making love to himself.

A rush went through me, part shame, part thrill. "How's it feel?" someone yelled, and Joseph/Josephine canted his hips and in a tremulous voice warbled, *"There is a house in New Orleans they call the Rising Sun."* People around me started to titter, mocking laughter filled with disgust. I tried to get my objectivity back by closing one eye and imagining how I would draw JJ, but the trick didn't work. Meanwhile, Joseph/Josephine seemed to be enjoying himself, strung out on the kick of applause. Maybe the carnival was the best thing that ever happened to JJ; maybe Fox was dead wrong.

When he finished another stanza of "House of the Rising Sun," Joseph/Josephine grabbed up his shirt and donned it. He faced the audience and bowed, displaying a ghoulish smile, his eyes as dead as marbles.

Fox put his mouth against my ear. "Have you had enough?"

"No," I said, and for the sake of pride, ripped past a set of adult male twins wearing identical red Goodyear caps, staggering into another curtained area.

"Hermes—Monstre et Prodige."

He reclined on a bamboo settee, a misshapen, boneless body attached to an overlarge head, majestic and terrifying. Instead of eyes, Hermes's two puckered flaps were slit like rodents' mouths, pink and raw-looking. He wore a starched blue shirt, a pair of ill-fitting checked trousers, and a beaded Indian belt and moccasins. His sparse hair was of no color, plastered over a bulging forehead. A harness of thick leather straps came up around his shoulders, and attached to this was another device with metal arms and a neck strap that held a harmonica inches from his mouth. A second man sat nearby on a bench.

Hermes was just finishing "Greensleeves." He removed his mouth from the harmonica and smiled, showing stubs of brown baby teeth. Despite his grotesque features, he had a heartbreaking smile. A woman next to me poked an elbow into my ribs. "Isn't he something? He can play anything! They say he fell out of a tree when he was a boy and broke his neck, but the music never left him. God was with him."

People began to shout requests, and the manager stood up and waved his hands. "One song at a time, folks." He looked over at Hermes, whose arms hung lifeless against his sides. "Now, will it be Bay-toe-vin or Chow-pin, my friend?" Hermes raised his great head and pushed his lips to the harmonica and played another soulful melody. Then, like a windup toy whose gizmo had run down, he suddenly stopped. His head tottered and fell back against the settee as if he'd died. A nervous twitch ran through the crowd. His sidekick got up again. "He's taking a little rest now, folks. Even angels got to take a rest."

Tears streamed down my cheeks. Hermes's smile was like the smile of a holy man who understood the world's sufferings and extracted sweet music from it, but who had to endure the world's ridicule and ignorance. What was huge in him was not his size but his goodness, and his gift, it seemed to me, was that he grasped our perversion but continued to rally. I closed my eyes, and the world swayed. I saw Hermes's future. He'd spend another year on the road, maybe two, then end up dying alone in some cheap hotel, left behind while the carnival traveled on. What would happen to all the goodness Hermes and his beautiful music put into the world? Did freaks think of themselves as freaks? Were they freaks to each other, or just Joseph and Selma?

It took me a minute to realize Fox was at my side. "Ready now?" he said, gently this time, and led me by the arm through the curtains and out of the big tent. We walked slowly through the dwindling crowds, away from the orange sky and toward the gravel mountains and the quarry. So much was going through my mind I couldn't talk. I needed to breathe the untainted night air.

"I'd like to sit by the lake," I said.

The quarry lake sat in a bowl of white cliffs that rose about twenty feet above the water's surface. The water was clear and black, and the moon threw a path of silver across its surface. We had come in under a warp in the fence. No one was around, but from the corner of my eye I saw two white swans glide across the water into ferns on the opposite side. In the rain-pocked pools eaten into the limestone, tiny iridescent snails sparkled. I bent to fish one out and examined the tiny, turret-shaped shell, already composing a drawing that would include the problem of representing the shell's empty spiral depths. Fox had been trying to teach me how to see with my emotions and draw beyond the literal, feeling my way into the subject. What did I feel for this snail? Nothing! I crushed it between my fingers and blew the dust from my skin. What had I just seen—actors or freaks? Or just plain human beings with something missing or something extra added? Or a bunch of rebel angels in disguise?

"Do you want to talk?" Fox asked.

"Hermes will haunt me for the rest of my life," I said. I started to unpin my hair and shake out the heavy waves. I had to move or I'd start crying. I needed to be alone. I flipped my hair over my shoulders and started unbuttoning my dress.

"Hey! What are you doing?" Fox said. His dry, slender fingers were on my wrist. I'd kicked off my shoes and socks and now stood unbalanced on a shingle of limestone above the water. The pressure on my wrist increased. "Come away from there." I felt a tug on my arm.

I said that I was going to swim across the lake, that I hated the carnival and never wanted to go to another one. The cool air off the water rushed up at me. All I could think of was declining the invitation of the June night, alight with stars, in favor of the dark and silent underworld. I rolled off the charm bracelet Fox had won and threw it on the ground. "Stop it, Eunice!" Fox said as I swatted at him and inched closer to the water lapping wide and glossy black. Fox caught the seam at the back of my neck, and as I strained against being captured, I heard the hideous rasp of the material tearing and felt the air lick over my skin. I no longer occupied myself; fury had borrowed me, and now I tore the rest of the dress down the front, the sound of popping buttons appallingly pleasing.

"You keep me locked away on your farm. You won't let me go anywhere. You won't let anyone near me. And look what you've given me to wear!" I plucked at the dress panels hanging at my waist in shreds. "Something my grandmother would have owned. You're a freak, Fox, and you're making me into a freak."

His hand came at me, and I felt the sting of his palm across my cheek. I was so shocked I didn't recognize the pain until a second later and put my fingers to the burning spot.

"If you touch me again, I'll kill you," I said, shaking, every inch of me covered with a fine sweat. "I'll kill you with my bare hands," I repeated, and fell into his arms.

He held me while I cried big, sloppy, openmouthed sobs that contained every sorrow I'd ever known. "I must have lost my mind," he said, draping his white shirt over my shoulders, wiping my tears on the cuff, kissing my eyes until the last bit of moisture had been squeezed out and the swollen lids closed. As if our bones had melted entirely, we sank together, Fox cushioning me against the crusty, uneven ground.

We lay quietly together, content not to speak, but after a while Fox lifted my hand from my chest, kissing the tip of each finger, his voice coming from a deep, calm place.

"I wanted a simple life," he said. "I wanted to keep you from harm. I haven't succeeded at either." He had been crying, too, a man's unblinking, stoical tears.

I shifted onto a hip, propping myself on an elbow to look at him, long and lean in his T-shirt and trousers. "Maybe it's not your place to protect me. But what did you think would happen when you kept coming back to Wedenbach's? You knew it would mean trouble." My tailbone ached against the damp, night-chilled stone.

Fox poked a finger into one of the eroded puddles and scooped out the same kind of snail shell I'd picked up earlier, rolling it in his palm. "Spirals," he said, turning the shell over, "they're part of nature, part of us. Our lifetimes aren't a straight march from here to there, birth to death. Each moment is a point on a spiral and many moments repeat themselves in slightly different form." He put the shell into my hand and closed his fist over it. "You've lost me," I said. Fox turned onto his back and looked up at the stars. "That's because it's almost impossible to put these things into words. I mean that our lives are governed by patterns, even though we don't see them or recognize them. But then we find ourselves in a place we've been before." There was a sudden flapping noise. Two swans rose from the water and disappeared above the grayish cliffs beyond. I had the eerie sense Rose had been near. I turned back to Fox.

"And...? So...?"

"It's time I tell you a story."

"What time is it?" I asked.

"Late," Fox said. He was tired. I was tired. The cold earth nibbled at my bones. "We have to get you home first," he said.

"I hope you don't feel sorry for me!" My voice sounded like an echo in my head.

"Why should I feel sorry for you?" Fox was standing up, reaching out his hand. "I don't feel sorry for you, but maybe you feel sorry for me, the old man." He stood away from me, pulling down the corners of his mouth with his fingers. I couldn't help laughing. He leaned forward and kissed me lightly, holding my face between his hands. The ache returned to his voice.

"I'm angry at myself. I shouldn't have brought you to the carnival, and certainly not to the quarry." He shook me gently by the shoulders. "You acted recklessly, but I never should have hit you."

"Can't we just forget what happened? Tonight was a mistake, a terrible, stupid mistake."

"A necessary mistake, however."

I was too exhausted to counter his statement.

Linking arms, we stepped carefully over the slippery rock, across the gravel and grass, under the fence, to the field of weeds that led to the truck. A mist hovered inches from the ground, and I held on to Fox's arm, shivering, the dress under his shirt utterly ruined.

When we got back to the farm, Fox led me directly to his room, off-limits since the day I'd arrived. The door fell open, and I stepped across the threshold for the first time, light from the hallway breaking the seal of darkness.

Everything in sight was subservient to the painting above his bed, a large portrait in a carved walnut frame of a girl wearing the beautiful, flawless, now-spoiled dress. I thought the painting was of me, but I saw the girl's face was rounder, her body slighter, her skin painted in tones of orchid, lavender, and peach, a darker shade than mine, the bangs I never wore swept off to the side, exposing a high domed forehead that gave her a fragile look. Her eyebrows were thick brown slashes, and she had the wide-eyed expression of a startled deer, the duck-toed stance of a dancer. I saw the resemblance between us—the dark hair and eyes and the long neck and something else I couldn't define—but more clearly, I saw the differences.

"Who is this?" I asked.

"Iris. My cousin. Matthew's daughter."

I reached out to touch the wall next to his dresser to hold myself up. Something in the way he said her name, the awakening of sorrow, the timbre of remorse, struck me that Iris was the story he'd wanted to tell me earlier. "I'd like some whiskey before you ask anything else. You?" he said. I asked if there were any cigarettes still around. I wasn't a smoker, but I needed to do something with my hands. He nodded, and I heard his boots on the stairs.

Other sketches were tacked on a sidewall between the dresser and his closet, drawings I remembered posing for. There was one of my head in profile that I particularly liked, a study of fly-away curls and one ear, its construction rendered with meticulous exactitude, a leprechaun's shape peeking from the cross-hatchings of hair, a maze of cartilage and flesh, and the ear canal as black as the entrance to a flue.

And then Fox was in the room again, and I realized I was relieved to see him.

"Do you want to hear about her?" he asked, holding the unopened bottle of whiskey and the pack of stale Chesterfields. "Is it too late? Do you want to bathe or change your clothes first?" I shook my head. He lit a cigarette and handed it to me. "Please," he said, gesturing to the bed or the floor, "make yourself comfortable." I slid down the wall with my legs straight in front of me, dragging on the little ember of tobacco as if it could warm my entire insides. Fox turned on a lamp and tucked a blanket around my lap.

"The dress you're wearing, the dress in the painting, Iris never wore. She died in thirty-six, long before I bought it. I found the dress in a San Francisco thrift shop that catered to society people with spent fortunes. I wasn't looking for a dress, but there it was." We both stared at the painting. "What attracted me was its color, the color of summer nights at Finch Cottage, the translucent deep violets and plums. And then"—he laughed self-consciously—"there's her name, Iris, suggesting the flower with its hidden folds and indigo-tipped petals."

Iris in the photograph, the girl lolling on Fox's back. Finch Cottage where Fox's storybook summers began and ended. Matthew, Fox's dead father's brother. I huddled over my knees, consumed by Fox's past. Things were falling into place.

"Between 1948 and 1950, I painted hundreds of canvases of Iris, how I remembered her, the woman I imagined she might have become. Sometimes I painted just the dress as still life—blowing in the branches of a gnarled cypress or thrown into the surf, about to be smothered by kelp and foam. The model in this particular painting is not Iris, of course, but Iris reconstructed in my mind. The model was someone I found who resembled Iris. As I may have said, but maybe I haven't"—he massaged his eye sockets as if hoping for better vision—"Iris had been dead for twelve years by then."

He stopped, took a gulp of whiskey, and looked at me, his brow wrinkling. "I'm hurting you, aren't I? This evening has been a disaster. I'd meant to take this painting down months ago and"—he opened his arms wide, a lawyer pleading before the jury—"never got around to it." His voice trembled. "My hope, my most sincere hope is that we clear the air and begin again, begin fresh. No secrets." He paused and cocked his head at me. "No secrets?" I let my head drop onto my chest, pretending to say yes, but I knew secrets always existed between people, even people who loved each other, and I was not ready to give up mine. I doubted Fox was either.

He continued. "The obsession of painting Iris taught me a lot about myself as a painter, but it did nothing to reduce the damage or heal the pain."

"What made you stop painting?" I asked, with more force than I knew I had.

Fox gazed at me intently. "I'm not sure I have, at least in my head. I'm always painting in my head."

"And now you have me."

"And now I have you."

"If I were you, I'd have kept Iris a secret too."

The remark was the end of a long, complicated unwinding of truth, the end of a thought, the beginning of a new idea. Emptied of revelation, we let it rest in the dim room, Iris looking on.

"How am I like her?" I asked after my second cigarette. "Was she moody? A daydreamer?"

Fox squeezed his temples. I could see him scowling, shuffling through his memories, superimposing Iris on Eunice. "You look like her, but the more I know of you, the less you two have in common. Iris hadn't a clue how annoying she could be. Matthew would invite me on a butterfly expedition. Iris would tag along and hold us up, scratching her mosquito bites, losing her butterfly net. I can picture her squatting among the reeds with her empty Mason jar, waiting for a frog to jump in." The dip into the past had brought forth his boyish impatience.

"And then she died."

"Yes, then she died."

"How?"

Fox rubbed the top of his head. "Summer of thirty-six. July sixteenth. It was a hot night. I let her drag me out of bed." She was fourteen; he was fifteen. They walked down the path to the canoe and took the old Grumman across the bay, Iris in the bow. A perfect night: windless, a fine moon. When they got to the island, they were suddenly awkward with each other.

Fox fell silent for a moment, stricken. "I told her the water was too cold for swimming." He'd wanted to go back but was ashamed to admit it. To keep warm, Iris did cartwheels on the sand. "I remembered thinking she was becoming a long-legged beauty."

I felt a stab of jealousy. But then Iris was dead, and I was alive. I *was* alive. I wrapped the flannel blanket tightly around my shoulders. Fox was sitting on the floor now, not next to me but facing me and facing the portrait.

"She liked being provocative. She wanted me to chase her into the water. I could swim, but I never liked putting my face in the water. She took off her shorts and stood in her bright blue bathing suit, and when I did nothing, she pulled off her suit and dashed naked into the shallows. I couldn't let her think I was a sissy, so I did the same. The next thing I knew, she had swum up behind me and jumped on my back, nothing between us but a skin of water.

"I pushed her off and held her head under for a second. She came up sputtering, and I kissed her, one brief, closed-mouth, innocent kiss. She lobbed a fist at my chest, and the next thing I knew she had climbed up onto a big boulder jutting over the lake and was shouting, 'Dare me, dare me.' I knew she was going to dive no matter what I said, and that's what she did. She took a step forward, lifted a knee, and dove. A second or two passed, though it seemed like hours, and she hadn't surfaced, and then she popped up in a dead man's float, arms and legs dangling below the surface, neck at a terrible angle." Fox bowed his head, his arms limp between his knees. "A long time ago," he whispered. "Before you were born."

So sad, I thought, so sad. I spoke quietly. "Was she dead?"

"She died three weeks later. Never regained consciousness."

"You never spoke to her again?"

"No."

"What did you tell her parents?"

Fox pressed his fingers to his eyes. "I didn't have to tell them. I paddled back with Iris wedged between the thwarts, her head flopped over onto her shoulder. Our mothers, Evelyn and Martha, heard me shouting and came running out of the cottage. That's all I really remember. And Matthew's black Buick arriving." His voice cracked. "If Iris had lived, she would have been paralyzed, a quadriplegic or worse. Broken neck, a common diving injury."

Blue moonlight was filling up my lap, painting shadows across my legs. I picked up the hem of my dress and caressed my cheek with it. I'd never have my portrait done in it now. Never.

"Are you still grieving?"

"Look, I've gotten used to it. I've had to."

"Have you ever loved anyone else?"

"Yes, but not permanently. Not with my whole heart."

I nodded.

"I'm not sure I'm capable."

Fox went out to check the gates and let Richard in. I ran a bath and let the dirt, grit, scraps of leaves float off my body. When I stood up to dry myself, I pictured Iris standing naked on the cliff above the lake.

I walked down the hallway and reentered Fox's room, climbed onto the bed, and touched the layered brushstrokes, passing my hand over Iris's face. A shudder ran through me. I gazed into her eyes. She gazed back, the slightest smile on her lips. I leaned over and kissed her mouth. Then I stared to laugh. It was the kind of laughter that didn't make any sense, that could not be shut down.

She never got to be any older than fourteen. She never even developed real breasts. Tears came. I closed my eyes and kissed Iris again, harder, the paint cold against my lips.

Chapter 28

The Sorrow Field

June 14, 1960. A huge oak was uprooted last night and nearly fell on the house but got caught in a maple instead. I can see Fox from my window trying to figure out how to get it down. I like to draw him when he doesn't know I'm watching, like now, a fist under his chin, like the famous sculpture *The Thinker.*

I wake half expecting to find Iris in the kitchen, twisting her hair around her finger or biting a fingernail, impatient for her friend Fox.

June 15, 1960. I helped Fox lug firewood to the shed. He acts cheerful, but there's something complicated going on in his face, like something's been stolen from it. I think he's waiting for me to accuse him. YOU ARE RESPONSIBLE FOR IRIS'S DEATH. But I won't. I don't believe he's responsible. I just wish it never happened.

June 15, 1960. PS. But accidents DO happen! Fox says so all the time.

June 15, 1960. PPS. But if Iris hadn't died, I probably wouldn't have met Fox!

June 17, 1960. Worked in the garden. The peas are in second bloom. The lettuce got eaten by rabbits. Summer has moved into the world. Soon we'll be haying.

June 18, 1960. I drew an imaginary circle around the farm to keep all sorrow and ghosts away.

June 20, 1960. Fox is going to an auction next weekend, and I asked if he'd bid on some bee boxes, if there were any. He scratched his head and smiled and said he learns something new about me every day. I wanted to say We Both Have Secrets, but instead I told him I'd had an aunt who kept bees. I don't know how to begin talking about my mother and father and Rose.

June 22, 1960. Needles of rain. I'm drawing them right now as they splat against the window. Fox watches the sky. Mare's tails or those big bushy clouds mean rain. The bad weather makes him grumpy. I'm glad he's in the shed all day fixing his stupid machinery. Sickle bars and hay rakes and augers! I brought him cupcakes with chocolate icing earlier. He grunted thank you, then went back to welding a chain. Richard trailed me back through the downpour. I let him into the kitchen with his muddy paws and fed him cookie dough from the beaters. Don't feel like writing today. Lonely.

June 24, 1960. Iris is fading from our conversation. I ask questions, Fox answers, and now I have nothing more to ask. I'd like to forget about Iris, but Fox still hasn't taken down her portrait. He keeps meaning to, but with haying coming up, he's got other things on his mind. I sort of understand. When we "do it," we use my bed so Iris isn't watching. Fox said when I'm ready to tell him, he'd like to hear about my childhood, but it makes me nervous talking about myself. The things that happened before Fox seem light-years away.

June 26, 1960. Fox brought me three hives from the Bernardsville auction. They look like they've been sitting in the corner of someone's barn for years and need a good cleaning and repainting. Tomorrow I'm going to hose them down and scrape out the old honeycomb. He's in the workshop right now tinkering with an engine he got in a job lot. I filled the brown jug with daylilies and phlox. While I was in the meadow picking flowers, I discovered a turtle egg near the drainage ditch. Eunice Turtle! You Restoreth My Soul.

June 28, 1960. We walked the fields today. Fox crushed tufts of alfalfa between his fingers, chewed the leaves to taste their readiness. We'll make hay before the fourth, if the weather holds. It will take three or four days to cut and bale the first crop. He's fixed up the John Deere, but now the baler has a problem. I'll be happy when haying is over, and Fox isn't so preoccupied and crabby. The warm, humid weather has brought out the flies. I find them repulsive but am trying to make myself draw what I don't like. Hundreds of flies on a dung pile clicking their wings! Here's my latest fantasy. I live with Fox the rest of my life. We keep bees and sheep. We clean out the chicken coop behind his shop and make it into a studio for me. I wear a beret from Paris and red lipstick when I paint.

July 1, 1960. Fox let me ride on the platform behind his tractor seat today while he drove the John Deere with the mower attached round and round the first field, the long arm of the sickle bar slicing through the grass, leaving wakes of silvery green swaths. I was giddy the whole time and had to hold on tight to the lip of his seat. The tractor bounced and sideslipped and once almost pitched me off the bar when we hit a gopher hole, but even that was exciting. In a day or two, when the loose grass dries, we'll go down the windrows and bale it. Fox said we're a good team and I'm doing the work of the Pulmacher boys! Iris is fading!

July 2, 1960. Question: how does an artist capture invisible things? Like the wind moving through the fields? The grasses bend, the wind passes, and the grass goes motionless again. How do I draw the wind moving on, its duration, its latitude? The problem is time versus infinity. I don't know how to explain what I mean except it's like love—like Fox's love for Iris—gone from here but not dead. So where is it?

I was in the yard, a bucket over each arm, on my way to fill the troughs, when Fox called from his high seat on the John Deere. "Going to bale the small field before it gets dark," he yelled, happiness broadening his smile. He stopped at the gate, jumping down to unlatch it, and waved his yellow straw hat. The tractor shimmied and shuddered, pouring its loudness and fumes into the flawless July afternoon. It was nearly five, the sky still an unaltered blue, the promise of a bright half-moon already visible. Men and their equipment! I thought. Fox was so happy among his hydraulics and hitches, the complicated innards of his machines. I watched him climb back into the cab, steering the big wheels up the lane, the baler waddling like a porcupine behind. I went to empty the buckets, the tractor's blue exhaust dissipating long before the metallic clatter drifted into silence, and then there was only the fact of my solitary self in the yard and Fox's disappearance over the hill and the stillness. I couldn't shake the urge to hurl myself up the road into the hay field. Some finely spun web of panic had dropped over me, and I couldn't move. I squinted into the sun at the empty lane, chunks of light falling through the tunnel of trees. I started running, not in the direction of the gate and Fox, but in the opposite direction, grabbing some rags off the line as I fled toward the barn where the bee boxes awaited my attention.

I slid open the heavy barn door and stepped inside under the high vaulted roof, into the cool dimness. The bee boxes, their mitered corners falling apart, their brood chambers clogged with old wax and cobwebs, were stacked against a wall. Ignoring them, I continued down the center aisle past the stalls, ruinous with decades of infestations and accretions, yielding to the impulse to visit the makeshift bedroom behind the curtain in the back.

A bedspread of Indian cotton had been thrown over the cot. The lantern was on its hook, Fox's flannel shirt next to it. I sank onto the mattress, letting my mind go loose and wide in the private, mote-dusky space.

A corner of white paper gleamed from a shelf to the right of the bed.

There were two drawings. One the size of an envelope, one the size of a paperback book. Very precise drawings, the lines heavy and dark—number eight B graphite pencil—in Fox's style. Even as I felt my scalp tighten and my heart drum loudly in my ears, I examined the two sketches with critical eyes. Fox had taught me well.

In the vertical drawing, Iris was poised to dive from a rock, the curve of her spine bent like a sapling. The rock itself was shaded with the side of the pencil in broad strokes, black and foreboding. Compared to the rock and water, Iris was fairylike. Delicate. Insubstantial. The peaked waves below reached up for her like enormous claws. The second drawing: Iris's face pushing up through the center of a circle of concentric ripples, her lips open, sucking air, water beading off her closed lids.

Iris. Iris. Iris. Here she was again, interfering with my life. My first impulse was to tear the sketches into confetti. I didn't even look to see if they were dated. All I could think was, *I should leave the farm right now.* I sprang off the cot, my fury needing something, someone to fling itself against. I needed to find Fox right now, confront him with the drawings, dig out the truth. I'd say, *Listen to me. I can't stay here if you love Iris.* I'd say, *I have something to tell you. You can't have both of us.*

Holding the drawings like an enemy's flag, the graphite smearing under my pinching fingertips, I stormed out of the barn and followed the wheel treads up the lane, rehearsing what I would say, the call of doves luring me on. The temperature was dropping. Fox would be pleased. Better for haying. Damn haying! Damn the farm! Damn Fox!

A loud, rhythmic *thunk-a-thunk thunk* and the thrumming of the tractor spilled into my consciousness. I was still some distance away when I saw Fox take the tractor out of gear, leaving the engine running, scoot down from his seat, the power take-off purring, walk around, and peer into the baler. He stood a moment, taking off his hat to scratch his head. I saw him squat lower, tilting his neck sideways almost parallel to the ground to examine the hay massed in the baler's long tines. He flung his hat out behind him and it landed near a back wheel like a piece of overturned crockery. A dozen bales spaced evenly over the cropped field shone with the spill of sunset. Fox straightened and kicked the side of the baler chassis. Nothing happened. He felt in his pocket for his bandana and wiped his forehead, then walked back to the tractor and lifted a long brass-colored metal bar from the tool case attached behind the seat, then went to the side of the baler and prodded the hay. The air was saturated with the sweetness of cut grass, the stars not yet twinkles of dust.

I approached cautiously from the next field, watching Fox's pantomime, aware that the sight of him, despite the drawings, brought a rush of desire. But desire felt like another betrayal.

I saw Fox toss the metal bar at a distance and get back onto his seat. The tractor lurched forward, and Fox was charging down the hay row. But only for a minute. The baler quit again. I was at the stile now, almost in his field, my anger returning. How could I expect to get his full attention if his mind was on his damn machine?

He jumped down in front of the wheels and shook his head. I could see by the tension in his shoulders that he was peeved. Good!

I was aiming for a down-and-dirty fight. I stepped onto the stile, and as I straddled the fence, I saw the curve of wide green earth meet the lilac-blue sky, and in the other direction, placed like pieces of brightly painted farm toys, the farmer in his rolled-up white shirtsleeves, the yellow straw hat atop the flattened grass.

I was standing on the stile when my gaze caught on the metal bar in a bed of grass. I felt a sudden chill and wrapped my arms around my chest. The drawings slipped from my hand.

Fox was crouching to the side of the long rake teeth, which snatched up the grass and fed it into the chamber where it was compressed. With his right hand, he groped for the stick or rock or wad of grass that had jammed the mechanism, his eyes closed, as if he needed to see only with his fingers. I was fifty feet or so away and opened my mouth to warn him but, as if in a nightmare, was unable to speak. Time faltered. I knew Fox shouldn't be doing what he was doing, but I also knew he was a careful farmer, solid and smart.

I saw him shift his weight onto the balls of his feet, kneeling on his left knee, his right leg bent at a right angle for leverage. Then I was running, calling over and over, moving with what seemed a robotic slowness. Fox turned toward me, his right hand still trying to excavate something stuck in the baler. I saw that he saw me just as a shrieking noise came from the baler followed by a sharp crack, followed by a slapping sound and a mechanical whine. And then another sound that seemed to erupt from inside the heart of the earth and spread over its fields. *Oh Christ! Oh Jesus help me.* Fox's free arm was pulling at the other arm being sucked into the baler, and in a heartbeat, both forearms disappeared into the maw.

I flew over the field, my vision precise and panoramic: a hawk carved figure eights above the line of poplars. The stuttering tractor glimmered lime green on the hill. Fox lay crumpled.

I fell to my knees beside him, a part of me clearheaded, alert, another part floating above, watching. Fox was ashen, a sheen of sweat coating his forehead. His knees had jammed against his chest, his feet pinned under him by the weight of his body. I touched his back, spoke his name, but wasn't sure I'd made a sound, the buzz in my head louder than words, my brain refusing to record what it was seeing. *Think! Think what to do!* Fox's left shoulder was raised and hunched at a distorted angle. His right shoulder was twisted back and down. His left forearm had disappeared halfway, his right arm eaten to the elbow joint. There was no blood, the color of skin on his upper arms no longer ruddy but sickly pale pink, the blood already being leeched away—the horror of it, like looking underwater and seeing a shark eating your leg.

He made an effort to talk, to stay coolheaded, but his thighs were pressed against his chest and his breath came in short gasps. I fell to clawing at his arms, clawing and grunting. He croaked out a single word. *Tractor.*

The tractor was still on, spewing exhaust, the heat of its engine, the smell of machine oil and hot metal coming in waves. I tore away to cut the ignition. "Tell me what to do?" I said, falling in next to him again, searching for a stick, something to ram between the rollers and release his limbs. "Legs," he whispered. I could see him struggling to throw off his confusion like a man shrugging off deep sleep. I fought my nausea and saw that I could make him more comfortable by straightening his legs behind him, which I did, one trembling leg at a time, a considerable effort. All the while I kept saying his name. *Fox. Everything will be okay.*

Flat on his stomach, the tension taken off his shoulders, he could breathe more easily, but his lips had a bluish tinge. He lay with his chin resting on the grass, eyes closed, breath shallow and rapid. He had wet himself, the smell of urine mingling with the rankness of his body odor. A vein angling up under his jaw beat like a separate heart.

"Fox," I said, running my hand over his scalp, the curls greasy with sweat. "Tell me what to do. Should I get help? Should I try to pull you out?" I made my voice calm, reasonable, the way you talk to a frightened child. His voice had begun to fail. "The bar," he said. I glanced to where the metal bar lay in the grass, scrambled to retrieve it, then hunted for a place to wedge its head. I tried several positions, each effort an attempt to regain a purchase on the now-slick ground as I strained to lift the rollers or jaws or whatever they were off Fox's crushed arms. It was getting dark and, because of the angle at which Fox lay, impossible to see what I was doing. A redwing sang out a piercing warning.

"My hat," he said suddenly, as if he'd just come awake, his biceps flexing as if he meant to fetch it. *Oh dear God, he wants his hat,* I thought. Surely I was losing him. I called his name sharply, fearful that in an infinitesimal span of time he might be gone. The sun was sinking fast behind the trees, the light flickering like a candle guttering out. With another surge of energy, Fox lifted his head, the force of his need calming him, but with the soft roar of pain in his voice. He thought he could feel his hands, he said. He was sure he could feel his thumb, wiggle it even, and if I would get behind him and pull, he thought he might be able to get his hands free. His breath was bitter, the skin around his eyes pulled tight to the skull.

I stepped over him, placed my left hand on his left shoulder, my right arm around his ribs. As my arm came around his waist, I became aware of the separateness of our bodies, the pain locked into his bones and tissue was his pain. There was no visible blood yet, but I could smell its brackish taint. I prayed Fox's agony would be short. I prayed for the strength to pull him free. Fighting to keep his dignity, Fox screwed up his face and endured my tugs with stony, single-minded devotion.

Under the strain of my efforts, the thin bridge of tissue connecting the lower crushed part of Fox's arms to the upper part ripped like fabric giving way. A hoarse *Ooh,* and he slumped against my chest, his mangled stumps hanging from their torn shirtsleeves. For a brief second I did not see mutilation; I saw crimson folds of muscle, stark protruding bone, the tangle of precious veins. Already the vessels were beginning to retract inside puckering skin.

I scrambled to change my position, to prop his body against the wheel of the tractor. He'd gone unconscious, his breathing shallower, a steady waterfall of bright red drops, not torrents, soaking the ground. I had to stop the bleeding, but my dry-eyed focus deserted me, and I wept against his chest, listening to the melodies in his body slacken, my mind already bickering with itself: why hadn't I run for help? *I couldn't leave him alone.*

Rose, or a specter of Rose, was standing in front of me, hands on hips. "There's no time to lose. You have to work fast before he bleeds out," she said, and pointed to the rags in my back pockets I'd forgotten. "Tourniquets on both arms," she coached as I laid Fox out. "Bands just above his elbows, not too tight, but enough to constrict the bleeding. Keep his feet raised." I tore the cotton into strips with my teeth, my hand moving quickly to dab the wounds and tie the knots. Blood on my face. Blood in my hair. Blood on my hands. Warm blood soaking into our clothes. When I looked up, my vision of Rose was gone.

Fox fell sideways, his spine curled against my thighs as I bent over to tighten the tourniquets above the spluttering wound. Once he opened his eyes and looked at me with searing intensity, his face speckled and grainy with darkness. My vision went blurry, my gaze sweeping over the field in search of help. Distinct sparks, the green sparkle of fireflies, skipped through brush; they might have been broken bits of stars. The earth itself felt porous. I dared not look at his face again or turn my eyes up to the sky, a vast pit into which I could easily fall.

"I have to go," I said into his ear. "I'm going to get help now. Please hang on, my love."

The cicadas had started their evening drill. Underneath the whirring was a hard cold silence. I tried to stay calm as I ran down the lane, tried not to trip, but the ground pitched and heaved under me. I tried to hang on to the plan in my head, to phone for help, but just before I reached the house, I had a sudden urge to run away. To flee and pound the memory of this night out of my brain. If I could forget, I might become a new person, resistant to love.

In the kitchen I was shaking so hard I could barely place my trembling finger into the rotary wheel. O for operator. The receiver was blood-slick in my hand. Behind me, across the linoleum, I'd left a trail of muck and blood, stubs of grass. When a voice came on the phone, I didn't bother to say hello. I simply yelled into the receiver, "Please. Hurry. Come right away. There's been a horrible accident." I looked down at my jeans. They were splattered with spongy maroon clots. I heard the person on the other end talking very slowly, telling me she'd call the sheriff, asking where, the name of the farm, telling me they handled emergencies all the time. "Hang up the phone, dear, and I'll call now." When I hung up the phone, I couldn't think what to do next. I ran upstairs and grabbed blankets, washed my hands and threw water at my face. I saw Iris's eyes follow me as I sped past Fox's room.

If only I'd suggested to him that it was too late in the day to bale. If only I'd asked for help with something in the garden. If only I'd enticed him into bed.

It was because of the drawings. He'd turned his attention from mowing because he'd heard me call.

When I got back to Fox, he was very still. Dark stains had bled through his bandages. I covered him with the blankets and took his head in my hands and kissed his eyelids. Richard had followed me up the lane, squeezing under the fence, and now crept up to Fox, ears back, tail between his legs, wary of the smell of blood. There were bald spots along his back where his fur had snagged on barbed wire. "Good boy," I said.

Chips of quartz in the far lane glowed under a stark moon. The sheep were calling to be fed. They could manage, I thought. An inky dusk spilled over the field. I rocked Fox in my lap, knowing the wait would be impossible, knowing there was no choice but to wait.

The sheriff's Plymouth sedan, its red top-light spinning, sped up the cow lane. Richard sprang to attention, barking, and raced to the gate. "Down boy," I yelled. I was the master now. I leaned to Fox's ear. "The sheriff's here. They're going to take you to the hospital." I brushed a wing of blood-stiffened hair from his forehead.

Sheriff Harry Rand was a heavyset man with a lived-in face like a baseball mitt, the roughness at odds with his respectful voice, which immediately put me at ease. He wore high leather boots, a gray twill uniform with flaring short sleeves, and a badge. There was a gun in his holster, a small gun, a pistol. The sheriff loosened Fox's collar and hunted for a pulse. Considering his bulk, he moved quickly and effort-lessly, squatting to stick a finger under Fox's tourniquets.

In one sweep he saw the stalled baler, Fox's bloody stumps. He nodded to me and said two words. "Terrible, honey." His eyes had the look of someone trained in sorrow.

His assistant leaned against the hood of the sedan and spoke into a staticky two-way radio. When he hung up, he dragged out blankets and a special collapsible stretcher from the backseat. They covered Fox with a blanket. The sheriff told Fox they were taking him to St. Claire's. They'd have everything ready for him there. A doctor was on his way.

Fox moved his lips. The sheriff put his ear to Fox's mouth, squinting, sucking in his bottom lip. "Can't hear him," he said, shaking his head.

"How you doing, my friend?" the sheriff asked Fox, bringing his ear closer to Fox's mouth as the assistant brought up the stretcher. "We're going to take care of you, buddy, don't you worry."

I wondered if Fox understood the sheriff's words. "Get him under the arms," the sheriff said to his assistant. "Keep his legs elevated and that blanket around him." There was nothing for me to do. I knew if Fox was conscious, he'd want to protect me from seeing this horror. He'd tell me to go back to the house. To take a bath. To try and sleep. Fox. Dear God, Fox.

The two of them placed Fox onto the stretcher. I ran alongside the men to the Plymouth, puzzled by everything. The sheriff gathered Fox in his arms as if he were a rag doll. I slid into the backseat and he laid Fox across my lap. The blood was like black pudding. Fox's face was unmarked, as pale as a death mask, but the rest of him looked like a man who'd beaten his way through a wall of thorns.

"Okay, honey. We're on our way," the sheriff said.

He made a U-turn and we headed down the lane. I glanced at Fox, trying to remember every detail of his right hand, his left, but already forgetting the specifics, the differences. As we drove away from the field, the moon disappeared and was lost in the back window. I placed my palm over Fox's chest and stared straight ahead. The sheriff eyed me in the rearview mirror. He said Fox oughtn't be feeling too much pain yet. Shock. It prevented the signals from getting through to his brain. But I didn't believe him. I'd heard Fox cry. My heart sent the sheriff the fierce message: *Save this man.*

We pulled onto the county highway and the dark shadows of spruce drifted over Fox's features like a black wedding veil. As we passed the bog, an owl called from the deep woods. In the front seat, the sheriff and his assistant gave each other a look. The long white beams of the sheriff's vehicle fell across the road like harness straps attached to some lumbering beast in whose belly we rode. I remembered something Fox had said about Iris's accident, about loneliness. Loss, he'd said, was not the same as solitude.

Chapter 29

Harry Rand

Under the emergency entrance portico at St. Claire's, floodlights flushed the Plymouth out of invisibility, a circle of brightness that pushed away the dark in all directions. The sheriff signaled me in the rearview. I heard him say, "We're here," and that Fox would pull through, but I was too dazed to respond. Fox's head was cradled in my lap, my thighs wet with his fluids, his intermittent moans of agony both impossible and horribly real. Two orderlies and a nurse were flying out of the hospital doors pushing a gurney, the nurse in her stiff white uniform barking orders. Harry Rand was already beside his vehicle making a sawing motion to explain the accident when the door on my side opened and a husky orderly swooped in to peel my fingers from Fox's body, plying each digit while I swatted at him with a free arm and clung to Fox with the other. A moment later, Harry Rand's own sizeable hand dropped onto my shoulder, the weariness in his voice evoking my own. "Let him go, sweetheart." I shook my head and held Fox more fiercely, my will shriveling along with my faith that anything I did or did not do could matter.

"You're not helping him," the sheriff said, firmly but kindly, reaching in to hold my wrists so the barrel-chested orderly, frowning now, biting the side of his lip, could haul Fox away. Lifting him from my grasp the minute I released him, he carried Fox in his arms as if he weighed no more than a child. Standing ready, the other orderly, a wiry, redheaded boy not much older than me, stepped up to help arrange Fox on the rolling cart, the nurse, half in shadow, there to stabilize his head and admonish the men to watch out for his filthy boots. Then they were running, the cart clattering on the asphalt, the first orderly holding down Fox's arms, the other securing his legs. The sheriff leaned through the car door frame and offered a handkerchief folded in quarters. The top of my shirt was soaked, but I hadn't realized I was crying. I pressed the heels of my palms to my lids, my skin embossed with Fox's scents, his blood, sweat, urine.

"They'll need you in Admitting," the sheriff said, adding softly, "when you're ready."

For such a big man, Harry Rand was surprisingly gentle. He draped his leather jacket mellowed with the odor of buffalo hide and stale tobacco over my shoulders. I managed to say thank you and that I needed a few minutes.

"All right, then. Take your time. No hurry. Nurses'll be cleaning your friend up. Get him stable. Doc Mueller's been called in, a fine surgeon. Saw plenty of action in the war."

Action in the war. Amputations. Deaths. That was what the sheriff meant. Images of a soldier-strewn battlefield crowded my head for a second, and then thankfully my mind went blank again. Respectfully, the sheriff allowed me privacy and walked off into the trees for a smoke. I didn't stay in the car very long because I didn't want to be alone. Beyond the hospital lights, earth and sky merged into a solid, threatening blackness, and I knew if I lingered alone in the backseat, I'd become a whisper of nothingness inside the great din of nothingness.

At Receiving, the nurse's desk was empty. I hurried down the corridor, the abrasive smell of disinfectants stinging my nose, and searched for someone to ask about Fox. I must have retraced my steps at least twice, panicking among the monitors beeping in hidden recesses, the garbled announcements calling for doctor so-and-so. I thought I might have been going around in a circle until I came to an alcove off the main hallway with curtained-off areas and heard a voice from one of the rooms calling for more morphine. An aide in a pink uniform swept past me, an incurious glance thrown over her shoulder as she rushed away, the sounds of her gummy-soled shoes diminishing on the linoleum. I pushed the curtain aside.

Fox, the person formerly known as Fox, was having a seizure, his head jolting back and slamming against the examining table, his body wrenching to the side as if trying to twist off the table, the heavier of the two orderlies reaching over to restrain him while a different nurse had her fingers in his mouth holding down his tongue. A mobile IV stand stood next to his head, and from it a tube fed liquid into his neck. The second orderly was trying to keep the tube from being jerked out. Fox's shirtsleeves had been cut to the shoulders, the seams of his trousers scissored open to the groin, his socks and shoes removed. His legs looked waxy and indecently exposed, abrasions from the baler's tines flourishing on his shins. The team worked swiftly, but in a controlled manner, too busy to notice me against the wall, their voices grimly methodical, consorting with my bleak thoughts. In less than a minute, the seizure was over, but now Fox's skin was putty-colored and his mouth had gone slack. "Are we losing him?" the aide whispered, and the nurse lowered her stethoscope to Fox's chest.

Now, again, a saving numbness stupefied me, stifling the emotions that might have stretched me beyond my endurance. I knew I was trembling, my knees quaking; a strange twitch was working at my eye. I knew I shouldn't be watching but I couldn't move.

Harry Rand arrived out of nowhere, his bulk shielding me from the scene. "Let's go, honey," he said, corralling me into the hall, his breath laden with the dregs of coffee, the doses of caffeine doing nothing to alleviate the bags under his eyes. The nurse had two fingers on the side of Fox's neck and was checking her wristwatch. The aide had started to remove the bloody towels from his arms, but the nurse, her narrow face and anxious blue eyes betraying the steeliness of her voice, scolded the aide to leave the towels alone. "You know how upset the doctor gets if we disturb the field."

The sheriff guided me to a waiting room furnished with industrial-style cocoa brown wing chairs and a love seat, tattered *Reader's Digest*s and ladies' magazines, a watercooler, tin ashtrays on every table. A man in a green serge work uniform slept in one of the chairs, a rosary dangling from his hand. The sheriff sat me down on the love seat, commanding my attention with his quietly forceful voice.

"You've had quite a shock, and I suspect you're dog tired." He waited for me to acknowledge this. "So here's what I suggest. You close your eyes and try to get some sleep. I'll go over to Admitting to give them the account of things. Then I'll check on your friend and give you a report. He'll be in surgery soon." I reached out for the sheriff's hand. He took it without a moment's pause, the touch of his skin reaffirmingly meaty and warm. "But first, I'm going to get you some Coca-Cola to settle your stomach. How's that?" He brushed my hair with his fingers, his smile a small miracle, the way it transformed his weathered face.

"Thank you," I said. After the sheriff left, I studied the man in the chair and wondered if a child of his was ill or had been in an accident. The man's mouth was slightly open, a string of spittle dribbling out. How could he sleep so soundly when someone he loved might be in danger? A chill took over my body and I sank into the comforting numbness, my arms wrapped around my waist. I felt utterly alone in the ugly hospital, rocking, alone, belonging nowhere else.

The sheriff returned with a Dixie cup of syrupy Coke, wedged himself onto the love seat, and looked at his watch. There was no news of Fox and nothing to do but sip the Coke and wait. To boost my morale, he offered up heroic tales about Doc Mueller's surgical skills and last-minute miracles performed on the wounded until I put my hand on his arm and asked him to stop. What I needed to hear was that Fox would live and that our story had a happy ending. "I've said enough," he agreed, and looked at his watch. It was after one in the morning. "Try to sleep now." He adjusted his jacket over my shoulders, ran his hands over his trouser knees, and stood up, his face puffy from lack of sleep. "I'm going over to Admitting. Now, look"—he sat down beside me again, as if he'd forgotten something—"you've told me what happened, and I believe you." I couldn't remember what I'd told him, the words spoken in his car, and before and after the car had vanished into a blur.

"We'll have to deal with the details of the accident later, after..." His hand covered his mouth to stifle a yawn. "I need to know your last name, though. For the forms."

Lastnamelastnamelastname. It had been ages since I'd thought of myself as a person with a last name. I groped for it now as the sheriff waited.

The laughter started in my belly and worked its way up, convulsing the muscles under my rib cage and into my throat until I felt the sounds spilling over my tongue and out my mouth, my eyes crinkling and tearing with a rumble of snorts. It was the same bizarre, uncontrollable laughter I'd had once before, frightening and wild in its stupidity and intensity, insanely without cause. The sheriff slipped beside me on the love seat and held my shoulders, and when I finally caught my breath, I realized what I'd been thinking. I was going to say my last name was Monroe and that I was Marilyn's secret daughter. It wasn't even funny. How could I explain to the sheriff that Mern was in the air? He looked concerned, and I thought he might be considering if I needed a shot to settle me.

"Do you want me to call anyone?" he asked, and clamped his big-knuckled fingers around my wrist to take my pulse. "You're a little shocky," he said, returning my arm to me. "And it's going to be a long night." He chewed the inside of his cheek. "You're not yourself right now." He suggested my name could wait until later too. I was disoriented, but it would pass, he said. *It's not going to pass*, I thought. It's not a matter of passing. Nothing will ever be the same again, period.

"How long?" I meant till we had news of Fox.

The sheriff shrugged. "Listen, I want you to know you saved a man's life, and I hope hearing this helps you now." We traded glances. The sadness was snitching its way back in.

"Isn't there anyone I can call for you?"

"My folks are gone," I said, sobering up. "I've been on my own for quite some time."

The sheriff cupped his fingers and examined his nails. "I have a feeling about you," he said, keeping his eyes on his cuticles. "Now you tell me if I'm wrong. This is how I see it. You're still underage, a minor, an orphan you say. All right." He gave one slow solitary bow of his head. I nodded in confirmation and felt the unwavering affection you'd feel for a favorite uncle. "You've been living with this man, Fox, who's a great deal older. You work for him maybe...? Farm help? Housekeeping?"

I nodded.

"He doesn't pay you, though? Not a business arrangement?" The sheriff sucked in his lower lip and crossed his arms over his belly. I knew what he was getting at and lowered my eyes. A pistol sat in Harry Rand's holster, and I imagined it would be a terrible thing for him to have to shoot someone in the line of duty. I imagined him coming home to his wife afterward, blubbering on her shoulder like a baby.

"So I figure, if Fox *had* done you wrong, treated you in some ill manner, you wouldn't have stayed around and waited until I got there. You might have left the fella to his fate. That's how I see it." He shot me a sideways glance. "Therefore . . . what to others might seem unconventional and improper in my eyes is evidence of plain and simple love."

I looked up and smiled.

"I'll be back in a little while, then," he said, kneading my shoulder, the sides of his face drawn up to his eyes in a smile. "Hold tight, honey, and try not to worry."

As soon as he was gone, I realized I didn't want to sit in the claustrophobic waiting room, a sickly odor clinging to its walls. I walked down the short corridor and took a left. Most of the rooms I passed were offices, names of doctors written on them. A nurse was on duty at Receiving. The seams of her white nylons ran straight down the back of her calves. She was filing something in a cabinet against the wall. I could not bring myself to ask about Fox and sped past her for fear she would turn suddenly, straighten her little white cap, and say, "Your friend is dead. He put up a very good fight." It was raining outside, puddling on the pavement, beating against the solid roof. The hospital hallways were quiet, empty. I passed the emergency room cubicle Fox had been in, the curtain pushed aside. There was the gleaming steel examining table, instruments in sterile packaging laid out on a rectangle of folded white linen. The clock ticked the passing seconds; the hands pointed to ten minutes after two. Plain and simple love, Harry Rand had said. Or was it pain and suffering love? Or simple pain and plain love? Or plain pain simply for love?

I turned right at the end of the next corner and traipsed along another corridor with rows of numbered doors, patients asleep behind them. An orderly coming out of one of the rooms asked if I was lost. "Yes," I said, without stopping. "I'm completely lost." The corridor ended at a set of elevators in front of which an empty gurney and a lone wheelchair had been parked. I spun on my heels, headed back, and kept going.

The news was good. Fox was in stable condition. Doc Mueller had tied off the blood vessels, cleaned up the torn tissue, stitched the flaps together. The sheriff held up his arm to show where the scars would be. Just below the elbows.

The tears started. "He's okay? He's going to live?"

"They couldn't save what was left of the forearms, but I'd say it's a good prognosis."

I felt suddenly awake. Truly awake. I knew where I was. In a hospital where Fox was alive, breathing. A miracle! Without thinking, I ambushed the sheriff with a rough hug, nearly poking my eye out on his badge. He held me cautiously at first. I felt his arms tighten, and I could hear his hammering heart. His big broncobuster heart. He said in my ear, "It won't be easy, but your man will be all right." His nose went flat when he smiled, almost touching his lip. I wondered if he'd broken it in a fight. I wondered if he'd been a tough kid.

"You're sure he's okay?" I asked. At least he hadn't said the usual *Now you can put this behind you*. There was no *behind*; the awfulness wasn't *behind* anything. It was in me, and there was no escape.

The sheriff patted my back. "*Sure* is not a word I'm comfortable with, but the odds are in his favor." He pushed up his cuff to check his watch. "Now, sis," he said, "I'm going to take you home."

I didn't want to leave the hospital. How could I leave Fox? Harry Rand noted my hesitation. "They won't let you see him now anyway." He took hold of my hand, and we walked past Receiving to the glass doors. The rain had eased to a drizzle, and the cool wet air felt refreshing. The sheriff fished inside his pocket for his Old Golds and offered me one, but I shook my head. He struck a match, protecting the flame in the curve of his palm. "Just so you know," he began delicately, squinting through the smoke, "I guessed you're a minor, not eighteen yet." *Here it comes*, I thought. Here come the authorities to ruin my life. Here comes the forced separation from Fox. What else did Harry Rand know about me? I held my breath while he took a few long drags, crushed the cigarette under his toe, and studied me, a smile in the corner of his mouth.

"But I'm not worried about you, honey. You've proven yourself in my eyes. From what I can tell, you're a mature young lady, qualified to make up your own mind. You did good under god-awful circumstances. I know that too." He placed his large hand on my shoulder, his gaze falling sympathetically on my face. "My wife, Mary, would like you. I'm thinking you grew up in tough circumstances like she did." He tweaked my shoulder in acknowledgment. "Now, another thing. I'm going to call the Pulmacher boys to come over to the farm. Jake Pulmacher can spare those older two. He's got a bunch of kids, and they all work long hours for him. You're going to need the help. Lots of help." The sheriff opened the passenger door to the Plymouth, and I got a whiff of cleaning fluid. I shuddered and climbed into the clean front seat.

"Life plays funny tricks on us, doesn't it, sister?" the sheriff said, turning on the wipers.

We drove back silently along the same route, passing the same dark woods, the same sleeping bogs and farms. The sky was growing lighter along the seam of earth, the unawakened planet still dark under it.

Richard was beside himself with excitement when we drove in. He raced the Plymouth into the yard, inciting the sheep, who rose on stiff legs and began to bleat. Beyond the gate and up the path, the tractor and baler waited in the far field. Someone would have to take apart the baler and clean it; someone would have to do the dirty work, flush out the crushed bone and gristle. Soon there would be a slice of electric blue on the horizon. Had Fox's blood already seeped into the soil? Were worms wriggling through bloody dirt?

"Let me see you in," the sheriff said as we crossed the yard to the back door. Richard was sniffing at my ankles, circling me, searching for clues of Fox. In our absence he'd ravaged the boot scraper, tearing out its bristles, leaving the bald rollers on the back step. I had my hand on the door handle but I couldn't make myself open it.

"I'd rather be by myself, if you don't mind," I said.

The sheriff looked surprised. "I guess that's all right," he said, massaging his temple, reluctant to go.

"I'll be fine," I said.

He took a memo pad out of his back pocket and wrote down his home phone. "I don't give this to everyone," he said, "but you call if you need me. Tonight or any other time."

I wondered why the sheriff was favoring me with his kindness. I hadn't earned it. I wondered if he had a daughter, if she'd left home early and had stayed away. Maybe love was like that, if it got dammed up one place, it had to flow out in another. I turned and waited for the sheriff to back down the drive, then went inside with Richard.

It was as we had left it, unwashed dishes in the sink, Fox's coffee mug, the gazette opened to the auction page on the counter. His flannel shirt, his rubber boots, his wire rims near the phone, the chill of his absence coming from bloodless things. I heard him saying, *Good morning*; heard him say, *Leave the washing up. I want to draw you.* There he was crossing to the mudroom, freshly shaven, the scythe slung over his shoulder. Singing, *There were three Marys in merry Scotland*...Everywhere. Everywhere. Everywhere. A house full of memories. I backed out of the room, out of the house into the lunar night.

Chapter 30

The Wound

What did I know? What did I know for sure? I knew I woke to a world indifferent to Fox's suffering. The same warblers sang in the maples; the same plump doves sat on the wires. Fat brown spiders tacked up their webs, and in the yard, the same rogue tufts of daisies sprang from the dirt. The same world and unspeakably different.

On the floor in the mudroom, I found one of Fox's grass-stained socks and rubbed it along my cheek. At the stove, I ran my finger down the center of the fry pan. *Fox's bacon and eggs.* The phone rang, rupturing my stupor, and I hung back, afraid to answer. "He died last night," a voice would say. But it was Harry Rand's gravelly bass conveying a favorable report. "He's not out of the woods yet, but he's holding his own. Vital signs are okay. He's weak but stable."

I stayed quiet for a moment, letting the sheriff's words imprint themselves into my brain. "You all right?" Harry Rand asked. I told him I was and asked if Fox was in pain. He was on morphine, the sheriff said. Could I see him? "Not yet. To be honest, sweetheart, he's not fully conscious. He wouldn't know you were there." In the background I heard a short bleep and a stream of muffled conversation on his two-way. Sheriff Rand was in his car, maybe on his way to another accident.

"You need anything out there? Now listen, can you hang on by yourself or should I come get you? My wife, Mary, is itching for some female company."

Did I need anything? I looked down at myself, as if that would tell me. I was barefoot, wearing one of Fox's flannel shirts, though I didn't remember changing my bloody, ravaged clothes. I glanced around quickly at the kitchen, staid and solid, as if the terror had never happened.

"Eunice? You there, sweetheart?" the sheriff was saying.

"I'm here. I'm fine," I said. The sun was making its morning passage across the yard, slabs of light veering off the disassembled generator in front of Fox's workshop and flooding the room. My clothes, I remembered, were on the porch in a heap by the blankets. Later, I'd take them into the yard and burn them.

"I trust you know your own mind, but call me day or night if you need me. The Pulmacher boys will be coming by to take care of things and finish the haying." I thanked the sheriff.

"You'll let me know about Fox?"

"Trust me."

The easing of sorrow was temporary, as fleeting as the touch of Harry Rand's kindness. I did two things: I went into Fox's room and lifted the painting of Iris from its hook and stashed it in Fox's closet, and I ran a bath. While the tub filled, I opened Fox's drawers and touched his shirts and underwear, ran my fingers over the odds and ends on a tray on top of the dresser, his key chains, comb, folded bandanas. I could not look at his tartan pajamas on the bathroom hook or sniff his towel, and when I lowered myself into the steaming water, I closed my eyes against the filaments of dried blood and tissue that floated from my body. The sheep had come down from the field and were bleating at the gate, their monotonous *baa*s suddenly enraging. If only the sheep would bark or growl, show some spirit, some independence. Who would care for the dumb creatures? Who would see that enough firewood got cut and check the fences? Who would pick the slugs from the cauliflower, pickle the beans, and can the tomatoes?

A little after two, I heard wheels on the drive and saw a blue Ford with blaze-red lightning bolts painted on the doors pull into the yard. The back of the truck was loaded with farm equipment. The Pulmacher brothers, I assumed. They knocked, calling through the screen door. I couldn't face anyone. Upstairs, I hid under my blanket and prayed they'd go away.

Mern would have called them Big Bruisers, and they certainly were bona fide, beef-fed, milk-mustached farm boys, as blond and neat and upright as two ears of corn. They waited by their truck for a few minutes and called again, and finally I went downstairs in old farm clothes, my hair in tangles, and let them in. Ty introduced himself properly, then Lloyd. Ty was clearly the spokesman, the leader. They were awful sorry for my troubles, he said. Their pop, their whole family sends their sympathy.

"I guess you know all about the accident," I said, hoping to be spared the ordeal of relating details.

Lloyd paled and looked at his feet. Ty rubbed his hand over his mouth and nodded. Holding their caps in their hands, they followed me through the mudroom into the kitchen. Their work boots, I noticed, were the same brand as Fox's. Red Duck, with rawhide laces. Ty said their father, Jake, had given them permission to be off their farm till Fox got settled. They'd come every day for a while, and the other Pulmacher kids would take over their chores.

Ty glanced over his shoulder out the window at the sky. "Good thing last night's rain missed your farm. If that loose hay sits too long, it's going to molder." He smiled uncertainly. "If it molders, it's no good for feed." When he turned again to look at the sky, the muscles under his T-shirt along his spine rippled. I had to admit he was handsome in a blunt, raw way, as if a sculptor had started to chisel a figure from stone but had left it unfinished. The squareness of his physique might be an advantage while he was young, but if he didn't watch it, he'd grow stocky, and the clean horizontals of his shoulders would begin to sag and rolls of fat would accumulate around his waist. Lloyd spoke up. He'd been working his thumb and index finger around the rim of his cap, pinching it like a piecrust. "It might take us a little longer than we've planned, depending on what we find today." He coughed into a fist. "With the baler and all." Ty smacked Lloyd on the arm with his folded cap. "She doesn't need to hear that, stupid."

Lloyd blushed. "Sorry," he said, running his hand over the back of his neck. His hair was strawberry blond, his skin baby pink, neither of these an asset on a teenage boy. He wasn't much of a talker.

"It's okay," I said. The three of us shifted from foot to foot, waiting for someone to politely end the conversation. The full weight of the moment got to me, and I started crying. Two big blond guys in my kitchen about to go into the field and ply the baler with their crowbars and wrenches, prying Fox's bone and gristle from the tines, the roller, the compressor so they could get the mechanism going again. I scrubbed at my eyes. Lloyd's face turned red, and he took a few steps backward toward the door, tripping over one of Fox's boots. My temper snapped. "Watch it!" I hissed. Did either of these oafs ever think twice about being able to put on a pair of boots and tie the laces, or cut their meat, or lift a cup of coffee?

Ty bent down to realign Fox's boot next to its twin and begged my pardon for the disturbance, his candid smile so full of good it embarrassed me. The phone rang just as I was about to collapse into more tears. The brothers retreated out the screen door as I picked up the receiver and heard the sheriff say Fox was improving. Another day or two and I could visit. After I hung up, I reclaimed Fox's boot and pressed my hand against the warm insole: how could that be? A single shoe can crush you, I thought.

I spent the rest of the afternoon in the garden, laboring on my hands and knees in the black dirt. Aphids had colonized on the tomatoes, leafhoppers on the beans. Even so, we'd have enough vegetables to put up and keep us for a year. I pictured Ty and Lloyd up in the field, hankies tied over their noses. Farm boys, I thought. Stoic. Used to blood. They were up to the task, had probably slaughtered a sow or two. Later, I let Richard into the house, and he ran around sniffing Fox's clothes and shoes, deliriously happy. When I dragged myself upstairs, Richard followed on my heels, burrowing himself against my side on Fox's bed in the cool dark, the blinds slapping lightly against the sash. Over time, I wondered, did the heart simply refuse more sorrow?

I was in Fox's robe when Ty and Lloyd called through the screen door. I'd forgotten they'd be working late and went down to let them in, but they said they were dirty and would stay outside. They'd be back tomorrow. Neither brother mentioned the baler or what they'd discovered. I sat on the back step and let Richard lay his head on my lap and combed my fingers through the nap of his fur, which was riddled with burrs and knots. Poor dog, I didn't have the energy to groom him.

The sky had darkened, and the stars came out all at once, like fireworks. There was a smell of ripeness and new hay. Owls watched for bunnies in the spruce. Maybe tomorrow I would see Fox.

July 5, 1960. I'm going to see him tomorrow.

July 6, 1960. 5:00 a.m. Didn't sleep all night. Ty and Lloyd will take me tonight.

It was strange to walk through the glass doors to St. Claire's again, strange to stand in front of the pleasant-faced woman at the information desk and say Fox's name. Strange to hear my footsteps echo down the hospital corridor, a girl in clean blue jeans not what she appeared to be—not someone's sister, not someone's daughter.

Most frightening was the stillness of his body under the sheets, his lungs barely lifting the weight of the linen: his arms pruned to stumps, his legs tied to the bed rails with soft gauze, his feet dressed in white anklet socks. Tubes and wires coming out of everywhere. He was not alone in the room; there were other beds, rods with curtains to close them off. A nurse sat in a chair next to his head, holding a glass of chipped ice, her inquisitive brown eyes raised toward me. "He's sleeping, dearie." Her voice had a chirpy Scots lilt. MARY DONNIGER her tag said. She looked at her watch, a man's watch with a heavy silver accordion band. "He's just had his meds, pet. I expect he'll sleep for several hours, but you can sit with him, if you'd like." Mary Donniger stood up and patted her chair. I walked to the bed and stood at the railing, touching the sole of his foot, his flesh cold through the sock, but his face dusky with heat. I didn't trust my voice; it sounded thunderous in my head, meager when I let it out.

"Is he in a lot of pain?"

"Aye. A wee bit, but we're getting it under control," Nurse Donniger said, and bent to drip ice water onto Fox's gluey lips. I held on to his foot a moment longer, not knowing where else to put my hands, knowing I could touch him anywhere and he wouldn't respond, knowing I knew nothing about what was ahead. I felt Mary Donniger's eyes appraising me.

"He has a low-grade fever, but nothing to worry about, pet," she said, turning back to wipe his mouth with a cloth. "We restrained the poor soul because he was thrashing about. Trying to run away from the pain, you see. A lot of them do." I stood mute and nodding. If Fox were awake, he'd find her motherly cheerfulness oppressing. I was afraid to ask if Fox had said my name. "You can stay a few minutes," Mary Donniger said, taking the cup of melted ice chips with her as she went out through the curtain, closing the heavy green twill behind her.

I let the tears come. I put my head on Fox's chest and listened to his heart. "I love you," I said. "I won't leave you. No matter what." A muscle in his thigh twitched, his gaunt face sickly gray, his eyes so deep in their sockets the lids passed as shadows. I bent and kissed the cracked lips where Mary Donniger had drizzled ice water. A couple were arguing in the hallway, a woman cursing a doctor and the man shushing, "Sweet Jesus, keep your voice down." Mary Donniger saying loud enough for both of them to hear, "Some people have no manners."

Life went on.

I stayed only a few minutes longer, Mary Donniger bustling in with a tray of meds. "You're a good lass for caring so much about your dad," she said.

I left quietly. Through the gap between the curtains, I saw her untie Fox's restraints and tenderly stretch each of his legs, run a finger under the anklet cuffs and rub his toes between her palms. Carefully, she rolled him onto his side, opened the ties of his gown, and sponged his back with alcohol. She had pudgy freckled hands, but she stroked him like a lover. "Poor soul," I heard her say. "Weren't you a strong one." I turned and walked away.

Ty and Lloyd had gone home to shower and eat and were waiting under the portico to drive me home. They smelled clean, ferny, the opposite of the medicinal hospital smells. Their hair was neatly parted, combed back from their foreheads. Their shirts smelled of hot starch. Good boys, I thought. Their mother must be proud.

Ty drove with his arm looped along the back of the seat but without touching me. Squeezed between them and the gear stick, I kept my elbows against my sides and gazed straight ahead. Both deferred to my wet eyes and said very little. The back roads were empty, the moon shunting between clouds. It wasn't until Ty rode over the cattle grate and up the drive and I saw the empty farmhouse with its blackened windows that I started to tremble.

"Do you pray?" Ty said.

"Not really," I said.

"Me neither," he said, "but it couldn't hurt." He hadn't meant it to be funny, but we both burst into laughter, breaking the tension. Lloyd repeated the joke. *It couldn't hurt.* Ty got out to escort me into the house. Their mother had packed a basket of chicken, dinner rolls, pickles, and brownies, which had been sitting under a blanket in the truck bed. At the door, Ty handed me the basket and told me his mother said there was a place for me at their table anytime. I was acutely aware of his piercing blue eyes and sunny expression, and for a moment I was just a girl getting home from a date, a girl saying good night to a handsome boy on a moonlit evening. I remembered the sheriff had said Ty was getting hitched soon, and I wondered briefly about his girlfriend. And then the moment fell away.

"She's a great baker, my mom," Ty said, smiling. "You'll love those rolls." He glanced up at the unlit house. "Hey, Eunice, you ought to leave the porch lights on when you go out. It's awful lonely to come home to a dark house."

"Do you think it would help?" I asked.

"Can't hurt!"

In bed I listened in the dark to the wind rough up the trees. When I couldn't sleep, I tried to write in my diary but no words would come. Writing in my diary seemed ridiculous now, beside the point, as did sketching. Why would I record my thoughts or use my vision when all I wanted to do was escape them? I thought of the stillness of Fox's body beneath his sheets, and I saw him standing by the side of the barn, sunlight lifting gold flecks from his hair. In another flash I saw his fingers unwrapping chocolate from its silver foil, a rich brown square held up between his thumb and forefinger to my lips. I saw him in the tub, his neck stretched back, the winter whiteness of the skin above his elbows, channels of green veins snaking to his heart.

Ty and Lloyd came at sunrise and drove up to the field without stopping at the house. I burst into tears seeing them disappear up the lane. Yesterday they'd felt like an invasion; today I wished they'd knocked to say hello. A little later, Marcus Wedenbach called. I thought for sure it was the sheriff ringing. It was late, after ten in the morning, and I couldn't imagine who else it could be.

Marcus said he'd heard about Fox's accident—a terrible misfortune, a crying shame. They couldn't get over it. What would Fox do now? I said I didn't know. "No, of course not," he said. "Too early to know." He asked if I would like to live with them again. There'd been talk about me in town, some of it nasty, "but people always talk," he said. His generosity touched me. I thanked him for his offer and told him I planned to stay on the farm. The line went silent. Lowering his voice, Marcus said, "I always liked you, Eunice. I never had any complaints." I thanked him for a second time and heard him clear his throat. "Tooty misses you," he said.

"I miss him too," I answered, my voice catching. If I let my mind go in that direction, I'd lose control, so I said good-bye and hung up.

Close to suppertime, Ty knocked on the screen door. They were finished for the day. They had stripped to their undershirts and were carrying their work shirts on a finger over their shoulders, ticks of green caught in the creases of their necks. They looked tired and somber, like soldiers returning from a skirmish they'd barely survived. "The big field," Ty said, "took us longer than we expected. Tomorrow we'll finish the baling. Got to get the hay up before it rains." They each guzzled a glass of lemonade as if it were beer. Coarse reddish blond hair grew out from Lloyd's armpits; Ty was beginning to get a burn. I observed the details of their bodies without fanfare or desire.

After twilight they returned to take me to the hospital, Ty all spruced up in a plaid shirt and clean jeans, leaning against the pickup swigging a Coke. The sheriff had phoned to say Fox had experienced some moments of consciousness and his condition had been upgraded from stable to good. "The doc's real pleased," the sheriff had said. I was elated and whooped like a banshee after I hung up. I told Ty the good report.

"Nice going!" he said, and gave me a thumbs-up.

Lloyd came out of the barn. He'd been checking around, and there were cracks in the barn's foundation, he said. He could patch them real good with mortar, no problem. Ty gave him an annoyed look. "Don't you think Eunice has got enough on her mind right now?" Lloyd swung his head down and studied his shoes. "Thought we were here to help." Ty slugged him playfully on the shoulder. "You're right, buddy. Sorry." Lloyd helped me climb into the passenger seat and Ty told him Fox was doing well. Lloyd shot me a winning smile. Ty turned on a country station and we listened to the nasal twang of the Everly Brothers' "Devoted to You." In the roadside ditches, the daylilies were closing for the night. The darkening sky had a slightly yellowish cast, hinting at rain. Ty caught me gazing up through the windshield.

"In case you're worried, you'll have plenty of hay for this year. And maybe some to sell after the next cutting."

"Oh!" I said, surprised. He seemed to have read my mind.

"Fox is a real good farmer," Ty said, in a way that made me think he'd been practicing how to say it. "He knows how to use the land. He's got good stock. He's someone a guy like me could learn a lot from."

I didn't want to discuss Fox and the farm, and Ty must have sensed me clamming up, so he said nothing more. Lloyd craned his neck out the open window and sucked in the night air like a happy pup. For the rest of the ride, I sat with my arms crossed over my waist, trying to imagine how it would be to finally talk to Fox.

A sign on a bucket near the entrance door said SLIPPERY WHEN WET. Though visiting hours had just begun, the corridors were empty. I shared an elevator with an Amish woman in a long black dress and white bonnet, both of us staring at the numbered buttons. The nurses' station was empty when I got off the elevator, and Fox was asleep when I entered his room. His dressings had been changed, there were fewer layers, and his legs were out of restraints. He looked thinner, as if his muscles had pulled closer to the bone. Overnight, the ridge of his brow had grown more prominent, his eyes sunken deeper into his skull. Gently, so as not to disturb him, I tiptoed to his bedside and put my lips on his neck. His skin no longer smelled familiar. It had been cleansed with something harsh, something that banished the smells of the field and of the animals. I could feel my face wanting to twist up the way it did when I couldn't control my sobbing and pressed my tongue against the roof of my mouth to stop the flow of tears. A minute later, Nurse Donniger appeared wearing a stethoscope and cherry lipstick, her nurse's cap balanced on a helmet of tight gray curls. I jumped away from Fox, as if caught in a vulgar act. "He asked for you today," she said. She had a curious look in her eye. There was a little more distance in her voice, less warmth. I suspected she knew who I was—not his daughter.

"You'll be happy to know the doctor checked his wounds this morning and found things quite satisfactory. His stitches are holding. The pooled blood has been drained." He was still on morphine.

Dislodging me from my place beside him with a subtle swoosh of her hips, she raised his head, her hand behind his neck, and placed a straw in his mouth. His eyes fluttered open, showing white crescents before the lashes closed again. Apparently the body could fall out of time and live in a kind of suspended animation. It took its nourishment. It swallowed; it passed gas. I knew for myself it was possible to have strength, to haul feed, dig up weeds, eat, breathe, and sleep, but to have no feelings whatsoever.

"It's only a couple days postsurgery, but all in all, Dr. Mueller is quite pleased with your Mr. Fox." *Your Mr. Fox.* She looked at her watch. "I suspect he'll sleep for a while now." I nodded and watched her go behind the curtain of the patient across the room. I thought, *He'll have to have everything done for him.* Someone will have to feed him. Someone will have to bathe him. Someone will have to unzip his pants. Someone will have to help him pee. Fox was resting but I could not; my mind would not quiet. I made myself sit in the plastic chair and concentrate on condensation sliding down Fox's water glass. The hands in my lap, my own hands, looked weird, the skin under my nails blue-white. Whose body was in the bed? Fox's stillness was a death. Why had they said he was better? I remembered the sensation of his fingers on my breasts and knew it would never be that way again, though now I thought to rouse him, to shake him awake and find him miraculously restored. What if he died without seeing me again? A great sadness overtook me just as an aide came into the room carrying a cup of apple juice. "You can give him a sip of this if he wakes up," she said. *If he can drink apple juice*, I thought, *he can't be dying*.

Fox slept on. I got up quietly and went outside and sat under the weeping willow on the hospital lawn, shivering in spite of the warm air. I had a savage desire to strip the wands of their feathery leaves. I felt cheated beyond words.

He was sitting up when I returned to his room. His pillows had been plumped, and in this new half-upright position, he looked awkward and vulnerable, more damaged somehow than when he was asleep on his back.

"Oh, Fox!" I said, running over, letting the tears flow.

Fox smiled weakly, fatigue or faulty vision or confusion dulling his eyes.

I lowered myself onto his bed. I was afraid any movement would cause him pain. I didn't know what to do with my hands, where to touch, where not to touch. I bent over and put my cheek against his, slicking his skin with tears.

"Don't cry," he said, his speech slurred.

It made me cry all the harder. I wiped my face and looked at him. Who now lived behind his eyes? "Have you been here long?" he asked, each word dredged up slowly, laboriously. There was acid on his breath, a rancid smell to his hair. He was excreting pain.

He closed his eyes. Maybe that was all he could manage.

I leaned over and whispered his name. He raised his eyelids slowly. Everything slow, breath slow, words.

"Sparrow," he said, trying to focus. He turned to kiss my cheek but couldn't. He was unable. The movement seemed to take everything out of him. An orderly had come in and was cranking up the bed opposite. The man in the bed had a spectral look. The noise disturbed Fox. I got up and drew Fox's curtain.

"Tired," he said, as if it was the last thing he would ever say, and closed his eyes. His pallor was bad. His eyelids trembled. I clung to the edge of his bed as if it were a lifeboat. The walls of his room, the gurgles and snores of his roommates, faded away. I watched Fox's chest rise and fall with effort. We were together at sea, in the darkness, no darkness we'd ever known.

Chapter 31
Hospital Days

July 12, 1960. Ten days. He'll never be able to touch me again with his hands. I hope I can bear it.

On a Tuesday, ten days after the accident, I went for my visit and Fox's curtain was open. He was fully awake for the first time, bolstered upright in his bed, the pillows beneath his stumps removed. His hair had been washed and parted and combed to the side. He looked almost normal, except for his bandaged arms, which made his shoulders hunch forward because of their weight and his withering muscles, normal except for his thinness, the austerity of bones visible beneath his skin. Mary Donniger was feeding him pudding, a napkin over her finger to wipe the dribbles. When she saw me, she set down the spoon and made a grand gesture toward Fox. "He's doing very well this morning, our Sir Galahad." That's what she called him—Galahad. Night after night in the plastic chair, I monitored Fox's turbulent sleep, obsessed with the rhythm of his breath, almost breathless myself until his chest lifted after the long ebbing away and his lungs refilled. Now, this early morning, sunlight glossing the walls and laying warm dashes along the floor, a roguish humor had been restored to his face, the amber flecks in his eyes revived.

"Look at you!" I said, aching but afraid to put my arms around his neck, afraid to damage him more. The space under my rib cage felt empty and full, as if a flock of birds had just taken off and left the air beating. I walked to his bedside, hugging myself, hands tucked under my armpits, my smile steady and bright, trembling on the inside, but I'd promised myself Fox would see only love on my face.

His voice broke when he said my name. He was still weak, his pupils dilated from morphine.

"How do you feel?" I asked, trailing my finger down his cheek.

"We're doing splendidly, aren't we?" Mary Donniger interjected, his gatekeeper with a thousand eyes. She'd collapsed his eating tray, and her expert hands were kneading his thighs down to his toes, which she massaged, one at a time. Bedsores were not allowed under her jurisdiction.

Color rose to Fox's cheeks, and I saw how quickly gratitude could turn to loathing, how swiftly it burned away in the fire of humiliation. She was tucking his feet back under the bedding, pulling the sheet up to his chin, his stumps hidden, turning him into an absurd papoose. "No straitjacket," he managed to croak. Donniger wagged a finger. "I see we haven't lost our sense of humor, pet."

I'd stepped back from the bed and noticed a plastic stick with a little sponge attached sitting in a glass with spit at the bottom. Toothbrush, I thought. Someone will have to brush his teeth. Mary Donniger, finished with her duties, called out, "Don't tire him" before leaving. I raised my hand. My heart was pounding. Her departure removed a buffer. I'd held so many imaginary conversations with Fox, but now alone with him, I didn't know where to begin. I closed the curtain. His silence felt violent. When he spoke, his chest heaved with each word. "Don't. Look."

"I've come every day."

"Don't. Remember."

I touched his hair, and his gaze followed my hand. "You've been..." I didn't know what to say. Ill? Drugged? Out of your mind?

He turned to look out the window on his left—transparent clouds, pale morning sky. His head seemed larger, stark. I had to keep my hands busy. I filled his water glass, straightened his blankets, asked if he minded if I sat on his bed. I cranked down the top half of his mattress, and his eyes turned up in their sockets. He let out a distressing groan. I jumped up, not knowing where to sit. An urgent tension pressed me into action. "Would you like some ice?" I asked, keeping up my patter, and pinched chipped ice from the glass to daub his chafed mouth. He had surrendered to the pain and lay inert, vaguely attending to my solicitations. "Everything's going to be all right.

You're strong. Everyone says so." My face was over his, close enough to see the blood-filled capillaries under his eyes that made his skin appear bruised. "Even Nurse Donniger says how well you're doing." Out in the corridor, after one of my visits, she had said Fox was coming around, gaining strength. But every amputee was different, she had told me.

"Mary—the Goddess Morphia," Fox muttered.

I put down the glass. "Fox, you're going to be okay. *We're* going to be...I am so sorry!" I blurted out.

"Don't...not now," he said, squeezing his eyes to get rid of me. He had no place to hide. But I didn't know if he understood what I meant, and why I was sorry. I was sorry for his suffering, and aching with sorrow for having distracted him the moment before the baler snatched his arm. Did he remember anything about the accident?

"We don't have to talk about it," I said, and positioned my body alongside his, my lips on his hair. Beneath the soap, there was a smell of destruction about him. I let myself sag against his side. We'd never be the same. *Before. After.* Words like a guillotine severing a head from its body, dividing what had once been whole.

"Don't want you to see me like this," he said, the trenches along the sides of his mouth deepening.

"Shush," I said, and touched his mouth, his throat. His body was foreign; I no longer knew how to read it. Another nurse had come in to see to the patient opposite, the sound of her rubber soles moving across the floor. "I think Nurse Donniger likes you," I said.

"She likes helpless men."

I cringed, certain he was going to tell me to leave forever. I stood up to go. He was going to tell me never to come back.

"I'll be here," he said, closing his eyes.

I nodded, the knots in my stomach releasing as I walked outside to wait for Ty and Lloyd under the dark pines.

He had setbacks. Fever. A slight infection, the surgeon called to drain his wounds. It weakened him, and I wasn't allowed to visit. Mrs. Sheriff drove over, bringing baskets of chicken or ribs, offers of her Patsy's bedroom with its own private bath. Harry Rand called every day. The sound of his voice gladdened me, the gentle way he probed the condition of my spirit, even while cautioning about the phases Fox might go through—anger, depression, withdrawal. "You gotta understand, he's lost his livelihood, his manhood. Goddamn, he can't even protect himself—he's lost his fists." *Lost his fists.* I made an excuse to hang up quickly and lit a cigarette, found the whiskey bottle, the liquor spreading through my body like bright faith. When I resumed visiting Fox, I vowed not to upset him and to refrain from talking about the future. I would talk about the abundant hay crop, the lambs on the hillsides, the good works of Ty and Lloyd replacing a fencepost here, brush-cutting there. I vowed not to further injure Fox, to be what he needed me to be, but despite my intentions, one beautiful July morning I arrived at the hospital carrying a bouquet of daylilies and unthinkingly extended the gift to him. His face blanched, something dying in both of us when, too late, I saw my mistake and the despair I'd caused. Fox turned his head away and in a horrified flourish, I rushed to the nurses' station to find a vase. There were other mishaps. I was holding a glass of water to Fox's mouth one day, miscalculated the angle, and knocked his teeth, and though he was chivalrous, I was beginning to understand the scope of our new trial-and-error life.

Mary Donniger conceded to me the most menial jobs. I peeled off his socks, ran my knuckles up and down his soles, and massaged his feet with lotion. Under her observation, I assisted with sponge baths, above the waist only, of course. Some days, I had to hide my revulsion. I wasn't used to the new smells his body put out, or the pitiful awkwardness of his limbs, the terrifying way they swung out to hold me; the queasy feeling that sometimes descended on me, and that shamed me, and I was sure Fox saw. One Saturday, an aide placed a tray over his lap on which sat a can of Barbasol and a Gillette razor. I lathered him up and gave him a shave. I felt I had turned a corner. The serious tasks belonged to Mary. Twice daily, she changed his dressings, a slow process, like undressing a mummy, carrying in special scissors, washcloths, and a small mauve emesis basin. She cranked up his bed, an arm across his chest to bar him from falling forward, and began the process. She had strong wrists, square blunt hands. "We're going to clean him up now," she'd say, and I was asked to leave. I left unwillingly, hunkering in the doorway, peering through the gap in the half-drawn curtain as she placed a thermometer under his tongue, the outline of her wide bottom visible as she bent over. She was a good nurse, a conscientious nurse, and Fox was lucky to have her, but I wondered about Fox: how did it feel to watch helplessly while Mary Donniger soaped his armpits and made her stupid banter? How did it feel when the washcloth slid down his belly to his groin, reaching farther to a thorough tour of his scrotum? I felt every insult to Fox's pride, the indecencies wrenching my guts.

The sheriff drove up on a day of oppressive heat, the air like soft lead pouring over everything. The sheep surged back and forth across the pasture hunting for shade, which they found under the mulberries, sharing it with the catbirds and crows and thrashers. The sheriff wanted to talk. We went into the living room and sat on the couch. He took my hands, narrowed his saggy eyes, and spoke bluntly.

"What kind of a life can you expect here? I've been thinking about it, and I'm kinda troubled by your decision to stay on."

"Sorry?" I said, and Harry Rand repeated his concern. But it wasn't that I failed to hear, only that I didn't know how to answer. "But what if I love him?" The sheriff wearily brushed a strand of hair from my face. "Love isn't everything, honey." He looked at me for a second, stared down at his bulging belly, and fiddled with his belt. "Exactly how old are you?" When I told him seventeen, he blew out through his lips. "Seventeen! Your whole life is ahead of you. Do you really want to spend it nursing an invalid?"

"You want me to leave Fox?" My hands twisted around each other in my lap.

"I know. I know," Harry Rand said. "You think I'm being disloyal to Fox, but Fox would be the first to agree with me. He wouldn't want you to sacrifice yourself for him. You know that, don't you? Let's call a spade a spade."

"But I love him," I repeated stupidly, as if those words could block out the reality behind the sheriff's little speech.

"I'm sorry to have to bring this up now," the sheriff said, his face florid with the effort it took to lift himself from the couch, his forehead coated with sweat. "But I gotta tell you what I think is right. I won't pull legal strings to make you leave, though, if that's worrying you." He set his big, warm paw on my shoulder, and we walked slowly from the living room through the dining room. There was no breeze outside, the leaves drooping in the heat. At the back door the sheriff put on his sunglasses and reached out to fold me against his chest. The bigness of his body seemed to absorb my fear and exhaustion. If I needed anything, I knew where to find him.

Mary Donniger said, "He's depressed, dearie," when Fox began to withdraw into himself during his third week in the hospital, and his silence, his monosyllabic responses, his downcast eyes were crushing. I did not let his moods keep me away. I went every night filled with my bag of tricks, jokes meant to tickle his funny bone, touches meant to claim his heart. "Please go," he would say in his sad, lethargic voice. Or once, "Stop trying so hard." I'd take a long sip of air and deny I was trying. *Afraid. Sad. Missing him,* I wrote in my diary. Scrubbing the carbon off the bottom of pots, brushing Richard until there wasn't a burr on his body, weeding the garden did not halt my morbid thoughts. Fox's decline was my decline. When I questioned him about his pain, he said joylessly it was like making love—it had a hundred variations. Sometimes he was churned up and restless, sometimes speechless and estranged. "They all go through this," Mary Donniger advised.

His bandages were off, his naked arms, what was left of them, exposed to the world for the first time. The tissue at the end of the stumps was swollen and pulpy, angry red and the purply green of mashed eggplant. The flaps of skin had been tucked under and sewn together, fine black stitches sunk deep into the flesh. I'd seen men with a trouser leg or sleeve pinned up, men with eye patches, and once, a man with an ear shaped like a piece of coral, but I had never seen a body that had been pruned. One evening I walked into his room while he was trying to stand up by himself. He heard my voice just as he was angling his upper spine forward, bringing his chest down almost to his knees to give himself the momentum needed to push off the bed but caught between not being able to lie back down or stand up. His face had gone completely gray, and he'd broken out in a sweat. I reached him in time to prevent him from toppling over, not knowing where to grasp his shaking body, how to avoid touching his wounds. While he braced his upper body against my side and caught his breath, I called for the nurse. Mary Donniger was there in a minute, easing him back against his pillows, instructing me to raise his legs onto the bed. It was a bad moment about to become worse. Mary settled him and had left the room when his shoulder went into a spasm and what remained of his left arm flew up and down. His whole body began to quiver, the spasms in his shoulder spreading to his neck, the muscles bunching and knotting visibly under the skin. He cried out from the pain, and I shouted for Mary again, Fox pleading with his wild eyes for me to leave. I knew he hated me to see him like this and believed that if I walked out, he'd never permit me to see him again. I believed that he could so easily hate me, and probably did.

He started rehab, nothing too strenuous, simple range-of-motion exercises with a physical therapist who visited St. Claire's twice a week. It was exhausting for him, Mary Donniger said, and made him irritable and we needed to encourage our Galahad to mix more with the others in rehab. "His type, dearie, the silent, independent ones, don't heal as fast as the talkers," she said.

I wheeled him into the lounge in the afternoons where he sat withdrawn and sullen among the other patients and listened to television. The news of the day became a focus for his anger. The mistreatment of Negroes in the South. The troubles in the Congo. Cuba. "All governments are bullies," he said cynically. I couldn't bear the agitation in his eyes. He didn't want me around. When I came the next time, he was out of his room. The aide at the nurses' station was fixing a tray of pills. "Where is he?" I asked. She stopped counting out the pills and sucked her lower lip. Her face reddened. "I'm sorry," she said. "I guess he just wants to be alone."

Later that afternoon, Ty found me crying with clothespins in my mouth. Though storm clouds were piling up in the west, I wasn't really paying attention to the weather, and I was pegging up the laundry. Determined to keep a positive attitude, to be steadfast, to not be put off by Fox's moods, I conjured happy pictures of Fox with his prostheses, plastic or rubber or wood, flesh-toned but pinker, not matching his real flesh, stiff and creaky at the joints, but workable. It would be my job to help him learn how to use his artificial hands. We'd sit at the dining room table and no matter how many hours it took, I would be patient and encouraging as he practiced picking up a glass. We'd practice over and over until he could feed himself, wash his face, comb his hair. A big oily drop landed on my arm, and I glanced at the sky. Sickly green clouds were moving in fast, the towels and sheets I'd just hung bulging with wind. Ty was hurrying through the gate, pushed forward by gusts that lifted his bangs straight up from his forehead. He pointed to the sky and yelled that Lloyd was driving the tractor down from the field and would put it in the shed.

In an instant, rain was lashing at us. Ty grabbed the laundry basket and ran alongside me as I tugged the shirts and towels from the line. "We're getting drenched," I said, laughing. It was the first time since the accident I'd felt alive. I was remembering how much I loved the fury of a summer storm, how Rose and I used to dance outside when the rains came, the wind ripping at our clothing, the pond frothing with whitecaps, and the crows in a jubilee. Now wind and rain went shrieking through the great oaks, tearing leaves from the branches, the grass boiling with instant puddles.

Ty seized my hand, the loaded basket under his other arm, and we dashed across the yard. Inside the mudroom, he set the basket down. The storm was moving away as quickly as it had come, leaving us soaking and tentative with each other in the quiet house. Ty ran his hand over his forehead, slicking back his hair. My own hair was dripping on my neck. "Would you like a towel?" I asked, reaching for one.

"You first," he said. I lifted the towel to my face, aware, as I raised my arm, of the transparency of my wet shirt. Ty was watching me with an intensity I could feel between my legs.

"Are you his girlfriend?" he said.

It was almost comical the way he asked, trying to sound offhanded, casual, his expression so earnest it almost hurt to look at him.

I dried my hair with the towel before answering. "I've been living on the farm with Fox since December. Some people would call that his girlfriend."

"I guess I heard that, but I wasn't sure it was true." His hands had slid into the pockets of his wet jeans. "You're not a cousin, then? Or some relative?"

I shook my head. The rain had stopped. The air was very still, the sun trying to break through a ridge of mottled clouds.

"What are you going to do . . . after?" he said.

"After?"

He shrugged, backing away, his arm extended behind him to push open the screen door.

I was about to say, *What about you? Aren't you getting married?* But he was halfway out the door. There was a rainbow.

"Look!" we said at the same moment.

The dispersing clouds were shot through with rays of sunlight, and below, closer to the earth, arcing over the width of the farm, was a shimmering band, the colors distinct as spools of thread—indigo, blue, yellow, red. "It's been a long time since I've seen a rainbow this bright," Ty said.

I stepped outside and came next to him. The earth was steaming, a fresh pungent smell rising from it. The rainbow had begun to fade, its colors a wash of pastels. A hornet flew out from under the wood siding and hovered around my ear. Ty turned and swiped at it with his broad flat hand, his palm grazing my cheek. I raised my fingers to where he'd touched me, the spot tingling as if I'd been stung. "You shouldn't try that on a hornet. It makes them angrier." I made a show of examining the eaves for the hornets' nest. The rainbow was now completely gone.

"I have to get going," Ty said.

I didn't want him to leave any more than I wanted the rainbow to disappear. We both knew we'd come to the end of something that had never begun.

Fox started to come out of the abyss. He looked forward to details about the farm, a positive sign. He began prowling after life.

At night I ran my fingers over the spines of his many books, hunting for subjects that would interest him. Soon we were discussing Adolf Hitler and vegetarianism, Mayan gods, cocoa beans, Matisse, the sunken Atlantis. He asked me about the bee boxes, and I said they were stored in the barn. "Have you ordered bees yet?" I shook my head. In my heart of hearts, I no longer wanted to be a beekeeper or be reminded of the wild and beautiful life whose sweetness I could still taste in my dreams. Getting Fox well was all that mattered, not the past. I'd begun to suspect that at Harry Rand's instigation, for my sake, St. Claire's was keeping Fox as a special patient longer than was usual. For my sake and for Mary Donniger's. She'd dropped her professional reserve and grown attached to us. "You've been a bonny lass," she'd said to me more than once. "Family is what gets a lot of them through," she said, and I was essential to Fox's recovery. I had entered a new era with Mary Donniger.

He had a new doctor. His name was Travis. Dr. Travis said Fox would have pains and itching until the bruising and lacerations healed and the tender lymph nodes drained. He wore a narrow tie, thick glasses, and a stethoscope around his neck. He explained about phantom limbs, the teasing of nerves that no longer existed, ghost sensations that inhabited ghost hands. His little pep talks to Fox about exercise and diet were delivered in a rote, impersonal voice. Mary Donniger said Dr. Travis had been a POW in Korea and was a strange duck. Dr. Travis wanted to send Fox for rehabilitation in another facility. I didn't want to think about our separation. I knew it would happen, but I pretended it would be a long time off.

Several days before the one-month anniversary of the accident, Fox seemed to have turned another corner. His hair, restored to its former glossiness, curled luxuriously over his ears. And though he'd lost weight and the outline of his kneecaps and ribs showed beneath his skin, he felt stronger. The pain was more diffuse, manageable. "Pain is a god," he said. "Pain rules. It has the final word." His appetite returned. The discolorations on his stumps were fading. His stitches were out; the redness was the redness of healing, not infection. He'd become grateful for the smallest things—the book-cart lady who read the latest Spillane mystery to him, the aide who still checked in on him almost hourly to see if he needed water. "Betty Boop" in a nurse's uniform he called her. He smiled so brilliantly it nearly broke my heart.

"Talk to me, Sparrow," he said one night. "Tell me how you are, really."

It was too big a question. I couldn't speak.

"Tell me," he said softly.

I didn't want to burden him. He'd suddenly become talkative, and I didn't know where to begin. The sad history of Mern and my father? Of Sam's departure, and Rose? Nights alone on the farm? I opened the window and let the near songs of robins enter the room.

"Let me guess. You're confused and afraid. The future is frightening you?" He was trying to make it easier for me, but I neither confirmed nor denied what he said.

"We have to talk," he said. "We can't *not* talk about certain things."

The breath of one of his sleeping roommates resounded like the surf, receding, returning again fuller. A nurse walked by in the hallway. Fox glanced at the door to see if it was Mary Donniger. It was not. His legs stretched like two toppled pillars under the hospital sheet; the tops of his toes wiggled.

"I miss you," I said. "That's the problem."

Chapter 32

Je Ne Regrette Rien

August 3, 1960. I bring him books and read aloud and the hours fly by. He likes Chekhov. Humans are tragic, jealous, conniving, heartbreaking. Undone by a seductive glance, Fox says. We've begun to talk about our pasts. He's confessed caramels are his favorite sweet from childhood. Tomorrow I'll bring him some. I'm happy to be drawing again!

August 3, 1960. PS. I forgot to say Fox was moved to a semiprivate room. He's off Mary Donniger's watch and she's crushed.

August 5, 1960. Put a caramel on Fox's tongue. He mugged like a kid, refusing to chew the caramel to prolong the pleasure. You have a whole bag left! I said. He and his mom used to eat caramels while they played mahjong on a Chinese set his father bought in India. His father had been Canadian, an engineer who designed bridges and who had once lived in India. His mom, Evelyn, studied to become a watercolorist in England. I told him his childhood sounded very exotic and asked if he'd ever heard of a pango! O Sam Podesta, where are you?

August 8, 1960. I'm reading *Great Expectations* by Charles Dickens to Fox. What will happen to Pip? I don't remember how he came up, but I told Fox about Dupere. Fox asked if I knew where my parents were. I said no. He asked if I wanted to find them. I told him he was my family. I'm not, he said. Tonight I examined myself in the mirror, and sure enough, impossible as it seems, Mern's face is alive beneath my usual one.

I brought Fox another bag of caramels. I was bringing him everything that I was, everything we'd been together. I was bringing myself and saying, Do you want me? You can have me. Say you want me. Say you want me to stay. I'll stay. Do you believe in sweetness, Fox? Say you do. Here it is; here I am. We can be sweet together again. Believe in our sweetness.

Fox was embattled, like a man who'd swum far out to sea and was exhausted but could not give up. He watched his leg muscles wither and his belly grow slack and pushed himself beyond endurance, always straining for more sit-ups than his physical therapist required. Hot skewers lanced his nerves, and his nightmares continued after he opened his eyes, but he shunned pity. "You can tell me?" I'd whisper. Fox shook his head, refusing eye contact. Occasionally he did share a dream, especially if the dream left him in good spirits—Fox throwing a football or waving a butterfly net in a field of lupine—images in which he was vibrant and whole. How shocking it was for him to awake to his stumps, the sensations in his phantom fingers painfully real, and how helpless and melancholy I felt sitting in the plastic chair, my hands joined in my lap. If only I could have carried him over my shoulder and out the hospital back to the life we once had.

"Pain is not the mortal enemy. Time is," he said, and in quiet panic we launched a campaign to halt time inside the cocoon of his hospital room—our own imperial palace. But, of course, time refused to stop. With the summer solstice well behind us, the hours of light shaved by minutes, dusk arrived imperceptibly earlier each night. The peas were spent, the lettuce done, the tomatoes swollen to ripeness. The farm informed me of time's swiftness and nature's collusion in the sweep toward death. I had my own nightmares, my own moldering flashbacks. One night I dreamed of butchered rabbits strewn over the pasture, a malicious tractor gloating nearby. Another night, I tried to wake myself by crying out and woke into a second dream of myself as a child alone in my bed in Wild Pea.

Midmonth, on a Sunday afternoon, Ty knocked on the back door to tell me that he and Lloyd had just rotated the sheep to the back pasture and that they were working on a pulley system to make doors easier for Fox when he returned home. They could put levers on the faucets to make them easier, too, if I'd like. It was one of those gorgeous August days when the sunlight soaked the leaves and ground, and Ty himself was like Adonis, all bronze and golden and shining with life. When I invited him in, he hung back from the doorway and rubbed his nose, saying he hadn't washed up. Our encounter that stormy day in July, too brief to be called a flirtation, had made us reserved around each other, which was probably further proof of our attraction. Just recently Fox had asked about the Pulmacher boys, emphasizing the word *boys* when inquiring if they stayed for dinner sometimes, suggesting that, if they were pressed for time before taking me to the hospital, they could use the shower rigged in the barn instead of coming into the house. I took Fox's interest as a sign of his improving health, jealousy, or curiosity, whichever it was, revealing a core of desire.

Ty kept our conversation to the immediate and practical. He'd checked the flock for bumblefoot, and they were clean. Did I know it would be mating season soon? With Raj dead, what would I do for a ram? His uncle had a Corriedale breeder. Lloyd could bring the ram over when it was time.

"I can't think about it now," I said, annoyed at being reminded of future ordeals. Pregnant ewes. Lambing. We'd just gone through that! Ty smiled apologetically, then added, "Fox has got darn good livestock and a good little piece of land, and it would be a crying shame to let this place fall apart." I assured him that I wasn't going to let things fall apart and that I'd talk to Fox about the ram. From his genial expression, I saw there was only virtue in his comment. He's so good, I thought. He'll make his sweetheart a fine husband. *Fine* was the word that came to me. It went with his quiet grace.

Not an hour after Ty left, Harry Rand stopped by. He was wearing his khaki uniform, no holster, no gun, no badge, carrying a sack of groceries in the crook of his arm and the basket Mary usually stuffed with muffins, cookies, and scones, whistling as he got out of his cruiser. *Now there's a happy man*, I thought, and a piece of my worry floated away. Harry Rand no longer visited at a designated hour and no longer called before coming. We'd developed an understanding and were friends. And while I longed to confide in someone older and wiser, Sheriff Rand, built of rock-solid kindness, was not the one. He'd spent so many years sorting out the messy entanglements of others by relying on logic, law, and ethical practicality, I suspected he wouldn't understand the complexity of my relationship with Fox. Not to sell Harry Rand short, but I didn't think he conceived of Fox the artist, Fox the lover, Fox the man with the sorrowful past. I knew he understood about genuine loneliness, and as sheriff, he'd certainly dealt with nastiness and ordinary lunacy, but I doubted he'd had personal experience with the wayward strivings of the heart.

The sheriff strode through the kitchen to the dining room table. A little circus of sparrows had gathered under the evergreens, and we sat thoughtfully for a moment watching their antics. When he turned to me, the sheriff wore a serious expression. Shortly, Fox would be sent to the Van Kessel Institute for extensive rehabilitation. If I hadn't considered so before, wouldn't I now consider moving in with him and Mrs. Rand until I made a decision about my future? Before I could get in a word about the farm, he said he'd already run the idea past Ty and Caroline, due to be married in September, and they agreed to move into the house and caretake the farm. Neither of them had been looking forward to living with old man Pulmacher.

It was a long sentence, and the sheriff had to catch his breath after he finished. "What do you think, sweetheart?" he said, stretching out his arms to crack his knuckles. I didn't say anything. There was something rehearsed and final about his suggestion, a neat package handed to me all tied up, the rough edges taped over.

"Does Fox know? Does he want this?" I said.

The sheriff patted himself for a cigarette. "Doesn't know some of it. Knows he's going to the Institute. Haven't told him about Ty and his sweetheart, Caroline." He lit a cigarette and blew smoke out the side of his mouth. He said he saw his plan as a chance for me to get on with my life. "I might even be able to get you an Elk's Club scholarship for higher education, if you choose that route."

I smiled weakly and hung back from answering. But Harry Rand wasn't blind. He waited, taking long pulls on his cigarette, grinding it out on a saucer when he was convinced my response remained less than eager.

"Think about it," he said. "No pressure." As I walked him outside, I could see that from his point of view, I was wasting my life.

We stood by his Plymouth, and to make the visit end on a happy note, he said, "Mary Rand has outdone herself this time. Wait till you taste her new oatmeal raisin recipe. She used honest-to-goodness maple syrup and them cookies are big as saucers."

I might have laughed at the idiocy of his statement at such a time if I hadn't been aware that Harry Rand was a prodigy of gallant gestures.

Later, I asked Lloyd to take me to the hospital early. Lloyd always begged my pardon for being quiet during the ride, as if silence were an affliction, but I told him I was grateful for the peace without the sound of sheep or dog.

When I got off the elevator on Fox's floor, a new aide named Lois was at his bedside. "Hello," she said. "We're just finishing." She must have known to leave when I came in. After she'd gone, I asked Fox how he felt. I wasn't going to tell him about the sheriff's visit. Not yet.

"I'm glad you're here," he said.

I went and sat on his bed, my hand on his thigh.

"I've been thinking you're a very brave girl," Fox said, in that way he had of making me feel proud and special. "You could have deserted the ship. No one would have blamed you."

A tear slipped down my cheek.

Fox sighed. "Many tears," he said softly.

"Many," I agreed.

"Me too."

"I know," I said.

Fox gazed out the window across the room at the sky, a deepening plum blue hung with peach-colored clouds. The bed under the window was empty, his roommate, Mr. Keane, dismissed the day before.

"Are you very lonely?" His voice came from far off.

"No, not very." My answer surprised me. I hadn't realized the ache was subsiding.

Fox shut his eyes and rested for a moment. "You look beautiful tonight," he said, his voice endlessly haunting, endlessly tired.

"Do I?"

"Close the curtain," he said.

I heard the change in his tone. I got up and closed the curtain.

"I wish I could hold you," he whispered. "Let me at least smell you." He had learned to make jokes about himself, referring to the misfortunes of other artists—Monet, blind with cataracts, painted with a brush tied to his wrist; Rembrandt, destitute and a drunk; poor van Gogh, mad as a hare. Fox said he would relearn to paint with a brush between his teeth and become rich and famous in his dotage.

I lay over him and fanned my hair across his face. He inhaled deeply, and I kissed his laughing mouth. I was hungry for him, and yet when I kissed him, it was with a new, more tender, less frantic passion, as if everything between us could be expressed in the meeting of our lips.

"Let me see you," Fox said.

"Here? Now?"

He nodded.

I started with my shirt, releasing each button from its hole with deliberate slowness, my shadow smoky and sinuous on the wall behind his head.

Fox's sex stiffened under the sheet. It was the answer we were both hoping for, the answer we needed. I leaned forward and pressed my hand over his hardness and felt it jump. His eyelids flickered, and he moaned like wind in a tunnel. I unhooked my bra, my breasts lifting in release, then quickly removed the rest of my clothes and straddled him. My wetness was extravagant.

Inside me his heat was combustible and urgent, turning my bones to water. If Fox felt pain, it was a delirious, beautiful agony. Our bodies were wise. They refused to lie. They were tactless and incapable of lying, and they held no grudges.

He knew they were sending him to Van Kessel but not about the sheriff's plan.

"St. Claire's isn't equipped for long-term therapy," he said. The Institute had the newest equipment, a proper gym, a swimming pool, special baths. They'd fit him with limbs. He'd work hard, he said, and hopefully return as close to who he was before, as close as diligence and determination could take him. He didn't know how long he'd be gone. Months.

I'd dressed and stood gripping the foot bars at the end of his bed, still tremulous from making love. I longed to get back on top of him, but visiting hours were almost over. I believed he'd work hard; he'd just proven how his body refused to be curbed. He had his eyes on me, and I had a presentiment he was about to say something serious.

"This isn't easy to talk about," he said.

"Are you sending me away?" I whispered.

He shook his head. "I'd never tell you to leave. I don't have the power to say those words. I'm incapable of it."

"What, then?"

His ardent eyes went abject in sorrow. "I don't know," he said, and gazed again at the sky and the black trees. "Maybe you should go. Maybe I'm being selfish. Maybe you should find another life."

I hadn't planned on saying what I said next, but with Fox leaving, I knew that if I didn't say something now, I might never tell him, and my not telling him would sully the thing between us. I found it difficult to breathe but forced myself to explain how I'd found the drawings of Iris in the barn and how I'd been coming up to the hay field to confront him before the accident.

Fox looked genuinely confused. "What pictures?"

Steeling myself, I described the sketches I'd found in the barn. Fox's face clouded, and I had an image of him putting a hand to his forehead, the way he used to when he was thinking about something, though his stumps lay useless against his side. It broke my heart.

"There may have been some drawings in that room, I don't remember, but the point is they were old drawings not recent ones." He closed his eyes. "Look, we have to live our lives differently now. Forget that day. Please. Let Iris rest in peace." He was breathing audibly. I went over and took his face between my hands and studied it. I kissed his forehead; he wrenched away. "I have to make you understand," he said. "You are not her. You were never her." He tried to push himself up in bed, his face twisting with effort. "I loved Iris, but not as a woman. We were kids, frustrated, horny kids. Two lonely adolescents caught in the confusion of our feelings." His eyes burned into me, defiant, enraged, captive, pleading. "I thought I loved Iris but everything between us was a fantasy. We were never sexual. After she died, she became a symbol of everything good and pure about love. The women I sought later..." He was struggling to make himself clear before his energy gave out. "I had many liaisons but never love." He shook his head convulsively as if to convince me. "But you...you with your ragamuffin charm, your orphan's paradoxical independence and need...you broke through my defenses...I couldn't resist."

I moved onto the bed and put my arms around Fox's head and laid my cheek on his scalp. I was discovering new ways to hold him. A hundred new positions for love.

An aide knocked on the door. "Past visiting hours," she said. I stood up and smoothed my jeans. The darkness had crept in stealthily, and now it was unbearable to think of leaving Fox for the night. "One more thing," he said as I approached the door. I turned back into the room. He didn't want me to go. He wanted me to stay on at the farm, in his room. Forever.

In the elevator, I thought, *He's going away for a while, but he'll be back. This is not a farewell. We are not parting ways.* But later, alone in bed, my small self embedded in the pitch-black heart of my room, the walls high embankments, I imagined more dinners alone, waking before dawn to an empty house. The weight on my chest was dense, impenetrable matter, like being buried under wet clay, the opposite of love's lightness but also a component of love.

The very next day, I did something I'd never done before: I strolled down the driveway and out the gate, pausing to look back up the hill at the farm, barely visible through the spruce. I turned and headed west down the county road into the glaring radiance of the afternoon, the locusts and maples and huge old oaks shimmering in the August heat. Everything—the dusty roadside lilies, the Queen Anne's lace, and the rusty stands of sumac—looked special, different, a vast new world as strange in the quiet of the late-day hours as if I'd crossed a border into foreign territory. Accompanied by the thrumming cicadas, I walked for miles, scanning the terrain with soft eyes, marveling at the shine on berries or the fragile blue sky. On the way back, I found a redwing blackbird, scarlet epaulets still blazing red, one smashed wing raised as if it had been trying to fly away. I carried the bird home in my cupped hands and put it on a white dinner plate, and as the sun descended, I sat down to draw.

I went to tell Fox I had an idea. My idea was that while he was in rehab, I would go back to Wild Pea, stay with Mr. Tabachnik, and together we would try to find my mother. I told him about the sheriff's plan to have Ty and Caroline live on the farm, and I said that of course I wouldn't be leaving for good, only for a little while. "Brilliant!" Fox said. "The perfect solution." And for a second, I pictured him jumping out of bed to twirl me in his arms.

I didn't see him off on the day he left—I was afraid I'd break down—but I went to the send-off party at the hospital, Mary Donniger outdoing herself, supplying ham sandwiches, shortbread, and scones. Her Galahad, she said, deserved nothing less than the queen's high tea. Dr. Travis had been his usual cool and cautious self, full of matter-of-fact instructions. Don't waste your chances, Mr. Fox. Be tough. Set your mind on the future. There are a lot of things you can do with your life. Good luck and good-bye. The sheriff said Travis's creed must have gotten him through the days and nights he spent rotting in a Korean POW camp.

"I hear you're leaving too," the sheriff said, one of Mary Donniger's scones crumbling in his mouth.

"I'm just going on a visit," I corrected.

"A visit?" the sheriff said.

While I elaborated, I kept my eyes on Fox's valise parked in a corner of the hospital nurses' lounge, its tarnished hinges and worn handle, Fox's tartan pajamas packed away. His brush and comb. Mary Donniger would dress him in slacks and a shirt, plant a kiss on each of his cheeks.

"Well, keep in touch, sweetheart," the sheriff was saying, pinching my arm. "Good for you!" His words echoed what Fox had said: *It will be good for you to get away. I'm glad you're going. Don't forget you're my brave girl. Come back to me soon.*

The day I left, I ransacked the kitchen drawers and cabinets, gathering in a large tin bucket anything that caught my eye. Aluminum cookie cutters shaped like flowers and stars, bits of old ribbon, homespun yarn, sheep bells. I took ladles and serving spoons from their hooks, a pair of Fox's wire rims that were missing the lenses, lead washers and slices of copper tubing, a daisy chain of daisies.

I was thinking, *This is foolish. This is insane.*

It was a glorious day. A hint of autumn in the impending shadows settling around roots and rocks. The flies were out in abundance, but they didn't bother me. Out the gate, up the lane, over the stiles, I started to run, feeling lithe and light, capable of covering a great distance without tiring, the objects in the bucket clanking against its metal sides.

In the orchard I went straight to the line of trees into which Rose disappeared the evening of the big snow and selected a wide-armed beauty hung with green fruit, its leaves shiny with health. With bells and ribbons, wool bits, cookie cutters, yarn and tinsel, I decorated its branches, blessing Sam Podesta and the catalpa. Bees were scouring last year's windfalls, and I remembered Rose telling me that honeybees were born with the hexagonal shape of their cells imprinted in their brains, and how humans were also governed by patterns we knew nothing about.

I imagined that when I found my mother, she would pester me with questions, nosing after the gory details. I'd tell her about Rose and Ruben, Fox and the farm, Hermes, JJ and the carnival, Fox's accident. She'd have stories of her own. Stories of pandemonium, disaster, travails over men. After she'd smoked her last cigarette and was pouring herself another shot of rum, I'd ask her what it was truly like, the true experience of my birth. What was it like the very first time you held me in your arms? I'd ask. What did you see when you looked into my eyes? Did you love me?

I stepped back, walked around the apple tree, and regarded my creation, the small, hard fruit flushing pink-green, the apple leaves trembling with silver light. I saw pictures—Buddy's Garden of Eden brimming with luscious fruit. I saw the Hanging Garden of Babylon, fig trees and palm trees, a lamb being licked by a wolf. I saw the shimmering blade of Iris's body diving into that black water. I saw Rose in a field covered with pulsing bees. I saw Fox's finger painting a flower of semen on my belly, and I saw that he would not be lost. We would not be lost. None of us. Somehow, someday, we would gather at this tree, a tribe of beloveds, the negligent and the errant, the forsaken, the wanderers and the lapsed wanderers alike.

The following week I said a temporary good-bye to the farm. I'd cleaned the house until every metal surface shone and not a loose hair was in sight. I baked a rhubarb pie to welcome the newlyweds and left Richard with a full bowl of food. I was sad to leave, but I believed the most painful time of my life was over. I pictured Fox on the day of his homecoming wearing his new arms. People who saw him would say his face had become almost saintly, bearing that strange, ravaged contentment I'd observed in paintings of St. Sebastian or St. Paul. I'd seen it in him already—that tested-by-fire look.

I imagined him walking from room to empty room, feeling as if his heart might shatter, but when he came to the doorway of his bedroom, he'd see the self-portrait I'd sketched of myself while he was in the hospital hanging in place of Iris above his bed. I'd give him a moment before surprising him with my presence, sliding my arms around his waist and whispering, "I'm here."

DALE M. KUSHNER

October 2004

Pyrus malus, the wild ancestor of our domesticated apple trees, biblical Tree of Forbidden Knowledge, Tree of the Forbidden Fruit. How appropriate I come here to the orchard to talk to you, Fox, to this Duchess apple, one of the few trees that hasn't succumbed to blight or rot. I sit among its knobby roots, my back against the trunk, and imagine we converse.

I haven't quite forgiven you for dying. Eighteen months now and the passage of days has not been swift, your death all the more shocking because I'd denied the fact of your aging. Till the last you defied time's ravishment. Till the end you strode erect and clear-sighted into the fields, your beauty and dignity unwavering. Which is why your stroke stunned me. *Stunned.* Do you know the origin of that word? It comes from the old French *estoner*, to astonish. The hollowed out person in the hospital was *astonishingly* not you.

Tears. So many tears, after which I went speechless, like you, the effort of putting thought into language too wearying. Everything wearied me. Leaden arms, leaden legs, my heart slashed through. Remember the night not long after you returned from Van Kessel and I from visiting Mern and Rose? We had a picnic here in the orchard and you said, *Would it be cruel of me to ask for a baby?* Cruel! You would have never used that word before the accident, and I might not have responded with an unfaltering, "I want your baby." *Two roads diverged in a yellow wood, and sorry I could not travel both*, Frost wrote. And isn't that how it is? We come to a crossroad and choose and our life is forever altered.

What would I have done these months without our daughter Iris? She took a leave of her busy practice to stay with me. Ocularists with her talent for simulating realistic prosthetic eyes are in great demand, but she wouldn't be talked out of it. She stayed for a month, and true to being her father's daughter, the first week she arrived, she marched me to my studio and told me "to let the paint speak." I was like a horse shown onto a familiar track: on cue, I walked straight to my easel, squeezed some color onto the palette, and poured my sorrow into ren-

354

ditions of your face, the cure for bereavement, it would seem, a scrutiny of its most harrowing and melancholic dispositions. I worked in a frenzy, dozens of portraits of you, finishing late at night sometimes but unwilling to leave before starting a new painting, fearing all endings, all that replication my effort to lift beauty out from the terrible, as Mr. Tabachnik would have said.

I don't believe in endings. Remember the day you said that? You'd been back from rehab nine months. With Ty's help, you'd gained confidence in managing simple farm tasks but you were still fragile and clenched against further shocks to the heart. We were fixing up the chicken coop for my studio: I was hauling out wheelbarrows of chicken shit and hay; you were leaning against a nearby tree embracing a plank of fresh pine. You'd instructed Pete at the mill as to the exact length and width for the lumber, but you couldn't hold a nail or swing a mallet. I was only half listening, and you must have felt bruised by my inattention. More than that, you must have felt useless. It does no good now to say I'm sorry and to tell you I'm ashamed of my cruelty and thoughtlessness. I think I was angry that day, angry and guilty, and pitying, the emotion you hated the most. It should have been your studio we were building. Fate had stolen a part of your arms and your fame, and I was angry at some indefinable Divine Will that had let it happen. But there you were, ever the teacher and mentor, ever my biggest fan, and I ached for your exposed soul.

You got off on a tangent about how an artist knows a work of art is finished. *At a certain moment you know in your marrow the painting is refusing you and you have to leave it and walk out of the room.*

I put down the wheelbarrow and studied you through a shaft of hay dust. What in the world were you talking about? *Walk out of the room!* Were you depressed, obliquely referring to quitting life? The lumber fell from your arms and crashed to the ground, setting off a cloudburst of dirt. I'd probably read too many Greek myths—Daphne into a myrtle tree—but I could feel myself turning to wood. The brevity of your smile frightened me, and my breath went shallow.

"All endings are artificial," you said, kicking at the wood with your boot. "Ten years after you've put a canvas in the closet, you pull it out and add a red sun. In another ten, you paint over the sun." You waited another moment before raising your gaze to mine. *We can't know what we are creating, Sparrow, until long after we've created it.*

What *did* you mean, Fox? We were having one of those layered conversations that can never be picked clean, but when I reflect on your words today, I think you may have been talking about reinvention and about hope. If I'm correct, months from now, your death will throw new marvels into high relief.

Are you there, Fox? Are you listening?

Speaking of endings... Did you always believe we'd have a happy one? The day I left you to find my mother, you must have worried I wouldn't return. I was barely eighteen. I might have traded my dungarees and work boots for a wand of mascara and a new boyfriend. I wasn't a martyr. I wasn't even that "good"—but that's another story. You were so brave to have trusted me! I was a child, really, your future, my future—the path ahead was murky and it must have frightened you to let me go, but you did, honoring my freedom to decide for myself, the way I once tested Eunice Turtle by setting her in a pond to see if she'd swim back.

If you believed I sacrificed myself for you, you must have also known I depended on your love. I was fervently dependent, and I don't see how any love of worth can be otherwise. Dependence and independence rightly coexist! I come here and am *expanded* by your presence, not made less. What a relief to discover our habit of lifelong companionship can't be broken by death. Time is a distinctly human and claustrophobic invention, but you, in the invisible realms, must already know this.

And yet... and yet... my physical desires persist. Some days I'm bent in half with a need to nuzzle and sniff your body, to lay mine over yours and to breathe in your breath. Instead, I swallow the bitterness that sorrow is and push away my childish wrath at your abandonment. Like everything else, my feelings are unpredictable and transient, but happily, Iris has given me a project to occupy my mind. Write a memoir, she says. Write about Dad. Write about crazy Mern and Rose. Her instructions: Don't think about what you are writing. Let your mind roam. No censoring allowed. I balked at first and got anxious and defensive—what do *I* have to write about? I wonder what you'd want me to say about us. I wonder what you would say. I hope you'll come in dreams and tell me. I feel a burden "to get it right." At the moment, however, a chill wind is rolling in across the meadow, and I hate to leave, but I'm getting cold. The time you found me nearly frozen in the orchard tool shed so long ago just flashed through my mind. We'd argued and I'd taken off in a huff and you'd come searching. That night christened a new era—the first time we realized we'd endure—and forty-four years later, here we are.

Jottings for Memoir

February 2005

It's raining heavily today, a good excuse to begin. I sit at the edge of my chair, pen flying across the yellow pages of a legal pad. Later I'll put it all on the computer, but at the moment, writing longhand activates the gears in my mind. I've decided that if there are no endings, then there are no beginnings either, and so I'm just plunging in.

Exhibit A: Photograph of Mern dated May 9, 1964. Paisley miniskirt, hair in a teased beehive, kohl-rimmed eyes hauntingly huge. On the back, in her bounding cursive: Mod me! Carnaby Street, USA.

March 1961. While Fox was in rehab, I went to visit Mr. Tabachnik and with his help, we found Mern living with Nick in Burbank, California. I got on a Greyhound, crossed tracts of corn and soy over to the mountains of Colorado and down through Arizona, cruising on into Nevada, where the desert was weirdly eclipsed by the lone brilliant hub of Vegas. I'd just turned eighteen, a fledgling traveler, naive and grieving the terrible accident that had claimed my lover's arms. Days and nights in the smoky posteriors of the nation's buses. The monotonous interspersed with stark-lovely landscapes. For company: knit-and-purl grandmas, sample-toting salesmen, the few unwashed, yet-to-be-called flower children. Greasy fries, undercooked burgers. Antsy but exhausted with anticipation. I hadn't seen Mern since the spring of 1959, the night of the flood, and had no idea what to expect.

Our meeting. The bus doors parted. I stepped down into the salty trade winds that had bumped the thermometer up to ninety degrees. Mern was at the curb squinting into her compact, reapplying lipstick. The first thing she said to me: "My gawd, kiddo! What happened to you??? You look a hundred years old!" She had on huge wraparound sunglasses and tears leaked from beneath the plastic rims. Pulling me to her bony chest, she kissed my forehead and rocked me like a baby. "Let's forget all the bad stuff and start again, okay?" I clung to her thin frame, laughing and crying, some vestige of familial blood quickening in me. Mern was her slapstick, innocent ignorant self! Her violent flirty kisses! She was impossible not to adore. "What do you want to do?" she asked. Before I could answer, she was dragging me toward her Chevy coupe, and then we were tooling down the highway to Malibu to look for movie stars.

The ocean on one side, mountains on the other. Air clear as glass. Sunlight as if refracted off a diamond. The scent of eucalyptus and kelp. Gulls over the breaking waves. Miles of beach, most of it, except for clusters of surfers, deserted. Something was different about my mother besides her dewy, sunblushed skin, something I couldn't identify until, over BLTs at the Harbor Café, I noticed she was less twitchy and sarcastic than she used to be, at peace among the local eccentrics, a blend of ranchers in cowboy boots, bronzed surfer boys, and bearded beatniks.

After lunch, we walked out onto the pier and then down to the beach. Mern took off her espadrilles and laced her fingers through mine. The tide was out, and we strolled along the packed sand, the beach slithering away from under our toes. At some point, I told her about Rose and Fox and about his accident. My mother stopped in her tracks and let out an unabashed, "Jesus H. Christ!!! No hands?" The words hung in the air, reverberating, and I might have gone down on my knees in tears if her outburst hadn't struck me as hilarious. A year-plus after Fox's accident and no one yet had spoken aloud the hideous truth. NO HANDS!!! A statement that made me want to wail and throw up and laugh all at the same time.

It might have been a little after that, after the wind picked up, that my mother removed her sweater and settled it over my shoulders. Taking my hand again, she thanked me for coming and asked me to forgive her for being a lousy mother. Behind her, the blue of the sea merged with the blue sky in a vanishing line streaked orange by the last bits of sun. "Forgiven," I said.

On the drive back to Burbank, Mern admitted Nick wasn't working out. "He's a good man and everything, but . . ." I was waiting for her to say he had no pizzazz, but instead she told me about a guy in her apartment complex. He was teaching her stuff. What kind of stuff? She pushed her glasses up the bridge of her nose. "Holy moly stuff." He'd been to Kashmir—cashmere—and was a clairvoyant. Really! I said. Yup, she said. He used to be Ted Ornstein, but now he was Lama Baba and sat on a straw mat, legs crossed, heels resting on knees, and chanted. He'd given away all his worldly goods and wore only a loincloth. He was twenty-eight years old and gorgeous. "Is he teaching you how to pray?" I asked. "Not exactly . . ." Mern's left hand slid from the steering wheel into a pocket. She handed me a brilliantly colored devotional card. "Lama Baba said this is me in my first incarnation." I stared at the extremely curvaceous and bejeweled dark-skinned lady rising from a giant pink lotus, gold coins spilling from her palms. "A Hindu goddess?" My mother smiled sheepishly, and I burst into laughter. Wouldn't Mern have loved to possess those ripe conical breasts, eyelashes as thick as a paintbrush, gold at her fingertips? "At least you weren't an ax murderer," I said.

I have to put down my pen and send up a cheer for the ever-hilarious Mern; even in death she makes me laugh. Now the rain has stopped and there's a sparkle to the air that reminds me of the clear Mediterranean light one sees in the coastal villages of Greece, a place I once visited during a siege with Fox when my own lights dimmed and I was lost to despair. Sadly, Mern never made it to the Aegean coast, but in a painting I did of her, she's at a harborside taverna wearing a big straw hat and sipping ouzo from a glass. Early on, I attributed my success as a painter to Fox and Milanka,* to their skillful instructions and

* Remember to tell about Milanka.

enthusiastic support and to Milanka's art world/gallery connections, but really, the mercurial Mern was my inspiration. To paint her was to know her in all her facets. I remember sending Mern the exhibition catalogue from my first show that included portraits of her. Recognizing herself as a subject, she sent it back with her picture circled in pink highlighter. Scrawled in the margin next to her face she'd written FAME AT LAST! She meant herself, of course, not me.

Mern. *Mernie.* She went out in a blaze of glory at the age of fifty-three after gall bladder surgery, attended by an intern she'd nicknamed Brando. I was inconsolable, unable to stop blaming myself for not flying to California to tell her I loved her before the surgery, though no one warned us she might die. On the anniversary of her death, Fox and I opened champagne, and I unveiled yet another painting that is now one of my favorites. She's seated at a vanity table wearing the apricot slip Sam gave her. On the table are her props—pots of rouge, powder puffs, makeup brushes of sable and squirrel. In the mirror, superimposed over her features, my own face appears in a gauzy blue mist, like the image of Jesus on the Shroud of Turin. The shadow in the doorway is my father. If the painting could talk, it would say, *A riff on family—what the Kodak missed.*

My crazy mother—ruined, ruining, and brave. I miss her every single day. I do.

Exhibit B1: My father. The photograph Mern kept in her underwear drawer when I was a child. Browning and curled at the edges. The handsome young Dupere in low-slung jeans and T-shirt, a swatch of dark hair falling over his forehead. My fantasy hero of a thousand days and nights. Mern and I loved him absolutely. (That he welcomed us only briefly into the shoddy spectacle of his affection did not seem to matter.)

Exhibit B2: His letters hidden in a box of old handbags at the back of Mern's closet. Ten letters held together by a rubber band and tied in a chiffon scarf still emitting a whiff of her Camels. Squint-eyed without her glasses, cigarette dangling, my mother slits an envelope with a cherry-red nail.

He'd developed retina problems and was living in a motel outside Gary, Indiana, nearly destitute. His letters span the seventies and stop a year before Mern's death in 1979. He outlived her by ten years.

Was it poverty or loneliness that impelled my father to write Mern? A request for money appears as a disjointed apology. We get what we deserve. Someone should have given me a swift kick in the butt for leaving you and Eunice. I hate to be asking. If you never answer this letter, I'll understand. *He wanted Mern to tell me a skunk could change its stripes.* Tell her I was a dumb-assed, selfish fool. Maybe you'll both come for a visit?

Mern must have refused him, at first. Then reconsidered. He thanks her with a promise "to make it up to her." I don't know if he did, or if they ever saw each other again. Then Mern died. Neither of my parents married, each other or anyone else, a tradition I have continued. (I'm calm rereading his words. Unanswered, unanswerable questions hover, but in the end I believe my parents' exchange of letters erased the guilt each felt. A friendship was reestablished, a lost world rediscovered.)

More Random Jottings for Memoir

March 2005

Today in the supermarket I thought I heard Rose's laugh, though this would be impossible because Rose died in 1995. Nevertheless, lured by blind hope and magical thinking, I whipped my cart over to the next aisle only to discover two clerks unpacking cartons, the girl sporting a nose ring and spiky blue hair laughing Rose's laugh. The mimicry jarred my composure and I fled.

There is no extensive public record of my relationship with Rose, no retrievable archive for posterity, which makes me the sole chronicler of who we were to each other, a responsibility I take seriously. And aside from the problem of where to begin her story, which for some reason troubles me more than writing about the others, there is the difficulty of setting into words the texture and flavor of our intimacy with its rich and complex nuances of mother and daughter, of sisters, and also of trusted friends.

Exhibit C: Snapshot, undated, probably late sixties. Rose outside her bakery in Brewster, Washington. Cobalt blue billboard advertising Rose's cardamom-spiced nectarine crumbler in background.

Exhibit D: Chunk of basaltic lava from the Columbia River Gorge. Chunk of crystallized zeolite from the same.

Musings: To this day, I don't know if the illness in Rose's body—most certainly TB—caused the illness in her mind. Not pride but a desire to spare me worry kept her from reaching out until she'd left the sanatorium and was healed in mind, body, and spirit. By mysterious and unknown means, she knew I was at the farm. I received a letter that arrived the week of Fox's accident (had she intuited a problem?) but I did not open it until weeks later.

On the same trip during which I visited Mern in Burbank (1961), I rented a car and drove up the coast to see Rose in Washington. She'd been released from the hospital and had a job helping a young couple establish a nectarine orchard. Her robustness now had a delicate side, as if all her equipment for listening and seeing, her attunement to the subtlest frets and scrabblings of invisible life had been turned up a notch. She was a quieter person but not without a big dose of her former glory. Her hair, wild as ever, rayed her face in coils of silvery gray. She was lean and strong, her color flush with health, but her voice betrayed the remnants of a cough that had roughed up her vocal cords forever.

We hiked in the Cascade Mountains under the benevolent watch of Douglas fir, their dense evergreen smell accompanying the sound of stampeding rivers. We had both just emerged from a dark time and it seemed natural to fill packs and walk deep into the forest. Now that we were together again, the troubles that so recently had burdened us evaporated. Everything had changed and nothing had changed, and I was still her darling girl.

But of course I was no longer a girl, nor had I the luxury of pretending I was one. After we had eaten our dinner and unrolled our sleeping bags, Rose rested her hand on my shoulder, the power of her gaze burning into me, as if to say, Relax, child. Trust life. No words needed to be spoken. Star fire burst through the immense black sky, and slowly the moon swung out above the mountain peaks. Rose sang quietly, and the backlash of tears I had been holding in flooded out.

The nights we slept under the stars were about as perfect an experience of sacredness as any questioning believer could hope for. Rose may have existed in the ordinary world but she wasn't of it. To be with her was to escape the petty, the trivial, the decorous and flimsy and to be housed in the grand.

Ten years ago a probate court–appointed administrator from a small town in Washington discovered my name and address among Rose's effects and contacted me. She'd been swept from a rocky trail during a rainstorm, her body found floating in a partially thawed lake by a pair of campers in the Pacific Northwest. The last time I'd seen Rose, she still owned the bakery in Brewster. She'd converted the place into a popular café and became a town legend. Then one day she sold the café and vanished. I did all I could to find her until finally admitting to myself she'd probably gone back into the wilderness and did not want to be found. (We'd had a half-dozen rendezvous prior to her disappearance, all of them on her turf. She never wanted to return to the Midwest.)

Two weeks after the attorney called, I received a box containing Rose's ashes. There was something else in the box as well: Belle's bronzed baby shoes. I held them up to the light, remembering that Rose had borne her sadness as a thing of great value and therefore had not been condemned to unhappiness. I felt almost giddy. Sorrow plied with patience and kindness, she'd said, feeds the spirit (another condition of love!), but my own theory is that unrelieved sorrow destroys one's cells, sucks the marrow from bones, and even sorcery is no antidote. I was hoping that in the end Rose would prove me wrong.

I sometimes think I invented her, Rose's life and character, the stuff of fiction. It's hard to imagine someone today so untouched by popular culture, so marginal, so feral, and yet so tuned in, so exquisitely aware and enlightened—*club moss to staunch bleeding, comfrey for ulcers*—but living in an alternate universe. Iris calls her the Good Witch. Who is the Bad Witch? I ask. Iris doesn't answer, but then Iris is more condemning of Mern than I. Were she alive today, Rose would be suspicious of the twenty-first-century infatuation with memoir-making. To her a story was worthless if it didn't impart wisdom, and a self-revealing, self-indulgent story the greater folly. I hope I am not betraying her. Forty-odd years later, I'm incredulous—no, disbelieving—how young and inexperienced I was when a strange woman plucked me from a tree on a stormy night and took me into the woods. We'd bonded and my life was forever altered—it might have been otherwise—and out of our loyalty and affection I constructed a faith.

Her death...an unfair ending. (And yet a perfect ending!) Hail in the mountains. Gusty winds. Mother Nature in all her unpredictable majesty. In my mind's eye, Rose is not bruised and unconscious tumbling off a mountain ridge, but a locus of calm awareness sailing down from the heights through the rain, eyes wide open, arms outstretched, the wind in her hair.

Exhibit E: Photo. Milanka Zuzoric and me standing next to a stone lion on the steps of the Art Institute, 1964.

The artist: June 1962. Dragana Zuzoric pulled up our drive looking to buy the Rambouillet lambs we'd advertised. She and her husband, Vasko, had bought a farm nearby and were planning to breed sheep. Plump Dragana, shawled and dirndled. Right away she noticed my studio, formerly the chicken coop, her sister an artist in Chicago.

Milanka, my henna-haired Milanka! Her smile of a thousand wrinkles, her wardrobe of gray and maroon. Restorer of frescoes, famous in her country for saving the peeling Magdalene in a monastery near the Albanian border. With Fox's blessings, in the fall of 1962, I went to study with Milanka in Chicago, sleeping on her antique sofa under the watch of dark Balkan landscapes and Oriental Madonnas on walls dingy from samovar steam and tobacco smoke. Fridays I walked to Union Station and took the Milwaukee Road home.

I reported to Fox my impressions of city life, the pawnshops and barred liquor stores, State Street at twilight engorged with last-minute shoppers.

Gypsy children, sandal-footed in the snow, hawking carnations under the soot and shimmy of the El. I sat at Milanka's drafting table and sketched high-rises of glass and steel, the steel as blue and icy as the huge slabs of frozen water jammed along the beaches of Lake Michigan. Urban life preoccupied me; I was no longer a witness to Fox's bouts of silence, the days he sat unshaven in the kitchen, kidnapped by despair. The acid facts of his accident would take us both years to absorb, but he understood better than I how healing required privacy and unlimited time, how he needed space to drop forks and break plates without me watching. How lucky I was that Milanka let me stay for six months while I soaked up all she could teach me in her non-museum hours. By day I wandered neighborhoods, visited abandoned churches, photographed a dancing mule on Maxwell Street, a Hasidic wedding on Devon. Cornices and stone lions, zoo-keepers and giraffes. The things we believe we are examining are examining us.

I returned to the farm in April of '63. I had just turned twenty and was pregnant. Fox was listening to Glenn Gould's Goldberg Variations *when I arrived. Before I could tell him the news, he said, "If Gould had lost his fingers, he would have still been a superb pianist." I set down my large portfolio and walked into the living room. "We're going to have a baby," I announced, unable to contain myself a second longer. A terrible trembling started in Fox's jaw and spread down his shoulders, his arms shaking so badly his hooks rattled in his lap. I knelt beside him and slid my hand under his shirt, pressing fingers against his heart.* Will this be good for us? *he asked.* Très bien, *I whispered.*

The unflappable Alice Knight delivered Iris Rose on a frosty morning at the end of October. Like all babies, Iris was noisy and wrinkled, a Lucille Ball of facial mimicry. Fox was experimenting with new prosthetic hands to replace his hooks, but they were numb and insensitive, his grip tenuous at best, and he worried how he would manage a baby.

Exhibit F: The paintings that made me famous—my middle style—a marriage of Mary Cassatt and Lucian Freud.

First painting: Male Interloper. *Me among the sheets, Iris Rose suckling at my breast. Fox in the doorway, naked from the waist up, skin glistening from the shower. Abbreviated arms heavy and aimless against his sides. Room tipped toward the frontal picture plane. Elongated purple shadows seeping over the floorboards.*

Second painting: The Adoration. *Fox in front of the bedroom window. Elbows and forearms pressed together to hold a swaddled Iris Rose. The incoming shaft of golden light.*

April 2005

Fox, I've almost completed my memoir, but lately whenever I start to write about you, some inner antagonist cuts it off. It's so much easier just to nestle against this apple tree and talk. I never told you that on my first visit to Mern and Rose I stopped at the small coastal village where you'd rented a bungalow-turned-studio above the Pacific, the one and only time you gave yourself wholly to painting and to exorcising Iris's ghost. I walked the same cliffs you must have walked above the roiling waves, wondering if your guilt over Iris's death had tempted you to take your own. (How old were you then? In your twenties?) Obviously, you didn't, but what protected you, what turned you back to life? (You probably understand why I'm asking this. I did, for a while, want to die after you died.) Did you wake up one morning, your sorrow shabby and outworn in the resolute oceanic light? Maybe that day you set up your easel and for one single hour attempted to forget. Or maybe—I'm guessing here—you drove into town and found a woman in a bar and lost yourself between her legs. Was it then you entered A Phase of Women, none important to you as individuals but the combination a restorative tonic?

You hid Iris from me for so long. What else were you hiding? Digging around in the past has raised questions.

Remember the day I showed up at your door? You answered with a bloody towel slung over your shoulder, and I wondered if I was stepping into Bluebeard's lair. I felt a strong instinct to run away, but when you asked if I knew about animals, your face softened, a secret sweetness you were letting me see, and I stayed. I'll never know what you were thinking at that exact moment, if you envisioned our long future together or if you smiled out of pity. In any case, I followed you to the barn and watched your deft hands deliver lamb from ewe.

I see you in the kitchen in your plaid lumber jacket, cheeks ruddy with cold. I hear you whistling in the yard and run to the window. I feel the warmth of your belly against me in bed. Only the flimsiest membrane separates your world and mine, and when you come out of the shadows to find me, I know it is because *you* need *me*. I have no proof of this, of course. If I did, I would be a famous scientist and not an artist who believes that love does not vanish across the border of death but is itself another word for eternity. This is a new century, Fox, a difficult century, I think, not turbulently radical like the sixties but transformative nonetheless. Not the Age of Aquarius but the Age of Entropy, and I wish you were here, flesh and blood, to share it with me. I blame you for all this musing today, you who asked the question without an answer. *What does a life signify?* More time, I want to scream. Please, more time!

Acknowledgments

The act of writing a book is a process of transformation and discovery. Though it is a solitary pursuit, along the way I have been accompanied by many benevolent souls including those unnamed here. I am humbly indebted to the following people who've honored me with their companionship.

Gratitude to my incomparably kind and brilliant agent, Gail Hochman, who instinctively understood what I was trying to accomplish and became my fairy godmother, complete with magic wand, and to her assistant, Jody Klein, from whose services I have greatly benefited.

Gratitude to Deb Futter, my editor at Grand Central Publishing, whose guiding vision, inestimable sagacity, and ready humor make working together a joy.

Gratitude to Dianne Choie for her abiding patience, exquisite attention to details, and gracious amiability.

Gratitude to Anne Twomey, Lisa Honerkamp, Jason Holley, and Jon Contino for their inspired rendering of my book jacket. Gratitude to Dorothea Halliday for her loving attention to the book's design, and to Carrie Andrews for her skillful copyediting.

Gratitude to friends who have sustained me with their loyalty and encouragement. For your unflagging enthusiasm and friendship, I bow in recognition: Hilde Adler, Kiva Adler, Dwight Allen, Susan Bickley, Mare Chapman, Alice Friman, Anders Hallengren, Rick Hilles, Bobbie Johnson, Agate Nesaule, Nancy Okerlund, Pam Porter, Nancy Reisman, Lisa Ruffolo, Ann Shaffer, Janet Shaw, Therese Stanton, Gladys Swan, Leslie Ullman, and the Madison writing group in all its incarnations.

Gratitude to Murray Stein, who initiated me into the archetypal realms and never let go of my hand. Gratitude to Michael Conforti for steadfastly holding up the lantern. Gratitude to Dave Roethe, who taught me to ride bareback with courage.

Heartfelt thanks to those whose skills greatly enhanced the refinement of this book:

Gratitude to Pamela Painter, friend and teacher, who supplied faith at the very beginning. Gratitude to Eileen Pollack for her astute suggestions and generous support. Gratitude to Janet Steen for the depth of her intuitions. Gratitude to Nan Gatewood Satter, who read and reread the manuscript and whose wise counsel shaped the final outcome. Thanks to Masarah van Eyck and Dean Robbins for early and late-stage editing.

Gratitude to Brooke Medicine Eagle, Darcie Gustine, Marissa Lins, David Nissenbaum, and Baiyan Zhou for their healing graces.

Gratitude to Greg Gecas, Richard Straub, Nancy Hutsen, and Joel Wisch for enlightening me about farm life, wilderness experience, and the medical world of the 1950s. I also consulted numerous books to increase the breadth of my understanding on these subjects. Among the most useful were: *The Life of the Bee* by Maurice Maeterlinck, *Northwoods Wildlife* by Janine M. Benyus, and *Richard Halliburton's Complete Book of Marvels*. Although Rose is a completely fictional character, two wilderness women, Justine Kerfoot and Dorothy Molter, served as models.

Gratitude to the Ragdale Foundation, Edenfred, the Wurlitzer Foundation, and the Fetzer Institute for providing solitude and sanctuary. Gratitude to the Wisconsin Arts Board for honoring me with a grant in the literary arts. Gratitude to the *Beloit Fiction Journal* for publishing an earlier story version of this work.

Inexpressible gratitude to my daughters, Jennifer Kushner and Jessica Kushner: You are my greatest teachers and the foundation of my ferocious love. Gratitude to John Hauser for our many conversations about art and integrity, and to Troy Gosz, who entered our family more recently and is a welcomed presence.

It would take another book to adequately thank my husband, Burt Kushner, for his unfailing optimism, strength, and unwavering love and for enduring the many sacrifices involved in the writing of this book. You daily enlighten me in the conditions of devotion. Without you all else would be impossible.

Lastly, the spirits that guide the creative arts are tricksters and demand acknowledgment. To those forces without name or habitation, and to the spirit of Carmelita, I offer my most profound gratitude.

About the Author

Dale M. Kushner has been honored by a Wisconsin Arts Board Grant, a Pushcart Prize nomination, and residencies at the Helene Wurlitzer Foundation, the Ragdale Foundation, and the Fetzer Institute as a participant in their first writers' conference on compassion and forgiveness. Her work has been widely published in literary journals including *IMAGE*, *Poetry*, *Prairie Schooner*, *Salmagundi*, *Witness*, and *Fifth Wednesday*. Her most recent poetry collection, *More Alive Than Lions Roaring*, was a finalist for the May Swenson Poetry Award at Utah State Press, the Prairie Schooner Book Competition, and the Agha Shahid Ali Prize at University of Utah Press. She is on the core faculty of the Assisi Institute and lives with her husband in Madison, Wisconsin. *The Conditions of Love* is her first novel.